"Erin, I'm going to get us out of this."

She said nothing.

"You don't think we're going to make it. Do you?"

"I've lost count of the times I thought we were both going to die. Whatever that thing is in that case you are hiding beside the bed, people are willing to kill for it."

"You still want me to leave it behind?"

He held his breath, waiting.

"No. My party died because of that thing, whatever it is. I've decided to see this through."

"For a minute I thought you were only willing to jump off trestle bridges after stray dogs."

"Jet isn't a stray. Her owners were murdered, just like my party." She lifted up on an elbow and stared down at him. Her hair fell across her face, shielding her expression. She stroked his forehead with a thumb.

"I just want you to stay with me. You know?"

"Planning on it." He cradled her jaw in his hand, and she turned to press a kiss against his palm.

PERILOUS MOUNTAIN PURSUIT

JENNA KERNAN

&

USA TODAY Bestselling Author

JANICE KAY JOHNSON

Previously published as *Adirondack Attack*
and *The Last Resort*

ISBN-13: 978-1-335-47370-7

Recycling programs for this product may not exist in your area.

Perilous Mountain Pursuit

Copyright © 2022 by Harlequin Enterprises ULC

Adirondack Attack
First published in 2019. This edition published in 2022.
Copyright © 2019 by Jeannette H. Monaco

The Last Resort
First published in 2020. This edition published in 2022.
Copyright © 2020 by Janice Kay Johnson

For questions and comments about the quality of this book, please contact us at CustomerService@Harlequin.com.

Harlequin Enterprises ULC
22 Adelaide St. West, 41st Floor
Toronto, Ontario M5H 4E3, Canada
www.Harlequin.com

Printed in U.S.A.

CONTENTS

Jenna Kernan has penned over two dozen novels and received two RITA® Award nominations. Jenna is every bit as adventurous as her heroines. Her hobbies include recreational gold prospecting, scuba diving and gem hunting. Jenna grew up in the Catskills and currently lives in the Hudson Valley in New York State with her husband. Follow Jenna on Twitter, @jennakernan, on Facebook or at jennakernan.com.

Books by Jenna Kernan

Harlequin Intrigue

Visit the Author Profile page
at Harlequin.com for more titles.

ADIRONDACK ATTACK

Jenna Kernan

This story is dedicated, with love and admiration,
to my mother, Margaret C. Hathaway,
who drove me to school, swim lessons,
summer camp, dance lessons, art lessons, the
Adirondack Mountains and the American West.
Who could have imagined the world was so big?

Chapter 1

On his first day off in three months, Detective Dalton Stevens shouldered his backpack and set out after his wife. He knew she'd be surprised to see him and possibly furious. She'd tell him that trial separations meant the couple separated. Well, the hell with that.

His wife, outdoor adventure specialist Erin Stevens, was up here in the Adirondacks somewhere. He had arrived last night, but as it was dark and he didn't know the location of her guided excursion, he'd had to wait until this morning. That meant she was well ahead of him. It seemed like he'd been chasing after Erin ever since he met her, and the woman knew how to play hard to get. But this time was different. This time he really didn't think she wanted to be caught. She wanted a separation. In his mind, *separation* was just code for *impending divorce*. Well, the hell with that, too.

Dalton adjusted the straps on his shoulders. He couldn't use the padded hip strap because it rubbed against his healing stomach wound.

The group she was leading had already been at it a full day. Normally he could have caught them by now. But nothing was normal since he'd told her he'd been cleared by the department physician to return to active duty.

"Did you hear anything I said?" she'd asked.

"I heard you, Erin," Dalton said to the endless uphill trail. Roots crisscrossed the path, and moss grew on the damp rocks that littered the way. He'd lost his footing twice, and the twisting caused a pain in his middle that made him double over in agony.

Cleared for duty did not mean cleared for hiking with a fifty-pound pack. It would have been lighter if he'd left the tent, but he knew his wife's tent was a single. He'd packed one that suited two. Ever hopeful, he thought. Now if he could just get her in there, he was certain the starlight and the fresh air would clear her mind.

She was always happiest in the outdoors. Erin seemed to glow with health and contentment in this bug-infested, snake-ridden, root-laden wilderness. Meanwhile, he couldn't tell poison ivy from fern, and the last time he'd carried a pack was in Afghanistan.

He stopped again to catch his breath, drawing out his mobile phone and finding he still had no service.

"Nature," he scoffed. He'd take a neighborhood with a quality pizza joint any day.

Erin's boss, and the director of the adult adventure camp, had given him a directions to the trailhead by phone and Dalton had picked up a topographical map. If he was reading this correctly, he should reach their second camping site shortly after they did. Yesterday they had used the kayaks to paddle the Hudson River before stopping for their first camp. This morning they should arrive here to await the scheduled release of water from Lake Abanakee this evening. This area of the Hudson was above the family rafting sites and would be wild running tomorrow, according to the director. The director said he would alert one of the rafting outfits to keep an eye out for him tomorrow, in case he needed a lift downriver.

Meanwhile, this trail from O-K Slip Road was all rocks and roots, and he seemed to catch his feet on each one. Recovery time from abdominal surgery certainly wasn't easy, he thought.

He reached the Hudson Gorge and realized it would be a miracle to find them, even knowing their general stopping point. If they changed the plan and camped on the opposite side, he was out of luck and up the river without a paddle or raft.

Gradually he left the pine forest and moved through birch and maple as he approached the river. He was relieved to finally come upon their camping site knowing she and her group would not be far.

Erin had chosen a rocky outcropping, away from the tall trees and on a covering of moss and grass that spread across the gray rock above the river.

The brightly colored tents were scattered in a rough circle. The trees below the outcropping made it impossible to see them, but he could hear their laughter and raised voices plainly enough.

He didn't see Erin's little single tent because she wouldn't camp very close to her charges. He was certain of that much, because his wife liked her privacy. Perhaps too damn much.

He found her camp in short order and dropped his pack beside her gray-and-white tent.

Erin's pack rested inside the tent, and her food was properly hung in the trees to prevent attracting animals. The peals of laughter and howls of delight guided him to the trail to the river.

A young man and an older woman headed in his direction, winding up the steep path from the water. The route inclined so sharply that the pair clung to saplings as they climbed. The skinny youth wore wet swim trunks and gripped a towel around his neck. His legs were pearly pale, but his face and arms showed a definite sunburn. The woman wore a one-piece bathing suit with jean shorts plastered to her legs and rivulets of water running down her tanned skin.

"Having fun?" Dalton asked.

The youth pointed a toned arm back the way they had come. "There's a rock like a diving board down there. Water's deep and still. It's awesome!"

The woman held her smile as her brows lifted in surprise. "Well, hey there. Didn't see another paddler."

He thumbed over his shoulder. "Came overland. The trail from O-K Slip Road."

She passed him going in the opposite direction. "Well, that's no fun."

He stepped off the trail to let them pass and continued, landing on his backside with a jolt of pain more than once.

"No fun is right," he muttered.

At the bank of the river, he saw the three remaining adult campers and their leader. He'd recognize those legs anywhere. Firm tanned legs pushing off the gray rock as she climbed, leaving wet footprints from her water shoes as she easily scaled the boulder that was shaped like the fin of a shark, using a climbing rope. It was his wife.

On the pinnacle of the sloping boulder she waited for a young woman in a pink bathing suit, which was an unfortunate match to her ruddy skin tone, to jump off and then followed behind, giving a howl of delight that made Dalton frown. He'd never heard her make such a sound of pure exhilaration.

The single male waded out of the water and came up short at the sight of him. Dalton judged the man to be early twenties and carrying extra pounds around his middle.

"Hiya," he said.

Dalton nodded and the young man crept past him on the uneven bank. The woman in pink swam and then waded after the man, followed by a lanky female with wet hair so short it stood up like a hedgehog's spines. Erin emerged from her underwater swim at the base of the rock, scaling the slope to retrieve her climbing rope before making a final leap with the coiled rope over one shoulder.

Dalton smiled as the pinkish woman, her face red from exertion, reached the muddy shore, her cheeks puffing out with each breath.

"Where'd you...come...from?" she wheezed.

"Your camp."

She gave him a skeptical look and paused, one hand on her knee.

"You don't look like an adventure camper."

"No?" He grinned. "What do I look like?"

She cocked her head and her eyes narrowed. "A soldier."

That surprised him as he had once been just that. But he'd left Special Forces at Erin's request.

"Why's that?"

She pointed at the hunting knife that he'd strapped to his belt and then to his boots, military issue and which still fit. Finally, she lifted her finger to the tattoos staining his left forearm from wrist to elbow. The overall pattern spoke of lost comrades, blood, war dead and the corps.

"You sure you're with us?"

"Erin's my wife."

Her entire demeanor changed. Her face brightened and the look of suspicion vanished.

"Oh, hi! I'm Alice. Your wife, she's wonderful. So encouraging and warm." Her smile faltered. "You're her husband?"

He didn't like the incredulity in her voice.

"Yeah." For now. His stomach gave a twist that had nothing to do with healing tissue.

"Hmm. Can't see it."

"Why?"

"She's fun and you're, well, you seem kinda…serious, you know?"

His brows sank deeper over his eyes. He was fun.

The woman glanced back down the trail where all but one hiker had vanished. "She didn't mention you."

"Feel free to ask her."

Alice waved. "See you at camp."

She moved past him and continued up the trail with her comrade on her heels. This other woman said nothing, just gave him a sullen look and glanced away the minute they made eye contact.

Erin reached the spot where she changed from swimming in the calm stretch to wading. He waited beside the kayaks.

Her tank top clung to her skin, and he could see the two-piece suit she wore beneath, along with much of her toned, athletic build. Her wet light brown hair, cut bluntly at her jawline, had lost its natural wave in the water. Her whiskey-brown eyes sparkled above her full mouth, now stretched wide in a playful grin. He took a moment to admire the view of his wife, wet and smiling.

He had the sudden impulse to hide before she spotted him.

Dalton didn't know how Erin knew he was there, but she straightened, giving him a moment to study her standing alert and relaxed as if listening to the birds that flitted across the water. Then she turned and her eyes shifted to her husband. The set of her jaw told him that she was not pleased.

Dalton was six-three and weighed 245 pounds, but Erin's scowl made him feel about two feet tall.

"Surprise?" he said, stretching his arms out from his sides in a ta-da posture.

Her gaze flicked to his middle, where she knew he still wore a bandage though the stitches were out now. She didn't manage to keep from uttering a profanity. He knew this because he read it on her lips. The Lord's name…in vain. Definitely. Then she tucked in her chin and started marching toward him in a way that would have made a lesser man run. Instead, he slid his hands into the rear pockets of his cargo pants and forced a smile that felt as awkward as a middle school slow dance.

"Dalton, if that's you, you had better run."

He did, running toward her, meeting her as she reached the bank.

He stopped before her, then reached, preparing to swing her in a circle, as he did after separations of more than a day.

She pressed her palm against the center of his chest and extended her arm, blocking him. "Don't you dare lift me. You shouldn't be lifting anything."

He was suddenly glad he'd dumped his pack.

She hoisted the coiled rope farther up on her shoulder and aimed her extended finger at him. Her scowl deepened and her gaze shot back to him. "How long have you been tracking me?"

"Just today. I signed up for your group."

Her fists went to her hips. "So I couldn't send you home, right?"

Her two female adults had not climbed up to camp, opting to linger and watch the awkward reunion. Dalton glared, but they held their position, their heads swiveling from her to him as they awaited his reply, reminding him of spectators at a tennis match. Dalton pinned his eyes on his wife, an opponent, wishing they were alone but knowing that the women bearing witness might just play in his favor. Erin's tone was icy, but she had not raised it…yet.

He grinned, leaned in for a kiss and caught only her cheek as she stepped back, scowling.

"I can't believe this," she muttered, pushing past him and heading up the trail. Her campers scuttled ahead of them and out of sight.

He trotted after her, ignoring the tug of pain that accompanied each stride.

"Did you bring a kayak?" she asked.

"No."

"You planning on swimming the rapids tomorrow?"

"I thought you'd be happy."

She kept walking, leaning against the slope. Her calf muscles were tight, and he pictured those ankles locked about his lower back. It had been too long.

"I'm taking a vacation. Just like you wanted," he added.

She spun and stormed a few steps away, and then she rounded on him.

"You didn't hear a word I said back there." She pointed toward a tree that he assumed was in the direction of Yonkers, New York, and their pretty little split ranch house with the yard facing woods owned by the power company and a grill on the patio that he had planned to use over the July Fourth weekend. Instead, he was adventure camping without a kayak.

She continued, voice raised. "A vacation? Is that what you got from our last conversation?"

"I missed you." He held his grin, but felt it dying at the edges. Drying up like a dead lizard in the sun. She didn't look back.

"You told me you understood. That you'd take this time to think…" She turned and tapped a finger on his forehead as if to check that there was anyone home. "Really think, about my concerns."

"You said a break."

"You knew exactly what kind of a break I wanted. But, instead, you went for the grand gesture. Like always."

He reached to cup her cheek, but she dodged and his arm dropped to his side. "Honey, listen…"

She looked up at him with disappointment, the hill not quite evening their heights. Then she placed a hand over his, and for a minute he thought it would be all right. Her eyes squeezed shut and a tear dribbled down her cheek.

Dalton gasped. He was making her cry. Erin didn't cry unless she was furious.

The pinkish woman appeared at the edge of the meadow, stepping beside them as her eyes shifted back and forth between them. She tugged on her thick rope of a braid as if trying to decide whether she should proceed or speak.

Dalton looked at his wife. She hadn't kissed him. When was the last time that she had greeted him without a kiss?

When she'd left for adventure camp yesterday, he recalled.

An icy dread crystallized around his heart. He would not lose her. Everything was changing. He had to figure out how to change it back. Change her back.

"Erin, come on," he coaxed.

She was listening, and so was the interloper. He turned to the camper.

"Seriously?" he said, and she scuttled away toward the others, who all stood together facing him and their camp leader, his wife.

Erin faced her group. "This man is my husband, Dalton," she said. "I wasn't expecting him."

The assemble stood motionless, only their eyes flicking from him to her.

Erin growled and strode away. She reached her tent,

paused at the sight of his pack and dropped the rope. Her hands went to her hips. She turned to glare at him. He swallowed.

When he gave her his best smile, she closed her eyes and turned away. Then she stripped out of her tank top and into a dry sweatshirt, leaving her wet suit on underneath. He tried to hide his disappointment as she dragged on dry shorts. She spoke, it seemed, to her pack.

"If you were listening, you would have respected my wishes."

"I heard everything you said. I did. I just..." *Ignored you*, he thought, but wisely stopped speaking.

"I don't think listening is enough."

"What does that even mean?"

"You always listen to me, Dalton. And then you do as you darn well please. My feelings don't change your decisions. They don't even seem to weigh into your thought process anymore. You want to go on living like you always have, and that's your right. And it's my right to step off the roller coaster."

"Is *stepping off the roller coaster* punishment, Erin? Is that what you're trying to do? Is that why you left?"

"I can't talk to you here. I'm working."

"I'll wait."

"It won't matter how long you wait, Dalton. You don't want to change."

"Because everything is fine just the way it is."

"No, Dalton. It isn't."

The way she said "it isn't" froze his blood. The flat, defeated tone left no doubt that she was ready to cut him loose.

Erin opened her mouth to speak, but instead cocked

her head. A moment later she had her hand shielding her eyes as she glanced up toward the sky. Her hearing was better than his.

He'd fired too many shots with his M4 rifle without ear protection over in Afghanistan. So he followed the direction of Erin's attention and, a moment later, made out the familiar thumping drone of the blades of a helicopter.

"That's funny," Erin said.

The chopper broke the ridgeline across the river, wobbling dangerously and issuing black smoke from the tail section.

Dalton judged the angle of descent and the length of the meadow. The pilot was aiming for this flat stretch of ground beyond the tents that ringed the clearing. Dalton knew it would be a hard landing.

He grabbed Erin, capturing her hand, and yanked her toward the trees. In the meadow, standing like startled deer amid their colorful tents, her charges watched the approaching disaster in petrified stillness.

"Take cover!" he shouted, still running with his wife. "Get down!"

Chapter 2

Erin cried out in horror as the rails below the chopper snapped the treetops above them. Branches rained down from the sky, and Dalton dragged her against him as the roar of the engine seemed to pass directly over her head. She squeezed her eyes shut as her rib cage shuddered with the terrible vibrations of the whirling blades.

She opened her eyes as the chopper tipped in the air, the blades now on their side rotating toward her and churning upright like a window fan gone mad. It was going to hit the ground, blades first, right there before her.

In the meadow, Brian Peters, the skinny seventeen-year-old who was here because his father wanted him away from his computers for a week, was now running for his life. She judged he'd clear the descending blade but feared the fuselage would crush him. Brian's acne-scarred cheeks puffed as he bolted, lanky and loose limbed. Behind him Merle Levine, the oldest of her group, a square and solidly built woman in her late fifties, lay prone beside her cheery red tent with her arms folded over her head. Merle was a single biology teacher on summer vacation and directly in the path Erin feared the chopper would take as it hit the ground.

Erin squeezed her face between open palms as the propeller caught. Instead of plowing into the earth, the helicopter cartwheeled as the blades sheered and folded under the momentum of the crash.

Erin saw Carol Walton lift her arms and then fall as debris swept her off her feet. The timid woman had reminded Erin of a porcupine, with small close-set eyes and spiky bleached hair tufted with black. Erin's scream mingled with Carol's as the woman vanished from sight.

The chopper careened toward the escarpment, some twenty feet above the river just beyond the meadow. The entire craft slowed and then tipped before scraping across the rock with exquisite slowness.

Richard Franklin, a twentysomething craft beer brewer from Oklahoma, was already close to the edge and he stood, watching the chopper as it teetered. He reached out toward the ruined aircraft and Erin realized he could see whoever was aboard. Then he ran as if to catch the two-ton machine in his pale outstretched arms. The chopper fell over the cliff and Richard dropped to his posterior.

Erin scanned the ground for the flash of a pink bathing suit. "Where's Alice?"

Not a bird chirped or squirrel scuttled. The wind had ceased and all insects stilled. The group rose, as one, staring and bug-eyed. The sudden quiet was deafening.

They began to walk in slow zombie-like synchronicity toward the spot where the helicopter had vanished. All except for Dalton.

Dalton released Erin and charged toward the spot where Carol Walton knelt, folded in the middle and clutching her belly like an opera soprano in the final act. Only Erin knew the blood was real.

Alice Afton appeared beside her, having obviously been hiding in the woods.

"Alice, get my pack. There's a med kit in there," Erin said.

Alice trotted off and Erin moved on wooden legs toward Carol Walton, knowing from the amount of blood spilling from her wounds that she could not survive.

Dalton cradled Carol in his lap, and her head lay in the crook of his elbow. In different circumstances the hold would seem that of a lover. His short, dark brown hair, longer on top, fell forward over his broad forehead, covering his heavy brows and shielding the green eyes that she knew turned amber near the iris. She could see the nostrils of his broad nose flare as he spoke.

"I got you," said Dalton. "Don't you worry."

"Tell my mom, I love her," said Carol.

Erin realized then that Carol knew she was dying. But there was none of the wild panic she had expected. Carol stared up at Dalton as if knowing he would guide her to where she needed to go. The confidence he projected, the experience. How many of his fellow marines had he held just like this?

Army never leaves their wounded. Marines never leave their dead.

"Can I do anything?" asked Erin. She couldn't. Nothing that would keep Carol with them.

"Take her hand," he said in a voice that was part exasperation, part anguish. She knew he'd lost comrades in war and it bothered him deeply.

Erin did, and warm blood coated her palm.

Alice arrived, panting, and extended the pack.

"Just put it down for now," said Dalton, his voice calm.

"Why doesn't it hurt?" asked Carol, lowering her chin as if to look at the slicing belly wound. Something had torn her from one side to the other and the smell of her compromised bowels made Erin gag.

But not Dalton. He lifted Carol's chin with two fingers and said. "Hey, look at me. Okay?"

Carol blinked up at him. "She's a lucky woman, your wife. Does she know that?"

Dalton smiled, stroking her head. "Sometimes."

Carol's color changed from ashen to blue. She shivered and her eyes went out of focus. Then her breathing changed. She gasped and her body went slack.

Dalton checked the pulse at her throat as Erin's vision blurred. He shook his head and whispered, "Gone."

From the lip of the cliff, Brian Peters called. "I can see someone moving down there."

Dalton slipped out from under Carol's slack body and rose. He glanced down at Erin, and she pressed her lips together to keep from crying.

"Come on," he said, and headed toward the rocky outcropping.

He tugged her to her feet and she hesitated, eyes still pinned on the savaged corpse that was Carol Walton just a few minutes ago.

"Erin. We have to see about the crew." His voice held authority.

How was he so calm? she wondered, but merely nodded her head and allowed him to hurry her along, like an unwilling dog on a leash.

And then, there they were on the lip of rock that jutted out over the Hudson. Twenty feet below them the ruined helicopter lay, minus its blades. One of the runners was snagged over a logjam that held the ruined chopper as the bubble of clear plastic slowly filled with river water. Inside the pilot slumped in his seat, tethered in place by the shoulder restraints.

"Is he alone?" asked Merle, coming to stand beside Dalton, asking him the questions as he emerged as the clear leader of their party.

"Seems so," said Dalton as he released Erin's hand.

"He's moving!" said Richard, pointing a finger at the river.

Erin craned her neck and saw the pilot's head turn to one side. Alive, she realized.

"He's sinking," said Brian. "It's at his feet now."

"We have to get him out of there," said Alice.

"He'll drown," added Richard.

"You have rope?" asked Dalton.

Erin roused from her waking nightmare, knowing exactly what her husband planned. He'd string some rope up and swing down there like Tarzan in a daring rescue attempt.

Except she was the better swimmer. Dalton was only an average swimmer at best and today he was four weeks post-surgery. His abdominal muscles could not handle this. He'd tear something loose, probably the artery that the surgeon had somehow managed to close. She squared her shoulders and faced him.

Erin regained control of her party.

"You are not going down there!" she said.

He ignored her and lifted a hand to snap his fingers before Richard's face. "Rope?"

Richard startled, tore his gaze from the drama unfolding in the river and then hurried off.

"Dalton, I'm the party leader. I'm going," she said.

He smiled at her. "Honey…"

Her eyes narrowed at the placating tone as she interrupted. "You might get down there, but you can't climb back up. Who's going to haul you back?"

He glanced at the drop and the chopper. The water now reached the pilot's knees.

When Richard returned with the gear bag, Erin dropped to the ground and unzipped the duffel. As she removed the throw line and sash cord, she kept talking.

"I'm a better climber. More experienced." She reached in the bag, removed a rope and dropped it at his feet. "Tie a bowline," she said, requesting a simple beginner knot.

His eyes narrowed.

She held up an ascender used to make climbing up a single belay rope as easy as using a StairMaster. "What's this for?" she asked, testing his knowledge of climbing.

His jaw tightened.

"Exactly. I'm going. That's all."

Erin showed Dalton the throw ball, a sand-filled pouch that looked like a cross between a hacky sack and a leather beanbag filled with lead shot. Its purpose was to carry the lighter sash cord up and over tree branches, or in this case, down and around the top of the chopper's damaged rotor. Finished, she rose and offered the throw ball and towline to Dalton because he was better at throwing and because she needed him to leave her alone so she could work.

"Knock yourself out," she said, leaving him to try to snag the helicopter as she slipped into her climbing harness and fastened the chin strap on her helmet.

"How deep is the river here?" asked Dalton.

"Twenty feet, maybe. The river is deeper and wider here, which is why there's no white water. The gorges close back in farther down and the water gets interesting again."

Twenty feet was deep enough to sink that fuselage, she thought.

Erin selected a gap in the top of the rocky outcropping for her chock. This was an aluminum wedge that would hold her climbing rope. The climbing rope, on which she would belay, or use to descend and then return, was strong and much thicker than the towrope, which was no wider than a clothesline. Belaying to the pilot meant using this stronger rope and the cliff wall to drop to his position and then return using two ascenders. The ascenders fixed to the rope and would move only in one direction—up. The ascenders included feet loops, so she could rest on one as she moved the other upward.

She set the wedge in place and then set up her belay system. Finally, she attached her harness to the rope with a carabiner and figure eight belay device. She liked old-school equipment. Simple was best.

By the time she finished collecting all her gear, a second harness and the pack with the first aid kit, Dalton had succeeded in snagging the chopper with the throw ball and pulled the cord tight.

"Got it." He turned to her and grinned, showing her the tight towline.

"Fantastic," she said, squatting at the lip of the cliff. Then she fell backward. She had the satisfaction of seeing the shock on Dalton's face before he disappeared from her sight. Only momentarily, unfortunately. When she glanced up he was scowling down at her. Holding the towrope aloft.

"What's this even for?" he shouted.

"It's like those spinner things, only for grown men."

She continued her descent, smoothly releasing the rope and slowing as she reached the river's uneasy surface. As she approached the chopper, she realized the wreckage was moving, inching back as the rotor dragged along the branch anchoring it in place.

The pressure of the water splashed over the dome in front of the pilot, who turned his head to look up at her. She could see little of the man except that his headphones had fallen over his nose and there was blood, obscured from above by his dark clothing.

Her feet bumped the Plexiglas dome and she held herself in place, dancing sideways on her line to reach the door on the downriver side. It was partially submerged, but the other one took the full force of the current. She'd never be able to open it.

The pilot clutched his middle and turned to the empty seat beside him. He grabbed a red nylon cooler and laboriously moved it to his lap.

"I'm going to get you out," said Erin, doubting that she really could.

Chapter 3

Dalton watched in horror as his wife opened the side compartment door and gave herself enough slack to enter the ruptured compartment of the wrecked chopper.

The pilot lifted his head toward her as she perched on the passenger's seat, now pitched at an odd angle. Her added weight had caused the chopper's runner to farther slip along the anchoring branch. When the chopper tore loose, it would sink and she might be snagged. Cold dread constricted Dalton's chest as he watched helplessly from above.

If he had been the one down there, he was certain the chopper would already have broken loose. She'd been right to go, though he'd still rather switch places with her. She'd been so darn quick with those ropes. Erin knew he was capable of belaying down a rope. And he could climb back up on a good day, but he didn't know how to use the gizmos she had in that pack on her back and jangling from her harness. And today was not a good day.

Beside him, the four surviving campers lay on their bellies and knelt on the rock, all eyes fixed on the drama unfolding below.

The pilot was pushing something toward Erin; it looked like a small red bag. Erin was unbuckling his restraints and shoving the harness behind his back.

The water foaming around the wreckage drowned out their words.

Erin succeeded in getting the waist buckle of the climbing harness clipped about him and was working on tugging the nylon straps of his harness under his legs as the pilot's head lolled back. Erin glanced up at Dalton, a frown on her lips as she exited the compartment and retrieved the towline he had thrown. She was signaling to him with the rope. Pantomiming a knot.

"She wants you to tie a climbing rope to the line," said the older woman. "I'm Merle, by the way. I used to do a lot of rock climbing before I got pins in my ankle."

She lifted the coiled climbing rope, expertly connected it through an anchored pulley that she tied to a tree some five feet from the edge, and then tied the larger belay line to the towline. Finally, she signaled to Erin. A moment later Erin was hauling the towline back down, dragging the connected larger rope through the pulley. She continued this until she grasped the belay rope, at which point she quickly tied a loop through which she connected the belay rope to the pilot's harness with a carabiner. Erin removed the pilot's headphones and fitted her own helmet to his head.

Merle lifted the other end of the line, which ran

through the pulley secured to the tree trunk, and returned to the rock ledge.

"Take this a minute." Merle offered Dalton the rope. "I know I can't haul that guy up." She then motioned to the others. "Brian, Alice, Richard, come take hold. We'll act like a mule team. Walk that way when I tell you. Slowly." She folded the rope back on itself and tied a series of loops every few feet. Then the others took hold.

Dalton dragged his hand across his throat while simultaneously shaking his head. This, of course, had no effect on his wife who offered a thumbs-up and then used her strong legs to haul the pilot toward the open side door. For a moment the pilot tried again to get Erin to take the red squarish nylon bag. When Erin rejected his attempts to make her take it from him, he gripped the seat, foiling her attempts to remove him from the compartment. Finally, Erin looped the small container over her arm using the black nylon strap. Only then did the pilot assist in his extraction.

Merle extended an arm and pointed at the struggling pair.

"It's moving!"

Dalton shifted his attention from his wife to the helicopter runner. He watched in horror as the twisted remains of one blade slipped free from the branch. In a single heartbeat, the compartment vanished beneath the surface, leaving the pilot, in Erin's helmet, dangling from the rope, half in and half out of the water. With his legs submerged, the pilot was dragged downriver.

Erin's rope went taut. Dalton's breathing stopped as he gripped his wife's rope from the surface of the rock before him and wrapped it behind his legs. He hadn't done this since he was in active duty. He remembered how to anchor a climber, but he had never had to anchor a climber who was below him. Dalton sat into the rope and pulled.

Merle shouted from behind him. "Pull!"

The pilot began to rise, his legs clearing the churning torrent.

Dalton ignored the pain of his healing abdominal muscles as he succeeded in inching back from the edge. How long could Erin hold her breath? What if she was snagged on something in that compartment? The rope stretched tight as if tied down at the other end. He scanned the water for some sight of her, fearing the chopper had rolled onto her line or, worse, onto Erin.

The rope vibrated. Was the fuselage settling or was that his wife moving? Dalton smelled the fear on his perspiration. If the compartment tipped to that side, she would have no escape. She'd be pinned between the compartment and the bottom. Dalton considered his chances of moving upriver and jumping into the water. He made the calculation and came back with the answer. He had zero chance of succeeding. The river would whisk him past the wreck before he could reach her.

Just then he saw movement on the line. He stepped closer to the edge and a hand submerged again as the pilot rose closer to the lip of rock where he stood.

Dalton tugged and Erin's hand appeared again. She clutched something; it looked like a metallic gold coffee mug handle. She slid the handle up the rope and her head emerged.

"She's using an ascender," called Merle. "Two! Holy cow, she set that up underwater? Your wife is magnificent. If I was ten years younger I'd steal that woman."

He saw her then, first her arms, sliding the ascenders along the taut rope. One ascender slid upward and her head cleared the water. Wet hair clung to her red face as she gasped. Her opposite hand appeared, moving upward while gripping the second ascender. The device fixed to a carabiner and then to a sling that she had somehow clipped to her harness. In other words, Erin had released her original attachment to the line and then succeeded in attaching two ascenders and slings to the free portion of the rope all while underwater.

Magnificent was an understatement.

Her torso cleared the water and he saw that the red nylon bag still hung from her shoulder, clamped between her upper arm and side.

"Keep going," called Merle to the pull team as the pilot appeared beside her and was dragged up onto the flat expanse of rock.

Fifteen feet below him, Erin made progress ascending as he leaned over the edge for a better look at her. This caused the rope to slacken and for Erin to drop several inches. Dalton straightened and sat into the rope. He lost his view of his wife, but Merle called the remaining distance to the top as the pilot's pull team, having finished their job, abandoned their posts to run to the pilot who was struggling to move.

"Five feet," called Merle, motioning him to hold position. Merle extended her hand and Erin gripped it, sliding the opposite ascender into Dalton's line of sight. Then she scrambled up onto the rock, rising to stand before them.

She didn't even look out of breath. He, on the other hand, had lost his wind. Seeing her disappear had broken something loose inside him, and his legs gave way.

He collapsed onto the moss-covered rock as he struggled to keep down the contents of his stomach. The climbing rope fell about Erin's feet, and she released the ascenders that clattered to the stone cliff top.

How had she escaped?

Merle was hugging his wife as Erin laughed. The men patted her on the back, and Alice got a hug as well, weeping loudly so that Erin had to comfort *her.*

"I'm getting you all wet," said Erin, extracting herself from Alice's embrace. She ignored Dalton as she turned to the pilot. "How is he?"

Dalton had a rudimentary field experience with triage and rallied to meet her beside the pilot.

"You okay?" he asked.

She nodded, still not looking at him. "Thanks for your help."

But she hadn't needed it or him. All he had done was dunk her as she emerged and possibly speed her arrival slightly by keeping the rope tight.

"Did you get pinned?" he asked.

"Just the rope."

"How did you get out?" he asked.

"Later," she said, and set aside the bag that he now saw was a red nylon lunch cooler. Why had the pilot been so insistent that she retrieve it?

Illegal possibilities rose in his law-enforcement mind, but he turned his attention to the injured man, checking his pupils and pulse.

"Where's your pack?" he asked her.

"Dumped it. Couldn't fit out the side window."

Erin dropped to her knees beside the pilot.

"Shock," he said. At the very least. If he had to guess, and he did have to, because there was no medical help for miles, he'd say the man was bleeding internally. He took a knee beside her and pressed on the pilot's stomach with his fingertips and found the man's skin over the abdominal cavity was tight and the cavity rigid.

"His leg is broken," said Merle, pointing at the pilot's foot, which was facing in the wrong direction for a man lying on his back.

So is his spleen, thought Dalton.

Chapter 4

"I don't like the sound of his breathing," said Erin, her brow as wrinkled as her wet tank top.

The pilot wheezed now, struggling for breath. His eyes fluttered open.

"Captain Lewis, this is my husband. He's a New York City detective. You wanted to speak to him?" The pilot had given them his name but little else.

The captain nodded. "Just you two," he said, lifting his chin toward the curious faces surrounding him.

Erin pointed at Merle. "Please go find my pack and get my phone. Then call for help. Brian, go find something to cover Carol up with and, Alice and Richard, can you gather my climbing gear?"

The campers scurried away.

"Now, Captain Lewis," said Erin. "What in this

cooler is so important that you were willing to kill us both?"

Lewis turned to Dalton and spoke in a guttural whisper. "I work for the Department of Homeland Security. Orders to collect this and transfer same to a plane bound for the CDC in Virginia."

Dalton felt the hairs on his neck lifting, as if his skin were electrified. The mention of the CDC or Centers for Disease Control indicated to him that whatever was inside was related to infection or disease.

"What's in there?" he asked, aiming an index finger at the bag.

"Flash drive with intel on terrorist cells within the state. Siming's Army, and those vials hold one of the three Deathbringers."

"The what?" asked Dalton.

"I don't know, exactly. Mission objective was to pick up a package, which contains an active virus—a deadly one—and the vaccine."

Erin moved farther from the cooler that had been dangling recently from her arm.

"So it's dangerous?" she asked.

"Yes, ma'am. Deadly. You have to get it to DHS or the FBI. Don't trust anyone else."

"Who shot you down?" Dalton had seen the bullet holes in the fuselage.

"Foreign agents. Mercenaries. Don't know. Whoever they are, they work for Siming's Army. And more will be coming to recover that." He pointed at the cooler.

"Where'd you get it?" asked Dalton.

"An operative. Agent Ryan Carr. Use his name. Get as far from here as possible."

"But you're injured," said Erin.

"No, ma'am. I'm dying." He glanced to Dalton, who nodded his agreement.

"Internal injuries," said Dalton through gritted teeth. Two deaths, and he'd been unable to do a damned thing to save them.

"I thank you for pulling me out. You two have to complete my mission."

"No," said Erin at the same time Dalton said, "Yes."

She stared at him. "I can't leave these people out here and I'm not taking charge of a deadly anything."

The captain spoke to her, slipping his hand into hers.

"It's a dying man's last request."

She tried to pull back. "That's not fair."

He grinned and then wheezed. His breath smelled of blood. "All's fair in love and war."

He used the other hand to push the cooler toward Dalton, who accepted the package.

She pointed at the red nylon travel cooler. "Dalton, do not take that."

But he already had.

"Get him a blanket, Erin. He's shivering."

She stood and glared at him, then hurried off.

Dalton stayed with the captain as he grew paler and his eyes went out of focus. He'd seen this before. Too many times, but this time the blood stayed politely inside his dying body. The pilot's belly swelled with it and so did his thigh. The broken femur had cut some blood supply, Dalton was certain, from the lack of pulse at the pilot's ankle and the way his left pant leg was now so tight.

"Tell my girlfriend, Sally, that I was fixing to ask for her hand. Tell her I love her and I'm sorry."

"I'll tell her." If he lived to see this through. Judging from the number of bullet holes in that chopper and the size of the caliber, staying alive was going to be a challenge.

Erin returned with her down sleeping bag and draped it over the shivering captain. Before the sun reached the treetops as it dipped into the west, the captain joined Carol Walton in death.

Dalton stood. "We have to go."

"Go? Go where? I've got two dead bodies and responsibility for the welfare of my group. I can't just leave them."

No, they couldn't just leave them. But there were few safe choices. Traveling as a group would be slow. "Get the kayaks ready. We're going."

"I am not taking this group into river rapids ninety minutes before sunset. Are you crazy?"

"Not as crazy as meeting them here." He motioned to the open field.

"Meeting who?" she asked.

"Siming's Army."

Twenty minutes later Erin, now in dry clothing, gathered the surviving campers and explained that the captain's helicopter was shot down, he claimed, by terrorists who would be coming for whatever was in that bag. She explained that leaving this evening was hazardous because of the volume of water at the forefront of the scheduled release from Lake Abanakee. Finally, she relayed that it was her husband's belief that they needed to leave this site immediately.

"I'm for that. Staying the night with two dead bodies gives me the creeps," said Brian.

"You can't just leave them out here for the predators," said Richard.

"You rather be here when the predators show up?" asked Merle.

"We called for help. They are sending an air rescue team for them," Brian said. "We should at least wait until they pick up the dead."

"We wait, there will be more dead," said Dalton.

"What do you think, Erin?" asked Brian.

"I would prefer to stay put and wait for help."

"What's coming isn't help," said Dalton.

On empty stomachs, the campers packed up their tents and gear, while Erin and Dalton headed down the rocky outcropping to ready the kayaks that had been stowed for their excursion the following morning. Dalton took Carol's gear and kayak.

"You really sure about this?" asked Erin, her gaze flicking from Dalton, who carried one end of Carol's kayak, and then to the frothing river behind him.

"Sure about our responsibility to deliver this? Yes."

"Sure about taking inexperienced kayakers into the roughest stretch of white water one hour before sunset. What if someone upends?"

He lowered the kayak onto the grassy bank. "What would you normally do?"

"Pick them up from the river and guide them to shore."

"We'll do that."

"In the dark?"

"You're right. We can't do that."

"So your plan is to leave anyone who gets into trouble. And here I thought you were the hero type."

That stung. He wouldn't leave anyone behind. She had to know that. "Erin, he said they're coming. Mercenaries. You understand? That means hired killers, and I know they are using high-caliber rounds from the size of the holes in the tail section of the chopper. We can argue later about specific logistics. Right now we need to…"

She was cocking her head again. Looking toward the sky. He didn't hear it yet, not over the roar of the river. But he knew what was coming.

Dalton looked at the three kayaks they had retrieved from cover. Her gear lay beside her craft, neatly stowed in her pack. Dalton slipped her gear into the hollow forward compartment of her craft and added her paddle so that it rested half in and half out of the opening.

Erin arched backward, staring up at the pink sky with her hand acting as visor. Dalton packed his gear into the bow of Carol Walton's craft and added the red nylon cooler, which now contained nothing but a river rock. The black case, recently within, held two small vials in a padded black compartment with a thumb drive. This precious parcel now rested safely in the side pocket of his cargo pants.

"They're here," she said, pointing at the red-and-white helicopter with Rescue emblazoned on the side.

The chopper hovered over the meadow, then began a measured descent. Erin stepped back toward the tree-lined trail that led to the meadow. Dalton glanced at the kayaks, packed and ready, and just knew he'd never get her to go without her group.

So he abandoned their escape plan and followed her. He could at least see that she wasn't one of the welcome party.

Dalton made sure he was beside her when they reached the sharply ascending trailhead at the edge of the open field. Before them, the chopper had landed. The pilot cut the engine and the copilot stepped down. Dalton studied the man. He wore aviator glasses, slacks and a button-up shirt. Nothing identified him as mountain rescue and his smile seemed out of place. As he crouched and trotted beneath the slowing blades that whirled above him, Dalton spotted the grip of a pistol tucked in the back of his slacks.

Erin moved to step from cover and he dragged her back.

"What are you doing?" she said.

He held a finger to his lips. "Wait."

Merle was first to greet the copilot. Their raised voices carried across the meadow.

"How many in your party?" asked the new arrival, straightening now. He was a small man, easy to underestimate, Dalton thought. The relaxed posture seemed crafted, just like his casual attire.

"There are six of us," answered Merle, omitting the two dead.

"Where's the crashed chopper?"

Merle pointed, half-turning to face the river. "Went into the Hudson and sank."

The copilot glanced back to the chopper and the side door slid open. The man within crouched in the opening. There was a familiar metal cylinder over his shoulder and a strap across the checked cotton shirt he wore. Dalton had carried a rifle just like it on many missions while in Special Ops. It was an M4.

"What about the pilot?" asked the newcomer. "He go down with his chopper?"

Brian answered that one, coming to stand beside Merle. "We got him out. But he died."

Dalton groaned.

"Too bad," said the copilot.

Alice smiled brightly, standing in a line beside Brian. The only thing missing was the wall to make this a perfect setup for a firing squad. Dalton had a pistol but it would hardly be a match for three armed mercenaries. They'd kill him and, more importantly, they'd kill Erin. So he waited, backing her up with a firm pull on her arm. They now watched through the cover of pine boughs.

Dalton knew what would happen next. He ran through possibilities of what he could do, if anything, to prevent it.

"Do something," whispered Erin.

"If I do something, they'll know our position."

"They're going to kill them."

"I think so."

"So save them."

"It will endanger you."

"What would you do if I wasn't here?"

He glanced at her. "You *are* here."

Dalton watched from his position. "Get behind that tree." He pointed. "Stay there and when I say run, you run for the kayaks."

"Dalton?"

"Promise me."

She met his gaze and nodded, then stepped behind the thick trunk of the pine tree. He moved beside her.

In the clearing, one of the new arrivals glanced in his direction and then back to Alice.

"You retrieve anything from the craft before it went down?"

"Yeah," said Alice,

Dalton aimed at the one with the rifle.

"What exactly?"

"A red cooler. We have to take it to the FBI," said Brian.

"That so? Where is it now, exactly?"

Brian seemed to have realized that he faced a wolf in sheep's clothing because he rested a hand on his neck and rubbed before speaking.

"Back by our tents," he lied. "I'll get it for you." He turned to go.

The man with the aviator glasses motioned for the pilot to follow. The copilot lifted his hand to signal the shooter. The rifleman raised his weapon and Dalton took his shot, dropping him like a sack of rags.

By the time Dalton swung his pistol away from the dead man, the copilot had Alice in front of him, using her as a human shield.

"Come out or she dies," said their leader.

He didn't, and the man shot Merle and Richard in rapid succession. They fell like wheat before the scythe.

From the brush where Brian had disappeared came the sound of thrashing. Dalton suspected the teen had made a run for it.

The copilot dragged Alice back toward the chopper, using the nose cone as cover, as he shouted to the pilot. Another shot sounded and Alice fell forward to the ground, shot through the head.

"Kill whoever is shooting. Then find the sample," said the copilot.

"The boy?"

"No witnesses."

Dalton leaned toward Erin and whispered, "When they find that cooler, they'll kill us. You understand?"

She nodded.

"Run!"

Erin didn't look back at the carnage. Instead, she fled down the trail toward the river. Dalton had a time trying to keep up.

At the bank of the Hudson, Erin finally came to a halt. She folded at the waist and gripped her knees with both hands, panting.

"They killed them. Just shot them down," she said.

Dalton thought he'd heard his wife express every emotion possible from elation to fury. But this voice, this high reedy thread of a voice, didn't seem to belong to Erin.

"Where's Brian?"

He wouldn't get far with two trained killers on his trail.

Erin, who had just belayed into a river and rescued a wounded man. Who had led this group here to disaster. Who had just watched three more people die. The first deaths she'd ever witnessed.

A sharp threat of worry stitched his insides.

She straightened, and he took in her pale face and bloodless lips. He felt a second jolt of panic. She was going into shock.

"Erin." He took a firm hold of both her elbows and gave a little shake. "We have to go now." Her eyes snapped into focus and she met his gaze. There she was, pale, panting and scared. But she was back.

"Brian," she whispered and then shouted. "Brian!" He appeared like a lost puppy, crashing through the brush, holding one bleeding arm with his opposite hand.

Behind him came the pilot. Dalton squeezed off two shots, sending his pursuer back into cover.

Erin and Brian crouched on the bank as Erin removed a red bandanna from her pocket and tied it around the bullet wound in the boy's arm.

She closed her mouth and scowled as a familiar fierce expression emerged on her face.

"Those animals are not getting away with this." She glanced toward the trail. His wife was preparing to fight.

"Erin, get into your kayak. Now." He tugged her toward the watercrafts.

She paused and looked at her pack and the paddle already in place for departure. Then she glanced at him.

"You knew?"

"Suspected."

She clutched Brian's good arm. "He can't paddle with one arm." She wiped her hand over her mouth. "And you don't know how to navigate in white water."

True enough.

The kayaks each held only one person. Dalton took another shot to send their attacker back behind the tree.

"He'll have to try," said Dalton.

"Get in, Brian. I'll launch you."

Tears stained the boy's pink, hairless cheeks, and blood stained his forearm, but he climbed into a kayak. Erin handed him a paddle and shoved his craft into the river.

"Now you," she called to him.

He knew what would happen when he stopped shooting. They'd be sitting ducks on the river.

"I'll be right behind you."

"Dalton. No."

"You promised," he said.

Brian was already in the current, struggling to paddle.

"Go," he coaxed, wondering if this was the last time that he'd ever see her.

She went with a backward glance, calling directions as she pushed the kayak into the Hudson.

"Get to the center of the river and avoid the logs. Hug the right shore going into the first turn and the left on the second. How far are we going?"

"Get under cover." They would be sitting ducks on the river once the chopper was airborne. He needed to kill that pilot.

"Got it."

He moved his position as the pilot left cover to fire at what he assumed was three kayakers.

Never assume. Dalton took the shot and the man staggered back to cover.

Body armor, Dalton realized.

He caught a glimpse of the man darting between the trees in retreat. He took another shot, aiming for his head, and missed. Then he climbed into the kayak. Erin's graceful departure had made the launch look easy. His efforts included using the paddle to shove himself forward, nearly upending in the process.

He moved by inches, shocked at how much his abdomen ached as he felt the grass and earth dragging under him. The river snatched him from the shore. He retrieved his double-bladed paddle, glancing forward to catch a glimpse of Erin before she vanished from his view. The pitch and buck of the river seemed a living thing beneath him, and this was the wide, quiet part.

He used his paddle to steer but did not propel himself forward. The river began to churn with the first set of rapids. He rocketed along, propelled by the hydrodynamics of the surging water.

Above him, the sky blazed scarlet, reflecting on the dark water like blood. Erin had never seen a dead body. Today she had seen six.

As if summoned from the twilight by his thoughts, he glimpsed Erin on the far bank, towing Brian's kayak to shore. He tried and failed to redirect her.

Erin reached the rocky shore and leaped out, holding both crafts as Brian struggled from his vessel. He didn't look back as he ran into the woods and vanished.

Dalton shouted as he slipped past her, using his paddle in an ineffective effort to reverse against the current.

He still splashed and shouted when Erin appeared again, towing an empty kayak. She darted past him, her paddle flashing silver in the fading light. She took point and he fell in behind her, mirroring her strokes and ignoring the painful tug in his middle that accompanied each pull of the blade through the surging water. She hugged the first turn just as she'd instructed him and he tried to follow, but swept wider and nearly hit the boulder cutting the water like the fin of a tiger shark.

She glanced back and shouted something inaudible, and they sped through a churning descent that made his stomach pitch as river water splashed into his vessel's compartment. He could hear nothing past the roar of the white water, and neither could Erin. He knew this because he spotted the second turn in the river at the same moment he caught the flash of the red underbelly of the helicopter.

Erin's head lifted as the chopper swept over them and took a position downriver, hovering low and then dropping out of sight. It would be waiting, he knew, low over the water to pick them off when they made the next turn.

Hug the right shore on the first turn and the left on the second. That was what she had told him, but his wife was very clearly making a path to the right on this second turn.

Dalton struggled to follow against the pull of the river that tried to drag him left. On the turn he saw the reason for her warning. There before him loomed the largest logjam of downed trees he'd ever seen, and it rushed right at them. Waves hit the barrier and soared ten feet in the air, soaking the logs that choked the right bank of the turn. The pile of debris seemed injected with towering pillars of rock.

It occurred to him then why most groups did not run this section of the river and never after a release from the dam.

Erin performed a neat half turn, riding a wave partially up the natural dam as the second kayak flipped. The river dropped her back and she pulled until she grasped a branch near the shore. She held on as the river tore the empty craft from hers. The empty vessel bobbed up beyond the logs and sped downriver as Erin struggled to keep hers from being dragged under the web of branches.

He tried to mimic her maneuver but instead rammed bow-first into the nest of branches. The water lifted the back of his kayak while forcing the bow down and under the debris.

"Grab hold," Erin yelled.

He did, managing to grip the slimy, lichen-covered limb as the kayak continued its path downward and into the debris. He used both feet to snag the shoulder straps of his pack as his watercraft vanished beneath him. His stomach burned and he knew he could hold his pack or the limb, but not both. His current physical weakness infuriated him, but he dropped his pack. It fell to his seat in front of the red cooler decoy. Both his gear and the kayak were pulled under.

He hauled himself farther up on the debris as his kayak resurfaced beyond the fallen tree limb where he clung and his craft was whisked away.

He sighed at the loss, but with his feet free he could now climb to a spot above where Erin was snagged. He help move the nose of her craft back and clear of a branch. Then she dragged and pulled herself toward the shore. Just a little farther and the current calmed. Erin shoved with her paddle and reached the shallows as he scrambled beside the log dam.

How many seconds until the chopper realized they were no longer on the river?

Chapter 5

Erin clambered onto shore, pausing only to tug her backpack from the inner compartment. Dalton dropped from the brush pile to land in the shallows beside her and dragged her kayak off the shore and well into the cover of the pines before halting to look back at the river.

No one ran that portion of the river on the day of a planned release. The water was too deep and too fast. She was shocked she hadn't rolled under the mass of twisted branches. Even experienced paddlers could be pinned by rolling water or submerged obstacles.

She looked back at the river now thirty feet behind them. The sound of rushing water abated. The roar lessened to a churning tumble, like a waterfall.

By slow degrees, the sound changed to something mechanical. The whirling of the chopper blades, she realized.

The killers had waited long enough. They were coming upriver.

Erin shouldered the second strap of her pack and crouched down as the helicopter swept low over the water, heading upriver. Dalton paused for its passing, then grabbed the towrope and hauled the kayak farther back into the woods until he and her vessel disappeared.

The helicopter raced past again and then hovered over the brush pile. Could they see Dalton's pack or his kayak? They definitely saw something.

How was this even happening?

Was Brian all right? He couldn't paddle with his wounded arm and she knew she'd never navigate the rapids towing him. The choice was hard, but leaving him gave him his best chance. They wouldn't know where or on which side of the river to find him. His wound was serious but he could walk, run actually.

Run and hide. When they're gone, when you're certain, you can find the river trail. The blue trail. Follow it upriver to the road.

He'd understood, she was sure, but with his pale cheeks and the shock, she didn't know if he could make it to safety.

"Please let him be all right," she whispered.

If her muscles didn't ache and her teeth weren't chattering, she'd try to chalk this up as some bad dream. Instead, it was a full-fledged nightmare. A waking one.

Her mind flashed on an image of Carol Walton, her stomach torn open by a soulless piece of debris that could have struck any one of them. Erin covered her eyes, but the image remained, emblazoned in her mind. That flying metal could have killed Dalton just as easily as Carol. And then she'd be dead in that meadow with her entire outdoor adventure group. Erin's shoulders shook.

Something warm touched her arm and she jumped. Dalton squeezed and she rolled into the familiar comfort of his embrace. She forgot the imminent doom of the men on the helicopter lurking just a few yards from where she wept in her husband's arms. He let her go after a few minutes, rubbed her shoulders briskly and drew back.

"We have to go," he said.

She nodded and sniffed. "Will they think we're dead?"

"Here's hoping. Will your kayak hold two?"

"No. We'd swamp in rough water."

"Then we go on foot."

"Where?"

"As far from here as possible."

She nodded and then looked around.

"They're gone?" she asked.

"For now."

Under the cover of the trees it seemed that night had already fallen, until you glanced at the purple sky visible through the gaps in the foliage.

Where was Brian?

"Do you think they'll catch him?" Erin could not keep the tears from coming as she spoke. "I had to get him to shore. I couldn't...he couldn't..."

Dalton gathered her in.

"It was the right choice. The boy has a better chance away from us."

"I was afraid he'd upend and drown. I told him to hide and then how to walk out, but he's bleeding and scared."

"He's young and strong." Dalton released her. "He'll make it."

Was he just telling her what she needed to hear? She didn't know, but if Brian survived, it was because Dalton did as she asked. His remaining at her request had saved the boy, at least. Or it might have.

"Which way?" he asked.

"Well," she said, adjusting her pack. "We should head downriver. That's the closest place to find help."

"Then they'll expect us to head that way." Dalton looked in the opposite direction. "What's upriver?"

"Brian, I hope, and the dead."

He turned back to her, and she knew that the tears still rolled down her damp cheeks.

"I'm sorry about them, Erin. If we are lucky and smart, you'll have time to process this and grieve. But right now we must get clear of this spot. We need full cover, and the more difficult it is to follow us the better."

"Maybe we should head west awhile. There isn't much in that direction. Not a destination. Then we can turn either to Indian Lake or Lake Abanakee. There are vacation cottages on both. Golf courses, some camping." She turned in a full circle tapping her index finger on the small indentation between her upper lip and nose.

"What?" he asked.

"You know, they'll expect us on this shore."

"Because they saw my gear on the jam."

"Yes, so what if we cross the river?"

He frowned, really not wanting to get back into that sucking vortex of death.

"How?" he asked.

"I'll cross with the towrope tied to my kayak. You

keep hold of the throw ball until I'm ashore. Then, you can haul back my kayak and use it to follow me."

"What if it tips on the way back? Then you're over there and I'm over here."

"Won't matter if it tips. It won't sink."

"Then we go together."

"The kayak won't sink, but it will be floating beneath the surface. We'll be swept out."

He nodded. "All right. One at a time. You first."

She gave him an impatient smirk for repeating her plan back to her, only this time taking credit, and then gave him a thumbs-up.

"Good plan. Let's do it your way."

He flushed as she sat to wait out their pursuers. The chopper continued to circle them like a shark smelling blood. Finally, their pursuers flew up and out of sight. Erin and Dalton waited for full dark so their crossing would not be noted.

Then she tumped the kayak, carrying it upside down on her head over the stretch they could not paddle. Dalton tried to take it, but the pain of stretching his arms too far above his head made it impossible. Erin carried the craft a quarter mile downriver to a spot beyond the turn. After that, he helped load her pack and held on to the thin cordage as she pushed off and flew out of his sight. He marked her progress by the line that slipped over his palms. He eyed the diminishing line, worrying that she would not reach the opposite shore before he reached the end of the towline. He wasn't sure that she'd calculated how far downriver the current would carry her before she could reach the opposite bank.

Abruptly, the towline stilled, then shuddered and moved two measured feet along. She was snagged or across. He counted the time in the rapid rasp of his breath and the sweat that rolled periodically down his back. Finally, he felt the four short tugs that signaled him to retrieve the kayak.

Dragging the craft back to him was not as easy as he had anticipated, and he was sweating and cursing by the time he sighted her kayak.

He took a moment to catch his breath and check the two vials he carried in their custom pack. Both they and the thumb drive were intact and dry. He zipped closed the case, returning it to his side pocket. Then he checked his personal weapon.

"Ready or not," he said, and climbed into the kayak, where he shimmied until the bottom cleared the bank and the river took him. Moving fast and paddling hard. The water seemed a glittering deadly ribbon. He could not see the rocks that jutted from the churning surface until they flashed past him. One pounded the underside of the kayak, making it buck like a bronco. He continued on, realizing that he was riding lower and lower in the water with each passing second. The kayak's bottom was compromised. He was certain.

The hollow core of the craft was filling with water. In other words, he was sinking.

Chapter 6

Erin's damp skin turned icy as she watched the dark shape of her kayak sinking below the surface. She caught a glimpse of the paddle sweeping before the craft and held her breath. Her husband was in the river, swimming for his life.

She grabbed her pack and cursed. It was a stupid dangerous idea to have him try to cross the river alone and at night. She knew this section and the location of the rocks that loomed from the water. Dalton did not and, as far as she knew, he had never kayaked before.

Brush and brambles lined the bank, but she raced along, searching for his head bobbing in the dark water.

"He's a strong swimmer," she told the night, but he wasn't. He was only average, his muscle mass making him what she called "a sinker."

And he should be at home on medical leave recovering from the abdominal surgery that followed the bullet wound.

She tripped, sprawled and righted herself.

"Dalton!" she shouted.

Where was he? The kayak had vanished and her paddle had been carried off. She judged the river's flow and imagined a line from where he went into the Hudson to where he might be.

He'd had loads of time in the pool and the ocean practicing escapes from crafts. He had jumped out of helicopters in to the ocean. So he'd know not to fight the river. The only thing to do was to use the forward momentum and patiently angle your stroke toward the shore.

How far would the river take him?

Her heart walloped against her ribs as she raced around tree trunks and scrambled over rocks.

What if he hit his head? What if he were unconscious?

She'd wanted a break, a time to think and a time for him to hear her fears. She didn't want him dead. That was why she'd called for a separation. He didn't see what he was doing, how dangerously he lived. And he didn't understand how his decisions affected her. If he died, oh, what if he was drowning right now?

He could be pinned against a rock or held down under a snag that wasn't even visible from above. Had he left her, finally, once and for all?

Something was moving up ahead.

Erin ran, howling like a wolf who had lost her pack, crying his name and wailing like a banshee. Her legs pumped. When had she dropped her pack?

Was it him? Had the Fates brought him back to her once more?

I swear, I'll never leave him again. Just don't let him die. Please, please, dear Lord.

It was big, crawling up the bank. A man. Sweet Lord, it was her man.

"Dalton!"

He turned his head—lifted a hand in greeting—and collapsed on the bank.

The roar of the river blocked any reply, but he'd seen her. She fell on her hands and knees before him. Gathering him up in her arms. Rocking and weeping and babbling.

He patted her upper arm, gasping but reassuring her with his action. It only made her weep harder. He shouldn't even be here. He could have died.

It would have been her fault. He was here because of her. He'd tried the river because of her, and he'd nearly drowned...because of her.

Dalton struggled to a seat on the muddy bank. His skin was as cool as river water and his clothing drenched. It didn't have to be that cold for someone to die from exposure. Being wet upped the chances. And being weakened from exertion and the healing wounds all made him more susceptible.

She needed her pack.

"Can you stand?" she asked.

He struggled to his knees and then to his feet, leaning heavily on her. The amount of weight that pressed down upon her nearly buckled her knees and terrified her further because he wouldn't lean so heavily if he didn't have to.

The sound of the river changed. There was a rhythmic quality that lifted to her consciousness and caused her to look skyward. A field of stars littered the velvety black and then, from upriver, came a cone of light.

"Helicopter," she said.

Dalton straightened and glanced up. "Cover," he said, and struggled up the bank. The tree line loomed like a dark curtain, impossibly far. They lumbered along, he the bear, she the fox. Nearly there when the helicopter shot past them.

The searchlight swept back and forth across the river's surface.

"They're on the logjam," he said, his voice shaking with the rest of him.

The chopper hovered, the beam shining on something beyond their line of sight.

"My kayak or my pack," he guessed.

"They'll think we drowned."

"Maybe."

"I don't understand. Why would they come after us? They must have found what they were looking for by now."

Dalton said nothing, just sank to his knees on the cushiony loam of pine needles.

"Where is your pack?" he asked.

"I dropped it."

He lifted his head and stared at her, his eyes glittering.

"In the open?"

"I'm not sure."

"Go get it, Erin. Hurry. Take cover if they go over again. Find it if you can."

"What about you?"

"I'll be here."

She stood, indecision fixing her to the spot. Go? Stay?

"We need that gear," he said.

They did.

"And if they spot it…"

Erin set off again as the helicopter continued to hover. She didn't look back as she returned to the shore and hurried upriver. She couldn't see more than a few feet before her. It would be easy to miss a green pack, but the frame, it was aluminum. She'd come too far, she thought. Must have missed it. She must have been carrying it here.

And then, finally and at last, she caught the glint of her silver water bottle.

She dashed the remaining distance and scooped up her pack. Then she turned to see the helicopter descending low on the river. Was it in the same place?

No, it was moving, shining its light on the opposite bank. The ruse was working. Still she hurried under cover and waited as it surged past her position. Then she retraced her steps.

"Dalton?"

She wasn't sure how far she needed to go, but this seemed the right distance.

"Dalton?"

"Here!"

She followed the direction of his call and found him sitting against a large tree trunk, arms wrapped about his middle. He wasn't shivering. Instead of taking that as a positive change, she saw it for what it was. When the body was cold and stopped shivering, it was dying.

Erin tore the lower boughs from the pines and set them beside the log. Then she unrolled her black foam mat and shook out her sleeping bag because the down filling needed to trap dead air within the baffles in order to insulate and help hold body heat.

When she finished, she helped him rise. He staggered and fell and then crawled as she urged him on, whispering commands like a hoarse drill sergeant. She stripped him out of his jacket, shoulder holster and personal weapon, then she tugged off the wet T-shirt and cargo pants that were predictably heavy and likely carrying his service weapon and extra clips for his pistol. All were wet, but that was a problem for another time.

"I'm not cold," he whispered, his words slurring.

He stretched out in the open sleeping bag and lay on both the mat and pine boughs. She zipped him in.

Erin thought about calling the emergency number of the Department of Environmental Conservation. The rangers could call the New York State Police Aviation Unit or the Eagle Valley Search Dogs, but she very much feared that rescue would be hours away. So she left her phone off and stowed for the time being. Right now she needed shelter and to get Dalton warm.

She was a survival expert and knew the rule of threes. The body could survive three minutes without air, three hours without shelter, less depending on the weather and their physical condition, three days without water and three weeks without food.

She fitted her pack half under the log at his head and then set to work on the shelter. Fallen sticks and branches littered the forest floor and she gathered them by the armful, making a great pile. Then she constructed a brush shelter around him using the log beside which he lay as the center beam and leaning the larger sticks against it. It was low to the ground, easy to miss if you were not looking. She did not know if the men who had killed her party would follow them into the woods, but she was taking no chances.

Her tent was too geometrical and too light to make good cover. But her camo tarp could work if she used it correctly. Erin laid the ten-by-ten tarp over the logs and sticks, then staked it down on the opposite side of the downed trunk. The remaining four feet she stretched out away from the log before securing it to the ground. Then she added evergreen boughs to further disguise their burrow.

Erin stepped back to study the structure she had built. The resulting shelter was roughly the shape of a lean-to and stood only two feet tall at the highest point, tapering to the ground from there and was no taller than the fallen tree trunk. The tarp would break the cold wind that was rising carrying the scent of rain.

As the helicopter searched the far bank, she finished all but the small gap needed to crawl inside. This she would close once she was beside her husband. The fact that Dalton did not move to help her frightened her greatly.

Shivering herself, exhausted and sick at heart, Erin crawled in next to Dalton. Before she closed the opening, she watched as the helicopter hovered beyond the barrier of tree trunks and crossed the glistening water. That too was a problem for another time. They could no longer run. So, it was time to hide.

Erin wiggled in beside her husband. His skin was cold as marble. She managed to get the zipper up and around them. The bag was designed for one, but accommodated them both with Dalton on his back and her tucked against him on her side. She knew how much body heat was lost from the top of a person's head so she tugged at the drawstring, bringing the top of the bag down around Dalton's head like the hood of a parka.

Still at last, she pressed her warm body to his icy one. Gradually, her temperature dropped and she shivered. Dalton lay unmoving except for the shallow rise and fall of his chest.

What if he was bleeding inside again?

She could do nothing if he was, and that was why her mind fixed upon it. Why was that?

When one shoulder began to ache, she pushed herself on top of Dalton. She inhaled fresh pine, damp earth and the aftershave that still lingered faintly on Dalton's skin. He lifted an arm across her back, holding her in his sleep. His movement made her tear up. By the time she shifted to his opposite side, he was shivering.

The helicopter rotors continued to spin and the beam of light crossed over them twice. She wasn't sure when the chopper finally moved off. Sometime after Dalton had stopped shivering.

She fell asleep with the uneasy feeling that the men who had murdered her party had not given up. A cold wind rushed through the shelter, cooling her face. She tasted rain.

Sometime later, the storm struck, hitting the tree canopy first, rousing Erin from uneasy slumber. Dalton's breathing had changed to a slow, steady draw and his heart beat in a normal rhythm. Eventually the rain penetrated the interlocking branches of the trees and the droplets pattered on the dry leaves. The torrent of water grew in volume until she could no longer hear the river rush.

The sky lit in a brilliant flash of white and Erin began her counting as she waited for the thunder. She didn't like being under the trees in such a storm. Tall trees were natural lightning rods, and the wind could bring down limbs and dead trees on hapless campers. It was why she had selected the fateful rocky outcropping.

She imagined the rain merging with the drying blood on the bodies of the ones she had left behind, and her chest constricted.

"Erin?" Dalton whispered.

"Yes?"

"You okay?"

"I don't think so."

"The chopper gone?"

"Yes."

"I thought I just saw the spotlight."

The thunder rolled over and through them.

"It's the storm."

He relaxed back into their nest. "Good. Make it harder to track us."

"Why would they want to track us?" she asked, and in answer heard his gentle snore.

Erin rolled to her side, pressing her back against him and curling her arms before herself. The thunder was still a mile off, but over the next quarter hour it passed overhead.

The cascade of water finally penetrated their burrow, soaking the evergreen and running down the needles and tarp away from where they rested.

Gradually the rainfall diminished, and the sound of the river returned, rushing endlessly. When she next roused it was to some unfamiliar sound. She stiffened, listening. The gray gloom inside their nest told her that morning approached. She could now see the sides of the shelter above her.

The sound came again, this time recognizable. It was the snapping of a stick underneath the foot of something moving close at hand.

Chapter 7

Erin strained to listen to the creature moving close to their shelter. Squirrel or possum, maybe. Or a deer, perhaps. When animals moved, they sounded much larger than they actually were. She'd seen grown men startle in terror from the crackle of dried leaves under the paws of a scurrying chipmunk.

The sound came again. That was no chipmunk.

Now there was another snap of a branch, this time coming from a slightly different direction. Dalton's eyes popped open and she pressed a hand over his mouth. Whatever was out there, she did not want to reveal their position.

Dalton woke with a jolt to feel Erin's warm hand pressed across his mouth. He shifted only his eyes to look at her. In the gray predawn gloom, he could see little. But his body was on high alert.

She had heard it, too. He was certain from the stiffness of her body and the way she cocked her head to one side, listening. Something was coming. To him it sounded like the even tread of boots. He had been on enough covert ops to recognize the sound of a line of men moving in sequence.

He lifted his head from the sleeping bag. Listening.

Where was his gun?

The sound came from the right and left. He counted the footfalls. He heard three distinct individuals moving together, searching, he guessed, the forest on this side of the river.

Had they already finished their sweep of the opposite bank?

Where the hell was his gun?

The group continued forward and then passed them. Why hadn't they seen them?

Dalton gazed up at the unfamiliar roof some eight inches above his head. They were in some sort of shelter constructed of broken sticks leaning on a large fallen log and then covered with a camo tarp. More branches on the outside, judging from the way the light cut through the tarp. His gaze swept above his head and down to his toes. Then he turned his face so that his lips pressed to his wife's ear.

"They missed us."

Now she turned her head to whisper into his ear.

"What if they come back?"

He did not answer. But he knew exactly. It was not to tie up loose ends or to silence them forever. It was to retrieve what had been stolen from them or from their employers. They were acting on orders to retrieve the contents of the red nylon cooler. Just as the pilot had told them. These men would keep coming until they recovered what he carried. And he would stop at nothing to get it into the hands of his own government.

But first he had to empty his bladder.

Erin was still for a very long time. Finally, she shifted beside him, lifting her knee across his thigh, rising up to one elbow to stare down at him.

"They were searching along this side of the river."

"Yes."

"Should we stay here or make a run for it?"

"I've got to get up. Let me do a little recon."

"Good plan, except you're naked, your clothes are wet, your gun is wet and recon means leaving me alone. Let me rephrase that. Bad plan. Really, really bad."

"I still have to get up."

"Me, too."

"After you then. I haven't climbed out of a foxhole in some time."

"It's a brush shelter."

Erin removed the sticks that obscured the opening. Then she wiggled out of the bag to crouch beside the tree. She saw immediately why they were invisible to their pursuers. Several more pine boughs had fallen during the storm. Her shelter seemed just more debris.

Not only that, the warm ground in the cool air had resulted in a low mist that crept around the tree trunks and hugged the earth. To disappear, one only had to lie flat.

She took her time listening and looking for the men. Seeing nothing, she called back to Dalton and then moved away to relieve herself. When she returned to him, he was crouching naked beside the shelter.

"It's freezing out here."

"The mornings can be chilly."

"I'm shriveled up like the... Do you have anything that I can wear?"

Erin moved to the shelter to slide her pack out of the gap. She sorted through her gear and retrieved the plastic rain poncho.

"Maybe this?" She offered the poncho and then added one of his olive green T-shirts.

He held the familiar garment aloft. "Why did you bring this?"

"Hey, don't read more into it than there is. It's soft and I like to sleep in it." She did not like his self-satisfied smile.

A moment later he had slipped into the T-shirt. As his head vanished into the fabric she glanced to his stomach. She always admired the heavy musculature of his chest and stomach, especially in motion. But this time her gaze tracked to the swollen red suture line at the flesh just above his hip bone. The man should be home, resting and not lifting anything over forty pounds.

Dalton tugged down on the hem of the cotton T-shirt and then donned the poncho. He chose to wear his damp cargo pants commando style. Then he spent the next twenty minutes disassembling, cleaning and drying his pistol. He dried every bullet in the four clips that he had stowed in the pockets of his pants.

Erin occupied herself scattering the branches used for her shelter. Then she stuffed the sleeping bag back into its nylon bag, rolled her foam pad and collected the tarp. She stowed all of these but the high density foam bedroll into her pack. That she tied on the top.

"Ready?" he asked.

"Which way?" she asked.

"Away from our company. When they don't find us, they'll backtrack."

"You want me to call the forest rangers?"

"Is your phone still off?"

"How did you know it was off?"

His mouth tipped down. "I tried calling you yesterday. Kept flipping to voice mail."

"I told you I wouldn't be calling."

"You did."

Now she was scowling. "I'll keep it off for now."

Dalton removed the strap from her shoulder and took her pack.

"You shouldn't carry that," she said, staring pointedly at his middle and the healing surgical scars that she knew were there.

"Circumstances being as they are, I am."

"We still have to talk about this."

He nodded and set off. Erin knew he'd likely rather face those mercenaries than have a talk with her, and that was exactly the problem, wasn't it? But they were going to talk, and even commandos were not going to keep her from saying her piece.

If he didn't like it, that was just too darn bad. Next time maybe he'd stay home when she asked him.

By the time Dalton finally stopped, the gray dawn had morphed into a fine drizzle that coated the leaves and dripped down upon them. It saturated her hair and dampened her clothing. Erin could see from his pallor that Dalton had pushed too hard and traveled too many miles.

".Where do you think we are?" he asked.

They'd been traveling in roughly a northerly direction according to her compass, paralleling the river, and she could guess the distance at three miles of scrambling down bramble-covered ravines and up lichen-covered rock faces. The topography on this side of the river was challenging, and the closer they got to the gorges the steeper the climb would become.

"Don't you know?" she asked.

He shook his head.

"Then just maybe you should let the one with the compass and maps lead."

He pressed his lips together in that suffering look, and her internal temperature rose to a near boil. She reminded herself that he'd nearly died last month and again last night. It seemed he was determined to leave her. Her leaving was intended to keep that from happening, but somehow it had just made everything worse.

She removed the bottle from the pack she carried and offered it to him.

"Almost empty," he said, refusing.

"I can fill it anywhere. I have a filtration system on this bottle."

"You mean I've been conserving all morning for no reason?"

"No, there was a reason. You didn't ask me."

His eyes lifted skyward as if praying for patience, and then he drank all that was left in the bottle.

"Why don't we just call DEC?"

"DEC?" he asked.

"Department of Environmental Conservation. The forest rangers. They can dispatch a helicopter and lift us out of here."

"No."

"Why not?"

He shook his head and looked skyward as if expecting a phantom helicopter. Honestly, the man seemed to want to do everything the hard way.

"Dalton, why?"

"The call for air evac would be via radio, and that transmission is being monitored by our pursuers."

"You don't know that."

"It's what I would do."

"Well, then, let me at least send search and rescue after Brian Peters and to my group." Her voice broke on the last word and she clamped her mouth closed to keep from crying.

"Your mobile is still off?"

"Yes. Why?"

"If the kid made it out, then they already know what happened and where."

She thought of the teen alone on the trail and the worry squeezed at her heart. "Do you think he's safe?"

Her husband offered no assurances and his expression remained grim. "He's a wounded kid and they're trained mercenaries. He went the way you told me that they'd expect us to go."

She had sent him straight into more trouble. Erin scowled. "I never should have left him."

"If you hadn't, we'd all be dead. His only chance was away from us. You made the right call. In any case, you are overdue to check in. When DEC finds your party, they'll know you are missing with three kayaks. But if you switch on that phone our pursuers will find us."

"How?"

"Forest Rangers will request GPS coordinates from the county 911."

Erin said no more as she studied the map for several minutes. "You want to backtrack to Lake Abanakee or continue downriver to the community of North River?"

"Neither. Those are the two directions they will expect us to travel. What else have you got?"

"Why are they even following us? Is it because we are witnesses?"

Dalton's gaze shifted away. Erin scowled as she remembered something.

"You took that cooler. The one from the helicopter. I saw it in your kayak."

"The pilot entrusted the information—"

"To me! And I left it behind. I left it because our lives are more valuable to me than some flash drive and a pair of glass vials."

He saw the look in her eyes, registering what he had done. He didn't deny it. But neither did he offer reassurance. She was right. He'd put them in danger.

"But you lost all your gear with your kayak. If they were searching, they should have found both. Even if the cooler popped out of your kayak…"

"It didn't. I tied it down."

Dalton's eyes shifted back to meet hers and she saw the guilty look on his face.

"Where is it?" she demanded.

Dalton lifted his hands in a gesture meant to placate. "Now, honey. Listen to me."

"Where?"

His right hand moved to the side pocket on his cargo pants. He gave the full pocket a little pat.

"Why in the name of heaven would you risk our lives for whatever trouble that pilot was carrying?"

Dalton reached for her shoulders and she stepped away. Then she released the waist buckle at her middle and dropped her pack. She spent the next several moments stalking back and forth like a caged animal, gathering her fury about her like a cloak. Finally, she came to a complete stop, pivoting to face him.

"You just don't get it. This is why I wanted a break. This…" She waved her hand in a circular motion and continued speaking. "This obsession with playing the hero. It's not our job to deliver that nonsense. It was his."

"This is bigger than that," said Dalton. "This could save thousands of lives. Maybe our own."

"If we don't get killed in the process." She turned her back on him and covered her face with her hands.

Tentatively, he wrapped an arm around her shoulders and turned her to face him.

"Erin, I'm sorry. But I didn't see a choice."

She shook her head. "And that's where you're wrong. There's always a choice. The choice to reenlist in the most dangerous arm of the Marines."

"I left them because you were unhappy."

"I wasn't unhappy being married to a marine. I was unhappy being married to a marine who insisted on being on the front line of every assignment."

"I quit because of you."

"You didn't quit. You just shifted from one dangerous assignment to the next. New York City Real Time Crime Center? Come on, Dalton. What is the difference between that and Vice?"

"It's not undercover work."

"You're a cop. You're a target."

"Is that what you think I am?"

"They shot you! They killed your partner."

"Not while I was on a call."

"What difference does that make? You were in a coma, Dalton. You didn't have to attend your partner's funeral. You didn't have to see them give a flag to his widow. You didn't have to comfort his children. I did that. I did that alone while you were recovering from internal injuries."

"I understand how you must feel."

"Clearly you don't or you would have stayed home as I asked. You would have considered that my fears are justified."

"And you'd be dead now."

"As opposed to in a day from now? If you really believe that those guys are after us, trained killers, what chance do we have? They have helicopters and guns. All we have is each other."

"Maybe that's enough."

She rolled her eyes. "Oh, Dalton. Just leave it. Put it on a rock on a bright red T-shirt with a note that says, 'Enjoy!' and let's get out of here with our lives."

"That's why I love you, Erin. You are a survivor."

She pressed her lips tight and glared. "The way you are headed, I'll have to be."

"Don't be like that."

"Like what? I'm trying to keep you alive. To save you from yourself because if I don't, one way or another, you're leaving me. Getting shot at, blown up in Afghanistan, coming home with knife wounds and now carrying a vial of something that, if it breaks open in your pocket, will kill us both."

She loved him, but she was not going to stand over

his coffin and accept a flag from a grateful city or nation. If you couldn't stop the oncoming train, sometimes all you could do was step out of its way.

He stared down at her with that hangdog look, and she tried and failed not to feel his sorrow.

"How do you see this ending?" she asked.

"We make it out and get this to the FBI in Albany."

"Fine." She shouldered her pack and stared up at the victorious smile on his handsome face, and she ignored the jolt of awareness that he stirred in her. "And then I want a divorce."

Chapter 8

Erin studied the topographical map. "If we walk along the gorge beside the Boreas River, we'll run into North Woods Club Road."

"How far?"

"Roughly three miles east to the confluence of the Boreas River and Hudson, bushwhacking because there is no trail. Then it's a two-mile uphill hike, steep for the first mile or so, on a marked trail to the gravel road. From there we can head west to a small community at the terminus of the road or east to Minerva. The community looks like about five houses. Either one is somewhere around five more miles."

"Ten miles."

"Only six to the road. We can get help there."

"Or get intercepted."

"The rain will fill the rivers and make the going slippery, but we should reach the road in a couple of hours. We can call the rangers."

He looked unconvinced.

"They can search for Brian, send help, and I'll tell them not to use radio communication."

"You can't guarantee it. With so many rangers, someone will pick up a radio."

"Who do you want to call, your detective bureau?"

"Too far. But I could have them call for help once we get out of the woods."

"What about my camp director? He can drive to the station. By now they've found—" she struggled to swallow "—my group. He'll believe me when I tell him we are on the run, being stalked. And if Brian got through, they'll know our situation. We know there's help out there. We just have to get to them or help them find us."

"When we get closer to the road."

"Fine." She kept hold of her pack and the map, leading the way back. "You know, there will be rafting groups on the river all day. We might get one of them to pick us up."

"No. They'll be at the terminus of every rafting trip."

"How many of these people do you really think there are?"

"Three in the chopper last night and three in the woods beside our shelter. Plus, the ones who shot the chopper down."

"They might be the same group."

"I don't know how many. Neither do you. So assume everyone we meet is one of them."

She'd seen what they could do, and she did not question her husband's assessment of their situation.

Erin led the way, using her compass only and staying well away from the Hudson. She stopped to fill the water bottle at a spring. All she had were several power bars she kept for emergencies, which this surely was. She handed Dalton the lemon zest bar and kept the chocolate chip for herself. She peeled back the wrapping and glanced up to see the second and last bite of the lemon zest disappear into Dalton's mouth.

"When did you last eat?" she asked.

"Yesterday morning."

He was a big man and burned a lot more calories than she did. She rummaged in her pack and offered a second bar.

"You have more?" His brows lifted in that adorable way that made her want to kiss his face.

"Yes, plenty." Plenty being one.

Midmorning, they paused at a stream and Dalton returned her poncho. He did fill out the shirt she slept in, and she surreptitiously enjoyed the view of his biceps bulging as he lifted the bottle to his lips and drank. The sight made her own mouth go dry.

Erin glanced away, but too late. She was already remembering him naked beneath her last night. Dalton's large, strong body never failed to arouse her. It was just his attitude that pushed her aside. Just once she'd like to have him choose them above protecting the city or the nation or whatever it was he thought he was doing. If he was right, the men hunting them were still out there.

Despite her reservations, her mind swept back to the last time they'd made love. Before the shooter had walked up to her husband's unmarked police unit and shot his partner, Chris Wirimer, in the head before turning the pistol on Dalton. The shooter had targeted the pair solely because they wore police dress uniforms.

They were en route to attend the annual medal day ceremony in Lower Manhattan. The gunman had managed to get a bullet between the front and back of Dylan's body armor. It had taken six hours to patch all the bleeders from the bullet, which had traveled between his body armor and his hip bone from front to back stopping only when it had reached the back panel of his flak jacket. A through and through with no internal organ damage, but Dalton had nearly bled out, nearly left her in the way she always feared he would.

From beneath the cover of the canopy of hardwood and pine, Erin again heard the rush of running water. A short time later they reached the Boreas River, flowing fast and swollen from the heavy rains. Here at the river's terminus, the water stretched forty feet from side to side. Erin knew that farther up, the river ran through narrow gorges on the stretch of white water known as Guts and Glory. Here, it tumbled and frothed, making for an excellent run.

She found the trail easily and turned north. Looking back, she could see where the two rivers met. She did not linger as she led them up the steep, muddy trail. Dalton's breathing was labored, and she paused to let him rest. She didn't like his grayish color and was angry again that he'd decided to ambush her instead of giving himself time to heal and her time to think.

She turned her head at the jangle of a dog's collar. A few moments later a young black Labrador retriever appeared wearing a red nylon collar and no leash. Its pink tongue lolled and it paused for just a moment upon sighting Erin, then dashed forward in jubilant excitement.

Erin laughed and offered her hand. The dog wore

a harness and was likely carrying her own food and water. Erin stooped to give the dog a scratch behind the ears. She glanced at her collar, fingering the vaccination tag and the ID.

"Jet, huh?" she asked.

The dog half closed her eyes and sat at her feet.

Erin glanced up the trail, waiting for the dog's owner to appear. She did, a few moments later—a fit older woman with braided graying hair who wore a slouch hat that covered most of her face, hiking shorts and a T-shirt, cotton button-up shirt, wool socks and worn hiking boots. In her hands she carried a hiking stick, and there was a day pack upon her back.

"Oh, hello," said the woman, drawing to a halt. "He's friendly."

Erin wrinkled her nose because the dog was clearly female. That was odd. There was something not right about that woman. Erin took a reflexive step back, trying to determine why her skin was tingling a warning.

"You been to the Hudson?" asked the woman.

The dog did not dart back to her master but instead sat beside Erin. A chill crept over her. She took another step away.

"Yes, it's only a mile and a half down this trail."

"You camping along here?" asked the woman.

"Yes."

"You alone?" the woman asked.

Alone?

Erin turned back in the direction they had come and was surprised to see only the dog at her side. Where was Dalton? Erin's skin prickled as if she had rolled in a patch of nettles. She turned back to face this new threat.

"Yes, why?" Erin thought the woman's smile looked

forced and she realized the hiker was younger than she appeared. She wondered vaguely if the gray braided hair was actually attached to this woman's head.

"Where's your partner?"

"What partner?" Erin asked.

"Detective Dalton Stevens." The female drew a small handgun from her pocket and pointed it at Erin's belly.

Erin's mouth dropped open and her heart seemed to pulse in the center of her throat. She could not have spoken if she had tried.

"Does he have it? Or do you?"

"I don't know what you're talking about."

The woman snorted. "Yes, you do. Drop the pack."

Erin did as she was told.

The woman waved Erin back with the barrel of the pistol. Then she moved forward, keeping her gun on Erin as she swept the surroundings with a gaze.

"Come out, Detective, or I shoot your wife."

Chapter 9

Erin faced the female pointing a pistol at her belly, clearing her throat before she spoke.

"Is this your dog?" Erin asked.

The woman's mouth quirked. "Took it off a pair that were camping back a ways. Unfortunately for them, I'm not so good with faces and I thought they were you. Should have checked before I shot them in their sleeping bags. Lesson learned."

Erin couldn't keep from covering her mouth with one hand.

"Don't figure they need a dog anymore and I thought it added to the whole look." She glanced at the trees on either side of the path. Then she raised her voice. "Detective? I'm counting to three. One…"

Erin jumped at the report of the pistol. Her hands went to her middle, but she felt no pain. Before her, her attacker sank to her knees. Dalton stepped from cover. Pistol aimed and cradled between his two hands as he moved forward with feline grace.

Her canine companion moved forward to greet him, but Dalton ignored the dog, focusing all his attention on the woman, who had released her pistol and sunk to her side. Blood bloomed on the front of her T-shirt and frothed from her mouth.

"How many are you?" asked Dalton.

She laughed, sending frothy pink droplets of blood dribbling down her chin.

"We're like ants at a picnic."

Dalton knelt beside her, transferring the gun to one hand; with the other he patted her down. His search yielded a second pistol, car keys, phone and several strips of plastic zip ties. Erin's stomach twisted at the thought of what she had intended to do with these.

She crept forward and removed the floppy blue hat. The gray braid fell away with the headgear. The end of the braid was secured with a hair tie to the hat's interior tag and looked to have been sliced from someone's head.

Had she stolen a woman's dog, hair and walking stick along with her life? Erin glanced at the plaid shirt and noted it was miles too big. Somewhere up ahead were the victims of this woman's attack. Erin feared she might be sick.

Dalton pocketed the key, one of the pistols, radio, phone and a folding knife. He extended the second gun to Erin.

"Take it."

She did, hoping it would not go off in her pocket.

"Who are you?" Dalton asked the downed woman.

"One of Siming's Army."

"Who?"

"You'll find out." Her smile was a ghastly sight with her lips painted red with her own blood. "The first Deathbringer. You have it. We'll get it back."

"Deathbringer," whispered Erin remembering the name.

The woman turned to look at her. "Oh! So you know them. Very good. One. Two. Three. Each body to his own fate."

The woman began to choke on her blood, struggling to draw air into her damaged lungs. Erin glanced at Dalton, who shook his head. She didn't need him to tell her that the woman was dying.

"Why are you doing this?" asked Erin, her voice angry now.

"A corrupt system must fall."

"You murdered hikers because of a corrupt system? That's insane."

"Acceptable—" she gasped and gurgled "—losses."

"We need to get off the trail," said Dalton.

He stood and Erin followed, hesitating.

"We just leave her?"

He nodded and offered his hand. "Come on. Off the trail."

The dog danced along beside them, and no amount of shooing would send her away.

"We'll have to take her," said Erin.

Dalton shook his head, adjusting the grip on the gun still in his hand.

"You will not shoot a dog!" she said, stepping between him and the black Lab.

Dalton smiled. "I was just going to tie her up on the trail."

"I'll do it." Which she did, but she also filled the water dish she carried in her pack and fed her dry food. When she left Jet, tied with a bit of her sash cord in plain view of anyone who came along here, she imagined the reaction of the poor next hiker who would stumble on this turn in the trail.

Then she petted the dog's soft, warm head and said goodbye.

When she returned, it was to find Dalton watching her.

"We should get a dog," he said.

Erin sighed and lifted her pack. "I don't like leaving her."

"We'll send somebody for her when we're safe. She'll be okay until then."

They bushwhacked uphill, staying well away from the trail and stopping when they heard people moving in their direction.

Dalton squatted beside her as they waited for the group to pass.

When he spoke, his voice was a whisper. "Once they report that death, Siming's Army will know our position. We need to move faster."

"Well, I lost my kayak."

They hurried up the rest of the slope, pausing only when they heard something tearing uphill in their direction.

Dalton motioned her to take cover and ducked behind a tree trunk. Then he drew his handgun, aiming it toward the disturbance. Something was running full out right at them.

She watched Dalton sight down the barrel of his gun, gaze focused and expression intent. She knew he would protect her and she knew he loved her. It should be enough. But who was protecting him?

The barrel of his pistol dropped and he relaxed his arms, his aim shifting to the ground. She saw him slide the safety home as he straightened.

"I don't believe this." Dalton stepped from cover.

Erin glanced around the tree trunk to see a streak of black fur barreling toward them.

"Jet!" she said.

The Lab leaped to her thighs, tail wagging merrily. Then the canine greeted Dalton by racing the few steps that separated them before throwing herself to the ground to twist back and forth in the dead leaves, paws waving and tail thumping.

Dalton holstered his pistol in the waistband of his pants and stooped to pet the dog's ribs. This caused Jet to spring to her feet to explore the area.

"She doesn't seem very broken up by the death of her owners," said Erin.

"Because she's decided we're her owners."

Erin grabbed Jet when she made her next pass. She sat before Erin, gazing up adoringly, her pink tongue lolling.

"She chewed through the sash cord." Erin held up the frayed evidence of her deduction. "She'll have to come with us."

"Not a great idea."

"I'm not leaving her again."

"She could give away our position."

She placed a fist on one hip. "If you can carry a deadly virus, I'm allowed a dog."

He twisted his mouth in frustration and then blew out of his nostrils.

"Fine. But let's go."

They scrambled over roots and waded through ferns that brushed her knees. She walked parallel to the trail that led to the gravel road, far enough away so as not to be seen. This made for slow going, and there were two places where they had to scramble up large sections of gray rock.

Mercifully, they did not see the couple that their attacker had mentioned before they finally reached the road. Dalton grasped her arm before she left the cover of the woods. Erin hunched down as he glanced right and left.

"Now we need to find the parking area for that trail. Good chance they might be there."

"We could call 911 with that woman's phone. If they're tracking her GPS signal, it'll just confirm she's where she's supposed to be—looking for us."

"Maybe. You know where the parking area is?"

"Usually right beside the trailhead. Sometimes across the road. That would be that way." She pointed to her right.

"Stay in the woods."

They picked their way over downed trees and through last year's fallen leaves, making a racket that Erin feared could be heard for miles. Under the cover of the pines, the ground was soft and their tread quiet. Jet found a stick which she tried unsuccessfully to get Dalton to throw.

Erin was willing and Jet dashed back and forth joyfully engaged in the game of fetch. Dalton came to a halt and Erin pulled up beside him. Through the maze of pine trunks she caught the glint of sunlight on metal. Automobiles. They had reached the lot.

She took hold of the dog's collar as Dalton scouted ahead. In a few minutes he returned, holding the key fob.

"This doesn't unlock either of the cars in that lot."

"What does that mean?"

"It means she was dropped at the trailhead, which means they are close."

Erin absently stroked the dog as she stared out at the lot. "What do you recommend?"

"Use her phone. Call the state police and wait for them behind cover."

They crossed into the open and then jogged across the mowed grass and over the gravel road to the opposite side. From a place in deep cover that still afforded a glimpse of the road, Dalton made his 911 call and was connected to NY State Police dispatch.

"I'm calling because my wife is on a kayaking expedition." Dalton gave the name of her camp and said that he had not heard from her. He flipped the phone to speaker so Erin could also hear the dispatcher.

"Yes, we have them listed as overdue. DEC rangers are searching."

"Should I be worried?"

"I can report that they located their camp from last night. No signs of trouble."

Erin scowled and opened her mouth to speak. Dalton held her gaze and shook his head.

"Whereabouts was that?"

There was a pause, and then the dispatcher correctly mentioned the bluff over the Hudson where her group had been murdered.

"I'll check back. Thank you." Dalton disconnected.

"What about the bodies? The helicopter piece that killed Carol? The tents, kayaks? What about the blood, Dalton?"

He gripped the phone in his hand. "The storm would have washed away the blood. Most of the helicopter sank in the Hudson, and as for the rest, someone had to remove all the evidence of the massacre."

"Just how darn big is Siming's Army?" she asked.

Chapter 10

"Call your camp director," said Dalton.

He passed her the phone and she placed the call. Erin gripped the phone in both hands as she held it out and on Speaker. The call was answered on the first ring. Her director, Oscar Boyle, a sweet, fortyish guy with tons of canoeing experience and a sunny disposition, picked up the call. Today, however, his voice relayed an unfamiliar note of anxiety.

"Erin! Oh, thank goodness. We've been going crazy. Your husband is here. He wants to speak to you."

"My husband?" She glanced at Dalton.

"Yes. He showed up yesterday to surprise you but couldn't locate your camp, so he… Do you want to speak to him? Wait, tell me where you guys are. Did you move camp because of the storm?"

Dalton gave her the cut sign and she ended the call. Then she handed back the phone.

"Do you think they'll have our coordinates?"

"Not yet. Your director will have to ask 911 to check this call and the coordinates. But they'll get around to it and they'll have this phone number, the registered owner, that is *if* it's not a burner, and after that, our position. We have to move." Dalton retrieved the phone and flicked it off.

"Which way?"

"They'll expect us to use the road and head toward Minerva. So either we go back into the woods in a direction they can't predict, or we walk on the road toward the fish and game club."

"Why there?"

"Food, shelter and possibly weapons."

"We need to get rid of that package. Just leave it on top of a car with the thumb drive. They find it and they'll stop chasing us."

He gave her a long look and she set her jaw.

"Is that really what you want me to do?"

She paced back and forth, and Jet crouched and leaped, trying to get Erin to throw the stick that the dog had carried across the road with her.

Erin stooped and took possession of the stick. Then she threw it with all her might. Jet tore off after it, of course. Erin turned to face Dalton.

"No, damn it, I don't."

He smiled. "That's my girl."

She rubbed her forehead. "We could hike over that mountain and come down at the town of Minerva. Or we could head west, past the gun club toward Lake Abanakee. Or we could backtrack to the Hudson."

"Distances?"

"Maybe twenty miles to the lake. Five up and over

the mountain to Minerva, and that's if we use the trail system."

"Maybe Minerva," he said, but his face was grim and she could feel the tension in him.

He didn't like their chances. She knew that frown, the deep lines that cut across his brow.

"They're getting closer, aren't they?" she asked.

He met her gaze and told her the truth. "Yes."

"And you think this is worth the risk of our lives?" she asked.

He glanced away. "It's worth the risk to my life." His gaze flashed back to her. "But not the risk to yours."

She swallowed down the lump, her throat emitting a squeaking sound.

"I have another idea," she said, and explained it to him. She knew there was an old trestle bridge that could take them safely across the Hudson and, from there, it was an easy eight-mile hike to the community of North River. "I don't think they'll be expecting us in the river now."

He nodded. "Yeah, that might work."

Was it the best plan? She didn't know. Dalton used their attacker's phone once more to call one of his comrades. Henry Larson had been in Dalton's unit for five years and they had come up through the academy together. He gave Henry, now in Queens, NY, their basic location and where they expected to be this evening. Henry would be calling the FBI the minute Dalton hung up. With luck they'd have help they could trust in about seven hours.

Dalton left the phone behind.

The walk downhill, off the trail, took most of the afternoon. She hoped they could reach the trestle bridge after the last group passed by. The rafters on this section were not looking for the kind of jarring thrills of the paddlers who shot the canyon. This trip was more family friendly. She had to be certain they crossed the bridge without any raft expedition or kayakers spotting them.

They paused just off the abandoned railroad bridge, behind cover and looked upriver. Erin had never crossed such a bridge and worried about the wide gaps between the horizontal wooden slats beneath the twin rails.

"What about the dog?" she asked. "Will she be able to cross the trestle bridge?"

"We'll see."

Erin heard the group before seeing them, their shouts as they descended one of the gentler falls. Dalton and Erin held Jet, remaining in hiding as the rafters floated by one after another. Only when they were out of sight did they stand.

"How deep is it here?" he asked.

"Deep enough to jump. I've seen teenagers do it."

Dalton looked over and down to the river some forty feet below. "Seems a great way to win a Darwin Award."

He spoke of the online list of folks who had, through acts of extreme stupidity, removed themselves from the gene pool by accidentally killing themselves.

He looked to her. "You ever try it?"

"I only like heights when I'm strapped into a belay system."

Dalton studied the river. "There might be lookouts."

"It's the only way across without swimming."

"Yes, that's what worries me. Ready?"

She nodded and started across. Jet whined and danced back and forth, anxious about following.

Erin turned back and called to the dog. Jet took a tentative step. Then another. The dog leaped from one slat to the next, jumping the eighteen-inch gaps. Dalton continued along, ignoring their four-legged companion and passing Erin.

Erin followed but then turned back in time to see Jet miss landing with her back feet, scrabble with her front and vanish between the slats. The splash came a moment later.

She glanced at Dalton, who was already kneeling, hands on the rail, as he judged his target and the distance down.

Erin ditched her pack, acting faster than Dalton.

"What are you doing?" he asked, standing now, reaching. She returned his frown and then jumped into the river after Jet. She heard his shout on the way down.

"Erin!"

The current was swift, even here on the wide-open section of the Hudson. She pulled and kicked, lifting her head only to mark the location of her new best friend. Jet paddled toward her, of course, instead of using the current, but the river swept her away. Erin swam harder, grabbing the dog's collar before turning toward the opposite bank.

Above, Dalton jogged along, carrying her pack, following her with an intent frown on his face.

She struggled against the current, using a scissor kick and one arm. Jet thrashed at the water, managing to keep her head up as they inched toward the southern bank. They made land at the same time as Dalton disappeared into the tree line above.

Racing, he reached her in record time.

"That was stupid," said Dalton.

She wiggled her brows.

Jet shook off the water, tail wagging as the dog immediately began sniffing the ground about them. Then she waded back into the river.

"Jet, come!" she shouted.

"You are not diving in after her again," said Dalton.

"No need."

Jet dashed back to her, tongue lolling and eyes half-closed.

"Someone will sleep well tonight," she said. When she turned her attention from Jet to Dalton, it was to see him scowling at her with both hands on his hips.

"You could have died," he said.

"Yes? How does that make you feel?" she asked.

"Mad as hell."

"Well, now you know how I feel every darn day."

His scowl deepened, sending wide furrows across his forehead.

"So it's all right to risk your neck for a dog but not for the safety of a nation?"

She lifted her chin, ready for the fight he obviously wanted. "I jumped to keep *you* from jumping."

"I wasn't…" He stopped just short of lying.

Erin shouldered her pack and turned to go and Jet followed. Dalton had caught up before they reached the highway.

"Do you think anyone saw us cross?" she asked.

"I don't know, but if there was anyone spotting, they couldn't have missed you and that darn dog."

Chapter 11

Erin changed into dry clothing and they ate the last of her food stores. Then they endured another four-mile hike over relatively flat terrain on the railroad tracks that flanked the river. Their trip was stalled twice by hikers and once by horseback riders. Thankfully, most travel in this area was by river rather than by land. Still, Erin was wistful as she watched the young women riding slowly past on a buckskin and a small chestnut mare. Her tired legs made it especially hard not to bum a lift.

She got her bearings when they reached the garnet processing plant, where abrasives were produced from the crushed red garnets mined nearby. She'd been on the mine tour more than once and knew the working mine was south of North Creek.

When they reached Route 28, Erin's ankles and knees pulsed with her heart, and her pack seemed exponentially heavier. Dalton drew to a halt and Jet groaned, then lay down, panting.

"You have anything we can pawn or trade for a hotel room?" Dalton asked, studying the mine plant from behind cover. "And maybe dinner?"

"No, but I do have three hundred dollars in my wallet. You lose your wallet?"

"I only have fifty bucks left," he admitted.

"Always prepared, except for things you have to pay for," she joked, and they shared a smile.

"How well do you know the area?"

"Drove through it, passed all the rafting outfits along the highway. Post office, roadhouse and bed-and-breakfast."

"Fancy. What about a motel?"

"I'm sure we could ask."

"I could. I'm traveling alone with my dog. You need to stay out of sight," he said.

"I can do that. I'll wait right here." The prospect of stopping and resting appealed.

"Let's get closer to town. That way?" he asked.

"Yes. A little farther past the garnet plant. We should see the highway and the river takes a turn. This is a really small community."

"Good and bad. Let's go."

They continued on the tracks until it reached the road. Erin suggested a state park that included cabin rentals, and they walked the remaining mile and a half on tired legs, reaching the ranger station after closing.

"Better off," Dalton said. "No paper trail. Should be easy to see if any of the cabins are empty."

They walked the looped trail past occupied cabins, waving at other campers.

"I could set up my tent," said Erin.

"I need a shower," he said.

She agreed that he did. So did she, for that matter.

"Bathhouse?" he suggested.

"Let's finish the loop."

As it happened, the ranger was making rounds to invite guests to a talk on the reintroduction of wolves to the Adirondacks that started at nine. Erin asked the tanned ranger in his truck if any of the cabins were still unoccupied.

"You two hiking?"

"Yeah. Going into the Hudson Gorge Wilderness and up Vanderwhacker Mountain."

"We should be able to set you up."

"Cash okay?" asked Erin.

"That'll work."

They accepted a ride back down to the station. When the ranger asked for ID, Erin held her smile but her gaze flashed to Dalton.

"I have your wallet still, I think," he said, and offered the Vermont license of the woman who had killed the pair of campers, stolen their dog and then tried to kill them.

Erin remembered the hair the woman had commandeered and shuddered. The ranger listed them in his book but never ventured near a computer. They were Mrs. Kelly Ryder and her husband, Bob.

The ranger handed over a key on a lanyard and Erin gave him seventy bucks. Transaction complete, Erin headed back out. Jet rose and stretched at their appearance. The ranger called from behind the counter.

"You'll need to put your dog on a leash."

Dalton waved his understanding as they left.

Cabin number eleven was a log structure with two bedrooms. Once inside, Erin removed her pack and groaned as she lowered her burden to the floor. Dalton flicked on the overhead light and glanced around at the living area, which included a full kitchen with a four-burner stove, refrigerator and small dinette. The living room had a saggy sleeper couch and a wooden rocker. A pair of crossed canoe paddles decorated the wall above the hearth made of river rock.

Dalton headed down the hall past the living area and found a bathroom with toilet, sink and small shower. The first bedroom was equipped with bunks and the second with a full-size bed, dresser and side tables holding lamps with decoy bases that resembled wood ducks. He really hoped he wouldn't be sleeping alone in one of the bunks.

When he returned, Erin was staring at the stove with folded arms and a contemplative expression.

"Kinda makes me wish I had some food," she said as she looked at the stove.

"We have to eat," Dalton said. A glance out the window showed that the night was creeping in.

"How are you going to pull that off?" She sank to the hard, wooden chair at the dinette and stared wearily at the knotty pine cupboards. Jet sat at her side and the dog rested her head in her new mistress's lap.

Erin stroked her dark head and said, "'Old Mother Hubbard went to the cupboard…'"

Dalton glanced out at the night. "I'll be right back."

He wasn't, but it didn't take him long. The ranger giving the talk was one of two, as he discovered upon knocking at the door to the rangers' quarters.

"I hate to bother you but those folks in cabin six-teen are shooting off bottle rockets. Guess the Fourth is coming early?"

The ranger cursed under her breath and headed out. Dalton waved her away and started off the porch, then retraced his steps after she drove off.

The door was unlocked and there were steaks in the freezer. He collected a paper bag full of groceries, left two twenty-dollar bills on the top of the drip coffee maker and headed out, returning to find Erin asleep on the sofa with her hiking boots unlaced but still on.

He didn't wake her. He let the smell of the steaks do that.

A few minutes later she opened one eye and then another. Her feet hit the floor and she rose stiffly to set the table.

"What have you got?"

He rattled off the menu. Fries and steaks, navel oranges and a box of chocolate-chip cookies. She started on those, offering Jet a one-to-three ratio on distribution, as Dalton tended the steaks.

"Where did you…never mind," she said. "I don't want to know."

He turned back to the steaks.

"Are these marshmallows?" She hefted the bag. "I love these!"

She had one toasting on a fork over the unoccupied burner of the gas stove as he used the salt and pepper before turning the meat. The only item of food in the cupboard other than salt and pepper was a ziplock bag-gie full of little packages of ketchup and mustard.

Dalton fed Jet from a box of breakfast cereal mixed

with pan drippings and the gristle from the steaks. Then he put the dog outside without a leash.

They ate at the kitchen dinette.

Erin smiled across the table at him, and he realized he could not remember the last time he had cooked for her or even the last time they had shared supper together. His job kept him gone for long hours and took him away unexpectedly and often—far too often, he realized.

"This is nice," she said.

"I've missed this," he admitted.

Her smile turned sad. "Me, too."

"Erin, I never meant for my work to take over. I don't even know when that happened." He was never home before nine anymore. By the time he got on the train and made it back to the suburbs, Erin was often asleep on the couch. Her days began early at the sports club where she taught rock climbing with frequent weekend jaunts up to New Paltz, NY, to head rock climbing outings.

"Your partner will be here tomorrow?" she asked, finishing her last fry.

"He should be here already with the cavalry."

"Great. How far do we have to go to get to him?"

"North Creek."

"A couple of miles."

He nodded and then reached across the table to take her hand, but at the last second, he panicked and instead retrieved her plate. He stood to clear the table and she followed.

"Boy, am I stiff," she muttered, rolling her shoulders. The action forced her very lovely bosom out and he took that moment to stare. She caught him of course and laughed. "I'm surprised you have enough energy for that."

"Looking doesn't cost energy."

He recalled the last time he'd loved her, the evening before the shooting. He had hoped that she'd attend the ceremony, but he'd been too preoccupied with loving her before bed to remind her and she'd been up and out before he rose. He never did find out if she had planned to be at the presentation. He and his partner were both being honored at the annual medal day ceremony, so he had been in full dress uniform. That uniform now had a small hole in the front above his right hip. That was nothing compared to the holes in his body.

Erin called his uniform a target. That day, she'd been right. Targeted for no reason other than the uniforms they wore, and the shooter in custody after clearing his psych exam. Not crazy, just murderous over old grudges stretching back through his childhood.

"Why don't you go shower?" he said. "I'll clean up."

She regarded him with mock surprise. "That's the sexiest thing you've said to me all day."

"The shower?" He couldn't help feeling hopeful.

"The cleanup." She dropped a quick kiss on his mouth and then spun away before he could reel her in. But she'd left him with something else.

Hope.

Hope for the night. Hope for their marriage.

He found himself humming as he went about clearing the table. The scratch at the door told him the canine had returned. He held the door open, but Jet danced off the porch and then paused on the spongy loam of pine needles, beyond the steps. She turned back, waiting.

The young female made a complete circle of the

cabin, encouraging Dalton to do the same. He stepped out of the doorway, his instincts making him uncomfortable being backlit in the gap. He headed after Jet and discovered that the rear of the cabin stood on stout logs and, behind them, the hillside sloped steeply toward the ranger station. Usually he would have done a quick recon at a new place, but his fatigue and hunger had taken precedence.

The stars seemed bigger here and he took a moment to gaze up and enjoy their brilliance. It had been a long stretch between now and the last time he'd noticed them, but they'd been there waiting. On the side of the cabin, making his return route, he paused at the light streaming from the cozy structure and at the sound of the shower running. Water was gliding over his wife's beautiful naked body. And he was out here with the dog.

"Idiot," he muttered, and continued back to the porch.

He still didn't understand how getting ambushed while in uniform, and nearly dying, had split them up. He'd explained it was just one of those things, and that just made her madder.

He hadn't really thought of her having to attend Chris's funeral alone. Of having to speak to the widow, see his partner's children's faces as they lowered their father's coffin into the ground.

It scared her. He got that.

"Come on, Jet," he said, opening the door.

The dog streaked past him, so fast she was a moving shadow. Back inside, Jet was already on the couch.

"Better you than me, girl," he said, and left her there, hoping he could hold the towel for Erin.

She met him at the door, her hair a wet tangle and her skin flushed pink. Steam billowed out behind her and she wore a clean white tank top and pink underwear. Both skimpy garments clung to her damp skin in a way that made his mouth go dry.

"It's all yours," she said, and slipped past him.

He caught her arm and she turned; her smile flickered and dropped away.

"Did you pick a room?" he asked.

"Yes?"

"Where do you want me?"

She lifted her chin, holding the power he'd given her.

"In my bed," she said.

He exhaled in relief. But she lifted a finger.

"We are still not okay, Dalton. You know that."

All he knew was that Erin would have him in her bed, and that seemed enough for now.

She regarded him with a serious expression that he could not read. He nodded and she left him the bathroom. He stripped and was in the narrow plastic compartment a moment later, leaving his clothing strewn across the floor. The water felt so good running over his sore muscles that he groaned. Then he washed away the sweat and grime. It seemed an eternity ago that he had showered in their small ranch-style home on a hill in Yonkers. Erin had left him a small liquid soap that was biodegradable for use on her hike. It barely foamed but did the job, leaving his skin with a tingle and the unfortunate scent of peppermint.

He scrubbed his scalp and the beard that had turned from a light stubble to the beginnings of something serious, and banged his elbows on the sides of the shower casing. The capsule had not been designed for a man who was over six feet and 245 pounds.

When he exited the shower, he found she'd left him

only the tiny towel she used when hiking. It was the size of a gym towel, but he used it to dry off. Then he used her deodorant, toothbrush and toothpaste—one of the advantages of marriage, he thought, working out the tangles in his hair with a pink plastic comb the size of his index finger.

Dalton touched the three punctures in his abdomen left by the arthroscopy. Blood loss had been the biggest threat. The scars from the bullet were pink and puckered, but his stomach was flat and showed no bruising from the recent ordeal.

He glanced at his cargo pants, underwear and the shirt she had commandeered. All of it was filthy and he was not wearing any of it to bed. He did rinse out his T-shirt and boxers, hanging them on the empty towel rack to dry.

Erin knew he preferred to sleep in the nude. He retrieved only the firearms and the black zippered case containing the thumb drive and vial case. He used the minuscule towel to hide them in one broad hand as he glanced at himself in the mirror over the sink.

"Wish me luck," he said to himself.

He'd never needed it before with Erin. She'd always welcomed him, but that was before the shooting and all the fury it had kindled in her.

Dalton stepped into the room to find the light already switched off and Erin sitting up against the pillows. The room was cast in shadows. He navigated to her by the faint bluish light from the night sky. He sat on the opposite side of the bed from where she lay stretched out and seemingly naked beneath white sheets. He set the weapons and case on the bedside table. A glance told him that the weapon he'd given her sat on the table beside her.

"There was a packet of sheets and a woolen blanket on the bed," she said, explaining the bedding.

"Nice," he said, slipping in beside her.

She nestled against him and inhaled. "You smell like my soap," she said.

He wrapped an arm around her and drew her close, resting his cheek on the top of her head. Then he closed his eyes and thanked God that she was safe and here with him.

"We're lucky to be alive, you know?" she said.

"Same thought occurred to me. People were shooting at you and you weren't even wearing a uniform."

This comment was met with silence and he wondered what was wrong with him. Reminding her of why she was furious with him was not a great way to slip back into her good graces.

"Will you call your friend and tell him our location?"

"Yes. I'll head down to the ranger station and give a call."

"They have a phone?"

"An actual pay phone. Hard to believe."

"Can you even reverse the charges to a mobile phone?" she asked.

"I guess I'll find out."

"Wait here or come with you?" she asked.

"I'll only be a few minutes."

He kissed her forehead and was surprised when she looped her arms about his neck and kissed him the way she used to. Now he didn't want to leave, and he was certainly coming back as fast as humanly possible.

"I'll be quick."

She released him and he waited until he was outside before jogging to the station to make his call. Henry sounded relieved to hear his voice. He promised to be there in thirty minutes. Dalton wondered if that would be enough.

When he got back, he was greeted by Jet. Alarm bells sounded as he drew his weapon and searched, room by room for Erin. He found her in the bedroom, curled on the blanket. She opened her eyes at his appearance.

"Everything all right?"

"Yes. They'll be here within the hour."

He sank down beside her. His shoulders definitely drooped with the rest of him as the fatigue he had pushed aside finally caught up with him. And then he felt her hand on his thigh, sliding north with a sure path in mind. His shoulders lifted with the rest of him, and he rolled to his side.

"Erin, I've missed this."

"Doctor said you needed time to heal."

"I think we've established that I am healthy enough for sex."

"I'll be the judge of that," she said, and kissed him.

Her mouth demanded as her tongue sought access. Erin's kisses were so greedy and wild that they scared him a little. Her fervor pointed him toward fear.

Did she believe they would not get out of this?

The desperation of her fingers gripping his shoulders and her nails scoring his back told him that something had changed.

Early in their relationship, he and Erin had giggled and wrestled and enjoyed the fun and play of intimacy.

Now, after three years of marriage, they had fallen into a general pattern. He knew what she liked and gave it to her. He liked everything and was always happy when Erin wanted to try something new. But this wasn't new. It bordered on manic.

Her hands flew over his shoulders and then down the long muscles that flanked his spine. Nails raked his skin as her kisses changed from passion to something that lifted the hairs on his neck.

He drew back, extending his arms on either side of her head and stared down at his wife.

"Erin? You all right?"

"I don't know. I just want… I want…" Erin then did something she never did. She burst into tears. All the horror and the fear and the fight drained out of her, and she wept.

Dalton rolled to his side and gathered her up, stroking her back as she sobbed against his broad bare chest. She sprawled over him, limp and still except for her labored breathing and the cries that racked her body.

Jet arrived and poked Dalton's bare leg with her wet nose. That made him jump and caused Erin to lift her head.

"Dog scared me," he said, in explanation.

She turned her head and reached, patting the mattress. Jet did not hesitate. She leaped up beside her new mistress and licked her wet face.

Erin laughed, hugging the dog with one arm and him with the other. Then she released them both, nestling in beside him. Jet, seeming to feel the crisis averted, hopped from the bed and left the room.

"Erin, I'm going to get us out of this."

She said nothing.

"You don't think we're going to make it. Do you?"

"I've lost count of the times I thought we were both

going to die. Whatever that thing is in that case you are hiding beside the bed, people are willing to kill for it."

"You still want me to leave it behind?"

He held his breath, waiting.

"No. My party died because of that thing, whatever it is. I've decided to see this through."

"For a minute I thought you were only willing to jump off trestle bridges after stray dogs."

"Jet isn't a stray. Her owners were murdered, just like my party." She lifted up on an elbow and stared down at him. Her hair fell across her face, shielding her expression from his view. She stroked his forehead with a thumb.

"I just want you to stay with me. You know?"

"Planning on it." He cradled her jaw in his hand, and she turned to press a kiss against his palm. "I've even signed up to take the civil service exam."

"You're going to be a supervisor?" Her voice held a squeak of elation that made him smile.

"Well, I can't run down crooks all my life."

She rested her head on his chest. "Oh, Dalton. That makes me so happy."

He didn't remind her that he still could be shot for just wearing his uniform, as was the case when he'd actually taken the bullet. Ironic that, when he had faced armed gunmen on the job, he'd never fired a round and that he'd escaped Afghanistan without catching lead, only to be shot at a red light.

And Erin wasn't immune from danger. She'd happened onto the worst of all situations, being the rabbit in a deadly game of chase.

He stroked his wife's drying hair as he calculated how far away Larson might be. The backup should be here anytime, and his friend was bringing the FBI, DHS and the New York State Police.

Odds were about to even up, he thought.

Dalton shut his eyes, determined to rest a few minutes before help arrived. But his eyes popped open when Erin slid up and over his body, straddling his hips as she indulged in a leisurely kiss that curled his toes.

Chapter 12

It had been too long, Erin thought as she deepened the kiss. Dalton's big body warmed her and she slid across him. His fingertips grazed her back and down over one hip, leaving a trail of tingling awareness.

His breathing rate increased, and she turned her head to allow them to snatch at the cool night air. Moonlight filtered through the glass window to splash across their naked bodies, revealing the tempting cording of his muscles as he caressed her.

Erin moved over him, showing him without words that she was ready for him, near desperate. He made a sound of surprise at her boldness as she took him, gliding over him to claim what was hers and remind him what he had missed.

The next sound he made was a strangled groan as his head fell back as he captured her hips in his broad, familiar hands. They rocked together in the night, savoring the perfect fit and rising desire. How had she ever thought that leaving this man would solve their problems?

She'd only increased them. Now she didn't know what to do. Except she knew she needed this, him, inside her and holding her and bringing her pleasure as he took his own.

He pulled her down against his chest, his hold becoming greedy as she reached her release, letting her cry tear from her throat and mingle with the sounds of the night.

Dalton arched, lifting her as she savored the receding echoes of pleasure and felt him reach his own. Together they fell, replete and panting, to the tangled bedsheets. Their slick bodies dried in the cool air. Their breathing slowed and Erin shivered. Dalton had reached for the blanket when something cold touched Erin's thigh.

She jumped. Dalton stilled, and a moment later the wet nose of their new addition poked him in the hip. Jet sat beside the bed, gazing up at the two of them as if asking if they needed anything.

"Jet," growled Dalton. "Git."

The dog stood, stretched and sauntered out the door.

Erin giggled. "How long was she there, do you think?"

Dalton threw an arm across his eyes. "I don't want to know."

Erin cuddled next to him and he dragged her close.

"I've missed you," he whispered. "Missed us."

"Me, too."

"I was so scared," he said.

She lifted up to see his face. Her husband was not

scared of anything or anyone. It was one of the things she both loved and hated about him.

"Of what?"

"Losing you. Losing us."

She tried for a smile, but it felt sad right down to her belly, which was tightening in knots.

"I was scared, too. You were unconscious for so long and they said there might be brain damage. I thought you'd already left me."

He threaded his fingers in her hair. "I'm right here."

"This time."

They lay side by side on the sheets as the cool night air chilled their damp skin. Her husband was not only able to keep up with her on a cross-country hike and kayak rapids—he was able to keep up with her in bed.

His recovery was complete, and she smiled at the proof that all systems were up and running. Dalton had always made her see stars, but tonight he'd given her something more—hope for the future.

"So, we have a house and a dog," said Dalton. He left the rest unsaid. He'd been after her to get a dog, seeming to think that would fix his late-night absences and ease her loneliness. But it wasn't loneliness that kept her awake at night. It was fear of the day he couldn't come home.

And it had happened. And, somehow, they had both survived.

This time.

She was with him again and he was with her. They were a team, and together they would deliver this devil's package and hopefully help the authorities catch these dangerous maniacs of Siming's Army.

Only a few more minutes and they would be safe.

"We should get dressed," she muttered, her voice slow with the lethargy that gripped her.

"Yeah. We should."

They could head home with Jet, who she already considered an important part of her family. Dalton would pass the promotional exams and become a supervisor. Then she could stop looking at her phone as if it were the enemy and treating every knock on her door as if she were under attack.

Erin slipped from bed to use the bathroom and on her return, she cracked open the window in the bedroom. She liked to hear the wind blow through the big pines all about them and hear the peepers chorus. She lay back beside Dalton and closed her eyes, feeling happy and satisfied.

He'd finally heard her and was taking steps to do as she asked. She didn't want him to quit the force. She just wanted him around to collect his pension. And in the meantime, maybe they could talk about kids again. She knew Dalton wanted them. She just never felt safe enough to try.

Widows and orphans were seen to by the NYPD, and that was only right. But she did not savor the prospect of joining their ranks. If Dalton wanted kids, he could darn well be there to raise them.

She had meant to get up and dressed, but instead she closed her eyes and drifted into a sleep like a feather falling to earth. She was in that deep sleep, the one that paralyzed you so that rousing felt like swimming up to the surface from deep water.

Someone was shaking her. She opened her eyes and looked around the dark room, struggling to get her bearings. From the hallway came the feral growl of a large animal.

"Dalton?" she whispered.

He pressed a pistol into her hand. "Get dressed."

"What's happening?" she said.

"Not sure. Jet hears something."

"Larson?"

"I don't think so."

She was about to ask who Jet was and where they were when the entire thing dropped into place. Her hairs lifted and the lethargy of sleep flew off. Her heart pummeled her ribs, and she sat up so fast her head spun.

The breeze from the window had turned cold and she was suddenly regretting opening it. The cabin was perched on a slope, so crawling in the window would be difficult—but not impossible.

"Have they found us?" she asked.

"Not sure. Might be a raccoon. Porcupine."

Or a man, she realized.

Dalton disappeared and returned carrying her pack and wearing his cargo pants and shirt. He sat on the bed for the few seconds it took to tug on his boots.

She set aside the gun to scramble into jeans, shirt, jacket and socks, and then realized her boots were in the living room.

"My boots are out there." She pointed.

"Come on," he said, offering his hand.

"Take the pack?"

"For now."

They reached the hallway and Erin called Jet's name just above a whisper. The dog came immediately and Erin grabbed her collar. Her hand at Jet's neck relayed that every hair on the dog's neck was standing straight up.

"Her hackles," she whispered.

"Yeah. Mine, too," he said.

Something large flew through the front window. Dalton lifted his pistol and aimed as the log rolled across the living room floor.

"They're trying to force us to go out the back," he said. "Safer than coming in here."

"They? Just how many are there?" Erin snatched up her boots. Quickly, she tugged them on.

He crept toward the door and the automatic gunfire exploded in the night.

"Down!" roared Dalton, and she fell to her stomach, sprawling as bullets tore through the frame and door.

Jet tugged against her, trying to break free.

"Two shooters, at least," said Dalton. "Get to the bedroom."

The gunfire came again as she scrambled down the hall, dragging her pack in one hand and Jet by the collar in the other. Then something else flew through the open window. She heard the object hit the wood floor and shatter, and the acrid tang of gasoline reached her.

"Molotov cocktail," he said.

She glanced back. Fire erupted in the living room. A log cabin, with wooden walls and wooden floors. How long until the entire place was ablaze?

"Forcing us back," he said, following her into the bedroom and closing the door against the wall of fire.

"What do we do?" she said.

Dalton moved to the window, keeping low, but the moment he lifted his head someone started shooting. He ducked back down.

"Are you hit?" she said, unable to keep the panic

from her voice as she crawled to him, dragging Jet along.

Smoke now billowed under the closed door. Dalton dragged the wool blanket off the bed and stuffed it against the base of the door.

"They've got infrared," he said.

"How do you know that?"

"Because he just missed my head and I can't see a thing."

Smoke continued to creep around the door.

"We have to use the window."

Footsteps sounded in the hall. The second shooter was out there. Bullet holes riddled the bedroom door and Dalton rolled clear of the opening, crouching beside her near the bed.

"When he opens the door, let go of the dog."

The shooter kicked the door open and Erin released her hold on Jet's collar. The dog moved like a streak of black lightning. The shooter fired as Jet jumped, knocking the intruder back. Erin held her breath as both intruder and canine vanished in the smoke.

Dalton charged after the dog with his pistol raised. She lost them in the smoke but clearly heard two shots. A moment later, Dalton emerged from the billowing smoke with Jet at his heels and kicked the door shut. In his hands was a semiautomatic rifle.

The shooter outside opened fire as Jet reached Erin. She swept a hand over the dog's coat, searching for the sticky wetness that would tell her that Jet had been shot. But her hands came away dry.

Dalton reached her. "I'm going to knock out that window. Then I want you to let the dog go again."

"He'll kill her."

Dalton said nothing for a moment. "She's fast. She's black and the shooter won't be expecting it. Jet's our only chance."

Erin did not want to die in this cabin.

"All right."

Dalton threw her pack outside. Gunfire erupted and then ceased.

"Now!"

She released Jet, who jumped out the window and vanished. Dalton went next. She heard him land. Then came the sound of someone screaming and shots firing.

Afterward there was only the crackling sound of burning wood.

"Erin! Clear! Come out the window."

She choked on tears and on smoke as she groped for the opening, grabbed hold of the sill and dropped to the ground some seven feet below. The slope sent her into an unanticipated roll that ended with her flat on her back against the roots of a tree.

Jet reached her first. Her dog licked her face until she sat up and then the dog charged away, likely back to Dalton.

"Where are you?" she called.

Dalton called back. She stood then and fell over her backpack. She groaned as every muscle in her back seemed to seize, but she righted herself and headed toward her husband's voice, carrying the pack over one shoulder.

Jet raced to her and then away. Behind her, the light from the blazing cabin illuminated the hillside. Sparks flew up into the sky, and she prayed that the ground was still wet enough to keep this fire from spreading to the forest surrounding them.

"Did you get him?" she asked.

"Yes."

Dalton returned up the hill for her and took hold of the pack, then dashed down the slope away from the fire.

"Shouldn't we wait for fire and police?"

"I'm not certain there aren't more of them." He tugged her along.

The ground was dark, and she stumbled over roots and through shrubs.

"If there are more, they can just pick us off from the woods."

"But if we get to the police."

Dalton didn't slow. "I don't know them. I know my people. We need to get to them."

They reached the other side of the roundabout on the cabin road and he paused, waiting. She heard the engine sound a moment later. Jet sat beside her and she grabbed her collar.

"She saved our lives," she said, and stroked Jet's soft head with her free hand.

"Yesterday she nearly cost you yours, so we're even."

She recalled her jump from the bridge.

"She fell."

Dalton said nothing as he watched the ranger's truck sweep past.

"How are you planning to get out of here?"

Chapter 13

Dalton doubled back and waited as other cabin dwellers gathered at a distance from the fire. He watched them, looking for some sign that one or more were armed. The first to arrive were the rangers, who quickly disconnected the propane tank outside the kitchen window and dragged it away.

They told everyone to keep back and asked if the two in the cabin had made it out. He waited with Erin outside the circle of light cast by the flames until the fire department and state police arrived. Only then did Dalton leave cover. He made straight for the police. Erin followed, despite his order for her to wait. She left her pack and the automatic weapon behind.

Dalton scanned the crowd. Everyone seemed intent on watching the cabin blaze. He worried about the surrounding dark. A sniper could pick them off with ease.

"What happened?" asked a park ranger. "Stove blow?"

Dalton pulled Erin down so that the ranger's pickup truck was between them and the woods above the cabin. Before them, flames shot out of the windows and smoke curled onto the roof of their cabin.

"I heard gunfire," said a woman in pink yoga pants and an oversize T-shirt.

"Automatic gunfire," added the tall, balding guy holding a half-finished cigarette.

The group clustered together, arms folded as they watched the firefighters set up. Erin held Jet and squatted beside a rear tire.

"Can you wait here just a minute?" Dalton asked.

She hesitated, chewing a thumbnail. "Where are you going?"

He pointed to the well-built trooper, his hat sloped forward revealing the bristle on the back of his head. He was tall and broad shouldered, wearing a crisp uniform with a black utility belt complete with all appropriate gear.

"That guy is the real deal. I'd bet my life on it," he said.

"Good, because you're about to."

"I'll be right back," he said.

"You said there might be more of them out here."

"We need help, Erin."

She stood and shouted, "Mr. State Trooper. I need help."

The trooper turned and looked their way. Erin waved. "Over here."

The officer strode toward them. Dalton had to smile. Erin had gotten help without leaving cover.

"Yes, ma'am?" said the trooper. He was young, Dalton

realized, without a line on his baby face. Still, he stood with one hand casually near his weapon and eyes alert.

Dalton identified himself to the trooper as an NYC detective and showed the officer his gold shield. Then he quickly described the situation.

"Two dead. One in the cabin and one behind the cabin."

The trooper lifted his radio. "Wait here."

"If you use that radio, anyone listening will know our position. Call it in with your phone."

The trooper hesitated, then nodded. "That your dog?" His gaze went to Jet, who sat calm and alert beside Erin.

Erin slipped an arm about Jet, suddenly protective.

"Is now," said Dalton. "Why?"

"Do you know anything about a couple murdered in the Hudson Gorge Wilderness? They were camping with a black dog."

"Plenty," said Dalton.

Erin interrupted. "Did you find a teenage boy, Brian Peters. He was in my party."

"Not that I'm aware of. But we do have a missing party of adult kayakers."

"That's my party," said Erin, pressing her palm flat to her chest. "I was the expedition leader."

"Erin Stevens?" asked the trooper.

"Yes. That's me."

"Where is the rest of your party?" asked the trooper.

Erin burst into tears.

Dalton took over. "I was with them when their camp was attacked. We escaped with the boy, Peters. He suffered a gunshot wound to his upper arm, couldn't hold a paddle. My wife towed him to the opposite bank from her camp and gave him instructions on how to walk out, then she and I proceeded downriver. The rest of her party aren't missing. They're dead."

"No evidence of that."

"There is. And there is a downed chopper in the river below the cliff."

"I'm going to need to bring you both in."

"Sounds good to me. Can you get some backup? I'm not sure that there aren't more out here."

"Who's after you?"

"Long story. You need to send help after Peters. Also, I need you to call New York City detective Henry Larson. He's here in North Creek. That was our destination."

"You can call from the station." He aimed a finger at them. "Wait here."

Dalton watched him stride away. It seemed to take hours, but he suspected it was less than forty-five minutes before they were transported to Trooper Barracks G in Queensbury. Another thirty minutes and four FBI agents arrived with two beefy guys from DHS.

It was five in the morning and the knot in Dalton's shoulders finally began to ease. They had made it. They were safe, though he still had the package.

Erin and he were separated, something that rankled and made him anxious. He felt the need to keep looking out for her, regardless of how many times she'd proved her own capabilities. He went over the events with the FBI agents Nolen Bersen and Peter Heller. Bersen took lead. He was tall, fit and had hair that was cut so brutally short it seemed only a shadow on his head. Heller stood back, arms folded, his freckled forehead furrowed beneath a shock of hair so red that it appeared to be illuminated from within.

By six thirty in the morning Dalton needed the bathroom and some food. He was informed that Henry Larson had been notified that they were now safe and had arrived, but Dalton could not see him. In the bathroom he discovered he was not to have a moment's privacy when a Homeland Security agent, Lawrence Foster, flashed his ID. He wanted a word. Dalton told him to get in line.

"Do you still have the package?" asked Foster.

This was the first person who seemed to know anything about the intelligence he and Erin had rescued. Dalton used the urinal and ignored him until he was finished. Then he faced the guy, who was heavyset with close-cropped hair, brown skin and dressed like an attorney in a well-fitting suit.

Dalton narrowed his eyes on the man. He knew all about interagency competition. His office hated it when the FBI came and took over an operation or, worse, took their collar. So he understood Foster's attempt to get something but still resented his choice of time and place.

"This is my first time being interviewed in a toilet," said Dalton. "You want to join us in interrogation room three, come on along."

Foster smiled and stepped away from the door he had been blocking. "I'll see you there."

Dalton headed back to the interrogation room. It was nearly eight when the room was cleared of everyone but two men in plain clothes. The elder one stepped forward. Dalton guessed him to be just shy of forty, with close-cropped salt-and-pepper hair, going gray early. He wore a slouch hat, fisherman's-style shirt, worn jeans and muddy sneakers. At first glance, he looked as if he'd been hauled off an angling excursion. Second glance made Dalton's skin crawl. He'd worked with CIA, and this guy had that look.

His gaze flicked to the younger man. This one would fit in almost anywhere. He was slim, with a thick beard, glasses and hair that brushed his collar. His clothing was banal, jean shorts and a white tee worn under a forest green plaid cotton shirt. He could be pumping gas or passing you at the horse race track. The point was you wouldn't notice him. The guy's gaze finally flicked to Dalton, and those intent gray eyes gave a whole other picture. A chill danced along the ridge of his spine.

"What agency?" asked Dalton.

"Federal," replied the older guy. His cap said he'd fought in Operation Iraqi Freedom, but somehow Dalton thought he was still active. "You got something that you want to give to us?"

"I don't know what you mean."

The men exchanged a look.

"Let's start again. We were expecting the delivery of some sensitive material. Our courier delivered that information successfully to one of our operatives. The helicopter he was flying crashed into your wife's party, killing Carol Walton."

"You all clean up that scene?"

He nodded.

"Terrible tragedy. Surprised you made it out. Looked professional. Helicopter, according to reports."

"You CIA?"

The second man took that one. "We are here to see just how much you know. Clearly you know something because you ran, survived, and we have not recovered our package. Judging from the trail of bodies, neither have your pursuers. Though, close one tonight."

"You recovered the two that came after us?"

"Bagged and tagged," said the Iraqi vet. "How did you end up with our intelligence and do you still have it?"

Dalton ground his teeth together for a few seconds, opened his mouth. Closed it again and then wiped it.

His initial interviewer passed him something. He drew back, leaving a folded sheet of paper on the desk. Dalton looked from the page to the man across from him at the table. Then he lifted the paper and read the contents of the letter.

It was from his direct supervisor returning him to active duty and notifying him that he was on loan to a Jerome Shaffer. Dalton recognized the signature. His gaze flicked up to the Iraqi vet, who had removed his wallet from his back pocket and laid a laminated ID card before him.

This was Jerome Shaffer and he worked, according to the card, with the Central Intelligence Agency.

The two stared at each other from across the table.

"I need to hear it from my boss."

The call was made and a sleepy, familiar voice verified that Dalton was now on loan to the CIA until further notice. He handed back the phone.

"Okay," he said.

Agent Shaffer nodded. "So where is it?"

Dalton opened the side pocket of his cargo pants and laid the black leather case on the table.

Both men stiffened. Shaffer rose and they backed toward the door.

"Don't move," said Shaffer. A moment later the pair were in the hallway and the door between him and the agents closed firmly shut. The click told him he was locked in the interrogation room. He looked to the mirrored glass, knowing there were others out there, but as he could not see them, he still didn't know what was going on.

Fifteen minutes later the door swung open and in stepped a woman in a full hazmat suit.

Chapter 14

They had separated Erin from Dalton shortly after their arrival at the troopers' headquarters. Dalton told her it would be all right, but as the minutes ticked by she became restless and had just given up pacing in the small interrogation room in favor of drinking from the water bottle they had furnished.

She looked up as the door clicked open, hoping to see Dalton. Instead, a trooper stepped in, preceding two men who were not in uniform.

Erin lowered the bottle to the table.

The trooper made introductions and Erin shook hands with each in turn. Agent Kane Tillman was first. He wore business casual, loafers and tan pants with a gray sports coat and a classic tie on a pale blue shirt. His face was cleanly shaven and his short hair had a distinctly military air.

Agent Tillman said he was a government investigator of some sort. She missed his title as the other man offered his hand. His associate was more unkempt with hair neither stylish nor unfashionable. His clothing was as drab as his features. She glanced away from him after the introduction and realized she'd only heard part of his name. Gabriel. Was that his first or last name?

She assumed that they were FBI agents, though Gabriel was not dressed like the other FBI agent, Jerome Shaffer, whom she had met on arrival. Her gaze slid to Gabriel. Was his hair dark blond or light brown? She wasn't sure, but Agent Tillman was speaking, so she turned her attention back to him.

They told her that they'd spoken to Dalton and that she'd be allowed to see him soon. The best news was that Brian Peters had been found alive.

"He was picked up by a ranger and driven to their station. We took charge of him from there."

"His wounds?"

"Superficial. He'll make a full recovery."

She sank back in her seat as relief washed through her, closing her eyes for a moment before the questions began again.

Her interviewer wanted to hear about the helicopter crash.

She relayed to Agent Tillman all she recalled of the attempted rescue of the pilot. They told her the pilot was a friend. Agent Tillman said that he'd known the man, and so Erin had been thorough. The other man, she could not recall his name now, only the letter *G*. The other one listened but rarely spoke.

"And he said to tell the authorities what exactly?"

"He said to tell you this was taken from Siming's Army."

"Right. And he gave you something?"

"Yes, a cooler."

"Which your husband carried."

"At first. Then he just carried the contents. We left the cooler to throw our pursuers off us."

"You believe they were after what you carried?"

She reported what they had overheard before running for their lives.

"Right," said Tillman. "We were looking for you, as well. Seems you outfoxed both pursuing parties. Even our dogs couldn't find you."

She shrugged. "Rain helped. We only left the river day before yesterday. I'm glad you didn't stop us. I'm afraid Dalton might have thought you were one of our attackers."

Tillman just smiled. "Well, this is better."

"Will we be able to go home?"

Tillman's smile grew tight. "I'm afraid not quite yet. You see, all the opponents you two faced are dead. But we believe there are several more in the region. We are very anxious to capture someone from this organization."

"I see." She didn't, and her face twisted in confusion. Why was he telling her this?

"Your husband has agreed to go back to the Hudson. He will be helping us catch the people who tracked you."

Her eyes narrowed. "Helping how?"

"He's a detective. He's worked undercover. We think it's our best option."

Erin straightened in her chair as her gaze flicked from one to the other.

"He said that?"

Tillman didn't answer directly. "He'll explain the details to you."

Something stank. Either he was lying or Dalton was ignoring every promise he'd made to her.

"What about his wife? He wasn't out there alone. Don't you think they'll notice that I'm no longer there?"

The other guy spoke and she jumped. She'd half forgotten he was even in the room and now he was right next to her, leaning against the wall beside the door.

"That's no problem."

What color were his eyes? she wondered, squinting. Green, gray, blue? It was hard to tell and he was only two feet from her.

He was smiling at her. It was an unpleasant smile that raised the hairs on her forearms.

"We have a substitute. Someone to play your part."

"The hell you say." She stood and faced them. "We just spent two days running for our lives and you want him to go back there without me? Phooey on that!"

"It's our best option."

"I want to speak to him now," she said, arms folding.

"Not possible," said Tillman.

"Now," she said, leaning across the table, looking for a fight.

Tillman backed toward the door. The other guy was already gone. She rushed the closing door.

"I want to see him!"

Tillman shut the door before she reached it, and the lock clicked behind him. Tugging on the handle only made her remember how sore her muscles were.

They allowed her to leave the vile little room to use the bathroom, escorted by a female trooper with umber skin and unusual height.

"I want to see my husband."

"I'll relay the message," she said.

"Where is my dog?"

"They are processing her for evidence."

"If you hurt one hair..."

The threat was cut short as the athletic woman lifted a thin eyebrow.

"She has bloodstains on her collar. They are taking samples."

Back in the interrogation room she found only the empty chairs and table. She walked to the one-way mirror and slapped it.

"I want my husband or my phone call now!" Who would she call? The camp director? She snorted and began her pacing again.

Tillman opened the door and motioned to someone in the hallway. In stepped a slim, athletic woman of a similar height to her.

Erin glared at the new arrival.

"Mrs. Stevens, this is DHS agent Rylee Hockings out of Glens Falls."

"My substitute," said Erin, standing to face her replacement. "She has blue eyes and she's blond."

"Contacts. Hair dye," said Tillman.

From the sidelong look Agent Hockings cast him, Erin guessed no one had told her about the dye job.

"It's a pleasure to meet you, Erin." Hockings extended her hand. Unlike Erin's hand, Hockings's was dirt-free, her nails trimmed into uniformed ovals and coated with a pale pink polish. She was clean and smelled wonderful.

"Look at her." She swept her hand at Hockings and then at herself. "Now look at me."

Erin wore damp, rumpled clothing and hair tugged into a messy ponytail. She knew she had circles under her eyes. She smelled of smoke and gasoline, and there were numerous scratches on her shins and forearms.

"I look like I spent the night in a bramble bush. But she looks like she just left a resort hotel."

Tillman's mouth went tight, but he said nothing.

Erin faced her replacement. "Have you been camping, Ms. Hockings? Do you know how to kayak in white water or set up a climbing rope?"

"I doubt that will be necessary."

"But it *was* necessary. Or I wouldn't be here."

Hockings glanced to Tillman, who offered no backup. So Hockings straightened her shoulders.

"I can fill this role, Erin."

"You are asking me to trust you to keep my husband alive. I don't think so."

"I'm an excellent shot."

"He's got that one covered all on his own."

Tillman stepped in. Erin had crept forward and was now right up in the agent's face. Funny, she didn't remember even moving closer.

"This isn't your call, Erin. She'll be in the field in less than one hour with or without your help. All you get to decide is if you help Hockings prepare or not?"

"Not," said Erin as she returned to her seat, folded her arms and scowled.

The two retreated out the door, leaving her alone again.

The door to the interrogation room opened, and Dalton turned to see both the small blond DHS agent and the CIA operative. Both of them were flushed. He stood for introductions. The woman, Rylee Hockings, chewed her bottom lip, and Kane Tillman had both hands clamped to his hips.

Dalton narrowed his eyes on them, speculating. Who did he know that could rattle both DHS and CIA?

He smiled. "You spoke to my wife."

Tillman nodded, removing his hands from his hips to lock his fingers behind his neck and stretch. He dropped his arms back to his sides and faced Dalton.

"Can you point out to us your route and specifically your position yesterday when you encountered the female shooter?"

Dalton's smile broadened. "Nope."

"The general location?" asked Rylee, hope flickering weakly in her gaze.

"Out of sight of the Hudson River on a hill." Dalton chuckled at their dismay. "I told you. You need her."

Tillman said nothing.

"She agree to help?" Dalton asked.

He shook his head. "She wants to see you."

"I told you it wouldn't work."

"You need to convince her to cooperate with us," said Hockings.

"You know that she asked for a separation. Right?" he asked Tillman.

"Yes."

"Do you know why?"

Tillman shook his head.

"Because I go undercover and stay away for days. She wants me to ride a desk and collect my pension. What she doesn't want is for me to play secret agent with a younger model who—no offense, Miss Hockings—looks like she does most of her traveling first-class."

"Business class," corrected Hockings.

"But not in the woods carrying a fifty-pound pack on your back."

"I can fill this role." She was speaking to Tillman now.

Dalton had told them that lying to his wife about his cooperation was a bad idea and that he wouldn't go without her consent, but they'd thought to trick it out of her.

He smiled. Erin was many things—stubborn, driven, protective—but not stupid.

"My wife rescued that helicopter pilot. Not me. She swam through white water, rigged him so we could haul him out and then got out herself, even though the wreck rolled on her tether rope. She got us downriver, through rapids. It was her idea to leave the kayaks on the opposite side of the river, to throw them off our trail, in the pouring rain."

"All very admirable."

"I told you that she won't want me to go back."

"You don't need her permission."

"No. But I'm not going without it."

"I don't understand. You're a professional."

"I'm a man about to lose his wife. I came up here to fix my marriage. Now you want me to go right back to telling her to wait at home and that everything will be fine when the last time I told her that I caught a bullet."

Tillman's hands slid back to his hips.

"We all know that these people are crazy, armed and dangerous," said Dalton. "She knows, too, firsthand."

"You willing to risk her life?"

"Heck no. But we have both been convinced of the importance of this. I think she should have a choice. She's right. I've asked her to sit on the sidelines too long. I wouldn't like it. Neither does she. I understand now why she didn't like it. Why she's been so angry. My thick head has been an asset in the past. But I don't want it to end my marriage."

"So what are you suggesting?" asked Tillman.

"Get her to help or let us go home."

Tillman looked at Hockings. "Sorry for dragging you up here. Seems we don't need you after all."

"This is bull," said Rylee. "I can do this job."

"We'll never know." He turned to Dalton. "That is assuming you can convince your wife to help us."

"She'll do what she thinks is best."

"For you or for her country?"

"Let's go find out. Shall we?"

Chapter 15

The door had barely closed behind DHS agent Lawrence Foster when it opened again, this time to admit Hockings, Shaffer, Tillman and her husband. Erin kept her face expressionless as she met Dalton's gaze but was relieved to see him. Something about DHS agent Foster had put her on edge. His questions were off, somehow, different from the others who had questioned her. Dalton winked at her and she could not keep the half smile from lifting her mouth.

"You going back there without me?" she asked.

Dalton turned to the three agents. "Give us a minute."

The two exchanged impatient looks.

"We don't have a lot of time," said Tillman.

"Understood," said Dalton. He wasn't looking at Tillman, and only Erin watched the others retreat and close the door behind them.

"I hear you've been less than cooperative with our federal friends," Dalton said, and drew up a chair beside her.

"I was cooperative with the DHS agent." She'd answered all his questions about the pilot's death, their escape and details about the woman who attacked them. He asked what was in the package that Dalton carried, and she told him it was vials and a thumb drive. The agent then asked about Dalton's colleague, Henry Larson, or "the NYPD SWAT officer," as Foster had called him. Maybe that was the thing that bothered her. Why didn't he know Larson's name?

"You weren't cooperative with the CIA," said Dalton.

"Because Agent Foster wasn't trying to replace me."

Dalton made a growling sound in his throat by way of reply that showed both skepticism and some aggravation. Then he took her hand and entwined her fingers with his.

"What should we do, Erin?"

"Don't ask me to let you go back there," she said.

"I won't," he said.

That got her attention. She waited, but he said nothing else. Just stroked his thumb over the sensitive skin at the back of her hand at the web between her index finger and thumb.

"They want to send you out with that woman."

"Yeah. They do."

"So you're going back without me," she said.

"That what they told you?" he asked.

She nodded.

"And what have I told you about interrogation techniques?"

Her brow knit and then arched. "You don't have to

tell a suspect the truth." She let out a breath and drew another. "They lied? To me?"

She smiled, but instead of returning her smile he was frowning.

"And you believed them."

"You've run off on dangerous business for years. Why wouldn't I believe them?"

"Because I told you that I wouldn't do that again."

Now she shifted, suddenly uncomfortable with the man she had once felt was an extension of herself. They'd moved apart now, like heavenly bodies changing their orbits. She wanted to align with him once more. Why was this so hard?

"What did you tell them?" she asked.

"I told them it's a bad idea to send our Ms. Hockings as your replacement."

She cocked her head. "You did? Why?"

"Because she can't fill your hiking boots. Because our pursuers are not stupid, and because I promised you that I wouldn't go out there."

"Without me."

Now he was off balance. She knew from the way he tilted his head as he narrowed his eyes. "What are you saying, Erin?"

"You think this is worth risking your life for?"

"I do."

"You ready to risk *my* life, too?" she asked.

"No," he said.

"Yet you think the information they could get from a living member of Siming's Army would be invaluable," she said.

"That information could save the lives of many innocent people. Might stop whatever is underway. But that is only if we manage not to get killed and they manage to capture someone alive."

"You believe they can keep us safe?"

"I believe they will try. But I don't think they can keep us safe *and* allow the bad guys to get close. So…" He lifted his hands, palms up as if weighing his options.

"They'll put us in danger."

"I'd say so."

"Thank you," she said.

"For being honest?"

"For not going without me."

"I'm done with that," he said.

"And I'm sorry for believing them."

He nodded, but the hurt still shone in his troubled gaze.

"Are we still okay?" he asked.

She forced out a breath between closed lips. "Let's talk about this after. Assuming there is an after."

"Erin, I came up here to save our marriage."

She nodded. "I know it. But trouble just has a way of finding you."

"Seems this time it found you."

Erin looked at the ceiling, taking a moment to rein herself in. They did not have time to hash out their differences. He might have told her that he was done taking chances and willing to change. But all actions pointed to the contrary.

"Where are they taking us?"

"Heck if I know. You know I can't read a map as well as you."

She rose then, went to the door and knocked. When Tillman's face appeared in the window, she motioned him inside.

"We've agreed to go back." She glanced at Dalton. "Together."

Rylee Hockings pressed her lips flat, exhaled like a horse through her nostrils and then stormed away down the hall, back to wherever she had come from, Erin hoped. Erin would not be sad to see the backs of either of the DHS agents—Hockings or Foster. One made her angry and the other gave her the creeps.

Tillman pressed a phone to his ear. "Yeah. They're in."

The Stevenses were left just outside the Hudson Gorge Wilderness on North Woods Club Road between the Boreas River and the small community of Minerva. This was the same side of the river where they had left the body of their female attacker and a reasonable distance for them to have traveled after that encounter. The dog, Jet, had remained back with their handlers. So at least one of them was safe.

Erin hefted her pack, knowing it was lighter but still thinking it felt heavier than before. Dalton carried the case of vials and thumb drive in his side pocket just as he had before. Only now the new thumb drive was inoperable due to irreparable damage and the vials were full of water.

"So we just use the road, after spending all that time keeping in cover?" asked Erin.

"That's the best way to be spotted."

"It doesn't make sense. We wouldn't do that, not after being attacked."

"At some point you have to leave cover and get help," he said.

"They said they'd keep us in sight," said Erin. "But there is no one here."

"How do you know?" he asked.

"Insects still singing. Jays and red squirrels aren't giving any alarm."

"It's a drone and it's up high enough that we can't hear it. But it surely can see us."

They also wore trackers. She had several. The coolest by far were in the earring posts she now wore.

"They might just shoot us and then search our bodies," she said.

Dalton groaned. "You are such a drop of sunshine today."

"Well, we don't have vests or armor, whatever you call it."

"Car," he said.

"What?"

He pointed to the rooster tail of dust growing by the second. It turned out to be a silver pickup truck. The driver came from the opposite direction. He slowed at sighting them but merely lifted two fingers off the steering wheel in a lazy wave as he passed them.

"Well, that was anticlimactic," Erin said.

"Could be a spotter."

She hadn't thought of that.

"Did Tillman tell you anything that I didn't hear?" she asked.

"Don't think so."

"So, this guy, this Japanese agent."

"Yes. A Japanese operative working out of Hong Kong," he said.

"Right," she said. "Hong Kong, which is where he obtained this information and put it on our flash drive."

"And he had the samples."

"Which he put on a commercial jet with hundreds of people and flew all the way to Canada."

"Toronto."

"And then, instead of meeting our government's agent, he changes the meeting to Ticonderoga."

"Fort Ticonderoga," said Dalton.

"See, that's why I'm going over this. You're the detail guy."

Dalton took it from there. "But they are attacked during the drop. Our guy gets away. Their agent takes off and leaves the country. The foreign agents chase our guy all over the place, but he made the pickup anyway and they send a chopper."

"And he makes the drop. But the helicopter—our helicopter—takes gunfire and goes down on my camping site."

"And queue the chase music. Both parties have been after us ever since."

"This Siming's Army seems more like a foreign agency."

"Backed by one."

"Which one?" she asked.

"They didn't say."

"To me, either." Erin rubbed the back of her neck. "Did they say how many people they have?"

"Sleeper cells, so it's hard to know. But you just imagine that they have people downstate. NYC is a target and it's my city. Damned if I'll let that happen if I can prevent it."

"If *we* can prevent it."

He wrapped an arm around her and gave a squeeze. "We."

"Did you tell them about the pilot? I heard him mention his girl."

"Yes, Sally. I told them. They'll speak to her. Relay his last words."

"Good. But it's so sad."

She heard the engine, the same truck returning toward them. The driver slowed and lowered his window. Erin stared at the face of a man in his middle years. His hat advertised the sports club that lay at the terminus of this road, but she knew the distance and he had not had time to have reached it and returned. The niggling apprehension woke in her chest, squeezing tight as her skin crawled. She shifted from side to side, unable to keep still.

"So we just let them take us?" she asked.

"That's right."

"What if they just shoot us?"

"I won't let that happen."

"Still time to run," she said, edging off the shoulder, eyeing the distance to the trees.

The truck stopped and the dust caught up, drifting down on them in a haze.

"Hey there," called the driver, keeping his hands on the wheel. Between his arms was a small, overweight dog that seemed to be both smiling and preparing to steer the truck. Her gaze flicked up to the man to note that he was clean shaven, with salt-and-pepper hair that touched his shoulders, making a veil from under his cap. His glasses were thick and black rimmed.

"You two need a lift?"

Accent was right, Erin thought.

"Appreciate it," said Dalton. His voice was calm and even.

Erin doubted she was even capable of speech. She

was good at the game of hide-and-seek, but less comfortable with the bravado required for confrontation. She thought of Rylee Hockings and straightened her spine. Her feet stilled and her jaw tightened.

Dalton moved to the truck, opening the passenger-side door. He motioned to Erin.

She spoke to the driver, her voice a squeaky, unrecognizable thing. "Okay if I put the pack in the back?"

"Sure thing."

Dalton took the pack and placed it in the truck bed. When he turned around, he had his pistol in his hand. He slid that hand back into his pocket and motioned for her to get in.

Dalton slipped in beside her and pulled the door shut.

"This here is Lulu. She's my copilot," said the driver.

The small pug moved to sniff Erin and then used her as a boardwalk to sniff Dalton's extended hand. She wondered if the canine smelled gun oil.

"Where you two heading?" The driver flicked on his wipers to push away the settling dust from his windshield and then set them in motion.

"Minerva."

"Oh, that's right on my way."

Erin let Dalton do the small talk. He'd always been better at it. She focused on the driver's hands as she wondered what he had in the pockets of his denim jacket.

"Surprised to see you two out here."

"Why's that?" asked Dalton.

"Ain't ya heard about the trouble?"

"No."

"Where you been then, you ain't seen the helicopters and K-9 units. Yesterday this place looked like a

TV movie set with all the cop cars. They all showed up like buzzards circling a dead woodchuck."

"Why? What happened?" Dalton asked.

"I don't know how to tell you this, but there's some maniac out here killing campers in their tents. Husband and wife. Right down that way on the trail to the trestle bridge."

Erin tried to look shocked but felt her face burning. This was why she had landed nothing more than chorus in the high school plays. Her acting left so much to be desired.

"That's terrible," she managed.

"That ain't all. There's a whole party of kayakers two days overdue. DEC's been out searching, but so far they're just gone."

She glanced out the window as they drove along at a break in the forest revealing a wide-open stretch of flat mossy land.

"What I heard is they ain't found hide nor hair of those tourists."

The mention of hides provided Erin with a perfect picture of Carol Walton's mangled body. The rest of the faces of her party flashed before her. Her stomach gave an unexpected and violent pitch, and she had to cover her mouth with her hand.

"That's odd," said Dalton as he gave Erin's arm a squeeze. She needed to get hold of herself before she gave them away.

Dalton frowned, his look concerned, before he shifted his attention back to the driver, the possible threat.

"It's all been in the papers." The driver frowned. "Course you wouldn't see them out here, I suppose."

Lulu settled back to the man's crowded lap, the wheel just missing the top of her tawny hide.

"That's why I picked you both up. Something terrible is going on up here. I'm Percy, by the way."

Dalton nodded and gave over their real names.

"A pleasure," said Percy. His smile dropped away as he saw something before them. "Oh, okay, they're still here."

Dalton's gaze flicked away, and Erin looked through the dusty windshield.

Before them was a roadblock consisting of two DEC vehicles. One was an SUV and the other a pickup truck parked at such an angle that approaching drivers would have to go around them. This was impossible on the northern side because of the bog. The open stretch might look like a meadow with brush and flowers and even clumps of tall cotton grass, but there were no meadows in these woods. Any cleared space was intentionally cleared by men, or it was clear because it was impossible for trees to grow there. That was the case here for, though the ground looked solid, it was in fact a thick well-adapted spongy mat of living sphagnum, a moss that knit together like raw wool. This bog was famous for both its size and proximity to the road. Hikers venturing onto the moss would quickly find the ground lower and themselves in water up to their ankles. Below was a secret lake.

She knew this because she was scheduled to take a canoeing trip on this very bog. Canoes carrying passengers were heavy enough to sink the moss below their keel so the party could glide along over the bog that sprang back in place after their passing.

Erin looked out at the tuffs where the thick brush was

actually cranberry bushes whose blossoms had given way to tight green berries. There were orchids and carnivorous pitcher plants, as well.

"Erin?" She glanced to Dalton. "Percy says we need to show our ID."

"Oh." She turned to look out the back window. "Mine is still in my pack."

She wondered if these were really DEC rangers or CIA agents in disguise. She couldn't ask Dalton, of course, so she just watched as a ranger stepped out from the truck and held up a hand for them to halt.

Percy laughed. "Think the truck in the road is all the stop sign I need."

The ranger wore the correct uniform and utility belt that included a gun. Many of the rangers here were tasked with law enforcement, so that was not all that odd. But the sight made her uncomfortable.

"Where's the other driver?" asked Dalton.

The ranger approached Percy's side of the truck.

Dalton opened his door and had one leg out when the ranger reached Percy.

"Hello again," Percy said.

The ranger dipped to look into the vehicle and then drew his pistol and fired.

Chapter 16

The pistol shot exploded so close to Erin's head that afterward she could hear only a high-pitched buzz. She gasped like a trout suddenly out of water. Percy slumped over the wheel. Her entire body went stiff with terror and sweat popped out all over her body.

Dalton wrenched her from the truck and down to the ground. His service weapon was out and he aimed forward toward the two vehicles, firing three quick shots.

Erin clamped her hands over her ears and squatted beside him, her back against the truck bed. The other ranger fell sideways in front of the truck.

Dalton rose, arms extended to quickly check through the open door to the place where the first man had been, ready to fire through the truck and past Percy. An instant later he dropped down beside her.

"He took the keys," he said.

Her ears still buzzed and his voice seemed distorted. Something moved in the truck and Dalton aimed.

"Wait!" she shouted.

Lulu leaped down from the cab, her coat spattered with Percy's blood. The dog disappeared beneath the truck.

"Where did he go?" she asked, referring to the shooter.

The road was now silent except for Lulu's labored, wheezing breath. Erin dropped to her belly to check the dog and saw the shooter's feet as he rounded the back of the truck.

She tugged at Dalton's sleeve and pointed. He nodded, motioning her under the vehicle. She rolled beneath the truck bed as Dalton dropped to his stomach and fired two shots.

There was a scream and the shooter collapsed to one knee as blood dripped from his foot. Dalton shot him again. Two shots. One in the knee. The other in his hand. The shooter dropped his gun and howled, scrambling back. Then he vanished from sight.

"No shot," said Dalton to himself as his target disappeared.

Erin remembered belatedly that she also had a pistol. She drew it now, holding the muzzle up and hoping she didn't shoot herself in the face. A pounding came from above her head.

Gunfire sent shafts of sunlight beaming through the new holes in the pickup's truck bed.

"We have to get to those vehicles," he said.

"My pack?"

"Leave it."

Dalton tugged her up and pushed her before him. She ran toward the SUV, dancing sideways to avoid the still body sprawled in the road. When she reached the SUV, she peered inside.

"No keys," she said.

Dalton had paused to check the corpse of the downed attacker, rummaging in his pants pockets. An engine revved.

Somehow the shooter had reached the cab with two bullets in his legs and one in his hand. Percy's body lay crumpled in the road beside his truck, and the wounded shooter was throwing the truck into gear.

Dalton made it to her as the truck raced forward. They dove from the road as the driver plowed into the SUV where she had stood. The SUV spun off the road toward them as the truck raced by. She fell to her stomach and slid as the SUV bounced down the embankment in front of them and rolled to its side.

"Where the hell is our backup?" he growled.

The pickup sped past and then turned around.

"He's coming back," said Erin.

Dalton lifted his weapon and fired continuously, every few seconds, with well-timed intervals, as the ranger smashed into the second truck pushing it along the road before him. The driver used Percy's vehicle to sweep the last useful getaway truck into the opposite ditch, where it tipped, engine down and back wheels clear off the ground.

"They did a good job grading this road," said Erin. The high ground was dry and out of the bog, even after that heavy rain.

"We have zero cover," he said.

"But he lost his weapon," she reminded.

"That truck is two tons of weapon."

Lulu sat on Erin's right foot and glanced up at her.

Something niggled in her mind. Two tons of weapon. The idea sprang up like a mushroom after a rain.

"Do you think he has another gun?" she asked, watching him back up.

"If he did, he'd be shooting at us." Dalton removed his empty clip and pushed the spare into place in the pistol's handle.

"You want to keep shooting at him?"

"Unless you have a better idea. We can use the culvert for cover."

"He'll just run us down."

He looked around. "We need to get to the SUV. Use it for cover."

"He can just hit that again."

He gave her an exasperated look. "What do you want to do?"

Their attacker spun Percy's truck back to the road and put it in Reverse.

"He's getting a running start," said Dalton, more to himself than to her.

"We could go out on the bog," she said, pointing.

He glanced at the open area broken only by tufts of grass and clumps of brush. "No cover."

"We won't need it. It's a bog."

He shook his head, not comprehending. "Here he comes."

"That moss is floating on a lake like a carpet or a giant lily pad. He can't drive on it because it's not solid ground."

Dalton turned his head, focusing on the bog now. "Can we run on it?"

"Yes, but we'll get wet. Sink a foot or so. It's spongy, like running on foam rubber and—"

He cut her off. "Okay. Okay. Go!"

She lifted Lulu off her foot and into her arms, then darted down the hill past the SUV. The tail section of the vehicle had already sunk into the moss, which accommodated the weight by moving out of the way.

Running out on the sweet-smelling, soggy sphagnum moss was like running on a field of wet loofah sponges, a rare experience that she would have enjoyed in other circumstances. The plant that most people only saw in wreaths and at the base of floral arrangements was a living sponge and just as easy to run upon.

Dalton swore as he stumbled and tipped forward. The bog absorbed his fall like a living crash pad, soaking his front in six inches of clear water. He scrambled to his feet, now standing in twelve inches of water as she raced ahead of him. She'd been on this bog before, looking for native orchids to show her expedition, and knew the best way was high steps and a little bounce. Her experience allowed her to get well out in front of him. Lulu whined in her arms and scrambled to reach her shoulder. Once there the little dog perched, looking back at the truck that was no doubt in pursuit.

"Erin?" Dalton paused, glancing behind him. They had made it some forty feet out on the bog.

Not far enough, she feared, seeing the pickup gaining speed in what she thought might be preparation for a jump from the road, some five feet above them, and onto the bog.

If he landed near them, the truck would sink down with the moss and take them with it. And the moss would tear... She had a dreadful premonition of what could happen to them. Stories told of early settlers rose in her memory. Entire mule teams vanishing with wagons and all. Swallowed up in an instant as the sphagnum moss rent like fabric, dropping men, animals and wagons through the spongy layer that instantly sprang back into place above them. Leaving them beneath the two feet of moss and as trapped as anyone who had ever been swept beneath ice by the water's current.

Her heart raced as she looked around for something to anchor them should the moss tear, keep them on the right side of the sphagnum mat, even if they temporarily sank.

"Grab the cranberry bushes and don't let go!" she yelled to Dalton.

She dove, using her one arm to grip Lulu and the other to latch onto the wrist-sized trunk of a hearty bush covered in tight green berries.

Dalton did not ask questions or try to take control. He just followed suit, landing beside her. Their combined weight sank them in eighteen inches of cold clear water. She lifted her head to breathe and looked back.

The truck was airborne. Lulu struggled, her body underwater. Erin held on.

The impact of the truck rolled under them like a wave. The vehicle landed upright, several yards away. Instead of speeding along the open field, it stopped dead as the tires turned uselessly and the motor revved.

The driver's hand went straight up as the moss sank instantly to the windows under the two tons of weight. She heard the wail and saw the brilliant red blood streaming down his shooting arm from his wounded hand. The moss yielded without a sound, the gash tipping the truck engine down before the vehicle vanished. The scream cut short as the moss sprang back into position, grass, plants and bushes appearing just as they had been, leaving no sign of the horror that must be playing out beneath them.

Erin rolled to her back and Lulu dog-paddled away,

her stumpy front legs thrashing until she reached a clump of grass that barely moved under her slight weight. There Lulu sat on a pitcher plant, panting.

Dalton lifted a hand to his forehead.

"Remind me to never cross you," he said. He sat up in the water that reached his hips, staring back at the empty bog. "It's like it never happened."

He was soaking wet, with bits of pale yellow-green moss sticking to his clothing.

"Why aren't there any helicopters or CIA agents charging from the trees?" Erin asked.

He glanced around. "Great question."

"You know what I think?"

"What?" He had one hand pressed to his forehead as he continued to look back at the tranquil expanse, disbelieving.

"They're dangling us like a worm on a hook," she said. "Doesn't matter what happens to the worm as long as you catch the fish."

"Only both our fish are gone."

She nodded. "We should get off this bog."

"I'll say."

"It's a protected habitat. I don't want to damage it any more than necessary."

"You're worried about the swamp?"

"Bog. It's a completely different ecosystem from a wetland. I'm scheduled to lead expeditions on this very site later in the week."

"Well, if I'd known that, I wouldn't have let you come up here." He tucked his gun into a pocket that was still underwater and shook his head in bewilderment. "And you think *my* job is dangerous?"

Chapter 17

"They wanted one alive," said Erin to Dalton as they stood on the road staring out at the bog. They were soaking wet and the breeze chilled him, but not as much as that sphagnum moss.

"You can't even see the tear. Nothing." Dalton shook his head. "It's the most terrifying thing I've ever seen." He glanced her way. "You canoe on that?"

"Walk, too. It's safe."

"Yeah, right. You'll never convince me of that."

She hiked Lulu up higher on her chest and scratched behind the dog's ear. "Now what?"

"The way I see it," Dalton said, "we can wait for the Feds to come and perform their catch and release. Try to capture another member of this terrorist outfit, preferably without getting killed, or we can get out of here and try to make it to someplace safe."

"Nowhere is safe as long as they think we have the vials."

"You're right, and I have a feeling Siming's Army will not take our word for it that it's gone."

"And we have no proof that the CIA took it from us."

"Or that we even met with them." He turned to her. "What do you think?"

Her brows lifted, and she stopped stroking the trembling dog. He wanted to take her in his arms and hold her, tell her that they'd get out of this. But he was no longer sure. Bringing her back out here now seemed the stupidest play imaginable. The CIA didn't have their back. His fanny was swinging out here in the breeze, and he'd dragged her with him.

The uncomfortable distance that had yawned between them, the one he had hoped to close, seemed to have torn open again.

"You're asking me what I think?" She didn't have to look so astonished.

"Yeah," he said, unable to keep the terseness from his tone. "I'm asking."

"I think we shouldn't have trusted those agents. I think we now have nothing to bargain with."

"Easy to catch us whichever way we go," he said. "And it's anyone's guess who will show up first."

"I hope it's not someone like Percy. That poor man."

Lulu licked under Erin's chin, the pink tongue curling up his wife's jaw.

"Oh, you poor thing."

"You keeping her, too?" asked Dalton, already knowing the answer.

"I'm not leaving her on a bog."

"Those pitcher plants might eat her," he said, referring to the cylindrical plants that held a sweet water designed to lure and drown insects. She'd told him about them once before. Not as flashy as the Venus flytrap, but just as deadly.

She didn't laugh at his joke. Lulu was tiny but not small enough to succumb to carnivorous plants. And not big enough to keep up on a hike, either.

Erin scratched under Lulu's chin. "Not a chance. Right, Lulu?"

The soft and sympathetic voice caused a sharp pang of regret. Not that he wanted her to speak to him this way; still he could imagine her, cooing and fussing over a baby. Their baby. But first they had to get out of this mess alive.

"I'm going to check the other one for keys." He thumbed back at the corpse sprawled in the road. Erin followed him and then turned to look at the sky.

"You think they're up there watching?" she asked, using her hand as a visor.

"Definitely."

Erin lifted her hand from her eyes and presented her middle finger to the sky.

Dalton laughed. "Feel better?"

She gave him a half smile as if that were all she could spare. He went back to searching the pockets of the dead man. His diligence was rewarded. The guy kept his keys in his front shirt pocket, which was why he'd missed them before.

He stood and tossed the keys a few inches, catching them again. Then he looked at the pickup truck, engine down and back wheels off the ground. The vehicle was diagonally across from the SUV, which lay on its side at the bottom of the opposite incline. Neither one of them was getting them out of here.

Lulu stood at the road alone. Erin had disappeared. His heart gave a jolt as he glanced to the bog. But Lulu was on the opposite side of the road, panting.

He headed that way at a run. Once he reached the chubby pug, he found his wife. Her head popped up out of the door of the cap that covered the truck bed. Because of the odd angle, the truck sat nearly vertical and the rear door opened out like a mailbox.

"Erin?"

She had something in her hand. "Did you find the keys?"

"Got them." He lifted the chain.

"Try the fob," she said, and scrambled out, sitting on the closed tailgate, legs dangling.

He hit the unlock button and the truck chimed.

He glanced down the bank and saw the truck sat nose down on the hill with the front tires resting on the incline and the grille buried in the ground beyond.

Erin tossed something from the truck. She dragged a length of chain from within. It rattled over the closed tailgate, extending to the ground. She looped the hook, at the end, around the ball-mount trailer hitch beneath the bumper.

"How did you even get up there?" he asked, looking to the truck's tailgate now above his head.

"Lulu boosted me."

He chuckled and looked at the dog, who sat on one hip, tail between her legs and eyes closed in the bright sunlight.

Meanwhile, Erin scrambled like a monkey over the

top of the truck and slid down the cap roof to the cab and then dropped to the ground.

"Keys?" she asked, and he tossed them down.

Erin disappeared into the cab and emerged a moment later.

"They're in the ignition and the truck is in neutral."

Dalton lifted the chain and gazed at the truck. Whatever she had in mind, he knew they would not be able to tug this truck up that incline.

She appeared up the hill a moment later.

"Riding beats walking when you are in a hurry," she said.

"How you planning to get that truck back on the road?"

She grinned. "The SUV has a winch on the front. "I figure we attach the two and see which one makes it up the incline and to the road first."

He pressed his lips together and nodded. "Let's go."

The chain reached across the road and the winch cable easily reached the chain.

"We don't have the keys for that SUV," reminded Dalton.

"City boy," she said. "This winch is electric. You don't need to turn on the vehicle to run it. Step back now. Where's Lulu?"

He lifted the dog and moved up the bank. She proceeded to flip a lever and then flicked a toggle switch.

"Holler when the truck is on the road."

The cable began to move, stretching taut. There was a hesitation as the cable vibrated, and then the SUV dragged on its side, inching to the hill below the road. The whine of the winch was momentarily obscured by the scrape of gravel and rock beneath metal. Once the

SUV reached the incline it paused as the cable continued to reel.

Dalton glanced across the road, following the cable to the upended pickup and saw it teeter. The back tires thumped down to the road and then the truck rolled with slow inertia up the hill. Since the SUV was lighter than the truck and not anchored, it was dragged up the incline as the truck crept along. By the time the pickup was on the road, the SUV was nearly up the hill.

"Good," he shouted.

The winch motor cut and the whining ceased. Erin instructed him to start the truck and drive it toward the SUV until the chain dropped so she could release the winch safely. He did and the SUV slipped back down the hill as he rolled forward. But the winched vehicle came to a stop before he left the road. Erin scrambled up the embankment and then released the winch cable, tossing it back into the culvert. She gathered the chain and threw it into the truck bed. A moment later she climbed into the truck. Lulu was ecstatic to see her, wiggling and wagging and then throwing herself to her back.

"Jet is going to eat that dog," he predicted.

She gathered up the little tan lapdog into her arms. "Where to?"

"That way has no outlet, just a loop to the gun club that will bring you back here," he reminded her.

"Right. Minerva it is."

He put the truck in motion. "You still have your pistol?"

She patted her jacket pocket. He flicked on the heater, hoping the air would help dry his clothing and warm them.

"I hate bogs," he mumbled.

She laughed and settled Lulu on her lap. Then she clicked her seat belt across her middle.

"Think we can make it to your partner in North Creek?"

"I doubt it. But that's where I'm heading."

She peered out the open window, gazing at the blue sky.

"They still up there?"

"Probably."

They did not even slow down in the town of Minerva and he was surprised that no one stopped them.

"How many people do you think are up here with Siming's Army?" she asked as they cruised past a gas station that advertised firewood and propane.

"Six fewer now," he said. "But I don't know. That could be all of them in one sleeper cell."

"Our attackers weren't in uniform," she said. "But the truck is DEC."

Erin busied herself searching the glove box. She found a bag of trail mix, the kind with chocolate mingled in with the nuts and raisins. She offered it open to him and continued her exploration while he munched.

"Nothing but the paperwork and some tools." She pocketed the universal multi-tool. Just as well, as she clearly knew how to use one better than he would.

He pulled into a KOA and drew up to the office. He handed back the half-empty bag and she lifted it, pouring some of the contents into her mouth and then offering Lulu a peanut.

"I need to make a phone call," he said.

She nodded and held Lulu, who tried to follow him out of the vehicle. Dalton used the office pay phone to call Henry Larson, who had not left the area, despite not being allowed to see him or, perhaps, because of it. The two made arrangements on how and where to meet, and then Dalton returned to Erin.

"Let me guess," she said. "You called Henry."

"I did."

"NYPD to the rescue," she said.

"I get it. You don't like Henry." He set them back in motion, pulling out of the campground's lot.

"True."

"Because when I'm with him, I'm not with you?"

"Because he thinks strip clubs are an acceptable form of entertainment and because he has a different girl-friend every time he comes to a party. Where does he get them all?"

Dalton wisely did not answer, but Erin's eyebrows rose, making the connection.

"So he's dating strippers?"

"They weren't *all* strippers."

"Oh, that makes me feel so much better."

"I don't want to fight."

"We aren't fighting," she said, as she always did. But they were.

"Do you know why I came up here after you?" he asked.

"To convince me to come home or at least not to ask for a trial separation."

"True. And because I don't want to become like Henry. I wanted to try, to keep trying."

This revelation had an effect that was the opposite of what Dalton had intended. Erin blew through her nos-trils and turned her head to stare out the window at the homes that had cut grassy plots out of the surrounding woodland. They were off parkland, he realized.

Dalton tried again. "Henry is a good guy. A solid guy. He loves his kids. He's a good father, but he has nothing but terrible things to say about his wife. He thinks that she's the reason for him losing his house and only seeing his kids on weekends. All his problems start and end with his ex."

She turned to stare out the front window. Listening, her face revealing nothing.

"I know how many cops are divorced. The statistics. I know the stats on drinking and drug abuse. It's a tough job. Stressful."

"On families, too," she said in a voice that seemed faraway.

"But I never thought that would be me. Be us. We were rock solid. I came home every night I wasn't working. I shared what I could instead of keeping it bottled up inside. Now I think that might have been a mistake. Telling you—I mean, because it frightened you. Some of the guys said I was stupid, letting you know the risks we take. The close calls. That this was the reason they didn't share work stories at home. Kids don't need to hear it and wives freak."

"I never freaked."

"You did. You left me and came here."

"Not because I was listening but because you weren't."

"I listened. But this is who I am. I'm a protector at heart. I live to get those criminals off the streets. To stop them before they can hurt anyone and see they never get the chance to try again."

"Which is why people are still shooting at us."

"Erin, I thought you agreed."

"That was before they ditched us. We have no backup or none that I have seen. I understand why we are here and I accept that what you do is important. I just can't live like this anymore."

"Erin. Please."

"I'm scared," she admitted.

She had good reason. The way this was heading, saving their marriage might be the least of their problems.

"We'll get through this."

She shook her head. "If we do, what then?"

"You come home. We work this out."

She stared vacantly at her scabby knees and offered no reassurance.

He extended his hand but, instead of squeezing it back, she just stared at it. He rested it on her leg, feeling the warm skin and firm muscle beneath. After a millennium, she moved her hand from the dog and covered his.

It was a start. Or he hoped it was.

"Are we going to get out of this?" she asked.

He set his jaw and nodded. "Yes, ma'am, we surely are."

"That just wishful thinking? Telling me what you think I need to hear."

He shook his head. "I can't believe there are this many of them. Erin, the woods are crawling with these terrorists. And I don't understand why we haven't already been picked up and brought back in."

"Because we didn't get a member of Siming's Army, not a living one anyway."

He shook his head again. Something was wrong. The Feds had not held up their end of the bargain, and that meant the deal was off. All men for themselves. He needed to look after his own and get Erin to safety.

Lulu shifted position, groaned and lay down on Erin's lap.

"Do you think she knows what happened to Percy?"

"No."

"Dogs grieve the loss of their owners, you know."

"I suppose." But Lulu's bulging eyes made her look more hungry than grief stricken.

"Are you regretting coming out here?" he asked.

She stared straight ahead, and he had the feeling something was really wrong. Mostly because she wasn't angry and she had a right to be. He'd trusted the system and they'd been dumped in a bog as reward. Finally, she spoke, and her voice was flat calm as the eye of a hurricane.

"I would have preferred that they put out an APB that we'd been picked up and processed and released, so everyone would know we don't have that darn black case."

She cut a sidelong glance at him and then rested a trembling hand on Lulu's back. She stroked the resting dog, seeming to draw comfort from the tiny creature.

That other woman, the Homeland Security agent, would not have known to take them out on the bog, and he very much doubted that Hockings knew how to use a winch. Maybe she could have shot and killed that second man. But he'd never know. He was happy to stay with the one who had brought him to the dance. But was she happy about it?

They reached an actual intersection and a stop sign. The dirt road ended against NY 28 and he turned south, away from Minerva and toward North Creek. The southern route flanked the Hudson on the opposite side from where they had walked yesterday over the trestle and all the way to North River. They covered the four miles in less than five minutes and crossed the river. Groups of rafters drifted by on the calm section before the upcoming set of rapids. Next, they journeyed through North River, with its white-water rafting outfits perched directly across the road from the launching sites.

Dalton didn't slow but continued toward North Creek. Henry was waiting.

"Did you speak to the CIA guys?" she asked.

"Yeah. They took the drive and samples."

"Tillman was okay. Seemed nice enough but that other one. What was his name, Danielson?" she asked.

"No, that's not it. First name was Cliff, I think. Or Clint."

"I don't think it was Clint. I can't even remember what he looked like." She rubbed her chin, thinking.

"There were a lot of federal agents. Two from the FBI. Agent Shaffer, also CIA and the Homeland Security agents."

Why had he mentioned them? Now she'd be thinking of Hockings again.

"Were you questioned by the guy? Forester?" she asked.

"Foster, Lawrence," he said. He thought of the agent he had met in the men's room realizing then that the guy had said he'd join him in interrogation but never showed "I met him, but we didn't have a formal interview. You?"

"Yes. He gave me the creeps."

"Worse than Clint or Cliff?"

"Different. He was the only one who showed up

alone. After the other agents left. I felt, not threatened, but cornered, I guess. He was with me until just before you arrived. He didn't ask the same things as the CIA men. He wanted to know about the pilot. Where he was and how he died. What happened to the woman who owned the dog and where we had been last night. He was the only one who asked about the contents of what we carried."

"They have the contents. Why ask you?"

"Maybe that's what bothered me. He also was the first to ask where we had been heading and which of your colleagues you had contacted."

Dalton's radar popped on and he scowled. "Where we were heading? Did you tell him about Henry?"

"Of course."

Dalton stepped on the gas.

Erin sat forward, grabbing the overhead hand grip. "What? What's wrong?"

Lulu startled awake as she nearly fell off Erin's lap to the floor mats.

"You see his ID?"

"I… I don't remember. I didn't see Hockings's ID. I know that."

"What if Foster is not DHS?" he asked.

"Then he wouldn't have been in the troopers' headquarters."

That wasn't necessarily true. All they had to do was to get someone to buzz them in and mingle with people in the building. It was alphabet soup in there.

"If he was legit, then he'd know that the CIA recovered the flash drive and vials."

"So?" she asked.

"He'd also know we aren't carrying anything. No reason to attack us back there."

That was true, unless their attackers had not gotten word from him or it was a different cell.

"But he asked about Henry?"

"Yes. All he knew was that Henry was NYPD SWAT. Not his name, even." She shook her head. "But Henry doesn't have anything they want."

"Neither do we, but those men by the bog still tried to kill us."

She didn't argue with that, just held on as he flew along the highway passing a Subaru with bikes fixed to the back end and a family SUV with canoes strapped to the roof racks.

Chapter 18

"I don't understand why we didn't have any backup out there," she said.

"That's just one of my questions," said Dalton.

They tore into the parking area of a chain hotel. Dalton leaped out of the truck and charged through lobby doors that barely had time to whisk open. Erin lowered the windows and told Lulu to stay. Then she followed him inside in time to see him leaning over the desk of the petite receptionist dressed in a polyester blazer with a gold-toned name tag.

"I can't tell you his room number." She lifted the phone. "But I can call his room for you."

Dalton flashed his shield to the receptionist. The wallet was soggy and much worse for wear, but the receptionist's reaction was instant. Her fingers started tapping on the keys.

"He's in 116. First floor, right down that hallway."

"Call 911. Tell them NYC detective Dalton Stevens requests backup for possible B and E."

"Yes, sir."

He pointed at Erin. "Stay here."

"Like hell," she said.

She'd seen enough cop shows to know how to enter a room with a gun. And if Rylee Hockings could do it, she could, too.

Dalton dashed down the hall toward his colleague's room and she followed at a run. When he reached the door, he motioned her to halt, and he stood to the side to try the handle. The door was locked. Then he lifted one booted foot and kicked in the flimsy hotel room door.

He entered with pistol raised and the grip cradled in his opposite hand. Erin watched him disappear and then heard nothing.

She crept farther down the hall and made out her husband's voice.

"Larson?"

Did he see his friend or was he just looking?

There was no reply. Erin peeked around the doorjamb and saw Henry Larson sprawled on the floor, his hands secured behind his back. Dalton squatted at his side.

"Is he dead?" she asked.

Before he could answer, Dalton rose to face her and his eyes went wild. He reached and took two steps toward her. Then she felt it, the hand clutching her jacket from behind, dragging her off her feet, across the hall and into the opposite hotel room. The fabric choked her, sending her hand reflexively to her throat.

Dalton reached the hallway as her captor kicked the door to the opposite hotel room closed and threw the bolt. The impact of Dalton's body against the door vibrated through the soles of her kicking feet.

On the second attempt Dalton crashed through the door. His gun was up and raised as he advanced with measured steps.

"Far enough," said her captor. She felt the hard pressure of the pistol pushing into her temple.

Dalton paused, as if playing some deadly game of freeze tag, but his weapon remained up and pointed at her captor.

"Foster, isn't it?" asked her husband.

"For now," said the man who had spoken to her in the darn troopers' headquarters just prior to Dalton's arrival with the three federal agents, Hockings, Tillman and Shaffer. He had identified himself as Lawrence Foster, an agent with the Department of Homeland Security.

"Lower your weapon or I kill your wife." He said it as a cashier might tell you to hold on while they print your receipt. The effect was chilling. The man was cold-blooded as a garter snake.

Dalton said nothing but his eyes were on her attacker. The gun barrel moved to her eye socket.

"All right. It's down," said Dalton. "What do you want?"

"To interrogate the two remaining witnesses. Find out how much they know about us."

"We don't have the package. It's with the agents at the troopers'—"

Foster cut him off. "I know that. Which is why I blew that building. That virus is now airborne. Anybody sifting through the ashes has a great chance of contracting our little superbug, and the vaccine, well, that doesn't go airborne." He made a *tsking* sound with his tongue on the roof of his mouth.

Was it true? Was that why there was no backup? Were they all dead?

The chill shook her. Was it really just her husband and her and this madman?

"Out," said Foster.

She didn't know where they were going and, right this second, she didn't care. What she did care about was seeing that Dalton did not get shot by some maniac terrorist. She and her husband were going to take Lulu and Jet home to Yonkers and give them a home. Dalton was going to make good on his promise to become a supervisor, and she was going to see that they spent every free minute trying to start that family.

If Foster didn't shoot her and her husband first.

What would Dalton do?

Something heavy pressed against her side. The pistol, the small one that she'd carried since Jet's captor tried to kill them. Her hand slipped inside her jacket pocket and she gripped the weapon. Her thumb flicked off the safety. He marched her forward. Sweat ran behind her ears and into her hair. It rolled between her breasts and down the long channel of her spine.

Dalton retreated to the hallway as they reached his discarded weapon. The man stooped and his pistol dropped toward her neck. He motioned with the gun to the floor.

"Pick that up," he ordered her. "Barrel first."

Erin slipped the pistol from her pocket and met Dalton's gaze. She'd never seen him afraid before. But that was what she saw now. Stone-cold terror in the hardening of his jaw and the hands extending reflexively toward her.

* * *

Dalton had stopped backing up when he saw Erin's hand moving in her pocket. His breath caught. His jaw locked and he saw stars.

No. No. No.

He'd only set down his gun to keep Foster from killing Erin. But she had other plans, as always.

Had she remembered to flick off the safety of her weapon? His gaze dropped for just an instant to the small silver pistol in her hand, but it was enough.

Foster's eyes narrowed on him and he lifted the handgun that was now pointing across Erin's chest.

Dalton took a step forward. Foster hesitated as if deciding whether to aim at Erin or back at him. Erin lifted the gun under her opposite armpit and fired back at Foster hitting him in the chest. He released her, staggering backward, still aiming at them. Dalton made a grab for Erin and missed.

Erin spun to face Foster and stepped between them as Foster fired a single shot.

Chapter 19

Every hair on Dalton's body lifted and his heart stuttered before exploding into a frantic pounding. Erin spun, staring at Dalton's shocked expression as Foster aimed at him. But he'd reached him now and grabbed Foster's wrist, then used his opposite hand to break Foster's elbow as he retrieved the man's pistol from his limp hand.

Dalton pointed his attacker's pistol at Foster, but his gaze flicked from his target to Erin, who sank to her knees, gasping. In that moment, Foster ducked past the doorjamb and out of sight.

The small pistol dropped to the carpet as his wife lifted her hand to her neck, pale fingers clamping down as blood welled from beneath her palm.

His head swam and he shook it in a vain attempt to wake from this nightmare. Erin stared at him, her eyes wide and round, showing the whites all about her brown irises.

"Erin. No," he whispered to himself as the truth ricocheted through him like the bullet that had struck her.

Erin was bleeding.

She toppled, her hand dropping away from her neck, allowing blood to pour out of her body, staining the carpet.

A wild shrieking came from the man darting down the hall to the lobby, his ruined arm flailing, his elbow jutting out at an odd angle. It took a moment for Dalton to realize that part of the screaming was the wail of approaching sirens. Help arriving too late.

Dalton let his suspect run as he dropped to his knees beside his wife. He gathered her limp body in his arms. She was going to die, leaving him after all but not in the way she had planned.

He tore back the jacket from her neck and saw the bullet hole at the point where her long neck gave way to her shoulder. A gentle probing told him that the collarbone was intact, and from the way the blood exited the wound he was certain that the bullet had not struck her carotid artery because there was no spraying of blood. But it had hit some blood vessel because the hole was a deep bubbling well of red.

She was going to leave him like his men back in Afghanistan. Like his partner, Chris Wirimer. Why was he still here when everyone he tried to protect…

"Dalton?" Her voice was weak, but her gaze fixed him steadily. "You okay?"

She was worried about him. Always. And suddenly he understood. This was exactly what she had feared, only their roles had reversed. How many times had she imagined him bleeding out at some crime scene?

This was what he'd done to her, year after year, because he couldn't stand being the one who made it out.

His broad hand clamped over her wound and pressed hard. He would not let her bleed out on the hallway like some...some...hero, he realized. She'd saved his life, possibly Henry Larson's life as well, if he wasn't already dead.

"I'm here. Help is coming. Hold on, Erin."

"Did he shoot you?" she asked.

"No."

She closed her eyes then, and relaxed against him.

"Thank God," she whispered.

Dalton felt the tightening in his throat, the burning as his eyes watered, vision swimming.

Then he started screaming for help. Doors cracked open as people crept cautiously out of their rooms.

"Bring help," he shouted. "Get her help!"

She had wanted to leave that package behind. Put it on a red T-shirt with a note, she had suggested. But he had to bring it along.

If Foster could be believed, he'd destroyed it anyway, and by bringing it out of the woods, possibly Dalton had jeopardized who knew how many lives, begun some Siming's pandemic for them. But now, the only life he cared about was Erin's.

He stroked her damp hair and stared down the hall until, at last, the EMTs arrived, charging toward him in navy blue uniforms, their bulky bags flopping against their thighs.

"Hang on, Erin. Don't you leave me."

They let Dalton ride in the first ambulance with Erin but did not let him into the operating wing. He was directed to a waiting area as Erin disappeared down a long corridor, followed by his partner, Henry Larson, on a second gurney. The waiting room had wooden chairs with mauve cushions set in a U-shape around three coffee tables holding a smattering of torn magazines and discarded paper coffee cups. There were two other men already there, and he was surprised to find both CIA agent Jerome Shaffer and FBI agent Nolen Bersen waiting.

"So it's true then," he said. "Troopers' headquarters is gone?"

Bersen nodded. "Agent Heller suffered injuries. He is in surgery now."

"So is Erin. Gunshot wound to her neck."

Shaffer stood and placed a hand on Dalton's shoulder. "Sorry to hear that."

"Anyone else hurt?" asked Dalton.

"Mostly minor injuries. The troopers have a K-9 dog. Former marine, and he found the explosives. They were clearing the building when it went off. Heller was hit by part of the ceiling. He's got a spine injury."

"What about the…" Dalton looked around. "What we brought in?"

"Long gone. Shaffer and Gabriel had it out of the station well before the blast. It's safe, Stevens."

Why didn't that make him feel any better?

"She's in there because of me."

"This isn't your fault, Dalton."

"I agreed to go back out there. I let her come along. Of course, it's my fault."

"I understand you're upset. With good reason. Your wife is injured and your colleague, Detective Larson, suffered head trauma in an attack," said Shaffer.

"Yeah, they just brought him in with her."

"What happened?"

Dalton's eyes widened as he realized that Shaffer didn't know about the impostor and therefore the agent from Siming's Army was getting away. "At the troopers' headquarters there was a man. We both met him. Said he was DHS, name was Lawrence Foster."

"Foster?" asked Shaffer. "I don't know him."

Dalton explained, finishing with, "He shot Erin. Don't let him get away."

Both men lifted their phones.

"So there is no Lawrence Foster of DHS?"

Shaffer lifted the phone from his mouth, pointing the bottom toward the ceiling. "No."

"Then how did he get into trooper headquarters?"

"I'll be checking that."

"What about the other one, Rylee Hockings?"

"She's DHS. On her way back to her offices in Glens Falls."

While Dalton paced, Shaffer and Bersen made calls.

He didn't realize that Agent Shaffer was speaking to him until he touched Dalton's shoulder.

"We got him."

"Who?" He'd been so lost in thought and worry that it took a moment to come back to his surroundings. Dalton was in the hallway now, standing on the wide tiles before the doors that read No Admittance.

"Lawrence Foster, or the man claiming to be Foster. Troopers caught him trying to board an Amtrak train in Glens Falls. Arm injury made him easy to spot."

"Sweating like a marathon runner," added Bersen.

"He had the proper ID for DHS. Either real or a very convincing fake."

Dalton felt none of the elation that usually accompanied a collar. He didn't care. Not unless they'd let him see him alone so he could settle up. And he knew that would never happen.

How many victims had asked him for that same thing?

"He alive?" Dalton asked, his voice mechanical.

"Yes, in custody. His real name is Vincent Eulich. He's a physicist, college professor in Schenectady with a bomb-making hobby."

"We already have agents at his home and office. But we have to go slow. Already found one IED," said Bersen, referring to the improvised explosive devices most commonly in use in the Middle East.

A man in blue scrubs emerged from the swinging doors and all conversation ceased.

"Anyone out here waiting for word on Henry Larson?"

"I'm in his department," said Dalton. And Henry was his best friend.

"Any direct family?" asked the surgeon.

"Not here. He's got an ex-wife and two kids."

The surgeon pulled a face.

"I'm Dr. Howard. Your colleague has suffered a spine fracture in three places. The rest is cuts and bruises and a mild concussion as a result of a head injury. The back injury is most serious. But the pressure is off the spinal cord and I've repaired a herniated disk. His prognosis is good. Barring complications, I'd say he'll be able to use his legs again after some physical therapy."

That news hit Dalton in the stomach like a mule kick.

"Walk? The man's a former Army Ranger. He bikes all over Westchester and runs Ironman contests."

The surgeon shook his head. "I doubt he'll be doing any of those things again. He'll need a spinal fusion once the swelling is down."

"Fusion?" Removal from active duty, Dalton realized. Just like that.

Dr. Howard nodded. "Got to get back at it."

Dalton grasped his elbow and Howard's expression showed surprise.

"Any word on Erin Stevens? She was shot in the neck?"

"Different surgical team. I'm sure they'll be out to you as soon as they can."

"Anything?" Dalton said, his voice gruff.

"Still in surgery."

He gave Dalton a tight smile and backed through the swinging doors.

Dalton walked slowly to the waiting area and sank into a chair. Bersen and Shaffer took up seats opposite. Dalton folded his hands and bowed his head. He had not done this in some time. Praying felt awkward and uncomfortable. Still he muscled through, asking God's help in saving his wife. When he finished he found both agents regarding him.

"You two waiting on someone?"

"Yes," said Shaffer. "You. And your wife. We need to be sure Siming's Army knows we have the intel they tried and failed to recover and that you two are safe. We've also got two agents outside of the operating room."

"After they know that, you think they'll try to hurt Erin again?"

"They seem determined to kill you both. So we've called some friends from WITSEC."

Dalton straightened at the mention of the witness protection program.

"That's extreme, don't you think?"

"Temporary placement. Until we get this organization shut down."

Dalton sat back in the uncomfortable little chair. They didn't think it was too extreme. What would Erin say? What about him? He had a mom, a dad and stepmother, plus two older sisters. Erin had a brother she rarely saw and a sister who lived on the same block.

His job... He'd have to leave his job and, even after relocation, he would not be able to work in law enforcement again.

A voice came from the edge of the carpet just outside of the waiting area.

"Mr. Stevens? I have an update on your wife."

Chapter 20

Erin woke in pain and in the company of strangers. She asked for Dalton and a nurse's blurry face appeared above her. When the nurse didn't understand, Erin tried to pull the mask off her own face. There was a sharp sting on her hip and she sank back into blackness.

The next time she roused, fighting every inch of the way back to consciousness, it was to a room of light and sound. Machines bleated and chimed. Alarms chirped and she squinted against the blinding lights above her.

"What time?" she tried to ask the attendant who checked the fluid bag that hung above her on a metal pole.

"You're doing great, honey," said a female voice.

"What time?" Her voice was the scratch of sandpaper on dry wood.

"It's nearly 9:00 p.m. You're out of recovery and in ICU. Your husband just left. He's a handsome fellow. Needs a shave, though."

"Dalton?"

"That right? I thought you said *Walton*. Anyway. He seems nice. You'll be here tonight and tomorrow. You do okay and you'll get a room. You in trouble, honey?"

"Trouble?" Other than getting shot? she wondered.

"There are two US marshals right outside. I know they aren't for me. So you in trouble?"

"Not anymore." Talking hurt so badly she had to close her eyes.

"You hurting?"

She nodded and immediately regretted it. The nurse used a syringe to add something to her IV line and Erin's body went slack. The pain dissolved like fog in the sun and she slipped away to a place beyond the needs of her body.

"Erin?"

She knew that voice.

"Erin. It's Dalton."

She tried and failed to open her eyes.

"Can you hear me?" He lifted her limp hand. "Squeeze my hand."

She tried, failed and swallowed. The pain was back. Her throat throbbed as if she were a tree trunk and a woodpecker was knocking a hole into her with repeated stabbing blows.

"Your sister, Victoria, is here."

Another voice, female murmuring. Erin tried again to open her eyes, but the deep pain-free well beckoned.

She let go and dropped. Just like rappelling down a cliff, she thought as she glided into blackness.

Dalton didn't see the surgeon until the following day. The guy had sent a physician's assistant out to see him in the waiting room yesterday, and his visits during the night had scared him silly. Erin had a bandage the size of a football on her neck. And she was on a ventilator.

Her sister, Vic, had arrived at nine and the physician appeared at bedside during the fifteen minutes they allowed Dalton each hour. Vic had stepped out at the MD's appearance so Dalton could step in.

"The loss of blood resulted in your wife suffering a cardiac arrest. To reduce her energy expenditure, I ordered a drug-induced coma. The medication is keeping her body from using any extra energy, easing the burden on her heart."

"How long will you keep her like this?" asked Dalton.

"Until her blood volume is normal and her bladder is functioning again." He motioned to the empty clear bag hanging from the bed rails. Had her kidney's stopped working?

Panic tightened its grip upon him.

"Days?" asked Dalton.

"Likely we'll wake her up later today. Your wife lost a lot of blood. It can damage organs. We need to be sure everything is working."

"If it's not?"

"One thing at a time."

The next twenty-four hours were the longest of his life. Because of him, his best friend had suffered a spinal injury and his wife was in a coma. As minutes ticked away, Dalton had lots of time to make promises to God and curse his own foolishness. Nothing was as important to him as his friend and his wife. He just hoped that he'd have a chance to tell them both.

Erin's eyes popped open. It was as if someone had just flicked a switch and brought her to full awake.

Tentative movement told her that she had not imagined her injuries.

Four unfamiliar faces peered down at her.

"Mrs. Stevens? How do you feel?"

"Thirsty," she said.

They asked her a series of questions that seemed designed to test her mental acumen. The day, month, who was president? What holiday was next on the calendar, and math problems.

"Is my husband here?"

"He is. And anxious to see you. But a brief visit. Right?" The physician looked to another attendee, who nodded. Brightly colored cartoon illustrations of popular candy bars covered this man's scrubs top.

Three of the gathering wandered out in conversation as the one male attendant remained.

"I'm Will. I'm your nurse today."

"Hi, Will. Um, water?"

"Ice chips for now." He fussed with the IV bag and then disappeared, returning with a plastic cup. "I did one better. Lemon ice. Okay?" He handed it over with a plastic spoon.

Erin discovered that she could not really work her left hand without waking the dragon of burning pain in her shoulder.

Man, it hurt to get shot.

Dalton arrived, hurrying forward and then slowing as he saw her. He looked as bad as she felt.

"Oh, Dalton!" she said.

"Erin?" He got only that out and then he did something she had never seen him do. He wept.

Both hands covered his big, tired face and his shoulders shook. She reached her good hand to him and called his name.

He peered at her beneath his dark brows and raised hands. The circles under his eyes startled and he looked thinner. Then he took her hand and allowed her to draw him to her bed, where he sat awkwardly on the edge.

"You're awake," he said.

She smiled. "They gave me an ice. But I can't manage holding and scooping."

Dalton took over both jobs, offering her wonderful sweet, cold bits of frozen lemon. Nothing had ever tasted so good, though the act of eating and swallowing hurt her neck. She didn't say so but was relieved when Will came to roust Dalton back out. The weariness tugged at her features and pricked at her skin.

"I'll see you soon."

She held her smile until he was out of sight and then groaned.

"Pain?" asked Will.

She nodded and then flinched. Will returned with the pain medication and then the throbbing ache retreated like a receding tide. She breathed a sigh.

"Thanks."

"Your sister is out there. I'll send her in after you take a little nap."

She murmured her acceptance and closed her eyes. What choice did she have? For the rest of that day and through the night, she had short visits with Victoria and Dalton. The following day she felt so much better that they removed both catheter and infusion bag. She ate solid food for breakfast. Victoria visited her at noon and then told her that she was heading home.

"You know there are armed guards outside your room?" Victoria asked.

"There are?" Erin asked.

"US Marshals, they said."

"Gosh. That's not good."

Victoria looked at her. "They do witness protection, right?"

"I'm not sure."

"I am. Dalton told me what happened out there. It's a miracle either of you is still alive. I don't know what I'd do without you."

Their embrace was tentative, but Erin survived it without too much discomfort.

"I'll see you soon," said Erin.

"I hope so. Love you." With that, her sister was gone.

Erin followed her with her eyes, stopping when she saw Dalton leaning on the doorjamb, obviously giving them time to say goodbye.

Something in his expression made her uneasy.

"What's happening, Dalton? Victoria said there are police out there."

He came in and sat in the padded orange vinyl chair beside her bed, the one she was supposed to be allowed to sit in this afternoon.

Erin offered her hand and Dalton took it in both of his.

"Are we still in danger?"

"We are. The FBI has turned us over to the US Marshals."

Her heartbeat pulsed in the swollen tissues at her neck, sending sharp stabs of pain radiating through her shoulder and arm.

"Witness protection services. Right?"

He nodded grimly.

"We have to go?"

"It's voluntary but until they know who is after us and if there are more…" His words trailed off.

"Does my sister know?"

"She saw them sitting there," said Dalton. "They frisked her."

"They did not!"

Dalton made a face that said he was not teasing.

"Have you spoken to your parents?"

"Just Helen. She's going to bring Mom up to see us."

"Your father?"

"If we decide to go, they'll bring him, too."

"What have we gotten tangled up in, Dalton?"

"Some very bad, very dangerous people who are unfortunately also well financed. Our guys don't know who is behind them yet. Have to follow the money. Large corporation or foreign government, I suppose."

"Are we going to have to leave?"

"They're recommending it."

She drew a breath and held it, studying him. "Together?" she asked.

He gripped her hand. "Erin, I know I put you in danger out there and I'm so sorry. You might not believe me, but you are the most important thing in the world to me and I hope you'll let me prove it."

"How?"

"I'm thinking I should see a counselor. See why I keep doing this."

"You think maybe that psychologist you were required to see after that deadly force thing might be right? That this has to do with your military service?"

His head dropped. "I was their platoon leader, Erin. It was my job to look out for them. Keep them safe."

"An impossible task."

"Maybe. But I failed." He met her gaze, and his eyes glittered with grief and helplessness. "They trusted me to look out for them."

"It was a war," she reminded.

"Military action."

"With bombs and gunfire and schools used as shields."

"Yes. All that," he agreed. "I just keep feeling responsible. That I don't deserve…"

"What?" she asked.

"You. My life."

She gasped at that. In all the time since he'd left the service, he'd never said such a thing before.

She thought about all the chances he'd taken since discharge from the service. He'd only ended his military career because of her and her threats of separation. Now the pieces began to snap into place. Was he looking for a second chance to save his men? Or a second chance to die with them?

How was it that she'd never realized that his risky behavior coincided with the loss of so many of his men over in what he called the Sandbox?

"Counseling sounds smart," she said.

"A beginning place." He dragged a hand through his hair and then let his arm drop wearily back to his side. "The marshals, if we choose relocation, told me I can't be involved in law enforcement."

"All I've ever wanted was to keep you around," she said, the tears burning her throat and making her shoulder throb.

He chuckled. "Funny way of showing me that. Throwing me out, I mean."

"I tried other things first. You didn't hear me.

Then after you got shot, I just couldn't stop worrying. Couldn't put it aside. It was consuming me. Eating me alive."

"I'm sorry. I don't think I understood that. I just thought you were being overly protective. That you'd get past it like all the other times. But seeing you out there, watching you get shot, well, it scared me to death."

Their eyes met and held. She knew it instantly. He understood. Finally and irrevocably, he comprehended what it was like to face the death of the person whose loss you knew you could not survive.

"I couldn't live if something happened to you, Erin. I'm sorry I didn't understand. That I didn't listen."

Tears streamed down her face as she gripped his hand. She wanted to hold him, but she could not lift her arm without hitting that morphine button and she needed a clear head.

"I just wanted you safe. It's all I ever wanted."

He gave her a sad smile. They'd come to an understanding, she thought.

"Dalton, I want to go home."

"It might be a new home."

"With the dogs?"

"The…" He laughed. "You *are* feeling better. I'll see if we can arrange that."

"Are they both all right?"

"Yes. Lulu has a new dog bed and Jet has already devoured two Frisbees."

"Where are they?"

"Your sister took them back home with her."

"I want to keep them. Lulu and Jet. Can the marshals arrange that?"

"I'll ask."

"So, the relocation…is it permanent?"

"Shouldn't be. Just until they sort out this group."

"Siming's Army."

He nodded.

She tentatively moved her arm and winced. "That will be hard, losing everyone, my family."

"It's a big decision."

Someone stood at the door and cleared his throat. They turned and Erin saw a man in green scrubs holding a clipboard. Was this the surgeon who had stopped the bleeding and saved her life?

"How are you feeling, Erin?"

She smiled at him as he approached the bed. He was handsome, with symmetrical features, of average size and above average physique. His brown hair needed a trim and the manicured stubble of a beard covered his face.

"I'm Ryan Carr," he said, and offered his hand to Dalton, who rose to shake his hand. The two released the brief clasping of palms and Carr continued around the bed, looking at her IV. She no longer had the solution dripping into her arm, but the needle remained in her vein.

"Did you say 'Carr'?" asked Dalton. Where had he heard that name before?

"How is your pain level?" asked Carr.

"I haven't used the morphine this morning."

He smiled. "That's good." He turned to Dalton and motioned to the chair. "Would you like to sit down, Detective Stevens?"

Her husband now had his hands on his hips and his brow had descended low over his dark eyes. She knew the look. Her husband sensed a threat.

Chapter 21

Dalton realized that Ryan Carr, though dressed appropriately for hospital staff, with the Crocs, scrubs and ID tag on a lanyard, gave off a totally different vibe.

Less like a healer and more like a predator.

"What did you say your position here is?" asked Dalton, not taking a seat and instead moving to stand between Carr and his wife.

"Very good, Stevens," said Carr. "You really are very good. Most people don't even notice me."

His wife spoke from behind him. "Women would notice you."

That made Dalton's frown deepen. He was attractive if you liked pretty boys.

"You need to back up out of this room," said Dalton, keeping his attention on Carr's hands, which held only the clipboard.

"I just wanted to warn you. Mind if I get my ID? My real ID?"

"I do mind. But go ahead. Slowly," said Dalton, prepared to body slam this intruder if he even looked at Erin again. He had touched her arm, checked her IV and demonstrated very clearly how easy it was to get to them.

And then he remembered. "Ryan Carr. The chopper pilot said you gave him the cooler."

Carr nodded. "That's right."

He removed his wallet. "The marshals checked my ID, bless their hearts. But they apparently don't have a list of hospital staff. If they did," he said, taking out his identification and passing it to Dalton, "they'd know that I don't work here."

Dalton glanced at the ID with a very prominent CIA in blue on the plastic card.

"How do I know this is real or that you are who you say you are?"

"Feel free to call in and check after I go. I'm here for two reasons. First to warn you that leaving for WITSEC sooner is advisable. You are not secure here."

"And second?" asked Erin.

"To thank you. I was the one who collected that intel from a foreign operative. And I *was* the one who put it on that helicopter and gave instructions, instructions that were passed to you, Mrs. Stevens. If I understand correctly, you swam out to the pilot, attempted a rescue and took what he offered as imperative to our country's safety. Is that right?"

She nodded.

"And I'd like to thank you, Detective Stevens, for not doing as your wife requested and leaving it behind…on a red T-shirt, is that correct?" He smiled.

Dalton knew that only the FBI and CIA who had interviewed them should know these details. Was this guy for real?

"I am who I say, Detective. A fact that Agent Tillman will verify."

"We've already been lied to by someone claiming to be DHS, so excuse my skepticism."

"Lawrence Foster, yes, he proves my point—about your safety, I mean. The Justice Department is a fine organization generally. Good for moving career criminals into nice new neighborhoods after they testify. But this group, Siming's Army, they are not your typical wise guy looking to get even. They are organized and funded, backed by foreign nationals, according to my contacts. The information you rescued will be instrumental in making my case and it has already reached its terminus. The CDC is analyzing the virus and vaccine. And all because of your bravery, Mrs. Stevens." He bowed to Erin and then turned to Dalton. "And your dogged determination. Thank you both. Your country owes you a debt."

"You're welcome," said Erin.

Carr backed away from the bed and then headed for the hall, pausing to meet Dalton's troubled stare.

"Call Tillman. Tell him Carr says we need to relocate you today."

"The CIA relocates people?" asked Erin.

"We are a full-service organization, ma'am. Best of luck to you both."

He disappeared into the hall. Dalton followed him as far as the seated marshal. Carr had vanished.

"Get your boss in here now."

* * *

Erin's stitches tugged as she transferred to the wheelchair under heavy guard. It turned out that their visitor, Ryan Carr, was exactly who and what he claimed. The real deal, apparently. An honest-to-goodness spy who had done exactly what he claimed, rescuing the package from repeated attempts at recovery by members of Siming's Army and then finally reaching the airlift location, only to watch the chopper be shot down.

Erin thought that he must have been only ten or twelve miles from where the helicopter crashed.

But right now, Erin's main concern was to not throw up as she was wheeled down the hall under the protection of a ridiculous number of men armed with rifles. The hallway to and from the elevator was absolutely devoid of people.

"Did we just go up?" she asked Dalton.

The elevator was making her sour stomach more upset.

"Yes."

"Why?" She swallowed back the bitter taste in her mouth.

"Evac helicopter is taking us out of here."

"Like the one that Siming's Army already shot down?"

Beside her, Agent Kane Tillman leaned close. "Appreciate it if you don't mention them."

She nodded her understanding.

The next twenty minutes were a blur. She only threw up once and the attending EMTs seemed used to this sort of disturbance. They gave her something that settled her stomach and something for the pain. But the analgesic made her sleepy. Now she struggled to stay awake.

The sky was a deep blue and the lights below them flicked on. Streets glimmered with lines of red tail-lights and white headlights, strung in parallel ribbons.

"Where are we heading?" she asked, watching the Adirondacks resume custody of the land now stretching below in darkness. She stared out at a complete absence of lights and land broken occasionally by the soft glow of dusk gleaming on a lake or river. Her stretcher pressed against one window and her incline allowed her to see forward to the pilots and down to the emptiness between them and the wilderness. She searched for familiar landmarks and saw what could only be the Hudson River, larger now and dotted with the occasional river town. She saw the Mohawk merge and the twin bridges that told her they were headed south. What was their destination?

She did not have long to wonder.

"Are we descending?" she asked Dalton.

"Seems so."

"Dalton?"

He held her hand. "Hmm?"

"I can't stay awake."

He kissed her forehead. "I got you, Erin."

The drug was seeping into her bloodstream like tea in warm water. She blinked and forced her eyes open, but they rolled back in her head and her muscles went slack.

"No," she whispered, or merely thought she spoke. Had her lips moved? She drifted, torn loose from the mooring of pain, knowing that if danger came it would find her defenseless.

* * *

Dalton had a long night and now sat on the front porch as the birds began their morning songs. They had arrived at the temporary safe house on a country road in a little village in a county called Delaware. He'd never been to central New York. Their hostess was a woman who ran an orchard. Peaches were in season and the bees already droned in the honeysuckle bush that bordered the porch.

Erin was in an upstairs room with Roger Todding-ton, a former army paramedic and an EMT who was also their hostess's son. Somehow Dalton had dropped into a crazy world of espionage and he felt like Alice slipping through the looking glass. Everything seemed so normal here, but it was not.

The outside of this farmhouse looked typical enough, but the adjoining outbuilding was not the garage it appeared to be; instead, it was a fully equipped operating room with an adjoining recovery suite that rivaled the ICU where Erin had convalesced from her surgery.

Their hostess, Mrs. Arldine Toddington, offered him a cup of black coffee. The woman was fit, thin and muscular with hair that was snow-white on top and red and white beneath. She looked about as much like a spy as Mr. Rogers, God rest him. But according to Tillman she was a former US marine, a nurse practitioner with unique experience with gunshot wounds and was, it seemed, even tougher than she looked. She also made an amazing peach-and-walnut coffee cake.

But if Agent Tillman was to be believed, they were safe here and would remain in Mrs. Toddington's care until Erin recovered enough to travel without drawing attention to her healing bullet wound.

"Estimate that will be twelve to fifteen days," said Arldine.

"Do you have a location?" Dalton asked Tillman.

"Two, actually." Tillman set aside his coffee to accept a fork and a plate with a large piece of coffee cake littered with sticky walnut bits. "Thank you, Arldine."

"We'll have a choice?" asked Dalton.

Arldine and Tillman exchanged looks, and Arldine withdrew to lean against the porch rail facing them. Tillman nodded and she took over the conversation.

"We understand your wife has asked you for a legal separation."

Dalton lowered the plate to his lap and forced himself to swallow. The moist cake had turned chalky in his mouth, and the sticky topping made the food lodge in his throat.

Tillman filled the silence. "Safer for you both if you go separate ways. You are a big guy. Distinctive looking. Erin is more attractive than most women, but with a change of hair color and wardrobe, she can fit in just about anywhere."

Sweat popped out behind his ears and across his upper lip.

"Now you're saying that if we stay together, I put her at risk?"

"We are," said Tillman.

"But a few moments ago you said you could keep us safe."

"Carr has uncovered more information on this outfit. Seems to be heavily funded from offshore accounts, and we do not have a handle on the number of recruited members or even how many more sleeper cells can be activated. The speed of their response is daunting. They definitely have our attention."

"Erin and I are no threat."

"But you are on a kill list."

Dalton sat back in the rocker, sending it tilting at a dangerous angle. He knew what a kill list was. Crime organizations used them. It was a bounty list of sorts with a price on the heads of people who had betrayed or wronged them in some way.

"How do you know?" asked Dalton.

"We've gotten that much from Lawrence Foster. It was why Carr made his appearance. He doesn't usually get involved with civilians. But you two protected the information he had carried. So he felt a certain debt. He was at the hospital when I arrived, watching over you and your wife."

The man gave Dalton the creeps, and that was saying something when you considered all the types of criminals and military badasses he had come in contact with over the years.

"Where will you send her?" asked Dalton, getting back to the crux of the situation.

"I'm afraid I can't tell you that. Only the location we plan to send you."

Dalton would not even be allowed to know where she was.

"We will give you regular updates on her condition and will notify you both immediately when we neutralize the threat."

Neutralized, he thought. Also known as dead, killed, KIA or otherwise squashed.

"I need to talk this over with Erin."

"Of course," said Arldine. "You should."

"But remember that the threat increases if you stay together."

Chapter 22

Dalton dreaded this conversation. He had come up here to win back his wife and save their marriage. Now he was going to blow it up again. Only this time he had a good reason. He was doing it to save Erin. To protect her, he had to leave her.

Impossible. Necessary.

He rubbed a knuckle back and forth across his wrinkled forehead trying to prepare for the conversation. She was just recovering, only off the morphine for one day, but he did not have time to waste. The longer he waited, the higher the chances that he would back out. Thinking of the look on her face and of never seeing that face again might just be enough to kill him. According to her, he'd been trying to do that—kill himself—ever since he came home from the Sandbox. He realized she had been right all along and so he would see a mental health professional ASAP. Or he could

throw himself right back into the action. He could de-
cline relocation and reenlist.

He felt as if his stomach was filled with tiny shards
of glass, cutting him apart from the inside. He stood
before her door, an upstairs bedroom of Arldine's farmhouse with southern exposure, lots of light and a fine
view of the hayfield across the road.

Dalton rapped on the door. Roger called him in.
When Dalton did not enter, the EMT appeared at the
door, his face fixed with a gentle smile.

"Come on in, Detective. I'm just finishing." Roger
looped his stethoscope around his neck and held the
ends as one might do with a small towel.

Dalton stepped in on wooden legs. Would she believe
him? He had to make her believe him.

"Hey there," Erin said.

She sat up in the hospital-style bed, a bouquet of
sunflowers in a blue ceramic pitcher beside her on the
bedside table. Beneath them rested a pill bottle, a half-
empty water glass and a magazine.

"How are you feeling?"

"Lonely. I asked Roger to let me move back with
you. I understand you have a queen mattress and a view
of the barn."

He hadn't noticed the view, except that there was
easy access to a flat roof beneath the window and a
short drop to the ground from there.

The thick bandage on her neck was all the incentive
he needed to do what he must. Dalton drew up the old
wooden chair and placed it backward beside her bed.
He sat, straddling the chair back, using the dowels as a
sort of barrier between them because he feared that if
he touched her, he'd never let her go.

Dalton cleared his throat.

"Honey?" asked Erin. "What's wrong?"

Erin felt the worry creeping up her spine like a nest of baby spiders, their tiny legs moving over her back, lifting the hairs on her body and washing her skin cold.

Dalton's expression was unfamiliar and deadly serious.

She hazarded a guess.

"Are they out there?" She motioned toward the window and winced, forgetting not to use her left hand. Her head was clear thanks to ceasing the narcotics, but the pain pulsed with her heart, and her healing skin and muscle burned with the slightest movement.

"No, they're not. Erin, we are going to different locations."

"What?" Confusion mingled with the fear, landing in her stomach and squeezing tight. She sat up, leaving her nest of pillows, ignoring the pain that now bloomed across her chest. "No."

"It's what you wanted. A separation."

"Trial separation and I explained that to you. I don't want a separation. I want you to stop taking unnecessary risks. To see a counselor as you said."

"I changed my mind."

Her mouth dropped open. She could not even formulate a reply.

"I'm not leaving the force."

"But…wait…no…" She was stammering. "You have to leave the force. We're relocating. You can't… Dalton, this makes no sense."

"You said I have a death wish. I'm agreeing with you."

"This is suicide."

He nodded.

"You have to come with me."

"I'm not."

"What are you doing, Dalton? Are they using you as some kind of bait again? We got them Foster. They cannot expect you—"

"They don't. Haven't. I just thought you deserved to hear it from me. I'm leaving *you* this time. I'm sorry, Erin. People don't change. Sooner or later, I'm catching a bullet. I'm ready. Ready to join those guys I promised to protect."

"Oh no, you don't." She reached for him.

He stood, looking down at her with regret. But not love. Somehow that was gone. The coldness in his dark eyes momentarily stopped her breathing, and her hand dropped to the bright pastel quilt.

"Goodbye, Erin."

The pain solidified like the surface of a frozen lake. She pointed a finger at him.

"Dalton, don't you dare walk out that door!"

But he was already gone, and the door slammed shut behind him.

Dalton made it only to the top of the stairs. Tillman stood on the landing a few steps below him. Dalton sank to the top step still gripping the banister.

"She believe you?"

He nodded, thinking he did not have the strength to rise.

"Good. You can leave now. I have your location information."

"Where?"

Chapter 23

Erin adjusted the wide-brimmed ranger hat on her head and proceeded toward her truck, the radio clunking against her hip with each stride. She paused to pass out a few stickers to the children in a visiting family who had stopped to read the nature trail board at the start of a gentle two-mile hike.

"Thank you!" piped the middle child. The youngest was already trying unsuccessfully to affix the sticker on her shirt without removing the backing and the eldest squatted in front of her to help.

Erin waved, feeling just the slightest tug in the stiff muscles of her neck. The cold in the mountains seemed to creep into the place where she had been shot.

She crossed the lot to her truck. Her new location was Mount Rainer National Park where she spent more time outside than she had on the East Coast. Unfortunately, she did not teach rock climbing or lead nature hikes for groups visiting from all over the world. That would be too much like her old life. So she did patrols, taught classes to youngsters in the nature center and manned the admission booth. At night she presented educational programs in the outdoor amphitheater for the visitors camping on-site.

Once in her truck, she unzipped her heavy jacket and headed back to the station past the yellow aspen and spectacular views of the ridge of blue mountains. She lived close to the station in the housing provided by the park to the rangers. Lulu and Jet greeted her at the door, as always. She had spent many nights alone back in Yonkers while Dalton worked his cases. And, though she had worried, she'd known he was out there and hoped he would be home eventually. Now that hope was gone. The cabin had a hollow feel and if not for the dogs, she didn't think she could take the solitude. Even with the other rangers she was alone, sticking to the story they had given her that made her five years younger and an only child.

September in New York was cool and lovely, but here in the Cascades the high altitude changed the seasons early. There was already snow predicted in the Cascades. In downstate New York, the earliest she ever saw snow had been November, and often just flurries, but here it was September 7 and predictions were for an accumulation tomorrow.

She didn't mind, could not have asked for a more perfect relocation. And the Company, as they self-identified, were optimistic that she would not have to stay here for more than a year. The information she and Dalton had furnished was likely to stop a pandemic.

Agent Carr kept in touch, appearing erratically to join a hike or as a solo camper applying for a wilderness permit. He said they were in the process of finding the three Deathbringers that were mentioned on the thumb drive.

The three Deathbringers, according to Carr, came from Chinese folklore, though even in myth form they were still considered dangerous by many. These "corpses" were believed by some to enter the body just after birth and determined the life span of each individual. Each corpse attacked a different system, brain, heart and organs. More specifically to the CIA, they would attack US citizens. The virus that she and Dalton had carried attacked the internal organs, causing a massive shutdown of the renal system. That was corpse number one and steps were underway to locate and intercept a shipment of this virus before it reached US soil. The second corpse, which attacked the brain, referred to a cyber attack, already in place, the brain being a metaphor for the infrastructure that kept communication open. Their people were working on that one now, as well. And the heart? Carr said that the Company believed this was an airborne toxin in production somewhere in New York State.

At the cabin she glimpsed a rental car. A man stood on the porch beside Jet, and for just a moment her heart galloped. But then she recognized that the stranger was too small to be Dalton.

She didn't look over her shoulder or jump every time she heard an unfamiliar sound. She just was not living her life like that. Erin was out of the vehicle and greeting Jet before she recognized the man in the cowboy hat.

"Mr. Carr," she said. "That hat makes you look like a Texas Ranger."

He slipped down the stairs to shake her hand. "A pleasure to see you again."

He smiled. "And you."

"Staying for supper?" she asked.

"No, unfortunately. Just wanted to tell you that the tech team has located the computer virus their hackers installed. It was set to disrupt two different systems. The rails in NYC, including subways, and the gas and electric grid in Buffalo."

"Can they stop it?"

"Working on that now."

She finished stroking Jet's head and the canine moved off to explore around the cabin. Erin hoped the porcupine she'd seen last night was now sleeping in a tree somewhere.

Lulu barked from inside. Erin let her out and Carr in.

"Can I fix you some coffee?"

He nodded.

She didn't ask if he'd like a beer, knowing he always turned her down.

"We are working to shut down the cell that came after you. Early indications are that they did not pass on any information about you or Dalton."

"What does that mean, exactly?"

"If we can ascertain that no other cell of the terrorist organization is aware of your involvement, it would mean you could return to your family."

It took only a moment for the coffee to brew. She used the time to force down the lump in her throat. To be able to return to your life would be wonderful, but one member of her family was absent. She missed

Dalton so much her body ached from the sorrow. Erin forced her shoulders back and she passed Carr a mug of black coffee.

"Erin?" he asked, his face showing concern as he accepted the mug.

"That's good news." She managed the words, but her voice quavered. "How are my parents?"

"Missing you. But fine."

"My sister?"

"Said to tell you that the middle one lost a front tooth."

Erin smiled. "That's Patrick. I hope he didn't knock it out." He was in second grade, and all his classmates had that same gap-toothed smile and whistling disability.

She never asked about Dalton out of a mixture of sorrow and fear. They would tell her if and when he was killed. Wouldn't they?

The panic that they wouldn't forced her to tip heavily against the kitchen counter. Summoning her courage, she fixed her gaze on Carr.

"What's the word on Dalton? Is he still with the New York City Real Time Crime Center?"

The mug in Carr's hand paused at his lip and he regarded her a moment in silence. Then he lowered the mug to the counter.

"What was that?"

"I'm asking if he's back with his unit?"

"Erin, we told Dalton that joint relocation was dangerous because Dalton is so…" He extended his arms, indicating Dalton's unusual size. Carr's hand then went up to indicate Dalton's above-average height. "So…distinctive. You both agreed to separate locations."

"I'm confused," she said. "Dalton turned down relocation."

Carr arched a single brow that told her instantly that she had something wrong.

"Yes. I was aware he told you that," said Carr.

"Turned it down," she said, trying to convince Carr as the panic constricted her throat. "He told me that he couldn't change and that he would miss the action, the danger. He told me…" She made a fist and scrubbed it across her forehead. "He said…" She lifted her gaze to Carr. "He relocated?"

"He was. He just didn't tell you."

Her knees went out and she sank down along the lower cabinets, stopping only when her backside hit the floor.

"He lied to me."

Carr was beside her in an instant, squatting before her. "You signed the papers agreeing to separate locations."

She glared up at him. "Clearly, I didn't read the fine print."

"That was unwise."

She rested her forehead on her folded forearms supported by her knees. She spoke to her lap. "I would never have agreed…"

And that was why Dalton had not told her.

"Exactly," said Carr his expression showing regret.

She concentrated on breathing through her nose until the dark moth-like spots flapped away from her vision. Then she lifted her head.

"Why tell me now?" she asked.

"It seemed wrong to me. And you are unhappy."

"I want to see him."

"Marshalls service will tell you that is impossible."

"Really?" she said. "Then I'm taking out an ad in the *Seattle Times*."

"That will get you killed."

"Want to stop me? Take me to Dalton."

"I can't do that."

She was up and snatching the keys from the bowl beside the door. Jet trotted after her. Lulu came at a waddle.

Outside she opened the truck door and Jet jumped in. Lulu needed a boost. She was behind the wheel when Carr reached her, on the phone, talking fast to someone and then to her. "Where are you going, Erin?"

"Yonkers."

He stood in the open door, keeping her from closing it.

"I could arrest you as a threat to national security."

"You told me what happened. Now you can take me to Dalton."

"He did this to protect you. If you leave WITSEC, his sacrifice is for nothing."

"The heck with that. I only agreed to this arrangement because he lied to me."

"Which is why he did this."

"I'll sue."

"You can't sue us."

Erin turned the key in the ignition. Carr reached in and flicked the engine back off.

"You knew what I'd do when I found out."

Carr shrugged. "Surmised."

He was playing her. Why did he want her to break cover?

"Why?" she asked.

"He's unhappy, too. Seems poor payment for your service."

"Take me to him," she whispered.

"All right," said Carr.

Chapter 24

Dalton returned from his monthlong job on an off-shore oil rig in the Gulf of Mexico on calm waters. The transport vessel slowed to dock in Mobile, Alabama. The replacement crew was behind them, and he and his new coworker were off for four glorious weeks. The gulf was the color of the Caribbean Sea today as they reached shallow water, and the sky was a pale summer blue. Though fall had taken firm hold up north, here the summer stretched long and warm.

He let the young ones hurry off the vessel first—those with girlfriends and new wives who still cared enough to greet them upon disembarking. The older men and the single ones had no one waiting and could make their way leisurely to their trucks and Harleys to head to wherever they went when not working thirteen-hour shifts. Dalton wondered where Erin was today.

Was she looking at a blue sky or gray clouds? Was it raining where she was? Was she safe? Did she miss him?

"See you soon, Carl," said one of the roustabouts he had come to know.

He touched two fingers to his forehead, tanned from all the outdoor work, and gave a sloppy salute.

His roommate, a motorman from the Florida Panhandle, slapped him on the back as he headed down the gangplank, which led to the receiving area where family sometimes waited.

"Bye, Carl."

"Safe drive, Randall," he called after him.

His position as an offshore installation manager was made easier by the real manager who was teaching him the job. Dalton's own experiences working on so many task forces definitely made the transition easier. And he was used to getting off duty only to be called back up the instant he fell asleep because that part of the job was exactly the same.

But he'd always had Erin to come home to.

He adjusted his duffel bag on his shoulder and exited the gangway over the pier and headed into the arrival facility. His body had healed, leaving only the entrance and exit wound from the bullet that had broken his marriage.

"Wasn't the bullet. It was you."

Had Erin's wound healed?

He crossed the lobby, passing the couples reunited after their offshore stints. He was surprised to see so many children here on a school day, greeting dads.

Nice, he thought.

The bureau had furnished him with a three-year-old red pickup truck and he headed to the lot, hoping it would start after sitting in the blazing sun for a month.

Dalton cleared the lobby of the company's dockside offices and was hit by the heat and humidity. Without the boat's motion, the breeze had ceased and he began to sweat. He hurried down the sidewalk toward the lot, anxious to reach the air-conditioning of his truck.

But where was he going? Back to his empty condo? Not likely. He'd have a meal first. One where he could pick what he wanted from a menu. And a beer. He'd missed having a cold one on a hot day.

He caught motion in his peripheral vision, his brain relaying that there was an animal running toward him. He turned to give a knee to any dog stupid enough to jump on him. Dalton dropped his duffel as his hand went automatically to his hip to find no service weapon waiting.

The dog was black, a skinny Lab with a new pink collar. The dog seemed familiar and wagged frantically as Dalton stared in confusion. It whined and bowed and fell to its back kicking all four feet.

That almost looked like…impossible.

This dog could not be that dog. But then, waddling around between a pigmy palm and a hydrangea bush awash in hot-pink blooms, came a fat pug dog.

"Lulu?" he asked. He turned back to the black dog as he dropped to one knee. "Jet?"

Jet's reply was a sharp bark. Then she threw herself into Dalton's arms, wriggling and lapping his face with her long, wet tongue.

Dalton scooped up Lulu and stared at her. The dog seemed to smile and panted as if the walk had been taxing. Dalton returned her to the ground and she dropped to one hip as he shot to his feet.

Erin. She had to be here. But that was impossible.

Dalton scanned his surroundings, fixing on the only running vehicle that had dark tinted glass.

He turned to see a woman stepping from the rear seat of a large, dark SUV, the sort you might see in a presidential motorcade. Sunglasses hid her eyes and her hair was shorter, darker and much more stylish. Her mouth lifted in a familiar smile. Was she wearing red lipstick?

"Hey, sailor," she said.

She slammed the door shut, giving him a view of the flowery, sheer halter top and short cutoff jeans. The pale skin told him that wherever she had been it was cold, for it looked as if she had not seen the sun since he last saw her.

Jet darted back to her and then reeled and dashed back to Dalton. Lulu sat looking at her mistress, content to wait for her to catch up.

From the opposite side of the SUV stepped CIA agent Ryan Carr. "I got a delivery for you," he said, tipping a thumb toward Erin.

"Where do I sign?" asked Dalton.

"We have an escort in the lot. They'll take you to your new location."

"Where?"

"New Mexico. Tourist town outside Sedona."

Erin lowered her glasses and studied him, taking a moment, it seemed, to absorb the changes. If he'd known he would have cut his hair, shaved his face. He rasped his knuckles over the stubble that was well on its way to becoming a beard.

He blinked at her, trying to understand and then taking two steps in her direction before the truth struck him.

They were blown.

Dalton turned to Carr.

"When?" he asked as he strode toward Erin. He needed her back in the car. Out of sight. What was the agent doing letting her be seen out here?

"When, what?"

"We're blown," he said.

Carr shook his head. "You're not. Just a change of plans."

Erin reached him now, slipped her arms around his middle and pressed herself to him. He gathered her up in his arms and lowered his head, inhaling the familiar scent as he took in the changes. She was thinner.

He drew back to look at her, seeing the puckering red scar at the juncture of her shoulder and neck. A shot through the muscle that had torn into a major blood vessel and nearly taken her life.

Erin flipped her sunglasses up to her head and stared up at him. The look was not longing or desperate unrequited love. It seemed more like a smoldering fury that he had seen too many times in their marriage.

She lowered her chin. "You said you wanted a separation."

"I said that."

"You never told me the reason. So what is it, exactly?"

He pressed his mouth shut, not wanting to spoil this. To see her again, it was too sweet, and even having her mad was having her.

"Dalton?" Her arms slipped from his waist and folded before her. One slim sandaled foot began tapping the hot sidewalk.

"They said you'd be safer away from me. That I stand out."

She threw up her hands. Then she slugged him in the chest. He absorbed the blow. He knew from experience that she had a better right than that. This was just a mark of displeasure.

"You were protecting me?"

He nodded.

"You still love me?"

He nodded again.

"Then get in the car." She motioned to the SUV.

"Yes, dear." Dalton slipped into the rear seat. Erin retrieved Lulu, who had collapsed to her side, and then snapped her fingers for Jet, who bounded onto the rear seat and sprawled across Dalton's lap.

Then Erin climbed in and closed the door, ordering the dogs off the seat.

In the front area Carr was already buckling into the driver's seat and put them in Reverse.

Erin touched a button on the armrest and the privacy window lifted. Once it had closed completely, she tossed aside her glasses and grasped his face between her two small hands. Then she gave him the sort of kiss that had his eyes closing to absorb the perfection of the contact.

When she drew back, they sat side by side, breathless, hearts racing. She curled her hands around one of his arms and lowered her head to his shoulder.

"I missed you every minute. I can't believe you'd do this without telling me."

"Would you have gone?"

She shook her head. "I love you, Dalton. And marrying you was my way of letting you know that I wanted to spend the rest of my life *with* you."

He closed his eyes as he wondered if being apart, safe and miserable was preferable to accepting the increased risk and being with his wife. Then he decided it was not.

"I was wrong," he said. "I know it. I knew it almost immediately after I left you, but it was too late."

"Apparently not."

"How did you get them to come for me?"

"Threatened to walk away, tell the papers all about it."

He sat back, stunned. "You can't do that. You signed an agreement."

She shrugged.

"You threatened the CIA?"

Erin's cheeks turned pink. "I did."

"They make people disappear for that."

"We're small fish. Best to just let us go."

"I'm glad you did," he admitted. "So glad. I've been miserable without you, Erin. You're more than a piece of me—you're my heart."

She hugged him. "Oh, Dalton."

They drove in silence behind the escort car and trailed by another, winding through the streets and toward the highway.

"Where are they taking us now?" he asked.

"Airport first. And then, who cares? As long as we are together."

He gathered her up in his arms, dragging her to his lap for another kiss. She was right again. It didn't matter where they went. It mattered only that she had never stopped loving him and that he had her back in his arms once more.

* * * * *

An author of more than ninety books for children and adults with more than seventy-five for Harlequin, **Janice Kay Johnson** writes about love and family, and pens books of gripping romantic suspense. A *USA TODAY* bestselling author and an eight-time finalist for the Romance Writers of America RITA® Award, she won a RITA® Award in 2008. A former librarian, Janice raised two daughters in a small town north of Seattle, Washington.

Books by Janice Kay Johnson

Harlequin Intrigue

Hide the Child
Trusting the Sheriff
Within Range
Brace for Impact
The Hunting Season
The Last Resort
Cold Case Flashbacks

Visit the Author Profile page
at Harlequin.com for more titles.

THE LAST RESORT

Janice Kay Johnson

For Barb, a great editor and even better friend,
and for her faithful sidekick, Panda.

Chapter 1

Leah Keaton eased up on the gas pedal too late to prevent her right front tire from dropping into an epic pothole with a distinct *clunk*. She winced.

Along with a gradual rise in elevation, the road was getting narrower, the dense northwest forest reclaiming it. The roots from vast Douglas fir, spruce and cedar trees created a corrugated effect as they crumbled the pavement. Long, feathery limbs occasionally brushed the sides of her modest sedan. Pale lichen draped from branches. Thick clumps of ferns and wiry branches of what might be berries overhung the edges of the pavement.

Her mother could have been right, that this was a wasted and even unwise journey.

All of which was assuming, Leah thought ruefully, that she hadn't taken a wrong turn. In her distant memory, a carved and painted wood sign had marked the turnoff to her great-uncle's rustic resort in the north Cascade Mountains, not that far from the Canadian border. She reminded herself this was rain forest, which by definition meant wood rotted quickly. Once the sign fell, moss and forest undergrowth would have hidden it in a matter of weeks.

Forcing herself to loosen her grip on the steering wheel, Leah caught a glimpse of Mount Baker above the treetops. At not quite eleven thousand feet in elevation, Baker wasn't the largest of the string of volcanoes that stretched from California to the Canadian border, but it was plenty imposing anyway with year-round snow and ice cloaking the mountain flanks. Leah remembered from when she was a kid seeing puffs of steam escaping vents at the summit, a reminder that Mount Baker still had the potential to erupt.

Weirdly, the memory relaxed her. This road felt familiar. If she was right, it would soon climb more sharply yet above a river carrying seasonal snowmelt that ultimately joined the larger North Fork Nooksack River. As a child, she'd hated the drive home from the resort because the edge was so close to the road, the drop-off so precipitous. She hadn't trusted the rusting guardrail at all.

What if a tumultuous spring had undercut the cliff and the road no longer went all the way to the resort?

The tires of her car crunched onto gravel as the pavement ended. She had to go slower yet, because potholes and ruts made the way even more perilous.

Although he'd closed the resort something like fifteen years ago, Uncle Edward had continued living here until his death last fall. Had he really not minded navigating this road when he had to stock up on groceries? According to Leah's mother, he'd declared flatly, "This is home," and remained undaunted by the perils of living in such an isolated location as an old man.

"Stubborn as that old coot Harry Truman, who wouldn't evacuate when Mount St. Helens blew," Mom had grumbled, mentioning the name of a rugged individual who'd refused to leave the mountainside before the volcano erupted in 1980. "He'll end the same way. You just wait and see."

Leah's dad had gently pointed out that, despite being in his nineties, Uncle Edward hadn't displayed even a hint of dementia and therefore was fully capable of making his own decisions. Dad had shaken his head. "He's lived up there most of his life. Imagine what it would be like for him to move to a senior apartment with busybody neighbors all around and traffic going by night and day."

"But we could find him a nice—" Mom had broken off, knowing she'd lost the argument. She just didn't understand her uncle, who'd spent his entire life in the north Cascade Mountains.

She did understand why he'd left the resort to Leah, the only one of his nieces and nephews who had genuinely loved vacations spent at the remote resort. Leah would have been happy to spend every summer there—at least until teenage hormones struck and hanging out with friends at home became a priority—but her mother refused to let her stay beyond their annual two-week family vacations spent in one of the lakeside cabins.

The road started to seriously climb, blue sky ahead. A minute later she saw the small river to the left, water tumbling over boulders and pausing in deep pools. This was July, the height of the melt-off on the mountain above. By fall, the water level would lower until barely a creek ran between rocky banks.

She stayed close to the steep bank on the right. After sneaking a few peeks at the guardrail in places it had crumpled or even disappeared, she decided she just might do the same thing coming down. It wasn't as if she was likely to meet any oncoming traffic, for heaven's sake. She could drive on whatever side of the road she wanted. And, while she'd brought a suitcase, sleeping bag and enough food to hold her for a night or two, she knew the old resort buildings might be so decrepit she'd have no choice but to turn right around and head back down the mountain. Uncle Edward had been ninety-three when he died. He wasn't likely to have done any significant maintenance in many years.

Still…the location was great, the view of Mount Baker across a shallow lake and an alpine meadow spectacular. There'd even been a glimpse of the more distant Mount Shuksan, too. Backed by national forest, the land alone had to be worth something, didn't it? She hoped Uncle Edward hadn't envisioned her building up the resort again and running it; despite good memories of the stays here, she'd grown up in Portland, Oregon, gone to college in southern California. Wilderness girl, she wasn't.

Learning about the inheritance had given her hope. She'd been dreaming of going back to school to become a veterinarian. The cost was one factor in her hesitation. Animal doctors didn't make the kind of income people doctors did, but finished four years of graduate school with the same load of debt.

Never having dreamed Uncle Edward would leave

the resort to her, she couldn't help feeling as if he'd somehow known what it would mean to her.

To her relief, the road curved away from the river and plunged back into the forest. Leah's anticipation rose as she peered ahead through the tunnel formed by the enormous old evergreen trees.

It was another ten minutes before her car popped out into the grassy meadow, spangled with wildflowers, and there was the resort.

Except...there were already people here. Her foot went to the brake. Half a dozen—no, more than that—SUVs were parked in front of the lodge and cabins. Not a single car, she noted in a corner of her mind. These all looked like the kind of vehicles designed to drive on icy pavement and even off-road.

This was weird, but...she'd come this far. Surely, there was a legitimate reason for people to be here.

After a moment she continued forward, coasting to a stop in front of the lodge. Head turning, she saw that some of the cabins had been repaired in the recent past. Several new roofs and the raw wood of new porches and window frames were unmistakable.

A woman on one of those porches looked startled at the sight of her and slipped back inside the cabin, maybe to tell someone else about the arrival of a stranger.

Two men appeared around the corner of the lodge, probably having heard her car engine.

Who *were* these people? Had Mom been wrong, and Uncle Edward had kept the resort open? But still, he'd died eight months ago. Could he have sold it, with no one knowing?

She'd braked and put the gear in Park, but unease stilled her hand before she turned the key.

What if—? But she'd hesitated too long. The men had reached her car, their expressions merely inquiring. There had to be a reasonable explanation. She should be glad the resort buildings hadn't begun to tumble down.

In the sudden silence after she shut off the engine, the car keys bit into her hand. Taking a deep breath, Leah unbuckled her seat belt, opened the door and got out.

One of the men, gray-haired but as fit as a younger man, smiled. "You must be lost."

The muscular guy behind him had full-sleeve tattoos bared below a muscle-hugging tan T-shirt. And... could that be a holstered pistol at his waist?

Dear God, yes.

Say yes. Claim you were heading anywhere else. Let them give you directions and then drive away.

She could go to the nearest small town—Glacier, population 211—and ask about the group staying here. There was only one highway in and out of this area. These people had driven here. They'd have been noticed.

But the older of the two men looked friendly, not hostile at all. There'd be a logical explanation.

"No, actually," she said. "Um... I own this resort."

His smile fell away. "You're the *owner*?"

"That's right. I inherited the place from my great-uncle, Edward Preston."

Outwardly, the man relaxed. "Oh, we've been wondering what was going to happen to the place. The old man let us mostly take over the resort these past few summers in exchange for working on it. We had no idea he'd died until we got here in late June and found it empty."

"Didn't you ask in Glacier or Maple Falls? Surely, people there knew he'd died."

"Some bed-and-breakfast owner I talked to said she hadn't heard anything." He nodded toward the lodge. "Why don't you come on in and we can talk? I don't know about you, but I could use a cup of coffee."

Conscious of the other man's eyes boring into her, she hesitated again, but what else could she do but say, "Sure. Thanks. I'd forgotten what a long drive it is to get up here."

The pair flanked her as they started toward the lodge, which sounded deceptively grand. The old log building only had six guest rooms, all upstairs, a large kitchen and living space and the owner's small apartment at the back. Mostly, Uncle Edward had rented out the ten cabins. What guests he'd allowed to stay in the lodge understood they had to bring their own food and cook for themselves. "Not like I'm going to wait on them hand and foot," he'd snorted.

Leah became nervously aware that several other men had stepped out of cabins, their gazes on her. Most wore camo cargo pants, as did the so-far silent man walking to her right. None of them called out. Their appraisal felt…cold.

She was imagining things. They were curious, that was all.

Only…why weren't there other women? Children?

The porch steps were solid, having obviously been replaced. The older man opened the front door and they ushered her in. *Herded me in*, that uneasy voice inside her head whispered.

She did smell coffee. In fact, a couple of empty cups

sat on the long plank table where guests had eaten or sat around in the evening to play board games or poker.

"Let me get that coffee," the gray-haired man said. "You want sugar? I have milk but no cream."

"Milk's fine. Just a dash, and a teaspoon of sugar."

"Coming right up. Have a seat." He nodded toward the benches to each side of the table.

Knowing she'd feel trapped once she was sitting with her feet under the table, she strolled instead toward the enormous river-rock fireplace where she had once upon a time roasted marshmallows for s'mores.

None of the men she'd seen thus far looked as if they'd do anything that frivolous. Chew sixteen-gauge steel nails, maybe. Graham crackers, gooey charred marshmallows and melted chocolate? Hard to picture.

The silent guy remained standing, a shoulder against the log wall right beside the door out to the porch. He watched her steadily.

Maybe he'd be friendly if she was. But before she could think of anything to say that wasn't too inane, the older man returned from the kitchen with a cup of coffee in each hand.

He glanced toward the second man but didn't offer to fetch him a cup, too.

Leah didn't feel as if she had any choice but to go back to the table and sit down.

He took a sip before asking, "Mind telling me your plans?"

"Um… I wanted to see what condition the buildings were in. And, well, probably I'll sell the place."

"Sell it, huh? You have a price in mind?"

"I have no idea what land is worth up here." If it was

worth anything. She had to be honest with herself. "Are you interested?"

"Could be. We'd hate having to relocate."

Feeling and sounding timid, she asked, "Do you mind telling me what you're doing up here? I'm assuming you're not all vacationing here three months a year."

The flicker of amusement in his eyes wasn't at all reassuring. He thought she was funny. Naive.

"No," he said thoughtfully. "No, this is a business."

More unnerved by the minute, she gripped the handle of the mug. She could buy herself time by throwing hot coffee in one of the men's faces if she had to run for it.

Just then, the front door opened and two more men walked in. Cool gazes assessed her. One of them raised dark eyebrows as he looked at the man acting as host. Leah had no trouble hearing the unspoken question.

Who the hell is she and what does she want?

One of the newcomers was short and stocky with sandy hair. Sort of Dennis the Menace, with the emphasis on *menace*.

The other was formidable enough to scare her more. Eyes a crystalline gray could have been chips of ice. Tanned and dark-haired, he had the kind of shoulders that suggested he did some serious weight lifting.

And, dear God, both men wore holstered handguns at their waists.

Paramilitary was the word that came to mind. What had she walked into?

Be up front, she decided.

"I'm starting to feel a little uncomfortable," she said, focusing on the older man who almost had to be the leader of this bunch. "Why don't I head back to Glacier and find a room for the night? I'll talk to a real estate agent, and if you'd like you can come down tomorrow, meet me for lunch, maybe. We can talk."

Still appearing relaxed, he said slowly, "That might work. Ah...in answer to your earlier question, what we do is run paintball camps. It's mostly men who come up here. They immerse themselves in the wilderness and harmless war games, have a hell of a good time. We've built up a serious seasonal business. Like I said, finding another location anywhere near as perfect as this one would be next to impossible."

Because this land was so remote. Leah had to wonder whether it was true Uncle Edward had let them use his place for several summers in a row, or whether they'd somehow heard he had died and moved in under the assumption no one would be interested enough in a falling-down resort in the middle of nowhere to bother checking on it.

She stole another look at the three men on their feet, now ranged around the room. "Those...look like real guns."

Boss Man across from her shrugged. "Sure, we have a shooting range set up. A bunch of us have been out there all morning. Gotta keep sharp, even if we're mostly using paintball guns."

Nobody else's expression changed.

"Well," she said, starting to push herself up.

The sound of the back door opening was as loud as a shot. Bounced off the wall, she diagnosed, in a small, calm part of her mind surrounded by near hysteria.

All of the men turned their heads.

Grinning, a man emerged from the kitchen. Over his shoulder, he carried a *huge* gun, painted army green.

Even as he said, "Hot damn!" before seeing her, Leah's blood chilled.

She'd seen pictures, taken in places like the Ukraine and Afghanistan. That wasn't a gun—it was a rocket launcher.

Son of a bitch.

Spencer Wyatt restrained himself from so much as twitching a muscle only from long practice. His mind worked furiously, though. Could this juxtaposition be any more disastrous? An unsuspecting woman wandering in here like a dumb cow to slaughter, coupled with that cocky, careless jackass Joe Osenbrock striding in with an effing *rocket launcher* over his shoulder? *Yee haw.*

Especially a young, pretty woman. Did she have any idea what trouble she was in?

Flicking a glance at her, he thought, yeah, she had a suspicion.

In fact, she said, in a voice that sounded a little too cheerful to be real, "Is that one of the paintball guns? I've never seen one before."

Good try.

Ed Higgs didn't buy it. "You know better than that. Damn. I wish I could let you go, but I can't."

She flung her full coffee cup at his face, leaped off the bench and tore for the front door, still standing ajar. Smart move, trying to get out of here. She actually brushed Spencer. He managed to look surprised and stagger back to give her a chance. No surprise, the little creep Larson was on her before she so much as touched the door.

She screamed and struggled. Her nails raked down

Larson's cheek. Teeth set, he slammed her against the wall, flattening his body on hers. Spencer wanted to rip the little pissant off and throw *him* into the wall. Went without saying that he stayed right where he was. There was no way for him to help now that wouldn't derail his mission.

He had more lives than hers to consider.

Ed snapped, "Get her car keys. Wyatt, go over the car. When you're done, bring in her purse and whatever else she brought with her. Make sure you don't miss anything. Hear me?"

"Sure thing." He knew that once he had the keys, he'd have to hand them over to Higgs, who kept all the vehicle keys hidden away. No one had access to an SUV without Higgs knowing.

Arne Larson burrowed a hand into the woman's jeans pocket. When he groped with exaggerated pleasure, his captive struck quick as a snake, sinking her teeth into his shoulder. Arne yanked out the set of keys and backhanded her across the face. Her head snapped back, hitting the log wall with an audible *thunk*.

Spencer jerked but once again pulled hard on the leash. If she would only cooperate, she might have a chance to get out of this alive.

Arne tossed the keys at him and Spencer caught them. Without a word, he walked out, taking with him a last glimpse of her face, fine-boned and very pale except for the furious red staining her right jaw and cheek where the blow had fallen.

She hadn't locked the car, which didn't appear to be a rental. He used the keys to unlock the trunk and pull out a small wheeled suitcase, sized to be an airline carry-on, as well as a rolled-up sleeping bag and a cardboard box filled with basic food. Then he searched the trunk, removing the jack and spare tire, going through a bag of tools and an inadequate first-aid kit.

He couldn't believe even Higgs, with his paranoid worldview, would think the woman in there was an undercover FBI or ATF agent.

She hadn't packed like one, he discovered, after opening the suitcase on the trunk lid once he closed it. Toiletries—she liked handmade soap, this bar smelling like citrus and some spice—jeans, T-shirts, socks and sandals. Two books, one a romance, one nonfiction about the Lipizzaner horses during World War II. He fanned the pages. Nothing fell out. A hooded sweatshirt. Lingerie, practical but pretty, too, lacking lace but skimpy enough to heat a man's blood and in brighter colors than he'd have expected from her.

Not liking the direction his thoughts had taken him, he dropped the mint-green bra back on top of the mess he'd made of the suitcase's contents.

There was nothing but food in the carton, including basics like boxes of macaroni and cheese, a jar of instant coffee, a loaf of whole-grain bread and packets of oatmeal with raisins. The sleeping bag, unrolled, unzipped and shaken, hid no secrets.

A small ice chest sat on the floor in front. No surprises there, either, only milk, several bars of dark chocolate, a tub of margarine and several cans of soda.

He took her purse from the passenger seat and dumped the contents out on the hood of the car. A couple of items rolled off. Plastic bottle of ibuprofen and a lip gloss. Otherwise, she carried an electronic reader, phone, a wallet, hairbrush, checkbook, wad of paper napkins, two tampons and some crumpled receipts for gas and meals. Her purse was a lot neater than most he'd seen.

Opening the wallet, he took out her driver's license first. Issued by the state of Oregon, it said her name was Leah E. Keaton. She was described as blond, which he'd dispute, but he didn't suppose strawberry blond would fit on the license. Weight, one hundred and twenty pounds, height, five feet six inches. Eyes, hazel. Age, thirty-one. Birthday, September 23.

She'd smiled for the photo. For a moment Spencer's eyes lingered. DMV photos were uniformly bad, no better than mug shots, but he saw hope and dignity in that smile. She reminded him of a time when his purpose wasn't so dark.

Did Leah E. Keaton know it wasn't looking good for her to make it to that next birthday, no matter what he did?

Chapter 2

Leah watched out the small window in an upstairs guest room with fury and fear as one of those brutes dug through her purse. He'd already searched her suitcase; it still lay open on the trunk of the car, the scant amount of clothing she'd brought left in a disheveled heap.

Everything that had been in her purse sat atop the hood. She felt stripped bare, increasing her shock. They would now know her name, her weight, that she used tampons. Her credit cards and checkbook were in their possession, along with her keys and phone.

That wasn't all. They had her, too.

Wyatt, if that was really his name, stood for a moment with his head bent, staring at the stuff he'd dumped out of her bag, before he began scooping it up and dropping it unceremoniously back in. Then he systematically examined the car interior, under the seats, the glove compartment, the cubbies designed to hold CDs, maps or drinks.

Following orders, of course.

Still gripped by fear, she saw him lie down on his back and push himself beneath the undercarriage. Looking for a bomb? Or a tracking device? Leah had no idea.

Her heart cramped when he shifted toward the rear of the car. How could he miss seeing the magnetic box holding a spare key?

From this angle, there was no way to tell if he pocketed it.

Eventually, if her parents didn't hear from her, they'd sound the alarm and a county deputy might drive up here looking for her, but that wouldn't happen for days. Maybe as much as a week. She'd been vague about how long she intended to stay, and they knew she was unlikely to have phone service once she reached the rugged country tucked in the Cascade Mountain foothills.

Would these men kill a lone deputy who walked into the same trap she had?

When the man below climbed to his feet and closed her suitcase, she took a step back from the small-paned window. He didn't so much as glance upward as he carried the suitcase and her purse toward the lodge, disappearing beneath the porch roof. The groceries, ice chest and sleeping bag sat abandoned beside her car.

A rocket launcher. Or was it even a missile launcher? Was there a difference? The image flashed into her mind again. Leah tried to absorb the horror. Her knees gave out and she sagged to sit on the bed, fixing her unseeing gaze on the log walls with crumbled chinking. She wasn't naive enough not to be aware that, with enough money and the right connections, anybody could acquire military-grade and banned weapons. But…what did these people intend to *do* with this one? And what other weapons did they have?

Her cheekbone throbbed. When she lifted her hand to it, she winced. The swelling was obvious at even a light touch. By tomorrow, a dark bruise would discolor half her face and probably crawl under her eye, too. Her head ached.

Leah wished she could hold on to hope that, whatever the group's political objective, the men might follow some standards of honor where women were concerned. After the stocky blond guy who'd slammed her against the wall had leered and tried to grope her while his hand was in her pocket, that was a no-go. Not one of the other men present had shown the slightest reaction.

But she was sure she'd seen a woman on the porch of one of the cabins. If women belonged to the group, would they shrug at seeing another woman raped? Somehow, she had trouble picturing this particular group of men seeing any woman as an equal, though. Armed to the teeth, buff, tattooed and cold-eyed, they made her think of some of the far-right militia who appeared occasionally on the news. Every gathering she'd ever seen of white supremacists seemed to be all male. If they had women here, they might be no more willing than she was.

But maybe…this group had a completely different objective. Could they be police or, well, members of some kind of super-secret military unit?

That thought didn't seem to offer an awful lot of hope.

Nausea welling, Leah pressed a hand to her stomach and moaned. She'd driven right into their midst, offering herself up like…like a virgin sacrifice. Except for not being a virgin. Somehow, she didn't think they'd care about that part, not if their leader decided to let them have her.

No one would be coming for her. She had to escape. Would they leave her in this room, the exit guarded? Feed her? Talk to her? Give her back any of her things?

Not her keys, that was for sure. She'd have to take the chance that Wyatt had missed the spare key. If not, she'd rather be lost and alone in the dense northwest rain forest miles from any other habitation than captive here. It would get cold at night, but this was July. She wouldn't freeze to death. At least she had sturdy athletic shoes on her feet instead of the sandals she'd also brought. Thank goodness she'd thrown on a sweatshirt over her tee.

The idea of driving at breakneck speed down the steep gravel road running high above the river scared her almost as much as those men did, but given a chance, she'd do it. If she got any kind of head start, she might be able to reach the paved stretch. Along there, she could look for a place to pull the car off the road and hide.

The hand still flattened on her stomach trembled. Great plan. If, if, if. Starting with, *if* she could get out of this room. *If* she could escape the lodge. *If*...

No, at least she knew she could escape the room. For what good that would do, given that she'd still have to pop out in the hall where a guard would presumably be stationed.

Footsteps followed by voices came from right outside her door. Her head shot up.

At war with himself, Spencer sat at the long table with a cup of coffee. Other men came and went, buzzing with excitement. They liked the idea of a captive, particularly a female. They were eager to see her. Only four of the guys had brought women with them, and they weren't sharing. Wasn't like the single guys could go into town one evening and pick up a woman at a bar. For one thing, Spencer hadn't noticed any bars or taverns any closer than Bellingham. The only exception, in Maple Falls, had obviously gone out of business. Higgs didn't let them leave the "base" anyway.

Their great leader had gone upstairs a minute ago. If he didn't reappear soon, Spencer would follow him. He thought Higgs intended to bring Leah Keaton downstairs. Let her have a bite to eat, try to soothe her into staying passive. The way she'd sunk her teeth into Larson's flesh, Spencer wasn't optimistic that passive was in her nature, but maybe she'd be smart enough to pretend. He was screwed if she didn't—unless he kept his eye on the goal and accepted that there were frequently collateral losses—and this time, she'd be one of them. Except, he wasn't sure he could accept that.

Footsteps.

He took a long swallow of coffee and looked as if idly toward the woman Higgs led into the big open space.

She'd come along under her own power, without Higgs having to drag or shove her. If she had any brains, she was scared to death, but her face didn't show that. Instead, it was set, pale…and viciously bruised.

Spencer's temper stirred, but he stamped down on it.

"Have a seat." Higgs sounded almost genial.

Leah Keaton's gaze latched longingly on to her purse, sitting at one end of the table. Wouldn't make a difference for her to grab it; Higgs had taken the keys and probably her phone, which wouldn't do her any good anyway, not here.

"Dinner close to ready?" Higgs asked.

The wives and girlfriends were required to do the cooking and KP. Spencer had heard a couple of them come in the back door a while ago. Soon after, good smells had reached him.

Tim Fuller leaned against the wall right outside the kitchen to keep an eye on his wife, who was the best cook of the lot. Now he wordlessly stepped into the kitchen and came out to say, "Ten minutes. Spaghetti tonight."

Higgs smiled. "Sounds good. That'll give us all a chance to settle down, talk this over."

Leah sat with her back straight, her head bent so she could gaze down at her hands, clasped in front of her on the plank tabletop. Her expression didn't change an iota. Higgs's eyes lingered on her face, but he didn't comment.

Spencer continued to sip his coffee and hold his silence.

Eventually, Shelley Galt, thirty-two though she looked a decade older, brought out silverware and plates, then pitchers of beer and glasses. She kept her gaze down and her shoulders hunched as though she expected a blow at any moment. Spencer wanted to tell Shelley to steal her husband's car keys and run for it the next chance she had, but he knew better than to waste his breath even if that wouldn't have been stepping unacceptably out of his role. Shelley had married TJ Galt when she was seventeen. She probably didn't know any different or better.

Spencer had read and memorized her background,

just as he had that of every single person expected to join them up here. He wasn't a trusting man.

The food came out on big platters, some carried by Jennifer Fuller, and the remaining members of the group filtered in, the men almost without exception eyeing Leah lasciviously. The four women were careful not to make eye contact with her.

Leah shook her head at the beer but took a can of soda—one, he suspected, from her own ice chest—and allowed Ed Higgs to dish up for her.

You can lead a horse to water, Spencer thought... but this one was smart enough to drink. And eat. She understood that starving herself wouldn't accomplish a damn thing.

Higgs tried to start a few conversations, earning him startled looks from his crew. He didn't do any better with Leah, who didn't react to any comments directed her way. What did he think she'd say to gems like, "Spectacular country here. Your uncle was smart to hold on to the land."

She blinked at that one but didn't look up.

Only when they were done and he said, "I need to talk to Ms. Keaton," did Spencer see her shoulders get even stiffer. "Wyatt," Higgs said, "you stay. You, too, Metz."

Rick Metz was an automaton, following orders without question, whatever they were. He carried the anger they all shared, but kept a lid on it. He rarely reacted even to jibes from the other guys. Spencer didn't see him raping a woman just because he could, which allowed him to relax infinitesimally.

Grumbles carried to Spencer, but none were made until the men stepped out onto the porch. If Higgs heard them, he offered no indication. Among this bunch, rebellion brewed constantly. Metz might be the only one who wanted to be given orders to carry out. The others accepted them, maybe seeing dimly that Ed Higgs, a former US Air Force colonel, was smarter than they were, his leadership essential to their accomplishing their hair-raising intentions. He reminded them constantly of his military service, happiest when the men called him Colonel. Compliance didn't mean they didn't seethe at the necessity and bitterly resent the inner knowledge that they were lesser in some way than Higgs. Spencer took advantage of that ever-brewing resentment when he could, giving a nudge here and there, inciting outbursts that had helped him climb to second- or third-in-command.

Once the other men were gone, Higgs said into the silence, "No reason for you to be afraid."

Leah did raise her head at that, not hiding her disbelief.

"We only need a couple more months. You'll have to stay with us that long. Once we're ready to move, you can go on your way."

A couple more months? Did Higgs really think he'd have this bunch whipped into shape that soon? Although maybe it didn't matter to him; he wanted to make a statement, truly believing that somehow an ugly display of domestic terrorism and some serious bloodshed would inspire a revolution. The men who shared his exclusionary, racist, misogynistic views were supposed to join the fight to restore America to some imaginary time when white men ruled, women bowed to their lords and masters, and people of color—if there were any left—served their betters. How a man of his education had come by his beliefs, Spencer hadn't figured out.

"What is it you intend?" she asked, voice clear and strong. She hadn't yet so much as glanced at Spencer or Metz, who stood to one side like soldiers at attention on the parade ground. Pretending they weren't there at all?

"For you?" Higgs asked.

"I mean, your plans. Once you *move*."

If there was irony in her voice, Higgs either didn't acknowledge it or didn't hear it at all.

He launched with enthusiasm into what Spencer hoped would be a short version of his rabid passion.

"What made this country great has been lost since we started paying too much attention to the elites, who believe in opening the floodgates to immigration—and it doesn't matter to them if plenty of those immigrants are the scum of society, criminals who sneaked into the US. What happened to the days when people whose ancestors built this great country decided what direction it would go? Now we have people running for office with such thick accents you can hardly understand them! People that don't look American."

Leah blinked a few times, parted her lips…and then firmly closed them. Definitely not dumb. Then she spoke after all. "That doesn't explain what you plan to do to get attention."

He smiled at her as if she was an acolyte crawling before him. Not that he'd accept her into the fold, her being a member of the weaker sex and all.

"You don't need to worry about the details. Just know it's going to be big. We're going to shake this whole, misguided country and raise an army while we're at it." More prosaically, he added, "You can see why we need to keep our plans quiet until we're ready to launch our op. I'm asking for your cooperation. I don't think I'm being unreasonable. After all, this isn't the worst place to spend the rest of the summer." His sweeping gesture was presumably meant to take in the vast forests, mountains, lakes and wildflowers. "Got to be one of the most beautiful places in the world."

"I don't suppose you're going to let me go hiking or fishing like I did when I was a kid up here."

"Once you've settled in, why not?" Higgs said expansively. "I think you might learn something while you're here, come around to my way of thinking." He paused, a few lines forming on his brow. A thought had clearly struck him. "What do you do for a living, young lady?"

Please, God, don't let her be an attorney or an activist working with migrant workers or... Spencer sweated, running through the multitude of dangerous possibilities.

"I'm a veterinary technician."

When Higgs looked blank, she elaborated, "I treat injured or sick animals under the direction of a veterinarian. I assist him in surgery, give vaccinations, talk to pet owners."

His eyes narrowed. "So you have some medical knowledge."

"I know quite a bit about health issues affecting dogs and cats, and even horses. Not people."

"Never stitched up a wound?"

She hesitated.

"You might be able to help us. In the meantime—" the colonel pushed back from the table, the bench scraping on the worn wood floor "—I'll have one of these fellows carry your suitcase upstairs for you, and wait while you use the bathroom." He nodded at Spencer.

Was he to guard her overnight? If so, could he let her club him over the head and flee into the night? He'd have to make it look good.

For the first time since she'd come downstairs, Leah looked at him. Her dignity might be intact, but the raw fear in her eyes told him she knew what she faced. He hated knowing she was afraid of *him*.

Earlier, her eyes had been so dilated he hadn't been sure of the color. Had he ever seen eyes of such a clear green? And, damn—the courage she'd shown hit him like a two-by-four. With her fine bones and the red-head's skin that wouldn't stand up to any serious exposure to the sun, not to mention the purple bruising on her puffy cheekbone and beneath her eye, Leah Keaton couldn't hide her vulnerability. It moved and enraged him at the same time.

She was a complication he couldn't afford, but knew he couldn't shrug off, either. Spencer couldn't pretend to understand men like Arne Larson and Ed Higgs who didn't feel even a fraction of the same powerful wave of protectiveness that he did at the sight of her, damaged but using her head and holding herself straight and tall.

He picked up her suitcase and nodded toward the staircase. She rose stiffly and stalked ahead of him as if he was less than nothing to her. He admired her stubborn spirit, but knew it would backfire big time if she tried it on some of the other men. He still couldn't risk offering her a word of advice.

If he had to step forward to save her, it would be only as a last resort.

* * *

Every nerve in Leah's body prickled as she climbed the stairs ahead of Wyatt. She'd felt his gaze resting on her throughout dinner and also while the apparent leader spoke to her afterward, yet his thoughts had remained hidden. It was all she'd been able to do not to shudder when some of the men looked at her. This one almost scared her more because he didn't seem to have a single giveaway. All she knew was that he might be the sexiest man she'd ever seen—and that he had the coldest eyes. Her skin crawled at the idea that he was sizing up her body from his current vantage point. Or was he wishing he didn't have to waste time on the woman who'd stumbled on their training grounds and in doing so became a potentially dangerous problem? One *he* might be assigned to solve?

At the top of the stairs, she hesitated, hoping he'd forget how well she knew the resort.

He said only, "Isn't your room at the end of the hall?"

Her room. Sure.

"We can put the suitcase down and you can get out your toothbrush and toothpaste."

Without looking at him again, she continued down the short hall and went back into the very rustic room that had been designated her cell.

He followed, setting down the small suitcase on the bed, unzipping it and then stepping back. Of course, the contents were in a mess. Thanks to *him*.

Resisting the urge to hide the bra that lay on top, she poked through the tangle of clothing, feeling for her toiletry bag and evaluating what was missing. Unfortunately, the closest thing to a weapon she'd packed was her fingernail clippers. Useless, but if they were still in the toiletry bag, she'd pocket them.

"Your name is Wyatt?" Appalled, she couldn't believe she'd blurted that out.

His hesitation lasted long enough to suggest he was deciding whether even that much information would be dangerous in her hands. "Spencer Wyatt." His voice was deep, expressionless and tinged with a hint of the South.

Finding the toiletry bag, she asked, "Are you supposed to go into the bathroom with me?"

Something passed through his icy eyes so fast, she couldn't identify it. "I'll wait in the hall."

He let her pass him leaving the room, clearly assuming she knew where the bathroom was. She took pleasure in closing that door in his face.

Honestly, there was enough space in here, he could have come in, too. There were two wood-framed toilet stalls, two shower stalls and two sinks. This bathroom had served for all six guest rooms. It was lucky they'd rarely if ever all been in use at the same time.

The fingernail clippers were there. She hurriedly stuck them in her jeans pocket, brushed her teeth, then used the toilet. Not exactly eager to face him again, Leah thought about dawdling, but couldn't see what that would gain her. Presumably, once he'd escorted her to the bedroom, she'd be left alone anyway. So she walked back out to find Spencer Wyatt lounging against the wall across from the bathroom door.

He looked her over, his icy eyes noting the bag still in her hand, and jerked his head toward the bedroom.

Head high, she obeyed the wordless command, walked into her room and shut the door. Her fingers hovered over the lock, which could probably be picked, and she made the decision not to turn it. Why annoy them?

They'd be annoyed enough in the morning when they discovered she wasn't where they'd left her.

Chapter 3

Lying on the bed in the dark, Leah waited for hours, even though eventually she had to struggle not to fall asleep. Twice she heard men's voices outside her room. The first time Spencer Wyatt's was one of them, the other unfamiliar. She tensed when one of the two walked away. Which man remained? Whoever he was, he didn't even look in.

Sometime later a muffled sound of voices had her hurrying to the door and pressing her ear to the crack in hopes of hearing what they were saying.

"…saving her for himself," growled one man.

The second man said something about orders.

She jumped when a thump came, followed by a scraping sound. Had they brought a chair upstairs so they could guard her comfortably? This had to be a change of shift, she decided.

Damn, she'd counted on one man being stuck on guard all night. He'd get sleepy, nod off, sure he'd wake up if her door opened. But if he stayed alert…

Or, oh, God, was the new guard the one complaining that someone was saving her for themselves? Who was he talking about? The gray-haired leader? Or Spencer Wyatt? What if grumbled defiance led to this latest guard deciding he could walk right into her room, and who was awake to stop him?

Rigid, she wished she'd locked the door after all. At least that would have slowed him down.

Receding footsteps were followed by silence out in the hall.

She needed to get out of here. In one way it might be smarter to pretend to be docile for a few days, until they lowered their guard. But the blatant sexual appraisal from so many of the men scared her more than any thought of being killed. Would she really be safe from rape if she played dumb and stayed?

Leah didn't believe it. At the very least, she could hide temporarily. She wished desperately that she knew what time it was. In her fear, she might have exaggerated the passing of time, until only a couple of hours felt like half the night. She had to go with her instincts.

After slipping out of bed, she put on her athletic shoes and tied the laces while straining to hear the slightest sound. Then she used most of the clothes in her suitcase to create a mound beneath the covers that might fool someone who glanced in to be sure she was really there. Finally, she tiptoed to the closet.

Earlier, she'd pulled the folding doors open. If Wyatt checked on her, she reasoned, he'd assume she was exploring, looking hopelessly for some out. Now, once inside the closet, she gently pulled first one door and then the other closed behind her. Kneeling on the floor facing the right side of the closet, she felt for the crack that betrayed the presence of a removable panel.

Uncle Edward had showed her and her brother the spaces between closets upstairs. She'd have been sunk if they'd locked her in either of the first bedrooms at the top of the stairs. But rooms two and three on each side of the hall had closets with removable panels that *connected* one closet to another. He guessed the builder had intended the few feet to be storage. Guests staying all summer could stow a suitcase away, for example. By the time Uncle Edward bought the resort, though, either the spaces—the passages—had been forgotten, or nobody had thought to tell him about them.

Apparently, all of the interior walls were what he called board and batten, which in the old lodge meant horizontal boards had been nailed up in rows. In the rooms and hall, they'd been covered by either plaster or wallpaper. Nobody had bothered in the closets. If you looked closely, you could see into cracks between the old boards, which might have shrunk over time. The whole subject had come up because her brother Jerry had cackled at the idea of spying on guests in the next room.

After issuing a stern warning against trying any such thing, Uncle Edward had smiled down at his great-niece and great-nephew. "Took me a few years here to notice the outline." He'd looked at the dark, dusty opening with satisfaction. "If we were down South, I'd think these were built to hide runaway slaves. 'Course, this place wasn't built until just over a hundred years ago, long after abolition."

He'd had to explain what abolition was for Jerry's sake. Leah remembered from school.

Now she held her breath, lifted the panel away and leaned it where she'd be able to reach it once she was inside. There hadn't been so much as a creak. If the next bedroom was occupied…she'd have to retreat.

Hesitating, she wished she'd brought a flashlight, instead of intending to rely on her phone. Although, that, too, would have been confiscated. Well, the spooky dark wasn't nearly as frightening as the men holding her captive. And yes, as she started to crawl through the opening and cobwebs brushed her face, she shuddered but kept moving. She could do this. She could deal with a few spiders.

Awkwardly turning around, she closed her fingers around the crude panel and tried to pull it into place. A quiet *clunk* had her freezing in place, but it wasn't followed by anyone swinging open the bedroom door and turning on the overhead light.

Dizzy, probably because her pulse raced, Leah used the short file from her fingernail clippers to pull the panel back toward her until it slotted into place—at least, as well as she could. Sliding her fingers over the edges, she thought it was snug. Her next challenge was to open the panel on the other side while preventing it from falling to the floor. *That* would make enough noise to bring the guard to investigate.

She scooted forward until her head brushed the rough wood that was the back of the panel leading into the next room.

Somehow, this wasn't nearly as fun as it had been when, as children, she and Jerry used these passages to perplex their parents.

She lifted her hand, feeling for the crack at the top...
and something crawled over her hand. Suppressing a
shriek she shook off the bug—a spider?—and made
herself start again. Finally, she applied a little pressure, then more—and when the panel gave way, she
grabbed the top of it.

And then she froze. She reminded herself that one
of the men might be *sleeping* in this room. Surely, the
group was using at least some of these upstairs guest
rooms.

Breathing as slowly and steadily as she could, she
told herself she'd made the assumption about empty
rooms for a good reason. She hadn't seen anyone go
up or come down the staircase, unless it was with her.
When the leader had dismissed the group, nobody had
headed for the stairs.

Which was reassuring, but hardly conclusive since
it had still been early evening when she was escorted
to bed.

Would she have heard someone come upstairs, a door
opening and closing? Surely, her guard and another man
would have exchanged a few words.

Her pulse continued to race and her teeth wanted
to chatter. Could she have chosen worse timing for a
panic attack? She took a deep breath. She wouldn't hesitate now.

Gradually, a surface level of calm and resolve sup-
pressed the fear.

If she was quiet enough, she could grope around the
closet and find out if someone was using it. She could
peek into the room without waking a sleeper. If there
was one, well, then she'd have a decision to make.

She eased the panel out and leaned it against the

back of the closet. Creeping forward, she patted her way along, cursing the complete darkness. She waved her hands over her head, not feeling any hanging clothes.

Would men like this bother hanging up a shirt, or would they just stuff clean laundry into a duffel bag? No shoes, either. But feeling confident the closet was empty didn't mean the room wasn't occupied. Somehow, she suspected these guys hadn't packed big wardrobes for their training session.

If someone really was sleeping in this room, he'd probably set his handgun aside. If she was quiet enough, she could take it. She might actually have a chance then.

If, if, if.

After Metz took his place outside Leah Keaton's door, Spencer had made a point of hanging around downstairs for a while. Higgs wanted to talk through the problem she presented. He rambled, Spencer mostly keeping his mouth shut.

"Would have been better if you'd been able to let her go in the first place," he couldn't resist saying.

The colonel grunted. "That idiot Osenbrock."

Knowing the variety of weapons of mass destruction the group had acquired, Spencer's blood still ran cold. Spencer refrained from saying the whole damn bunch were idiots, including and especially Air Force Colonel Edward Higgs, retired. Spencer could almost wish to be present to see Higgs's face when he learned that he had a snake in his cozy hideaway.

Yeah, not really, Spencer thought, even as he nodded and made supportive noises.

Eventually, he'd had no choice but to announce he was heading for bed. He'd rinsed out his cup and set it on the dish drainer, gone out the front door after a last good-night and headed straight for his cabin. He had no doubt there were eyes on him. At least three of this crowd resented him bitterly. So far, they hadn't risked laying it on the table and thereby earning Higgs's displeasure. Sooner or later, someone would find a good enough excuse to throw down the gauntlet. The longer he could put that challenge off, the more likely he'd get out of here alive.

Although the likelihood of that had plummeted with the arrival of a gutsy woman who didn't deserve to become a victim.

Grimacing, he clumped up on the small front porch of the cabin he'd claimed, unobtrusively drew his weapon and went in for the usual search before he could relax at all.

And before he slipped out again, this time staying unseen, to maintain a long-distance watch over Leah.

The room proved to be vacant, and likely had been for a decade or more. A broken bed frame left the mattress tipping. A front on one of the dresser drawers had split in half.

Light from the hall showed beneath the door.

When Leah tiptoed over to the sash window, she felt a draft. Standing to one side, she felt the cold glass until she found the corner that had broken out.

Taking a chance, she stood right in front of the window, turned the window latch and tried to heave the lower sash upward. Absolutely nothing happened. The warped, painted-too-many-times frame didn't so much as groan. For an instant she thought she saw something—some*one*—move out at the edge of the treeline, but then decided her eyes had tricked her.

She could break out the rest of the glass—but that would alert the guard. If she could swing out, dangle and drop, she might make it to the ground uninjured...but they'd be on her right away. And what if she sprained or broke an ankle? She might not be able to drive, even if the hideout key was still there, and she sure as heck couldn't run away.

If only she knew what time it was. If the door to the hall would crack open without a squeak of rusting hinges.

She stopped herself from creating a list of dire consequences for every decision she made. She'd come this far. She had to peek into the hall and see if there was the slightest chance at all of making it unseen to the stairs. Maybe even whether there were any lights on downstairs, or whether she'd be able to descend into blessed darkness.

No floorboards creaked underfoot as she crossed the room. Prayed the door and frame had been as solidly built. Holding her breath, she very gently turned the knob, then drew the door toward herself a fraction of an inch at a time. It was quiet, so quiet.

Until she heard a muffled sound. A curse?

She had the door open wide enough to allow her to poke her head out into the hall. When she did, she saw a tattooed, muscular guy who hadn't stood out to her if she'd seen him at all. Chair pushed aside, he sat on the floor, leaning back against the door to her original room, legs stretched out. His head sagged to one side, and another snort came from him.

He was snoring. Asleep.

If she'd opened that door, he'd have awakened instantly. As it was…she slipped out into the hall and tiptoed toward the stairs. There was a light on down there somewhere—the kitchen?—but not in the main room.

First step, second, third. She hesitated. One of the stairs had squeaked on her way up. The next— she thought. Gripping the handrail, she stretched to reach the step below, then kept going. Once she was far enough down, she turned her head, searching for movement. For a second guard. For a Rottweiler. For anything, but all remained still.

Within moments she was at the front door.

Spencer kept staring at the window into the middle bedroom upstairs in the lodge. He'd seen someone; he'd swear he had. Durand, who was currently on guard? Maybe he'd heard something outside, was doing some rounds? But he was an exceptionally big guy, and the figure Spencer had seen had been slight. But how in hell could that woman have gotten past Durand and into a different guest room? He shook his head. Maybe it had been a damn ghost.

He waited. Waited.

Something happened in the deep shadows of the front porch. A person, moving tentatively, emerged into the moonlight and started down the half dozen steps.

Careful, Spencer urged silently. She reached the ground, apparently unheard and unseen except by him, and ran for her car. She went straight for the back fender, crouched out of sight and then stood and rushed around to the driver's side.

A light came on in one of the cabins. For an instant, the woman froze, looking in the same direction.

It was probably just somebody out of bed to take a leak, but you never knew. Spencer had crossed paths with some other night owls from time to time. Paranoia had that effect on a man.

She opened the car door, still unlocked, and jumped in. She was smart enough not to turn on headlights, but seconds later the engine purred to life. Given the silence out here in the forest, it sounded more like a roar.

Lights in other cabins came on.

The car didn't move.

Goddamn. Somebody must have taken the precaution of screwing with her car. Disabled the transmission, maybe, or the CV joint.

Why hadn't Higgs mentioned that to him? Spencer wondered.

Men were running toward her. She flung open her door, fell out and scrambled back to her feet, then took off for the trees.

He couldn't intervene. Even feeling a crack tear open in his iron control, Spencer knew there was too much to lose, and she wasn't going to make it anyway.

It killed him to stay back in the darkness and watch her be tackled by the fastest pursuer. Even down, she screamed and fought furiously. Finally breaking, he started toward them, but too late.

A second guy reached her, and the two of them wrenched her to her feet, still struggling but in an uncoordinated way, as if her limbs no longer worked right.

It was TJ Galt who'd reached her first. Curt Baldwin second. They'd pay for the unnecessary brutality, Spencer swore.

By the time they dragged her to the foot of the lodge steps and dropped her on the ground, the porch light had come on and lights shone in all the cabins. They'd all been awakened and closed in on her. Spencer circled until he could join them in a way that would appear natural.

"What the hell happened ?" Spencer asked, just as Higgs pushed his way to the center of the group.

The colonel swore viciously before turning his head. "Where's Durand?"

"Here."

Everyone else drew back from the man who'd failed at his appointed task. Higgs didn't accept failure.

"How did she get by you?"

"She couldn't have." Seeming dazed, Don Durand gazed down at the woman lying in the dirt at his feet. "That bedroom door never opened. Maybe...the window."

All but Spencer looked up at the obviously closed windows.

Was she conscious? It was a minute before he could reassure himself that at least she was breathing. He should have run to her first, pretended to smack her around to avoid this. He gritted his teeth, wishing she'd made it into the woods.

"Get her up!" Higgs snapped.

Galt pulled her up in one vicious motion. One of her eyes was swollen completely shut. The other was open, but dazed. How aware was she?

"Who has a gun?" Higgs demanded.

After a heartbeat, Durand handed over his. Higgs grabbed a handful of her hair and yanked hard while grinding the barrel into her temple.

"How'd you get out?"

It was a long time before she spoke. Then her voice

was a mere thread, so faint Spencer found himself leaning forward to hear.

"Way to get from one bedroom closet to another."

Spencer stirred. When he was a kid, his still-intact family had vacationed at a rustic resort on one of Georgia's barrier islands. He remembered discovering that a panel could be removed in the back of the closet to expose an additional space.

Higgs swore some more. "Why shouldn't I kill you?"

Half the men clustered around her wore avid expressions Spencer had seen too often before, the kind you'd see on faces in the audience at an MMA fight when blood spattered, or in the crowd at a car race after a collision that might leave fatalities. These men were excited, wanted the shock of seeing blood and a young woman go down right in front of them. If Higgs's finger tightened even a fraction...

Spencer pushed forward. "That'd be an awful waste."

"What?" Higgs's head jerked around.

"You heard me." Spencer smiled slightly and leaned on his Southern accent. "She's a real pretty woman."

A chorus of agreement broke out. "Hell, yeah. We can keep her too busy to get in trouble."

Spencer looked into Higgs's eyes. "Give her to me, and I'll guarantee no more trouble from her."

The two men stared at each other; Higgs's eyes narrowed. Spencer didn't dare relax enough even to see how she had reacted, or if she had. Arguments broke out around them. They wanted to share her, or a few of the men thought they were entitled to have her, sure as hell more than that Southern bastard who'd joined the group late. This was a gamble that Higgs would acknowledge him as second in charge by giving him what he wanted.

Higgs's hand holding the gun dropped away, and he used his grip on her hair to twist her toward Spencer. Then he gave her a hard shove, sending her flying into Spencer, who pulled her tight against him.

"She's all yours," Higgs said in a hard voice. "You screw up, on your head be it."

Spencer nodded at their fair leader, then half carried Leah through the crowd, ignoring the chorus of protests and the glares. Every hair on the back of his neck stood up as he broke free and steered her toward the refuge of his cabin.

How the hell *was* he going to control her?

Chapter 4

Supporting most of Leah's weight, Spencer propelled her up the steps to his porch and into his cabin. He laid her down on the futon that would have once served a dual purpose when a family rented this cabin. The damn thing was uncomfortable, but he didn't suppose she'd notice right now. Aware that they'd been watched all the way, he was glad to be able to close and lock the door.

The damage to her face was severe enough this time; he wondered whether her cheekbone might be broken. He worried even more that her brain had been traumatized. Knowing there wasn't a thing he could do if that was so, Spencer gritted his teeth and went to the corner of the room that served as a kitchen. She hadn't moved when he returned with an ice pack and a T-shirt he'd left lying over the back of a chair.

He sat beside her on the futon, wrapped the ice pack

in the thin cotton T-shirt and gently laid it over her cheekbone, eye and brow.

She jerked and flailed.

"Hey," he said quietly. "I know this doesn't feel good, but it's only ice. You've got some major swelling going on."

Her eye—the one that wasn't swollen shut—opened, looking glassy and uncomprehending.

"That SOB clobbered you," Spencer continued, working to keep his voice reassuring instead of enraged. "I'll give you something for the pain once the ice has had a chance to help." And once she demonstrated some coherence. If she didn't...well, that was a bridge he'd cross when he had no other choice.

Her eye closed and a small sigh escaped her.

His hand was cold, but he didn't move it, just kept looking down at her, taking in every detail of her face, from the old and new damage to her lashes and eyebrows, both auburn instead of brown. Just long enough to tuck behind her ears, her hair was ruffled but obviously straight. A high forehead gave her some of that look of innocence and youth he'd first noticed. She had a pretty mouth, now that it wasn't pressed into a tight line.

With a grimace, he corrected himself. What he'd really meant was, *Now that it was lax because she was semiconscious.*

"Leah?"

His anxiety ratcheted up a notch when she didn't respond.

He tried again. "Can you hear me? I need to know how you're doing."

Her lashes fluttered and the single eyelid rose. She

tried to focus a still-dazed eye on him. "Why—" she licked her lips "—would you care?"

He'd bent his head closer to hear a question that was more a prolonged breath than words. There were any number of possible responses, but he went with, "You didn't deserve this."

"Tried...run away."

"I know."

"You...missed car key."

Okay, she was with him, if still feeling like crap. He smiled. "I didn't miss the key. I left it for you."

"Car wouldn't drive."

"I didn't do that. Didn't know anyone else had, either."

Tiny lines formed on her forehead above the ice pack. "Why would you want me to get away?"

The side of him that was utterly focused on his mission hadn't. A police response would have majorly screwed up this operation. He'd invested too much in it to want it ended prematurely. But he hadn't been able to stand back and watch her be raped or killed, either.

"I don't hurt women," he finally said.

Was that a snort? He wasn't sure, and she'd closed her eye again.

"If you can hold this in place—" he lifted her hand and laid it over the ice pack "—I'll get you some painkillers."

"'Kay," she murmured.

He kept a sharp eye on her for the short time it took him to dig in his leather duffel bag in the bedroom and return to the main room with a bottle of over-the-counter meds. He had some better stuff tucked away, too, but he'd hold off on that for now.

Bringing a glass of water, too, he helped her half sit up and swallow the pills, then gently laid her back again.

"Have you gotten any sleep tonight?" he asked.

Her nose wrinkled. "Maybe...hour or two?"

That was what he'd thought. "Once the pain lets up a little, I'm hoping you'll be able to get a few hours."

She didn't comment. Spencer had to wonder if her busy little brain wasn't already plotting how to escape. As in, waiting until he had fallen asleep. And, damn it, he did need some sleep. He didn't like his best option here, and she'd like it even less, but he didn't see a workable alternative. Now that he had her safe, he wouldn't let her risk herself unnecessarily...and he was back to focusing first on what he needed to do.

She paid enough attention to him to lift her arms when he asked, and tell him where else she hurt. He manipulated her right shoulder and decided it, too, was inflamed and deeply bruised from when she hit the ground with TJ's weight atop her.

He cracked open another ice pack and applied it to her shoulder. When she started shivering, he grabbed his fleece jacket and spread it over her.

Leah peered suspiciously at him from her one good eye.

Finally, he said, "Okay, tell you what. I'm going to move you to the bed so you can really get some sleep. We'll ice any swelling in the morning." Which wasn't very far away.

She didn't move. Spencer took away the ice packs and tossed them in the small sink. Returning to her, he slid an arm behind her back and said, "Upsy daisy."

"I want to stay here."

"Not happening," he said flatly.

"Why not?"

"You didn't get away. There won't be a second chance."

She twisted out of his grip. "I won't!"

"I didn't ask you." This time he lifted her using both arms.

Her pliancy vanished. She fought like a featherweight champ, landing blows with her small fists. He averted his face and endured as he walked to the bedroom, but when she managed to clip his jaw, he snapped, "That's it," and dropped her on the bed.

Of course she rolled for the other side and thudded off onto her knees, then scrambled to her feet. "If you think I'm getting in that bed with you—"

"I'm not giving you a choice," he said grimly, and pulled a set of handcuffs from his back pocket.

Already scared, Leah completely lost it then. Gripped by a suffocating terror, she knew only that once he clicked those cuffs on her, she'd be utterly helpless.

He was already shifting toward the foot of the bed, expecting her to come around. She threw herself across the bed instead, her shoulder hitting his hard belly when he moved to intercept her. Fighting mindlessly, Leah used every weapon she had, including her teeth and nails. He let out a stream of invectives when she raked her fingernails over his cheek and sank her teeth into his biceps. Sobbing for breath, she kept fighting even as he subdued her with insulting ease, throwing her again onto the bed and, this time, coming down on top of her.

Even that didn't stop her. She bucked and kicked and screamed until he covered her mouth and half her face with a big hand, somehow managing to capture both her wrists with his other hand and plant them above her head.

Now she couldn't breathe at all. With that powerful body, he was crushing her. She wrenched her head side to side until she was able to bite the fleshy part of his hand below his thumb.

"Enough!" he snarled, and before she knew it he'd pushed her to her side and clicked the handcuffs around one wrist. Her face was wet with tears and probably snot as she continued to fight uselessly against his greater strength.

He snapped the other side of the cuffs onto the old iron bedstead and rolled off both her and the bed to land on his feet where he glared down at her, his teeth bared, his hands half curled into fists.

Leah went still, hurting everywhere, terrified in an all new way. She had no doubt at all that he intended to rape her.

I don't hurt women.

Sure. Right. Her shoulder screamed and her head throbbed. One hip hurt, too, and she tasted blood. Her gaze flicked to his powerful biceps where she saw the bite mark. It was *his* blood in her mouth.

"Damn," he said suddenly, and scrubbed one of his hands over his face. When he looked back at her, his expression had changed. Instead of triumph, she thought she saw regret. No, probably pity. But even that was good news, wasn't it? If he felt sorry for her, would a man still rape a woman?

"Let me get a wet cloth to wipe your face," he said unexpectedly, and left the bedroom.

She tugged at the cuffs, just to be sure they really had

clicked shut. The metal bit into her wrist. Leah turned her face away from the door.

A moment later she heard his footfall.

"If I sit down, will you attack me again?" he asked in that deep voice tinged with a softening accent.

Did he wear a pistol? She couldn't remember noticing. If she could get her hand on it...

She had to roll her head to see.

No gun.

He held a wet washcloth.

"No," she whispered.

Watching her, those oddly pale eyes unblinking, he sat beside her, much as he had out on the ancient couch. When he'd tried to take care of her, Leah couldn't help remembering.

That didn't mean she was safe from him, though. Why would he have claimed her if he didn't want sex from her?

But she only closed her own eyes when he laid the warm washcloth over her face and very carefully wiped away her tears and probably some blood and, yes, snot. The heat and rough texture felt so good, she heard herself make a tiny sound that might have been a whimper.

"Better?" he asked quietly.

She bobbed her head. Pain stabbed both shoulders, now that her arm on the uninjured side was stretched above her head, but everything was relative.

"Then we need to talk." He paused. "I want you to look at me."

Leah rolled her head enough to be able to see him out of her right eye. The other one had to be swollen completely shut despite the ice this man had applied to it. Why would he have bothered unless...

"You're not going to escape at this point," Spencer said, his gaze steady, his tone rock hard. "You're alive, and not in the hands of one of those animals, because I took responsibility for you. Everyone here will respect that unless they see me as failing. Say, if you make any kind of serious attempt at taking off. It'll be a free-for-all then, and you could end up in anyone's cabin. Or shared between them. Do you understand that?"

After a moment she nodded. She did see that; she just didn't know what kind of threat *he* represented.

"You have to cooperate. For both our sakes, I wish you could stay holed up in this cabin, but that's not an option. I have to participate in training exercises and planning sessions. That would leave you alone. What you need to do is join the other women and imitate them." He paused. "You saw them at dinner."

This time her nod was uncertain. She hadn't paid that much attention. Mostly, she'd hoped for…she didn't know, maybe a signal from one of them? Any hint that one or all of the women would help if they could?

"They're abused women." His expression was grim. "They each try not to meet the eyes of any man but their own husband or boyfriend, and that rarely. They tend to keep their heads down, shoulders hunched. They scuttle across open ground."

Could she act that well? Leah thought so. Fear was a great motivator.

He continued relentlessly. "The women are expected to do all the cooking and cleaning. They don't complain, because they know their role in life. They talk among themselves only when they're working together in the kitchen, and then it's quietly, and about their work. One of the men—the husbands and boyfriends—always keeps an eye on them while they're together. The message is that they can't be trusted."

Feeling growing horror, she whispered, "You'll do that, too?"

"Damn straight I will, as often as I can."

He startled her by planting a hand on each side of her torso and leaning over her. Dominating her, so she couldn't look away from him if she tried. The triple scratches she'd inflicted showed vividly on his angular cheek above dark stubble. A small bump on the bridge of his nose wasn't her fault.

"*I* am your only protection," he continued relentlessly. "You can't forget that. Right now they're all afraid to cross me."

"Even the boss?"

"Colonel Higgs?"

The irony in his voice had her blinking. "That's what he's called?"

"He is a retired US Air Force colonel. He doesn't let anyone forget it."

"That's scary."

His eyebrows twitched. Leah couldn't tell if he agreed or was pleased to have a leader with a legitimate military background.

"I wouldn't say he's afraid of me," Spencer continued. "Wary, maybe. Preferring to keep my loyalty. Apparently, he has no interest in taking you on himself."

She shuddered.

"You might have been safer with him," the big man with the icy eyes told her. "Nobody would have thought to argue with him. I'm...not popular with a few of the men. We may run into trouble if someone works up the guts to challenge me."

We? This bizarre conversation had her bewildered. *Us against them.* Did he imagine she'd be *happy* to be one of those stoop-shouldered, timid, obedient women?

Or... Leah replayed everything he'd said. His expressions, subtle though they were. His actions, if it was true he'd left the hideout key to the car deliberately to give her a chance to get away. His care with her injuries, the flickers of rage she'd seen. Even when she fought, when she hurt him, he'd still been careful not to hurt *her.*

Very slowly, she said, "You're not one of them, are you?"

Spencer quit breathing as he stared at her. Only long practice allowed him to keep his face impassive despite his shock. After a moment he said, "That's not a smart thing to suggest. Not to me, and especially not to anyone else."

Her eyes searched his. The impulse to confide in her took him by surprise. Part of it, he understood. Seeing her so terrified of him that she'd fought with crazed ferocity had hit him hard. If she hadn't calmed down, he might have had no choice. As it was…he shouldn't even *think* about trusting her to that extent. One careless word, a reaction that seemed off to one of the men, and he and she both would be dead. She *had* to be seen to be scared of him, unwillingly bowing to necessity, or somebody might get curious. No cover was good enough if someone was willing to dig deep.

No.

Bending even more closely over her, he said softly, "Do you hear me?"

She shrank from him. "Yes."

"Good." He straightened so that he was no longer caging her body with his.

"You can't tell me—" she began.

Spencer almost groaned. She was either very, very perceptive, or just naturally rebellious. Neither quality served them well right now.

"I've got to get some sleep," he said abruptly, bending to pull off his boots and socks. "I don't think you have a concussion—your eyes seem pretty focused to me—but I'll keep a watch for any problems. You can try to sleep."

Her eyes widened.

Ignoring her, he pulled his belt from the loops, then unbuttoned and unzipped his cargo pants.

Wearing only the T-shirt and knit boxers, he went out to the living room to check locks again, pick up his Sig Sauer and turn off lights. Returning to the bedroom, he briefly thought about switching the cuff from the bed frame to his wrist but decided against it. She couldn't go anywhere, and if she attacked him again, he'd wake up in the blink of an eye and deal with her. He might have slept on the futon so that she could relax a little—but he couldn't afford for someone to look in the uncurtained window above the sink and see that he was pandering to Leah. Besides—even rocky ground would be an improvement over the futon.

He adjusted the bedroom curtains to block anyone trying to steal a look, turned off the light and tugged the covers out from beneath her so that he could pull them over both of them. Then he claimed one of the two nearly flat pillows, doubled it over and stretched out beside her.

Leah lay rigid, as close to the far edge of the bed as

she could. Given that the bed was only a full size—his feet hung over at the bottom—that wasn't very far away. Besides...the mattress was as old as the futon and the stained kitchen sink. Once she nodded off, she'd roll to meet him in the middle.

A rueful smile tugged at his mouth as he pictured how happy she'd be waking up plastered against his body.

Chapter 5

She dreamed about being stretched on a medieval rack. At the same time she was weirdly comfortable, the cozy warmth feeling as if it came from a heated blanket, but more…solid. Comforting.

Leah surfaced slowly, realizing that she lay on her side with her head resting on her upper arm. That arm was stretched above her, and ached fiercely. Not stretched, she thought on a sudden memory; pulled.

And somebody spooned her, his hips pressed to her butt, thighs to the backs of hers. A heavy arm lay over her, his hand tucked—Leah quit breathing. If his hand wasn't so relaxed, it would have enclosed her breast.

His chest felt like a wall. Was it possible she could feel his slow, steady heartbeats?

He. Spencer. The man who'd claimed her and now expected complete obedience as payback. How had she let him wrap her in such an all-encompassing embrace?

When he climbed into bed with her as if that was routine, she'd resolved to stay awake. Obviously, that hadn't gone so well, and no wonder, considering how desperately tired she'd been by then. Not just from lack of sleep. Shock and pain and fear had taken a toll.

Lying completely still, as if she could fend off the reality that she shared the bed with a very large, muscular man who might well have squeezed her breast in his hand while she slept, Leah understood how poorly prepared she'd been for any of this. She'd grown up in a middle-class home with loving parents, had a good relationship with her sometimes irritating little brother, enjoyed college and even her job, although she did want more. Her only major stumble had been being so blind where Stuart was concerned, and compared to her current predicament, that was…normal. Her letting love, or some facsimile thereof, blind her. And to think of the agonies she'd suffered over that jerk. If only she'd known.

Now she had to face the fact that there was a really good chance she'd be gang-raped or—no, make that *and*—killed in the next few days. It would seem her only chance at survival was to obey the stranger who shared this bed.

His pelvis wasn't all that was pressing into her butt, she became gradually aware. That hard bar hadn't been there when she first woke up. His breathing had changed, too.

"I have to use the bathroom," she said loudly.

His chuckle ruffled the tiny hairs on the back of her neck. "Gotcha."

He gently squeezed her breast, gave a regretful sigh,

and he rolled away from her. The mattress rebounded without his weight.

"Now, what did I do with that key?" he said.

She growled; he laughed.

A moment later he'd unfastened the cuff on the bed frame. Leah scrambled to get out of bed. She hadn't thought about her bladder until she'd told him that, but now she *really* needed to go.

Amusement on his face, Spencer stepped out of her way. She rushed for the small bathroom. The warped door didn't quite latch, but stayed closed. Relief.

The mirror was spotted, but she inspected her face. It wasn't pretty. She could see out of both eyes, although the one side was still really puffy, the discoloration gaining new glory. The last time she'd had a black eye, a scared Labrador mix had head-butted her in an attempt to escape. This one would be way more spectacular before it was done.

She surveyed the bathroom before she went back out, but didn't see anything useful. A good, old-fashioned straight razor, or even a disposable kind of razor, might have come in handy. But no; a rechargeable shaver lay on the pedestal sink.

Arming herself might be stupid at this point anyway. A razor blade would look wimpy to men all carrying semiautomatic pistols. And really, given her inexperience, even a gun in her hands might get her in more trouble than it would solve.

Whatever else she could say about the man who'd stepped forward on her behalf—an optimistic way of phrasing it—he exuded danger. So much so, none of the other men had been prepared to challenge him, as he put it. That made him the best weapon she could have acquired…assuming he didn't have an end game that had nothing to do with her welfare.

She ran through a plus list. A) he hadn't raped her when he could easily have done so; B) he had done his best not to add to her injuries, even when she was attacking him; and C) he had actually seemed to care that she was hurt and had tried to make sure she was comfortable.

Plenty of negatives came to mind readily, too, starting with the fact that he was a member of a frighteningly well-armed white supremacist militia with big, scary plans. Moving on to B, if she tried something, he could handle her without breaking a sweat; and C, she had no idea how much of what she'd seen was facade and how much real.

She didn't know him, and one of the greatest threats right now was an unreasoning belief that he wasn't a member of the group at all, that he despised them and was really an honorable, good man. Oh, yeah—and she would have been sexually attracted to him in any other circumstances at all.

Maybe even *these* circumstances, which meant… she didn't know. Was this a primitive response to the fact that he claimed to be standing between her and the world?

Not happening, she told herself firmly. She'd do as he asked, for now. What choice did she have? But she'd watch for an opportunity to escape, and she couldn't afford to soften toward Spencer Wyatt—or to entirely trust him.

Spencer felt antsy from the minute he left Leah in the large kitchen at the lodge and headed out to the shooting range with the others. The women were washing

up from breakfast, Lisa Dempsey planning lunch while
Jennifer Fuller handed out cleaning assignments. Spencer wasn't sure he could have made himself walk away
if TJ Galt had been the one "supervising," but Dirk
Ritchie was staying behind this morning. He'd brought
the fourth woman along, Helen Slocum.

Helen didn't seem so much terrorized as mentally
slow, Spencer had come to think. Dirk could be unexpectedly patient with her, even showing flashes of genu-
ine caring. In fact, he seemed like a decent guy in many
ways, which left him the low man on the totem pole in
this crowd. Decency registered as weakness here. Spencer made a point of supporting the guy. Dirk's background suggested a reading disability, a lousy school
district and a father who was disappointed in his only
son's spinelessness. As with Shelley, Spencer wanted
to quietly tell Dirk to take Helen and drive away—and
not go home to daddy.

He'd as soon not feel sorry for any of this crowd, but
couldn't entirely shut down that side of himself.

Obviously, or he'd be able to keep his mind on business. As it was, he should have taken this shot two
minutes ago.

He lay prone in the dirt looking through a scope at
a target that he'd calculated was five hundred and seventy-five yards out, give or take a little. It was crystal
clear. He breathed in, out, in, out…and gently pulled
the trigger.

Higgs squatted beside him, peering through military-
grade binoculars. "Hell of a shot."

As had been every one he'd taken today.

Higgs was in love with the Barrett M82 rifle, not because of accuracy, although it was fine. What he liked—

and why he'd acquired several of these rifles—was that they fired the exact same .50 BMG cartridge used in the heavy machine gun. The heavy-duty round excelled at destroying just about everything up to armored vehicles. Higgs wasn't interested in subtlety. He wanted a big boom.

One of the downsides of this particular rifle was the lack of accuracy for truly long-range shots. In fact, anything over nine hundred yards. Personally, Spencer had preferred the M40A5, one of many descendants of the Remington 700 rifle commonly owned by hunters. He had comfortably made shots at twelve hundred yards and farther, although there were military snipers who could make longer ones. So far, Higgs hadn't asked for anything remotely difficult for a man with Spencer's experience, which meant a simple assassination wasn't on Higgs's agenda.

Now Spencer peeled off his ear protection and rose to his knees still cradling the rifle. "That's it for me. You know I had sniper training at Fort Bennett. I've spent enough time on a range to stay sharp. Let's focus on some of the guys who need the work."

Happy with what he'd seen, Higgs stood, too, letting the binoculars fall to his chest. "I agree. We'll be lucky if any of the men become reliable at even a hundred yards out. We could use another real sharpshooter, but unless you have a former army buddy you can recruit, we'll have to get by with what we have."

Temptation flickered at the opportunity to bring in another agent, but Spencer was inclined to think the risk was too great. Aside from backup, how much could a newcomer achieve anyway? He was well enough established to be in a good position to be included the next time Colonel Higgs met with his arms dealer. Nailing down who was stealing and selling contraband US Army weaponry to the group was one of his highest priorities, along with finding out the final details of the spectacular attack that Higgs was so convinced would not only deal a major blow to the government, but also fire-start a civil war.

The crack of shots interspersed their few words. Spencer didn't need binoculars to see how badly Tim Fuller, stationed closest to him, was shooting.

Another week or two, he told himself, but he'd thought the same before. Ed Higgs was being cagey even with Spencer, who wanted some serious time alone with Higgs's laptop. As it was, he had to hold out for that upcoming exchange of cash for arms.

He'd had better luck tracing the source of the funding, and managed to share that much with his superior the last time he'd been part of a supply run to Bellingham and had had a minute to get away to make a call. Some names weren't all, though. A lot of the money was coming from someone who remained cloaked in shadows. Even the one chance to share what he'd learned had been a few weeks ago, but now instead of hoping he'd have the chance again, his gut told him bad things would happen if he left Leah for an entire day.

In fact, when he looked around he didn't see Joe Osenbrock.

"Where's Joe?" he asked sharply.

The older man's gray head turned. "Don't know. Taking a leak?"

The AK-47 Osenbrock had been using lay in the dirt where he'd apparently left it. Spencer had spent time drilling these idiots in how important it was to treat their weapons with care, but nothing he said had sunk in. They thought they were ready, their impatience building almost as fast as their confidence, until they had begun looking at their great leader with doubt. What use was more target shooting? Hand-to-hand combat? Why did they need any of this, when they had the weaponry to shoot planes out of the sky? Spencer had heard the whispers.

Just the other night, for example. Thinking he was alone with Shawn Wycoff walking at the edge of the trees, TJ had said, "I'm starting to think he's all talk." Hidden in the darkness, Spencer hadn't been ten feet away. He didn't miss so much as a mumble. It never occurred to them anybody could be near, far less breathing down their necks.

That arrogance was good. It would bring these fools down.

Unfortunately, it also explained Higgs's continuing hesitation as well as his unwillingness to trust anyone.

Speaking of trust, Spencer said, "I need to go check on Leah. Make sure she's behaving herself and that Joe hasn't forgotten who she belongs to."

Leah's face had looked better this morning, but that wasn't saying much. He still feared she'd suffered a concussion. He'd checked on her a few times in the night and not seen anything too worrisome, but he wanted to be vigilant.

Higgs's eyebrows rose, but he nodded. "I don't need you out here. Let's talk after lunch, though."

Yes. Why don't we talk about who's footing the bills, he thought. *Better yet, some details about your endgame.*

But Spencer only nodded and, carrying his rifle, walked toward the lodge. He was careful to keep his pace unhurried until he was out of sight of the range set up in what had been a beautiful high alpine meadow. They'd undoubtedly destroyed much of the fragile eco-system.

Then he broke into a run.

Leah was on her hands and knees scrubbing the floor in the downstairs bathroom when she heard someone stop in the hall. She stiffened, sneaking a look. Without lifting her head, all she knew was that a man stood there, and he wasn't Spencer or Dirk.

Feet in heavy black boots were planted apart, meaning he filled the doorway. Camo cargo pants didn't hide powerful legs.

"May I help you?" she asked timidly.

"You sure can," he said.

Oh, God. She'd heard his name at breakfast. Joe Osenbrock. He hadn't been one of the two who'd tackled her during her escape attempt, but his perpetual sneer didn't make him likeable. Plus, she'd seen hunger in his eyes when he looked at her. Almost as tall as Spencer, he was broad and strong.

Swallowing, she stayed on her knees and kept her head bent.

"See, Wyatt's got no reason to keep you to himself. What he don't know won't hurt him, now, will it?"

She bit her lip so hard she tasted blood. Where was Dirk Ritchie? Had he seen Osenbrock come in?

"You think he won't know?" she asked, still diffident.

"If he finds out, so what? Not like I'd be spoiling the goods." His voice changed, hardened. "On your feet, woman."

Her mind scrambled for any way to get away from

this would-be rapist. She couldn't just let this happen. Finally, she straightened her back, lifted her head and met his eyes, holding his gaze. "If you touch me, he'll kill you."

"Nothin' to say I won't kill him, you know."

A dark shape materialized behind him. "*I* say you won't," Spencer said, voice as cold as his eyes.

Joe whirled to face the threat he hadn't anticipated. "What're you talking about?"

Spencer spoke softly, but with a sharp edge. "I'll also tell you right now that if you bother her again, if you lay a finger on her, she's right. I *will* kill you."

"I was just teasing her a little. That's all. Ain't that so, Leah?"

She kept her mouth closed, even though agreeing might lessen the tension that made the air hard to breathe.

Spencer leaned toward the other man until he was right in his face. "Do you hear me?"

"I hear you!" Joe yelled, and stormed forward. His shoulder bashed Spencer's, but he kept going. A slam seconds later was the front door of the lodge.

Spencer took Joe's place in the doorway. "Where's Dirk?"

"I don't know." She used the hem of her T-shirt to wipe her forehead. "He might still be in the kitchen. Why?"

"I expect him to watch out for you when I can't be here."

"I thought he's here to make sure none of us make a run for it."

The grim set of Spencer's mouth didn't ease. "Well, that, too."

"Will you expect TJ Galt to watch out for me? Or Jennifer's husband? Or... Is Lisa married?"

"Not married. She lives with Del Schmidt. And no, I wouldn't ask any of the other men to protect you. Which leaves me with a problem."

How reassuring. "Leaves *you* with a problem? That sounds like *my* problem."

He shot a glance over his shoulder. "Keep your voice down."

Leah opened her mouth again but had the sense to close it. She hadn't sounded meek or deferential at all, which would set any of the others wondering about him, too.

"I'm sorry," she whispered.

As usual, his expression remained unemotional, even as his gaze never left her face. "Did you have a choice of jobs?" he asked after a minute.

Leah shook her head. "I wouldn't expect to when I'm the newcomer. They don't know me."

"No." He rubbed a hand over his face in what she'd decided was the closest to betraying frustration or indecision that he came. "Finish up here. I'll decide what we're going to do after lunch."

She nodded, hesitated...and went back on her hands and knees to resume scrubbing. Not that this ancient linoleum would ever look clean again.

"I'll take over here this afternoon," Spencer said during a break in conversations around the table while they ate.

Heads turned, the silence prolonged. When Higgs said, "I'll stick around, too," the atmosphere changed.

Many of them had the same interpretation: their

leader intended to discuss plans with Spencer, the chosen, while everyone else, the mere grunts, continued
physical training.

And yeah, Spencer thought with some irony, he'd
been guilty of plenty of apple polishing to achieve just
this outcome. What he earned today were some hateful
glances directed his way only when the colonel wouldn't
see them.

Only Rick Metz kept chewing with no visible reaction. It wouldn't have crossed his mind that he could
have a planning role. The question was why Dirk looked
relieved. The same man was never allowed to hang
around the lodge all day. Spencer wondered if Dirk
knew the other women weren't safe from TJ or Tim
Fuller.

By God, maybe he should slip Leah a knife so she
could protect herself.

Nice thought, but even if she could bring herself to
stick it into her attacker, the ultimate outcome wouldn't
be good.

Fear of him was her only real protection. He had to
say a few quiet words to men besides Joe Osenbrock.

As he and Higgs waited while the other men left the
lodge and the women cleared the long table, Spencer
tried hard to focus on what might be an important step
in closing this damn investigation, instead of on the
woman who had become his Achilles' heel.

Leah wished she could hear what the two men were
talking about at the table, but she couldn't make out
a word. She had a feeling it was important, but she
couldn't think of an excuse to sidle close enough to
eavesdrop. Jennifer Fuller was in the pantry making

sure she had everything for tonight's dinner, which was to be lasagna. Leah had noticed that she poked her head out pretty regularly to survey her worker bees. As intimidated as she was around the men, she seemed to relish lording it over the other women.

Helen was well aware of when they were alone. Now, as she handed over a rinsed pot for Leah to dry, she whispered, "Spencer said something to Dirk that shook him up real bad. Do you know what happened?"

Just as quietly, Leah said, "Joe Osenbrock got me alone when I was cleaning the bathroom and threatened to…you know."

Helen blushed and ducked her head.

"Spencer heard him and was really mad. I guess he thought Dirk should have kept Joe away from me."

"Dirk didn't know nothing about Joe being back here in the lodge. He wouldn't have let anyone hurt you if he'd known!"

Leah hadn't known a whisper could sound indignant. She smiled at the small, anxious woman. "I believe you. He seems nice."

She didn't actually know any such thing, but at least he didn't look at her the way most of the other men did, and she hadn't been able to help noticing that Helen didn't seem afraid of Dirk.

"Spencer was mostly mad at Joe," she confided.

"I bet." Elbow deep in sudsy water, Helen wielded a scrubbing pad with vigor on the pot that had held the baked beans that were part of the lunch menu. They'd been really good, considering the limited resources anyone cooking had to draw on. Plus, the commercial stove and oven had been installed at least thirty years ago. The miracle was that they mostly still worked.

Possibly that was because Uncle Edward had hardly ever used them himself. Most of the time, he'd insisted the hot plate in his apartment was all he needed. Why make baked beans from scratch when you could open a can? Leah remembered her mother's rolled eyes. Mom had bought him a microwave their last summer here, which had intrigued him. It was safe to say that, as her great-uncle got older and crankier, he would have been even less likely to be inclined to bake a cake or cook anything from scratch.

Too bad he hadn't lingered as a ghost. If he could know, he'd be horrified by the consequences of his gift to her. If he'd actually rented the resort to this group in previous summers—and she increasingly doubted that story—he couldn't have known what those men believed, and especially not what they intended. He'd been courtly, old-fashioned in some ways, but also accepting of people's vagaries. Not for a minute would he have condoned hate-mongering or a threat to the country he loved. Having served as a paratrooper in World War II, Uncle Edward had spent time in a Nazi prisoner-of-war camp. Maybe those experiences explained why, upon returning, he'd chosen a solitary life in the midst of one of American's wildest places.

Handing Leah the next pan, Helen whispered again. "Dirk says you *own* this place."

"My great-uncle left it to me in his—"

Helen jabbed her hard in the side. "Sshh!"

"What...?" Oh. Spencer had settled himself in the doorway between the main room and the kitchen, his posture relaxed, his gaze shifting between the two women. Leah almost whispered that Helen didn't need to worry about Spencer—but if his reputation as the baddest man here was to survive, she needed to keep her mouth shut. If Helen told Dirk what she'd said, he could tell anyone.

She was supposed to be afraid of him, and she needed to act the part. In fact, she immediately imitated Helen's fearful posture. But her forehead crinkled as her hand stopped in the act of wiping out the pot. *Wait*, she thought in alarm. *I am afraid of him.*

Wasn't she?

Chapter 6

"How would you feel about going for a walk?" Spencer asked once they left the lodge, post Leah's KP duty after dinner. He felt restless, but didn't dare take a run and leave her behind. The sky was still bright, with night not falling at this time of year until close to ten o'clock. Then he took another look at her. She moved without any noticeable pain, but she'd been brought down to the ground hard yesterday. "Scratch that. You're probably beat."

Flashing him a surprised look, Leah said, "Beat? Why...oh. The cleaning. You do know I don't sit behind a desk all day back home, don't you?"

He hadn't thought about it, but of course she wouldn't.

"I'm on my feet all day long. I see patients, package bloodwork to send out or run screens myself. Medicate and give fluids. Assist in surgery. Like just about everyone else, I help clean kennels and runs. And I subdue everything from snarling Dobermans to raging bulls while one of the vets does an exam or procedure. Oh, and then there's the wildlife. We do the care for a local refuge, which means holding down an eagle with a broken wing or a cougar dented by a car bumper. A little house cleaning is nothing."

Spencer would have laughed if he hadn't felt sure they were being watched. He appreciated this woman. Leah's bravado was welcome in place of self-pity.

"Of course," she continued, her tone musing, "on the job I wouldn't be worrying whenever a man walked into the room whether he had in mind raping or murdering me. That does take a toll."

"Yeah," he said, a little hoarsely. "It would do that."

"A walk sounds good. After all," she added wryly, "as Colonel Higgs said, I couldn't be held captive in a more beautiful place on earth."

Spencer turned his head, for a rare moment letting himself take in the extraordinary panorama. It had been many years since he'd spent time in the Pacific Northwest, a fact he suddenly regretted.

White-capped Mount Baker dominated the sky to the southeast, while more jagged, and farther distant, Shuksan would have been impressive enough. Other mountains were visible almost everywhere he looked. This was rugged country, and yet not far from the Puget Sound and Strait of Georgia to the west. They were surrounded by forests that had never been logged, an arc of vivid blue above, thin grasses and a dazzling array of flowers. Once they passed the last cabin, he found himself picking his way more carefully than usual because of the wildflowers.

"This is one of the prettiest times of the year here, with so much in bloom," Leah remarked.

Grimly focused on his task, he'd hardly noticed the flowers until five minutes ago. After a moment he said, "I know a few of these. Who hasn't seen a foxglove or a tiger lily?"

For some reason the idea of him gardening in some distant future crossed his mind. Not like he wanted to spend another decade living this way. Once this was over...what if he bought an actual house? Even thought about a wife, having children. What would it be like, coming home at five most days?

His picture of that kind of life was vague, not quite in focus, but he discovered it did include a bed of flowers and a lawn. He hadn't mowed a lawn since he was a boy.

As if she'd followed his thoughts, Leah looked around almost in bemusement. "My mother is a gardener. I always figured someday I'd have a house and yard, too." She went quiet for a minute, likely reflecting on the very distinct possibility she'd never have that chance. But she forged on. "I remember Uncle Edward telling me about the wildflowers. There." She pointed. "That's an easy one, a red columbine. And yarrow, and bleeding heart, and monkshood."

"Isn't monkshood poisonous?"

"I think so. I don't remember if it's the leaves or the flowers or what." She looked pensive, then shook her head. "Oh, and that's goat's beard and..."

He let the recitation roll over him. He wouldn't remember which flower was which, but he liked that she knew and was willing to talk to him.

"When's the last time you were up here?" he asked at one point.

"I think I was twelve, so it's been forever." A pained expression crossed her face. "I'm thirty-one. I don't know why I never thought to get up here to see Uncle Edward. I loved our visits when I was a kid."

"We tend not to look back." He was ashamed to realize how many friends he'd let go over the years. He couldn't even claim to have a close relationship with his own brother or parents anymore. Disappearing for months at a time wasn't conducive to maintaining ties with other people.

Leah stopped walking feet away from the bank of the lake that filled a bowl probably scoured by a long-ago glacier. That was not where she was looking, though. Instead, she turned a gaze on him that was so penetrating, it was all he could do not to twitch.

Instead, he raised an eyebrow. "See anything interesting?"

"Yes. Is there a single other man up here even remotely interested in the names of wildflowers?"

"It's not the kind of thing we talk about," he admitted, although he knew the answer. No. "Anyway, who said I am?"

She frowned. "Do you have any hobbies?"

He ought to shut her down right now, but she'd taken him by surprise, as she often did.

"I target shoot. That's relaxing." More reluctantly, he said, "When I can, I play in a basketball league." Baseball, too.

"All militant white supremacists?"

"Ah…we don't talk politics." For good reason.

"Why didn't you assault me last night?"

Spencer was offended enough, he was afraid it showed.

"I told you, I don't hurt women," he said shortly. "It doesn't turn me on at all." Except that she had to have felt his morning erection, so she knew that she did turn him on. For all she knew, though, he woke up with one every morning.

She nodded slowly, the green of her eyes enriched by the many shades of green surrounding them. His fingers curled into his palms as he resisted the desire to cup her good cheek, trace her lips with his thumb.

Damn, his heartbeat had picked up.

But she wasn't thinking about him kissing her, because what she said was, "I don't believe you'd blow up innocent people to make a point."

This time he felt more than alarm. "Who says we intend to kill anyone who's innocent?"

"How can you not?" she said simply. "Unless you plan to blow up Congress…"

That idea was enough to make him break out in a cold sweat. He was beginning to fear that Higgs's plans really were that grandiose.

But she shook her head. "I refuse to believe there aren't good politicians."

Having met some decent men and women who had run for office because they believed in service, he conceded her point. "What are you saying?"

"I think you're an undercover federal agent."

He should laugh. Jeer, tell her to take the rose-colored glasses off. He should slap her, which would fit with the role he played.

Instead, he growled, "I told you how dangerous it is to suggest that."

"We're all by ourselves."

She'd made mistakes today. Carried herself with

too much pride, looked people in the eye when she shouldn't. Would she be more careful, or less, if she knew the truth?

"If I tell you why I'm here, you have to become an Oscar-worthy actress," he said harshly. "I can't afford for you to get mouthy with anyone, or say something to me when we can be overheard. Do you understand?"

Her expression altered. "Yes. That little episode today with Joe was a good reminder that not only am I in danger every minute, but you are, too."

"I would be either way." He shrugged. "Me demanding an exclusive on you came on top of what some of the men see as Higgs's favoritism. I wasn't popular anyway. Now it's fair to say jealousy and dislike have become hate."

"Isn't hate their reason for existence?" Leah pointed out.

"For the men." Whether the women took the same world view, he had no idea. And it wasn't all of the men. He wished he could figure out how to get Dirk out of the hole he'd dug, but nothing had come to him. There were a couple of others he'd wondered about, but it wasn't his job to separate the deadly fanatics from the ones who were willing to go along. As Leah put it, to blow up innocents.

She didn't say anything else, just waited.

While undercover, Spencer had never, not once, told anyone his true identity or purpose. He'd also never let himself get tangled up with a nice woman who depended on him for her very survival, and who was handling a terrifying experience with dignity and determination.

He sighed, half turning away from her. "You're right. I'm FBI. I've been under with this group for five months now, although we only moved up here for intensive training four weeks ago. Higgs has been on our radar for a long time. Even before he retired, he'd expressed some really marginal ideas. In fact, his obvious contempt for his boss at the time, a two-star general who happened to be black, led to a behind-the-scenes push to early retirement. Unfortunately, it appears that enraged him, helping motivate him to turn militant."

Out of the corner of his eye, he saw that she hadn't done much but blink during this recitation. She'd seen right through him, all right, which made him question how convincing *his* act was.

"I have plenty of evidence to bring down everyone here. We can't let them get to the point of launching their attack. But there's more I need to know. Like when that main event is scheduled for, and what the target is."

"Does that matter if, well, you prevent it from ever happening?"

"Yeah. What if there's another cell training for the same attack? I've seen no indication Higgs is working with anyone else, but we don't have phone service up here. A few times he's made a trip down to Bellingham. Nobody knows what he does while they're shopping for supplies. He could be meeting someone. If he's emailing, it could be from a computer at the library." Frustration added extra grit to his voice. "He has added new posts to a couple of extremist sites, but they're so cryptic we suspect they might really be messages." He gave his head a shake. "We need to keep walking."

"Oh!" She cast a nervous glance back toward the lodge. "Yes, of course."

Circling the lake, he walked fast enough she had to ask him to slow down. He kept talking, telling her his larger goals: making sure they knew who was backing the group, and who was supplying the arms. Moneyed, powerful men were his real target.

"That really is a…a rocket launcher?"

His jaw tightened. "US Military issue. We have two of 'em."

Leah breathed what was probably really a prayer. He agreed with the sentiment wholeheartedly.

Well before they neared the tree line, he said, "I shouldn't have told you this much, but I don't see that it matters. Just remember, even the smallest hint of any of it is a death sentence for me."

She wasn't looking at him. "And me."

"Unless you get the idea you can bargain with Higgs."

Her shoulders stiffened and her chin came up. "I wouldn't!"

"No." He let his tone soften. "I don't think you would."

She sniffed indignantly.

The color of the sky was deepening, the purple tint making it harder for the eye to see outlines.

"This is the end of our discussion," he told her. "I can't be a hundred percent sure the cabin isn't bugged. From here on out, your job is to avoid notice as much as you can."

"What if…if I was able to get a look at Colonel Higgs's room when I'm cleaning?"

"Don't even think about it," he said flatly. "You are not a federal agent. You're a vet tech."

"My life depends on you learning what you have to so we can leave, you know. I'm not going to sit and wait if I can help."

"If you found names or numbers, you wouldn't recognize their meaning. I would. I repeat. The answer is no."

Her chin went back up but she didn't argue again. Spencer wasn't entirely reassured. This was why he shouldn't have told her so much. That said, people talked within earshot of the women as if they were pieces of furniture, much as servants might have been treated in a big house in eighteenth-century England. They could get lucky—but he didn't mention that possibility, because she was too gutsy for her own good. If she got caught where she shouldn't be, *trying* to eavesdrop—she was dead.

They were dead, since he couldn't stand back and let her die, whatever his priorities ought to be.

As they approached the line of cabins, she whispered, "Is Spencer your real name? Or Wyatt?"

Damn her insatiable curiosity.

"It doesn't matter," he snapped.

A faint squeak came to his ears. In response to his irritation, Leah's step hitched and she hunched a little, probably not realizing that she was looking cowed. As little as he liked having that effect on her, her timing was impeccable. That little creep Arne Larson had just stepped out on the porch of his cabin, the one at the end.

"Got her trained, I see," Arne remarked.

Spencer gave her an indifferent glance. "She's smarter than Osenbrock. She knows what's good for her."

Arne laughed, acid in the sound. "Yeah, I heard you told Joe what's what. He didn't like it, you know."

Spencer shrugged. "He's not thinking about what counts. I watched you shooting today and saw a big improvement."

Arne might not like him, but he preened. Spencer's sniper creds inspired some awe among this bunch.

Then he and Leah were past Arne's cabin and the one beyond it, finally reaching his. She trailed him up the porch steps like the obedient little woman she wasn't. She stayed right inside next to the door, too, while he did his usual walk-through with his Sig Sauer in his hand.

The shower afforded only a tepid stream of water, but it was adequate for Leah to wash her hair. The shampoo dripping down her face stung, though, and had her mumbling, "Ow, ow, ow."

Somebody had absconded with her hair dryer before Spencer grabbed her suitcase. He had even reclaimed her purse, minus everything important.

"I have your wallet," he told her, not offering to return it. "Phone and keys are in our great leader's possession."

She'd heard him use that phrase before, equally laden with sarcasm. Never in anyone else's hearing, of course.

She couldn't wrap her mind around everything he'd told her. He'd confirmed her suspicion and more, but... could he have lied to ensure her cooperation? Of course he could have—but she didn't believe he had. The very fact that he'd gone out on such a limb in the first place for her sake was a strong argument for his honesty and, yes, possession of what some people would call the old-fashioned quality of honor. Personally, Leah was big on honor right now. Where would she be without it?

She towel-dried her hair as well as she could, brushed it and left the bathroom.

Spencer looked up from where he lounged on what she'd realized was a futon in the living area. Every time she saw him, she was hit afresh with awareness of how sexy he was. Partly it was a matter of bone structure and the contrast between icy, pale eyes and deeply tanned skin, but that wasn't all. He had a brooding quality that got to her. And he'd tried to protect her.

He hadn't even taken off his boots, and his gun lay within easy reach. He was prepared for anything at a moment's notice. The tension really wore on her, but he seemed to take it for granted.

"What are you reading?" She nodded at the book.

"Huh?" He seemed to turn his eyes from her. "Oh. It's Calvin Coolidge's autobiography."

"Really? Is he that interesting?"

"You might say he's become relevant again." If there was dryness in his tone, Leah doubted anyone else would have noticed it. "Coolidge endorsed a law in 1924 that cut immigration by half, with national origin quotas. He considered southern and eastern Europeans to be genetically inferior. The law led to something like forty years of reduced immigration. Higgs thought I'd like to read this. I'm not sure he paid any attention to Coolidge's other policies."

"Is it interesting?"

"His prose isn't riveting." With a grimace, Spencer stuck a torn strip of paper between pages as a bookmark. "You ready for bed?"

"I guess."

He ushered her into the bedroom, then returned to the main room to make his rounds of the windows and check locks. For what good they'd do, she couldn't help thinking. There were new, shiny dead bolts on the front and back doors, but two of the windows had cracked panes, and the frames would splinter under one blow. Of course, that would alert him instantly, and she'd already seen how fast he could move.

When he returned, she still stood beside the bed.

He raised his eyebrows.

"You aren't going to put handcuffs on me again, are you?"

"That depends. Can I trust you not to try anything?"

Somebody could be listening, she reminded herself. "I won't." She went for very, very humble. "I know you'll take care of me."

He cracked a smile that made her mouth go dry, so drastically did it alter his face. Not soften it, exactly, but a hint of warmth along with wicked sensuality shifted her perception of him. Sexy when somber, angry or expressionless, he might be irresistible if he just kept smiling at her.

Of course he didn't. Dear Lord, he wouldn't dare get in the habit! Imagine what the others would think if they saw him.

His eyes burned into hers. Had he read her mind? Well, thinking he was sexy, and okay, feeling a yearning ache deep inside didn't mean she was having sex with him.

She managed a glare that resulted in the corners of his mouth curving again, but once she climbed into bed, he did turn off the light before he stripped and slid in beside her.

Even his whisper held a little grit coming out of the darkness. "I'd complain about the mattress, but I like knowing what'll happen the minute you fall asleep."

The trouble was, so did she.

Chapter 7

Leah had zero chance to get anywhere near her great-uncle's apartment, appropriated by Colonel Higgs. Jennifer Fuller had the privilege of cleaning it, although only when he was there. Otherwise, another of those shiny new dead bolts kept the nosy out.

However tempting an opportunity would be, Leah wouldn't have seized it. Spencer was right; she'd have no idea what she should be looking for. Anyway, she had no desire to find herself in another spot like she had when Joe Osenbrock cornered her. If Spencer hadn't shown up, she wanted to think she could have fought back effectively or that Dirk would have intervened, but she wasn't stupid enough to buy into comforting lies. Joe was muscular, mean and lacking in a conscience. Dirk had an athletic body, but his muscles didn't bulge quite as much, and he struck her as a little quieter and less aggressive than most of the others. Even if he'd tried to step in to protect her—albeit for Spencer's sake, not hers—he'd have had the shit beaten out of him. Then Joe would have been mad.

Today, in between breakfast and lunch, Leah volunteered hastily for cleaning jobs that would keep her in the main spaces and working with at least one of the other women. There were four of them here, instead of five; TJ said Shelley wasn't feeling well.

Lifting benches around the table while Lisa Dempsey swept under them, Leah tried to start a conversation. If she made friends, she might learn something, right? Well, it wouldn't be with Lisa, who completely ignored her, responding only when Leah said something relevant, like, "I see something under there you missed."

She never looked Leah in the eye, either, which was a good reminder to her that she was supposed to imitate the other women, not befriend them.

Jennifer cracked briefly when Leah said, "That lasagna you made was amazing. You must have worked in a restaurant."

"Thank you," she said grudgingly. "I learned from my mother, that's all."

"Oh, well, I hope you have a daughter who'll learn from you."

Jennifer turned her back and walked away.

A few minutes later Helen whispered, "You shouldn't've said that to her. She's had miscarriages. I think—"

A footstep presaging the appearance of Del Schmidt silenced her.

Chagrined, Leah scraped frost out of the old chest freezer. Could Jennifer's body just not hold on to a fetus? One of the veterinarians Leah worked with had had two miscarriages. She and her husband had been devastated.

In this case, though, Leah couldn't help wondering whether abuse from her husband had ended each pregnancy. Maybe that was unjust, but she didn't like the way Tim talked to his wife, or how he'd shoved her hard up against a wall when he thought she was giving him some lip. It was all Leah could do to pretend she hadn't seen what happened.

Spencer was one of the last to show up for lunch, shredded beef tacos and Spanish rice today. He glanced at Leah when she was the last to sidle up to the table and take a seat, but he was immediately distracted by something the man beside him was saying. Shawn somebody. Or was that Brian… Thompson? Townsend? These guys looked an awful lot alike, all Caucasian although tanned, hair shaved or cut very short, big muscles, tattoos on their arms or peeking above their collars. Arne Larson's looked a lot like one arm of a Nazi swastika, which she thought was more than a little ironic, given how the Scandinavian countries had resisted the Nazi invasion. Obviously, he identified with the invaders and maybe even their genocide.

Leah had a sickening thought. What if her mother had married a black or Latino man? Things would have been different if she, a woman with dark skin, had driven up to announce that she owned the resort. Would Spencer have had any chance at all to save her?

No. How could he have? Higgs wouldn't have bothered giving her his impassioned speech about inciting a civil war to restore this great country to the *true* Americans, because she wouldn't have been one in his eyes.

Her appetite scant, she picked at her food and kept her head down by inclination as well as orders, not even looking toward Spencer.

Toward the end of the meal, though, she heard Tim Fuller say into a lull, "We're running low on food. Jennifer made a list."

Higgs mulled that over for a minute before saying, "Wyatt, you take Lisa tomorrow." He scanned the men around the table. "Schmidt, you go, too."

Leah didn't dare look at Spencer to see if he'd betrayed any emotion at all. She hoped she'd succeeded in hiding how she felt, but she was quite sure she wouldn't be able to take another bite, not when she couldn't swallow it. Fear squeezed her throat as if a powerful hand had closed around it.

Higgs turned a cold stare on Spencer, who had stopped in front of him with crossed arms. The two men were on their way toward the obstacle course built their first week up here, taking in part of the meadow and forest. "I don't want to hear it."

Spencer said what he was thinking anyway. "You didn't like me taking Leah out of your control."

Frosting over, the colonel said, "*Nobody* here is out of my control. Did you forget that?"

He had, misjudging how Ed Higgs would see him stepping in to remove Leah from the chessboard. Damn, Spencer thought incredulously, he was going to have to take her and run, tonight while they still had a chance.

"Are you planning to have her yourself?" he asked.

Higgs's eyes narrowed. "I don't rape women."

"You just encourage your followers to do it."

"Is that what you think?"

Jaw jutting out, Spencer couldn't back down. "I think that's what you're threatening. Take me out of the picture, show me how I rate."

"I've developed a lot of respect for you. I thought I could trust you. Since you set eyes on her, I'm having to wonder."

What was it he'd said to Leah? *You have to become an Oscar-worthy actor.* That was it.

He scoffed, "You seriously think I'd let a sexy piece of tail divert me from our plans? I took her because I don't like doing without, and I figured I was entitled. If you want her—" *I'll have to kill you. Nope, shrug as if she's nothing to you.*

Higg's relaxation was subtle. "I don't."

"Then what's the problem?"

"The problem is you getting in my face because I chose you to run an errand and you don't want to do it because you're afraid someone will put a move on her in your absence."

"No," Spencer said coolly. "I'm afraid someone will think they can get away with taking what's mine, and then I'll have to kill him. You don't want to lose a soldier in our war, do you?"

"You said yourself, she doesn't matter worth shit," the colonel said impatiently. "What's your problem?"

"My problem is that I laid my reputation on the line. *That* matters to me. If you expect me to exert any authority over this bunch, it should matter to you, too. If someone hurts her and smirks at me when I get back tomorrow, what's it going to look like if I back down from what I promised?" He let that settle for a minute before shaking his head and raising an eyebrow. "I'm not willing to do that. I'll do your errands tomorrow, but if I find out anyone touched a hair on her head, there'll be violence. I'm just telling you, that's all. Don't be surprised."

Higgs muttered an obscenity. "Fine. I get it. I'll reinforce your message tomorrow. If that'll satisfy you, General?"

Spencer snapped a salute. "It's Captain, as you know quite well."

"I never could verify your service." This was an old complaint.

"The army can be secretive, even with an air force lieutenant colonel. More so when it comes to the records of spec-ops soldiers."

"Especially snipers," Higgs grumbled. "I got nothing out of them at Fort Bennett."

"Well, it's not as if that's something I could fake," Spencer pointed out. "You want to get me a different rifle, I can make a kill shot from over a thousand feet out."

"Why not the rifle you're using?"

Spencer had said this before, but he didn't mind repeating himself. "The M82 loses accuracy over nine hundred yards. It's a mallet, not a stiletto."

"A mallet's what we want, and you're right. You've proved your abilities and more. I'd take one of you over ten of the rest of these grunts."

"They have their uses."

Higgs smiled. "Indeed they do."

Repelled by that smile, Spencer stifled his need to hear Higgs promise that they had a deal. Demanding any such thing would undo all the good he'd just accomplished.

If he had to kill someone tomorrow, he was prepared, but that would do shit for Leah.

His self-control was rarely strained, but as he held back a growl, he was freshly reminded that she'd put more than a few cracks in it.

Scuttling along at Spencer's shoulder in the morning, Leah asked, "Won't Higgs be outside most of the day, like usual?" Spencer hadn't wanted to talk about it last night. In fact, his mood had been foul.

"Probably." His long stride ate up the ground. "He promised to reinforce my message where you're concerned. He knows what will happen if anyone bothers you."

"Well, that's reassuring," she mumbled. Nothing like knowing he'd take revenge for her, even if by then she was a bloody, bruised piece of pulp.

"Stick with the other women and you should be all right," he ordered before they reached the lodge and there was no more chance to talk.

Should was not the most reassuring word in this context.

Since she'd been designated cook for the first time this morning, she had to shove her worries to the back of her mind. With only a little advice on the quantities needed to feed nineteen men and five—no, four—women, she competently turned out pancakes and two platters piled with nice crisp bacon. Nobody said, "Hey, good job," but as they served the food she felt part of the quartet in a way she hadn't before.

Of course they'd pretend not to see if someone like Joe Osenbrock assaulted her in the middle of the kitchen.

During the meal Spencer ate mechanically, never so much as glancing at her. The table was barely cleared when he, Lisa and Del Schmidt went out the door. Feeling hollow, Leah pretended not to notice.

While the other men headed out for whatever training scheduled for today, Tim Fuller took up a position in the kitchen, his irritation plain.

Did he hate this detail? His wife seemed more self-effacing than usual, which made Leah suspect either he'd been posted out of rotation or was missing something especially fun—say, they were going to find out today what happened when they fired a rocket into a big pile of boulders.

Had they tried out their rocket launchers yet? They surely wouldn't dare shoot one upward. Wouldn't that be picked up on air force or civilian airport radars?

As she was setting the table for lunch, two men walked in. Joe Osenbrock and Carson somebody, another look-alike. Joe's expression turned ugly as he looked at her.

"Coffee," he snapped.

She set down the pile of silverware on napkins and wordlessly returned to the kitchen.

"Joe and Carson want coffee," she said.

"I'll pour it," Helen offered.

Leah smiled weakly. "Thanks."

A minute later she set the mugs down in front of the two men, careful to follow Spencer's instructions. Head bowed, shoulders rounded, avoid meeting their eyes. She hoped they couldn't tell that her pulse was racing so fast she felt light-headed.

Neither thanked her, of course. Joe flicked a glance

past her, as if checking to see whether anyone was watching.

Knowing she had no choice, she continued setting the table. She finished and headed for the kitchen just as she heard the front door open again, followed by a burst of voices. She hadn't realized Tim had come out to the dining room until she almost bumped into him.

He stopped her with one hand on her arm. "You're a lucky bitch," he murmured. "Don't count on that lasting."

Leah shuddered. The minute he released her, she hurried into the kitchen. Had he been assigned to watch out for her? Was that why he'd followed her from the kitchen...and why Joe had kept his distance?

Maybe...but she knew a threat when she heard one.

Getting away from Schmidt long enough to make a phone call wasn't easy, but Spencer managed. He'd ordered Schmidt to stay with Lisa while he used the john. Then he helped himself to a phone he had spotted at a momentarily empty cashier's station and took it down the hall toward the public restrooms, an office and what appeared to be an employee break room. It was likely password protected, of course, and he had a phone he could use, but he couldn't be a hundred percent sure that it was still secure. Even if it had been found, he doubted anyone in the group was sophisticated enough to know how to record his conversation or trace numbers he called, but better safe than sorry. If he could get away with borrowing—

Yes. He'd gotten lucky.

Thank God Ron answered. "Special Agent Ron Abram."

"This is Wyatt." No, that wasn't his name, but he didn't use his own name even in theoretically safe moments. He had to *think* of himself as Spencer Wyatt. "I've only got a minute."

"I'm glad you called. I've been worrying."

A woman emerged from the restroom, head bent over her own phone as she passed.

"I have problems," Spencer said. He summarized the events of the past few days, from Leah Keaton's arrival to the "deal" he'd made with Ed Higgs to ensure her safety. "Even though I don't want to quit until I have all the info we need, part of me wants to throw her in my SUV and take off. Trouble is, I'm not even betting we'd get away with that. Del Schmidt drove today. I'm wondering if I won't find the starter or alternator have kicked the bucket. Or worse, it runs for five minutes and then dies. As it is, Higgs keeps the keys when we're not using the vehicles."

"You're not driving today?"

"No. I wasn't given the option, which is one reason I suspect sabotage. By standing up for Leah, I awakened suspicion. Higgs has called me on it. I think I talked him around, but I can't be sure."

"If you have to cut and run, we'd have no choice but to raid the resort and pull the plug on the operation."

"Exactly." He watched two teenage boys laughing and bumping shoulders as they headed for the men's room. "Leah's smart. I think she can play her part for a few days. Higgs wants me with him for a meeting Saturday." The day after tomorrow. "I think it'll be a meet to acquire some new arms."

"That's worth holding out for," Abram said.

"I hate keeping a civilian in the mix," Spencer said.

Abram was quiet for a minute. "Damn. I wish you had a panic button."

"You and me both. I can't promise when I'll be able to call again." He saw a woman wearing a checker's nameplate at the cashier station where he'd swiped the phone. "Gotta go."

He quickly deleted a record of his call, shoved the phone in a pocket and strolled that way. Just as he reached it, he said, "Hey! Somebody lost a phone," and bent over, rising with it in his hand.

"Oh, thank goodness!" she exclaimed. "You'd think I'd have heard it drop."

"It's not damaged, is it?"

"Well, there's no crack anyway." She beamed. "Thank you."

"No problem."

When he rejoined Lisa and Del, now heaping packages of meat into one of the two carts, he asked, "We get any desserts? My sweet tooth has been aching."

Lisa almost forgot herself so much as to smile. "I'm supposed to pick up some flats of strawberries and blueberries for pies, and rhubarb for a cake."

"What about some apple pies? Let's get plenty of ice cream."

Nodding in agreement, Del said, "We need to load up on chips, too."

"I'm supposed to keep to a budget," she said nervously.

"If it looks like we're going to run over, I'll pick up

the extra," Spencer said. "Remember, we're feeding an-other mouth, too." Even if Leah hadn't eaten enough to keep a bird alive, as far as he could see. He'd have to get on her about that.

"Thanks," Lisa said shyly. "I don't want to make anyone mad."

"I'll be mad if I don't get an apple pie," Spencer joked.

The mood stayed good as they shopped and then packed huge quantities of food in the rear and on one backseat of the big SUV. Spencer made sure neither of the others saw even a trace of his growing tension as they made the drive heading northeast on increasingly poor roads.

If he found Leah hurt, he wasn't sure he wouldn't grab the closest fully automatic weapon and start spray-ing bullets.

When at last they pulled up in front of the lodge, he hopped out, waited for the rear hatch to rise and grabbed bags of potatoes and a couple of flats of canned goods, then took the steps to the porch. He had to shift the load a little to reach the knob, shouldered the door open and walked in. The first person he saw was Joe Osenbrock, sitting beside Tim Fuller at the long table. Spencer clenched his teeth until his back molars hurt.

He passed the two without a word, without paus-ing long enough to read expressions, and went into the kitchen.

One of the other women was off to his right. He didn't even know which one. All he saw was Leah, turn-ing from the sink, her hands encased in plastic gloves,

a scrub brush held in one of them. The relief and something more that suffused her face did a number on him.

"Leah," he said hoarsely.

Can't drop my load and take her into my arms.

He couldn't even ask if she was all right. He hated that.

Her eyes widened at whatever she saw on his face.
What she did was flush, draw a deep breath and say,
"Oh, good. I was hoping potatoes were on the list. I'm
not sure we have enough…" She bit her lip and ducked
her head. "I'm sorry."

Sorry for? But he knew. Some men here would have
backhanded her for that artless chatter, especially given
the implication that he might have screwed up by not
buying everything that was needed.

He tore his eyes from her, saw Jennifer watching
them. "Where do you want this stuff?" he asked.

"Oh, in the pantry." Maybe reading his expression,
she added hastily, "Or…anywhere is good. We can put
everything away."

Footsteps behind him heralded Del's arrival with
more food. On his heels, Lisa carried more than she
should have to.

"Wherever is best," he said shortly, and went to the
pantry.

As he made three more trips back and forth from the
SUV, he couldn't help wondering what Jennifer thought
she'd seen, and whether she talked to her husband. Or
whether he listened to her if she did.

After depositing the last load, he said, "I hope dinner isn't far off. I'm starved."

It was Jennifer who answered, the tiniest edge in her
voice. "No, not if Leah gets on with that potato salad."

"I'm hurrying," Leah said, sounding chastened.

Turning to stalk out of the kitchen, Spencer knew he'd be happy never to hear her sounding so diminished again.

But if they were going to hold out long enough for him to make this mission a success, that was one wish he wouldn't get.

Chapter 8

They didn't talk during the walk back to the cabin. With the sun still high in the sky, it might have been midafternoon. Days were noticeably longer here than even in Portland, Oregon, she'd noticed.

Inside, Spencer did his usual walk-through, then said, "Waste of a goddamn day."

"We…we really were running out of food."

He made a rough sound. "Higgs should have sent Ritchie or Jack Jones."

Leah only vaguely knew who the second man was. Would Spencer dare talk like this if there was any chance at all of a listening device?

Maybe. This barely muted contempt went with the arrogance he projected so well. Deliberately, she thought. Higgs would expect it from him.

"I want apple pie tomorrow," he said. "See to it there is some."

Seeing her bristle, he winked.

In her best "I'm nobody important" tone, Leah said, "Jennifer makes up the menu. She doesn't like it when any of the rest of us make a suggestion."

"Tell her it's from me." He flat-out grinned now. "Lisa knows what I want."

Leah rolled her eyes.

Smile gone, he growled, "Did any of the men bother you today?"

"I... No."

His gaze bored into hers. "You're mine. If anyone so much as laid a hand on you..."

"No. I think they're all scared of you."

"They should be."

Neither of them had sat down. It was too early to go to bed. Leah felt restless and could tell he did, too, but they couldn't go for a walk every evening.

Eyes heavy lidded, he took a step toward her, his fingers flexing. The hunger on his face ignited her own. Leah swallowed. Sex was something they could do. In fact, if the cabin was being bugged, they definitely *should* be having sex. And if that wasn't an excuse, she'd never heard one before.

But he seemed to pull down a shutter, turning away from her and saying gruffly, "You have some books in your suitcase. Why don't you get one? I want to read before we go to bed."

Would anybody buy that? But she knew; he didn't really believe there was a bug, he was just being cautious. She should be grateful he wasn't the kind of man who would use "we need to convince any listener" as an excuse to get her naked.

So she only nodded, went to the bedroom and grabbed one of the books at random. She didn't want to read; she wanted to hear whether he'd had a chance to call his office today and, if so, what he'd learned. She wanted to tell him about the threat issued by Tim, and about the inimical way he and Joe Osenbrock had stared at her. She wanted to know what his lips would feel like on hers.

And she wanted desperately to know when he thought they could leave—if there was any way they could without getting killed.

But he'd finally lowered himself to one side of the futon, stacked his booted feet on the scarred coffee table and opened his book. He appeared to immediately immerse himself.

Leah sat at the other end of the futon, which really meant she could have stretched out an arm and touched him, and opened her own book. She read a few pages, realized she hadn't taken in a thing, and turned back to start over. She thought the one side of his mouth she could see curled up. So he wasn't any deeper in the biography than she was in the romance she'd picked up.

The next hour dragged. She read, reread and finally plunked the book down without bothering to save her place. She was going crazy here, and Spencer continued to read as if unaware of her. She felt quite sure that wasn't true.

Her mind wandered.

He hadn't answered her question about his name. She *liked* the name Spencer Wyatt. What if his real name was something like…she entertained herself by coming up with a list of not-so-sexy possibilities. Elmer. Homer. Barney. Cornelius. Wilbur.

All names, she realized, that would have been her grandparents' or even great-grandparents' generation. If she'd been born then and *her* name was Dolly or Kitty or...or Winnie, she'd probably have been fine with Barney.

The name Barney wouldn't reduce the man beside her in any way, she admitted to herself in dismay. She couldn't think of much that would.

I can't fall in love with him, she thought in shock. What a ridiculous idea. This gooey mess of emotions in her were completely natural, considering he'd dedicated himself to saving her life and virtue. And *that* was a silly way to think of a vicious crime like rape.

She sighed. She couldn't exactly whine that she was bored.

Only, she didn't want to know when they'd get there; she wanted to know when they could *leave*.

"Why don't you go take a shower?" he said irritably.

"Fine." Leaving her book where it lay, Leah stomped into the bedroom, grabbed clean clothes and went straight to the bathroom without so much as looking in his direction.

The fixtures were all chipped and stained, but they worked. At least she'd be bored *and* clean.

Or scared for her life and clean.

She was sitting on the toilet to take off her shoes and socks and tug her shirt over her head when the bathroom door opened again, almost bumping her knees in the tight space. Startled, she looked up at Spencer.

He crowded her even more to allow him to shut the

door behind himself. Then he squeezed past her and turned on the shower.

"What...?" she whispered.

He crouched in front of her. For a second she fixated on the power of his forearms before being distracted by the long muscles in his thighs outlined with the camouflage fabric pulled tight. Then she lifted her gaze to meet his eyes.

"I thought we should talk," he said in a low voice. "I worried about you all day."

"I really am fine. There was only one weird moment." She told him about Joe and Carson coming in, the glance Joe exchanged with Tim and then what Tim had said.

"That son of a bitch threatened you."

"It wasn't that overt. I mean, he didn't say, 'I'll hurt you.' It was more like, 'Next time I won't stop Joe.'"

"I still want to shove his teeth down his throat." Spencer rolled his shoulders. "Damn. Saturday I'll be gone part of the day again."

A greasy ball lodged in her stomach. "Why?"

"Don't know for sure. Higgs asked me to accompany him for a 'meet.'"

"To buy weapons?"

"That's what I think."

The pale silver of his eyes was almost like glass, except not so transparent. Quartz crystal. Shimmering, clear, but still hiding the secrets inside.

"That was one of your goals, wasn't it?"

"Yeah." He cleared his throat. "But I'm asking a lot of you."

What if she said, *Too much?* Could she persuade him

to take her and leave? Leah didn't know for sure, but thought he might choose her if she begged.

It took her only a moment to steady herself. "What you're doing is important. If all goes well, you'll prevent a cataclysmic attack on this country." If her voice shook a little, well, who could blame her? "It's my country, too. What's more, anybody stealing weapons bought with my and every other American's tax dollars needs to be locked up for good."

She'd swear that was pride in his eyes. He lifted a hand to her face, gently cupped the injured cheek and said, "You're an amazing woman, Leah Keaton."

Her tremulous smile probably didn't enhance the kick-butt speech, but it *was* a smile. "And don't I know it."

Now he grinned openly. "Pretty bra, too."

"What?" She looked down at herself and felt her face heat. The vivid green satin probably made her skin look pasty, but she liked the color.

If she wasn't mistaken, his gaze lingered on the swell of her breasts above the fabric, not the bra. He was so close, his hand still holding her jaw, his face nearly level with hers. If she scooted forward...

His pale eyes speared hers. "I won't do that to you." Low, his voice was even grittier than usual.

"Even if I want you to?"

"Even if. You know the balance of power thing. It's swinging heavily in my favor right now."

Leah couldn't deny that was true. But... "I know what I want."

He rose to his feet, letting her see his arousal, but his gaze never left hers. "I want, too," he said quietly. "But we can wait."

She managed a nod, and he left the bathroom.

Did they *have* enough future to allow for some distant, ideal day? she asked herself. But…he was right. Of course he was. What if they triumphed and made it out of here and then she realized she didn't really like him that well? Mightn't she question whether she'd used her body as bribery so he'd keep her at the top of his priority list?

And no, she didn't think he was that man, or she was that woman.

Maybe what she needed to do was believe in him and herself. Believe they'd make it.

She could do that…but she was more aroused than she could ever remember being just from a touch, an exchange of looks.

Now that Spencer knew Leah was willing, he didn't know if he could survive many more nights with fullbody contact but him blocked from being able to make a single move. He seriously considered sleeping on the futon, but that would be as torturous in a different way. He still had the original issues, too: he didn't want to be seen sleeping separately from her, and he didn't like the idea of her alone, a room away from him.

Her cheeks were pink when they met in the bedroom, but she wore a long T-shirt over panties that did a number on his libido, slipped into bed and turned her back on him without saying anything.

Spencer swore silently, set his gun within easy reach and stripped down to his own boxers and T-shirt. He turned his back on her, too.

It was not a good night. Far as he could tell, Leah slept better than he did. He couldn't get comfortable, couldn't control his body's reaction to having hers pressed against him, and when he wasn't brooding about why he hadn't taken her up on her offer, he worried about Saturday.

If Tim's suggestion to her meant what Spencer thought it might, she could be in big trouble. Individually, they were all afraid of him, and rightly so. But what if, when he returned, he wouldn't be facing a single man, but several? Would Higgs intervene, or let them tear him up? If he did step in, would the simmer of resentment boil over?

Did Higgs know a couple of the guys were cocky enough to think they could take his place?

Spencer knew he had allies, guys that were glad he could hold the vicious ones in check. Joe Osenbrock, Tim Fuller, TJ Galt and Arne Larson weren't popular with the rank and file. The question was, how many of the others would have the will and guts to stand up with him?

Who should he talk to before he left Saturday with Higgs? Or was there someplace he could stash her before he left? She probably knew this mountainside better than any of them did. She might have an idea.

But then, could he afford the fallout from her temporary disappearance?

Spencer groaned and rolled over again.

One day, a lot of decisions to make—and another night tucked into bed beside Leah.

The following evening, as they left the lodge after dinner, he said curtly, "We're taking a walk." Well aware several men were within earshot, Spencer ignored them. Beside him, Leah ducked her head and nodded.

He strolled down the line of cabins, Leah keeping up. A single sidelong glance let him see her bewilderment.

"What will they think about us doing this?"

He used an obscenity to tell her how little he cared. He *should* care; he and Leah had been so careful to fly under the radar. Somehow, today, he'd met his breaking point.

Leah looked alarmed but was smart enough to say nothing.

When they reached the meadow of wildflowers, he pointed at one with deep pink, almost bell-shaped flowers. "You know that one?"

"Um…a penstemon, I think. There are clumps of hybrid penstemons in my mother's garden."

Last time they were here, he hadn't noticed the faint trace of a path. Left from the days when the resort would have been filled with guests? He followed it toward the lake.

"What did you want to tell me?" Leah asked.

He appreciated her directness.

"I want to talk about tomorrow, but I needed to get away," he admitted.

"Oh. Me, too."

"Everything okay today?"

"Sure. It was a relief having Dirk there again."

"You're getting Del tomorrow. I don't think he'll bother you."

She didn't say anything, but Spencer knew what she was thinking. Would Del stand up to any of the dangerous men on her behalf? Why would he?

Spencer asked himself again if he was doing the right thing. He didn't know any of the potential victims of the planned attack. He knew, liked, admired, wanted

Leah. She was the first woman in years who'd gotten to him like this, and he'd only known her for a matter of days. Maybe it was her spirit, relentless in the face of adversity. Or her courage, facing up to dangerous men while suppressing her fears. She'd sure as hell complicated his life. If they had the chance, he could see being happy to have her go right on doing just that.

"Once you sell this place, what'll you do with the money?" he asked, going for the positive. The question was out of the blue, but he was hungry for a few minutes of normalcy. At least, what he vaguely remembered as normalcy.

Obviously surprised, Leah stayed quiet for a minute. Then she said, "I want to go back to school to become a veterinarian. I'd have done that instead of training as a vet tech, except the idea of graduating with such a massive load of debt is really daunting. I'm pretty sure I have the grades and now the experience to be accepted. The money…would make a difference."

"Your parents can't help?"

"I don't want to ask. Mom's a teacher and Dad works for our local utility district. They make a decent living, but they're not rich. They put me through college, and now they should be saving for retirement."

"You intend to specialize as a veterinarian?"

"I don't know. Surgery fascinates me, and I think I'd get bored if I had to do spays and neuters all day, even if they're important." She shrugged. "One step at a time."

Unfortunately, her next step wouldn't be talking to a real estate agent or filling out graduate school applications.

He said gruffly, "I never asked whether you have a boyfriend."

Leah shook her head. "It's been a while. What about you? I suppose it's hard, given your job."

He fixed his gaze on the mountain, gleaming white, somehow pure. "Next to impossible."

"I don't believe that," she said stoutly. When he didn't say more, she asked, "Was becoming an FBI agent always your dream?"

Dream? Spencer wasn't sure he'd ever had one, the way she meant. Given his lousy mood, that struck him as sad.

He didn't love talking about himself, but he owed her. No, he corrected himself immediately; if he had any thought of pursuing these unexpected feelings for her, he had to open up, at least partway.

"My goal was to get away from home." He hoped she couldn't hear the sadness. "My father and I butted heads for as long as I can remember. I think he loved me—loves me—but his way of showing it was by being a harsh disciplinarian. I joined the army two days after my high school graduation. Barely looked back."

They'd reached the lake now, the surface of the water utterly still, mirroring the rich blue of the sky. Some plants that probably thrived in wetter conditions grew on the shores, but he didn't ask about them.

"I spent ten years in the army." Too much of it killing people. "Got my college degree along the way. A friend who'd left earlier suggested I apply to the FBI, too. I was feeling less sure that the US military was accomplishing anything. I thought I might do more coming at problems from a different direction."

"Isn't one of their biggest divisions counterterrorism?"

"Yeah, I'm in domestic counterterrorism. Unfortunately, we never have the chance to get bored."

"You said you've done this before."

"Gone undercover? Oh, yeah. I'm good at it." His struggles this time all had to do with her.

"I can't imagine living under that kind of stress."

"Right now you are," he pointed out.

She made a face. "That's why I know I wouldn't like it long-term."

"This may be my last time," he heard himself say. "I've almost forgotten who I am."

Ignoring her role, Leah reached for his hand and squeezed.

He turned his body to block anybody watching through binoculars from seeing the physical contact. When she started to withdraw her hand, he held on.

Her cheeks turned pink, but she didn't look away from him. "To me, you're a hero. That's a good place to start."

Spencer shook his head. "Undercover, you get your hands dirty. It's too easy to forget the moral standards you began with. That's one reason—" He broke off. "If I'm ever going to have a life outside the bureau, I figure I ought to get on with it. I'm thirty-seven."

They had reached the edge of the forest on the far side of the lake. His gaze strayed to shadowy coves between tall fir and cedar trees. It wouldn't be such a sin to draw her out of sight and kiss her, would it? If things went south tomorrow... But he refused to think like that. No reason to believe anyone would be stupid enough to attack Leah. He'd made himself clear enough. And what he'd told her last night would hold true until they got free of this bunch. What if she kissed him back mostly because right now she needed him desperately?

Shoring up the walls of his reserve, he released her

hand but moved to face her. "Let's talk about tomorrow," he said. "I'd rather you follow your usual routine, but do you know anyplace you could hide if necessary?"

"Now I wish I hadn't given away the hidey-holes between the closets."

He wished she hadn't, either. "No other secret passages in the lodge?"

Leah shook her head. "If I could get as far as the tree line…"

"That would work only if you had a serious head start. Otherwise, they'd be on you like a pack of wolves."

Seeing her already creamy white skin blanch, he was sorry he'd been so blunt, but she needed to know what she faced.

He'd ruled out giving her his backup gun. It would be a disaster if anyone noticed her carrying. He'd also had to consider whether, in a struggle, she could bring herself to pull the trigger quick enough, or at all. However courageous, Leah was at heart a gentle woman, if he was reading her right. Even if she did manage to shoot and kill or at least disable her assailant, then what would happen? He didn't have a suppressor fitted to either of his handguns. The sound of a shot in the vicinity of the lodge versus at the range would bring everyone running.

"Chances are good I'll only be gone for a few hours. Nobody has said anything, so I don't think the rest know Higgs and I are going anywhere tomorrow. I'd try to get you the key to my SUV, but I can't think how to check it out for sabotage without drawing notice."

She was shaking her head even as he spoke. "Even if I could take off…what would happen to you when you get back?"

"That doesn't matter."

Her expression turned mutinous. "I'm not going to just run away and desert you."

"Leah." Unable to help himself, he took her hand again. "If you ever see an opportunity—a good one—take it. Let me worry about myself. You got that?"

She searched his eyes in that way she did, undoubtedly seeing more than he wanted her to. Finally, she said, "I'll think about it."

Always stubborn.

"You do that," he murmured, and turned away to resume their walk.

Chapter 9

"Turn in here." Higgs leaned forward, the action pulling against his seat belt. "Go around behind the building."

The long, ramshackle log structure along the old highway might once have been a restaurant or tavern. "What's this place?" Spencer asked as he braked and turned into a weedy gravel lot.

"Somebody told me it was a visitor's center back in the fifties or sixties. Then a restaurant and gift shop." The older man shrugged. "Not sure what else. Not a lot of traffic up this way anymore."

The reason this meeting had been set for here.

Given how little traffic he'd seen in miles, he was surprised the highway was maintained this well. About all he'd seen in ten miles or more was beautiful forest, a waterfall plunging off a cliff only feet from the road and moss and ferns everywhere. Pale, lacy lichen draped like tinsel over branches. When they first set off, mist had clung in dips of the road, blurring the outlines of the evergreens. Half an hour ago they'd risen above it.

Spencer tensed as he drove around the building and saw a pickup already here, parked facing out. It was a dually built for especially heavy loads; black plastic tarps crisscrossed with cord hid whatever was being hauled in the full bed.

"Park so we can load easily," the colonel suggested.

As he backed in, two men climbed out of the pickup, slamming their doors. Even before he saw faces, he noted both men were armed. Of course Spencer was, too, and he felt sure Higgs was, as well.

Turning off the engine and setting the emergency brake, he was slower getting out than Higgs was. He and the older of the two men were already shaking hands when Spencer walked forward.

He knew that face. It set off alarms in him, even if a name to go with it didn't come to him immediately. He just needed to figure out the context where he'd seen the guy before—or his photograph.

Photograph, he decided. In his line of work, he studied thousands. Soon, he'd have a name to go with that face.

The high and tight haircut on the younger man looked military. His scrutiny suggested he, too, was trying to fit Spencer's face into a context. The older guy's was more buzz-cut, graying like Higgs's hair. Same generation, sure as hell their paths had crossed during their military careers. Both, maybe, getting more and more dissatisfied with the direction their country was going as gay marriage became approved, a black man was elected president of the United States and now women wearing hijabs had been elected to congress.

They'd believe passionately that the violent mission they'd chosen was patriotic. Spencer didn't see any hint of deference between them. They saw themselves as equals, he decided. The younger guy was just muscle. Hey, maybe that was all Higgs considered Spencer to be, too.

Spencer exchanged nods with both. The closest to an introduction came when Higgs said, "My second-in-command." Two pairs of eyes raked him appraisingly. He lifted his eyebrows but didn't otherwise react.

"Let's get this done," Higgs's buddy said.

Spencer unlocked and opened the rear doors on the Suburban. Evaluating the load, he thought it would fit. Then he joined the younger guy in pulling the cord off so the tarps could be removed.

This was just like Christmas Day, he thought sardonically. What would be inside the wrapping?

That morning Leah and the other women hadn't even started clearing the table before Colonel Higgs swung his legs over the bench and said, "I'll be running an errand."

Everyone around the table looked startled, except for Spencer, of course. He nodded. "Shall I drive?"

Higgs took a set of keys from his pocket and tossed them to Spencer. "We'll take my Suburban. It has more hauling capacity."

Spencer gave a clipped nod, took a last swallow of coffee and rose to leave with Higgs. His gaze passed over Leah without pausing on her, but she made a determined effort to hold on to this last sight of his face as if she'd taken a snapshot.

None of the men moved until they heard the engine start outside. Tim Fuller looked at her.

"Where are they going?"

"I don't know," she said softly. "He doesn't tell me anything."

Every man in the room was staring at her. The effect was unnerving, making it easier to act scared. She stood up and began gathering dirty dishes.

"We're running low on some of the ammunition," one of the men she didn't really know commented.

"He's been promising a new rifle the army is supposed to be testing. I wouldn't mind getting my hands on that." Brian Townsend.

They threw out wilder and wilder ideas. But when somebody said "bomb," a deafening silence ensued. Apparently, there were some things they weren't supposed to talk about in front of the women.

Leah had been pushing through the swinging kitchen door and hoped they all thought she'd already gone back into the kitchen. Carrying a teetering load of dirty plates, Helen was right on her heels. Leah set down her pile, then took some of Helen's.

Jennifer clapped her hands. "Let's hurry! Along with lunch, we should do some baking."

By all means. Bake goodies while the men planned to build bombs.

Not waiting to be assigned a task, Leah filled the sink with hot, soapy water and began washing while the others brought in the remaining dirty dishes and Lisa carried a coffeepot out to top off mugs.

Leah let most of the talk about the menu go over her

head, but when the women turned to discussing what to bake, she decided to volunteer. Staying in the kitchen, in company with other women, would be smart today.

"I make a really good apple-raisin cake." She suggested they think about picking huckleberries, too, currently ripe. "They're as good or better than blueberries, and they'd stretch our supplies."

Picking huckleberries would give her a reason to be well away from the lodge, too. She might be able to give herself a significant—no *serious*—head start. Wasn't that how Spencer had put it? She couldn't help remembering the rest of what he'd said, too.

If you ever see an opportunity—a good one—take it. Let me worry about myself. The ache in her chest told her it wouldn't be that easy.

"I'll ask Tim," Jennifer said briskly.

Leah only nodded. She wasn't sure she'd ever been truly timid a day in her life, and she could only hope all this deference didn't get to be a habit.

Finished with the dishes, she joined the other women in the baking, putting together a double recipe of her apple-raisin cake while they worked on blueberry pies.

After lunch Jennifer reported that Tim said they could maybe pick berries tomorrow, but not today.

Damn.

She assigned Leah to mop the floor in the main room. She was to do beneath the table by hand, Jennifer said firmly.

The scarred fir planks really needed a new finish. After this many years, the original varnish had been almost entirely worn away. Soap and water weren't really good for the wood, she couldn't help thinking, in one of those absurd moments. Because, gee, did it really matter if the floor rotted and collapsed? As things stood—no.

At least the task shouldn't leave her isolated. Helen had to clean the downstairs bathroom today, Lisa to sweep the front and back porches and clean the mudroom. Jennifer intended to reorganize the pantry and continue baking.

The benches pulled out, Leah was underneath the table on her hands and knees when she saw Del go into the kitchen and let the door swing shut behind him. On a sudden chill, she stopped scrubbing. From here, she couldn't hear voices in the kitchen. He'd probably gone out the back to check on Lisa, she realized. He might stay there for a few minutes talking to her. Helen, here in the lodge, wasn't that far away, but more sweet than a lioness at heart.

Leah made herself get back to work. Any minute Del would return as part of his appointed rounds. Anyway, the men were all too scared of Spencer to mess with him. She'd *seen* Joe back down. Still, she listened hard for any sound at all.

Like the sound of the lodge door opening. She froze. Del might have circled around. That would make sense—

Booted footsteps approached. From her low vantage point, Leah peered out. This wasn't Del, who wore the ubiquitous desert camo today with desert tan boots. This man had on black boots with heavy cleats and forest-green camouflage cargo pants.

Joe Osenbrock.

Staying as utterly still as a mouse that had seen a hawk's shadow nearing, she even held her breath. Did he see her beneath the table?

Who was she kidding? How could he miss her bucket filled with soapy water and probably her lower legs? In fact, he walked right to her.

"Alone at last," he gloated.

Go with ignorance. "Who's there?" She dropped the sponge in the bucket and turned to sit on her butt facing the threat. "Joe? Do you want a cup of coffee?"

"You know what I want."

Maybe she ought to hold to her timid—now terrified—persona, but she couldn't make herself. Still unable to see his face, she said, "Have you forgotten what Spencer said?"

"He's not going to mess with our team. What we're planning is more important than any piece of ass," he scoffed. "He told Higgs that himself." He crouched to look straight at her. "Don't kid yourself that he gives a damn about you."

"I don't." Scared as she was, Leah knew her chin jutted out at a defiant angle. "But I know he *does* care about his reputation. You'd be a fool to challenge him."

Seeing the fury on his face, she knew she'd just made a big mistake. *She'd* issued a challenge. To save face, now he almost had to rape her and face down Spencer. What she'd forgotten was that Spencer wasn't the only one to value his tough-as-nails reputation.

Lightning quick, Joe grabbed her ankles and wrenched her toward him. Leah screamed and grabbed for purchase, not finding anything. Her butt slid on the wood floor. No, there was the bucket. Even as he was still dragging her forward, she snatched it up and flung the water, followed by the bucket, too, in his face.

Joe bellowed and momentarily let her go. Maybe the soap stung his eyes. Leah seized the chance to scramble backward, desperate to come out the other side of the table within reach of the kitchen.

Water dripping from his hair and face, he ducked to grab her again. His head clunked against the edge of the table. By now he was yelling a string of invectives.

At that moment the swinging door slapped open and she heard the thud of running footsteps. Whimpering, Leah crawled out from the shelter of the heavy table right beside Del.

He didn't even look at her. His hand rested on the butt of his pistol, though. Beyond him, Jennifer hovered in the doorway, watching.

Joe snarled as he rose to his feet. "Get out of here."

Leah hardly dared take her eyes off Joe, but she turned her head anyway to see Del. What if he shrugged and walked back into the kitchen?

But his hard gaze stayed on Joe and he said, "No. She's Spencer's girl. You got no right."

"He had no right to snatch her away right out from under our noses."

Del's expression didn't change. "You could have done something then. You didn't."

Joe's eyes narrowed to mean slits. "You calling me a coward?" And—oh, God—his hand slid toward the butt of *his* gun.

"That's not what I said."

Preparing to drop to the floor at any sudden movement, Leah hoped Jennifer was smart enough to fade back into the kitchen. Couldn't they feel the tension?

As the two men held a staring contest, she prayed for Spencer to appear. He hadn't expected to be gone long, and it had already been at least four hours.

Joe said in a low growl, "Butt out of this, Schmidt. She's not your business."

"My job today is to watch out for the women. All I'm saying is, you need to take this up with Spencer, not sneak behind his back."

"You and who else will stop me?"

That should have sounded childish, but didn't. The threat of violence had a weight; it raised prickles on the back of her neck. These men wouldn't take a few swings at each other. They'd pull semiautomatic weapons and start shooting. Killing.

Over her.

Would either of them notice if she eased back until she could dart for the kitchen? And would that do any good if Del lost this confrontation?

A man's voice came from the kitchen. Then heavy footsteps. Two men walked in. Jennifer was no longer visible.

Shawn Wycoff, tall, lean and blond, was accompanied by another of the men who'd so far remained anonymous to Leah. He didn't say much around the table, and like too many of the others, was distinguished by a shaved head, a powerful build and full-sleeve tattoos.

When the men took up positions to each side of Del, Leah did edge backward.

The guy she didn't know was the one to say, "What's this about?"

"None of your goddamn business!" Joe snapped. "Get lost."

"He wants Leah," Del said, not taking his eyes off Joe. "I told him to take it up with Spencer, face-to-face, not stab him in the back."

"What's he done to you anyway?" Shawn asked.

"He's suddenly giving us orders? Where was he six months ago? Where'd he come from? Does anybody even *know*?" Joe asked.

No-name said with surprising calm, "I'm betting Colonel Higgs does, or he wouldn't be here. And the only orders he's given are during training. The guy can shoot like no one else I've ever seen, and I had two deployments. I hear while he served he was spec ops. You don't think you can learn from him?"

Joe made a disgusted noise. "He's so sold on himself, I wouldn't be surprised if he didn't make up that shit."

"You think the army would keep a guy who can make his shot from a thousand yards plus as a regular grunt?"

Joe let them know, obscenely, that none of that mattered. Spencer had overstepped himself when he claimed exclusive rights over the only decent-looking woman any of them had seen in six weeks or more.

"Del doesn't have to do without." He was trying for persuasive, which scared Leah enough to have her inching back again.

Should have gone sooner. Should have run for it.

"What say the three of us have a good time? I mean, come on. What's Spencer going to do? Take us all on?" He grinned. "I've seen you looking, Wycoff. You can't tell me you haven't." He tipped his chin at the other man. "You, too, Zeigler."

Zeigler shook his head. "Not me."

"Looking ain't the same thing as taking," Shawn Wycoff told him. His lip curled. "*I* can get women without raping them."

By goading such an unstable man and appearing to

enjoy doing so, Shawn might as well have lit the fuse on a stick of dynamite.

Joe's face turned ugly again with a snarl. "You saying I can't?"

"I'm not saying nothing, 'cept Del's right. Take it up with Wyatt. We're teammates. We gotta trust each other. That's the right thing to do."

Hear, hear! Except the idea of Joe Osenbrock "taking it up" with Spencer scared her. He hated Spencer and would kill him in a second, if he could.

Before, he hadn't had the guts to face off with him. After this standoff, with not one but three of the other men looking at him with doubt, he'd think he had no choice.

And, oh, dear God, did she hear a vehicle outside?

Following orders, Spencer drove around behind the lodge to the sturdy outbuilding that served as their armory. It was a natural. Constructed of logs, too, it appeared to have been added some years after the lodge and cabins had been built, which meant it was solid. Even the shake roof was in good shape. Mostly empty when they first opened it up, it had held only a few chainsaws, a heavy-duty weed whacker, assorted hand tools and an old Jeep with a custom-mounted snowplow. A quiet guy named Jason Shedd had given the Jeep a lube job and oil change, replaced a few belts and gotten the thing running. It was too small to be of much use, but Spencer figured you never knew. He'd been thinking a lot about that Jeep in recent days. The key hung on a string from a nail just inside the rusting steel garage-style door.

The trick was that a heavy hasp and padlock on the

door ensured it could only be opened by Higgs, a fact that pissed off some of the men. The ones who'd begun to question his leadership.

Spencer really wanted to get his hands on that key.

Now he backed the Suburban up to the outbuilding door, set the emergency brake and turned off the ignition.

"I'll look inside and see if anyone's there to help us unload," he said, careful to betray none of the edginess he felt.

"Do that." Higgs reached for the door handle.

Spencer crossed the twenty-five yards to the back door into the lodge with long strides. His nerves had been buzzing since they left this morning. Pretending he was unconcerned had taken everything he had. There wouldn't be any relief for him until he saw Leah unhurt, safe.

The unlocked door opened into a mudroom and then the kitchen. Lisa and Jennifer hovered just outside the entry into the pantry, their anxiety palpable.

His heart lurched. Ignoring them, he walked quietly to the swinging door that stood open.

Before he reached it, voices came to him.

"I'll wait." Joe Osenbrock. His voice turned vicious. "But sweetheart, I'll win. I know better than him how to treat a woman."

"Gee, that might be why you're so desperate," Leah said flippantly.

Spencer hoped no one else heard the slight tremor in her voice.

One part of his tension abated. She was still on her feet swinging, which meant she had to be all right.

The ugly epithet from Joe sent Spencer into another

state of being, one all too familiar. He felt...very little. Combat ready, he walked into the dining room just as something big crashed.

On the far side of the table, Joe must have just picked up and thrown one of the long benches. He stood above it with his teeth showing, breathing hard, face flushed with rage.

Only a few feet from Spencer, her back to him, Leah faced Joe...as did three men, all in battle stance, hands hovering over their guns.

Voice arctic, Spencer announced his presence. "Seems I missed some excitement."

Chapter 10

Leah and two of the three men spun to face him. Del Schmidt had the presence of mind to keep his attention on the armed idiot throwing a temper tantrum.

Both gladness and fear shone from Leah. He wanted her to fly into his arms, but at the same time he hoped she'd know better than to do that. They needed to maintain their cover—and he needed to keep his mind on what was coming.

The two men looked relieved at the sight of him. From the sweat and dirt coating them, it appeared Garrett Zeigler and Shawn Wycoff had just come from running the obstacle course.

Harder to tell with Joe. He was either sweat-soaked or had dunked his head under running water.

Spencer nodded at the two backing up Del. He didn't like owing any of this bunch, but this was different. "Thank you."

Garrett Zeigler's lip curled as he glanced over his shoulder. "He thinks he can take you," he said quietly enough not to be heard by Joe.

"He can try." Would he really have to kill Osenbrock? Yeah. Probably. "Higgs and I need help unloading."

Quick as a rattlesnake striking, Joe started to pull his weapon. In the blink of an eye, Spencer had his own in his hand. "I wouldn't mind blowing your head off, and you know I don't miss."

Joe's face went slack with momentary fear, but he blustered, "Hand to hand. Winner takes Leah." His eyes slid to Leah, who looked strong in spirit but physically fragile as she stood with head high and expression defiant.

Not seeing a way out, Spencer inclined his head, even as he held his Sig Sauer in a two-handed stance aimed at Joe Osenbrock's heart. "Tomorrow morning. In the meantime, put that gun down. You've shown us all you're not trustworthy." Seeing such hate in another man's eyes disturbed Spencer, even as he stayed cold inside.

When Joe didn't move, Spencer said, "Del?"

The other man walked around the table. "He's right, Joe. Give it to me. You can have it back later."

That burning stare turned briefly to Del. "I won't forget this."

"Let me have it."

Spencer took a step closer, making sure even Osenbrock couldn't miss his deadly intent.

With a jerky, furious motion, Joe yanked the handgun the rest of the way from the holster and slapped it on Del's outstretched hand. Then he wheeled around and stormed out of the lodge.

There was immediately relaxation in his wake, although Spencer didn't share it. Joe probably had half a dozen more weapons stockpiled in his cabin. Whether he'd go get one and commit cold-blooded murder in front of his fellow "soldiers" was another matter. This was all about ego, and if he really wanted respect, he had to make the fight seem aboveboard.

Spencer straightened and reholstered his own gun. "Higgs must be wondering where I am. Let's go unload," he said as if nothing had happened.

Leah stood ten feet away, her face parchment-pale, her eyes dilated. Her hands were clenched in small fists. He wanted to know everything that had happened, how it was that not only Del had stepped in, but the other two men, as well. But that had to wait. Right now appearances were everything.

"Don't you have a job to do?" he asked.

Some emotion flew across her face, too fast to read, which was just as well considering they weren't alone. She nodded, but also stole a look toward the front door.

"Del," Spencer said. "Can you stay?"

"That's the plan."

"I need to refill the bucket," she said tightly.

"Throwing it at him was smart," Del said unexpectedly, addressing Spencer rather than her. Still, he'd gained some respect for her, which might or might not be good.

So the bucket hadn't spilled because someone tripped over it. A pail full of soapy water explained Joe's dripping wet hair, and some of his temper, too.

Ignoring all the men, Leah circled around the table

and picked up the bucket, then trailed Spencer, Zeigler and Wycoff into the kitchen. As she went to the sink, the other two women stared at the men.

Walking out the back door and across the bare yard to the Suburban with Zeigler and Wycoff, Spencer asked, "How'd you two get mixed up in that?"

"Del sent Lisa to get help. We were, ah, heading up to the lodge to take a break."

Shawn grinned. "What he means is, the women did some baking this morning. Blueberry pie and an apple-raisin cake. Decided we needed seconds."

"I'll look forward to dessert tonight."

Higgs had the garage door lifted and the back of the Suburban open. "What took so long?" he grumbled.

"Osenbrock was up to the same crap," Spencer said as if unconcerned. "These guys and Schmidt told him he had to take it up with me."

Higgs's attention sharpened. "He attacked Leah?"

"Appears so. She fought back. Del came running. He sent Lisa to get these two."

The colonel flicked a glance at the other two men, then leveled a steady look at Spencer. "Can you handle him?"

"We agreed to hand to hand in the morning." He nodded at the packed rear of the SUV. "Let's get this done. Be careful. Some of the boxes are heavier than they look."

He wasn't sure what was in all the boxes, except the one crate he'd watched Higgs inspect. It held at least a dozen rifles. Markings on some of the boxes indicated they were the property of the US Government. A lot of those contained ammunition to replace what they'd used. Then there was the something mysterious that had had Higgs and his confederate talking quietly for quite a while.

Given half a chance, Spencer intended to find out what other weapon had just been handed to a bunch of alt-right nutjobs.

The men worked in silence, Higgs directing where he wanted each box put.

"Getting crowded in here," Wycoff remarked at one point.

Higgs frowned at the Jeep. "We can move it out of here if we have to."

Spencer liked the idea but didn't want to go on record saying so. Even if the key stayed on the nail inside the armory, he was confident he could hot-wire a vehicle as old as this one. The Jeep was a standard CJ-5, probably dating to the sixties or seventies.

Five minutes later Spencer turned with deliberate incaution and bumped into Zeigler, who bashed a hip into a sharp corner of the old Jeep. Cursing, he barely held on to the box he carried.

"Oh, hell," Spencer said. "I'm sorry."

"Let's get the damn thing out of there." Higgs took care of moving it himself, parking it to one side of the armory. "We can throw a tarp over it if it looks like rain."

"I wonder if you could sell it to some classic car buff?" Wycoff suggested.

Spencer laughed. "I doubt you could give it away. You know how common these were?"

"Yeah." Wycoff studied the rusting metal and tattered remnants of a canvas cover that had snapped on. "It's no beauty, I'll give you that."

They continued to work. Once the Suburban was

empty, Spencer moved it to its usual parking spot out front of the lodge and handed the keys to Higgs.

The two men were now alone.

"Osenbrock is becoming a problem," Higgs remarked.

"Becoming? He's an arrogant hothead."

The boss grunted. "I'd boot his ass out, except that would mean turning him loose. Resentment and a big mouth make for a dangerous mix."

"He's a fighter," Spencer said more mildly than he felt. "He believes in our goals."

Higgs's brows climbed. "You plan to leave him alive?"

"Depends how it goes."

"Whatever you have to do." Higgs nodded and walked away.

Spencer followed him only as far as the dining area, where Leah seemed to be finishing up. Sweaty and disheveled, she looked worse than the men who'd come to her rescue—but she was still on her feet, doing what she had to do.

She was also beautiful, even now. In the intervening days, the discoloration and swelling on her face had diminished significantly, making more obvious the delicacy of her features. The pale, strawberry blond hair was sleek enough to fall back in place whatever she put it through.

"Can I get some coffee?" he asked.

He especially liked the glare that should have incinerated him.

She grabbed the bucket and rose to her feet. "Anything else?"

He barely refrained from grinning. "How about a piece of that cake?"

Leah stomped into the kitchen.

It was Helen who delivered the cup of coffee and a generous square of a rich, dark cake. He could see the apples and raisins in it.

"Leah made this," Helen said softly.

"Did she?"

She backed away. "If you need anything else…"

"I'll be fine." He nodded, watching as she hurried away and out of sight. It was unlikely any of the women would go to prison, but he wondered what would happen to her without Dirk.

Shaking the worry off, he took a bite of the cake. The taste lit up all his synapses, as rich as it looked. Sweet, but with enough spice to offer complexity. Damn, Leah could cook, too.

She appeared ten minutes later, hesitating when she saw him but then advancing. "Do you want a refill?" She nodded at his cup.

"Sure. That's fabulous cake. Helen says you made it."

"My grandmother taught me. It's my go-to recipe when I have to contribute to potlucks."

He nodded and lowered his voice. "You're really all right?"

"Yes. He…was dragging me out from beneath the table when Del came running. He tried to talk Shawn and—"

At her hesitation, Spencer supplied the name. "Garrett."

"Garrett into having some fun with him. He suggested you wouldn't take on all three of them."

Enraged, Spencer ground his molars. "They didn't consider going for it?" If they had...

But she shook her head. "Joe said he'd seen Shawn looking. I had the feeling Shawn doesn't like him."

She was right. With very few exceptions, these were aggressive men, angry at the world. Small as the group was, it had broken into cliques, the alliances shifting.

Leah continued, "He sort of sneered and said *he* could get women without raping them. It was like he wanted Joe to blow."

"Joe's got friends here, but not those three." His voice still sounded guttural. If Joe had had Arne and Chris Binder and TJ Galt backing him, Leah would have been gang-raped. TJ wouldn't have let a marriage certificate stop him.

Slammed by how he'd have felt if he'd gotten back to find Leah huddled in a small, battered ball, forever damaged by that kind of assault, all the violence in his nature rose in outrage. That was a mistake none of them would have survived to regret.

"Are you all right?" Leah still hesitated several feet away.

"Yeah." It was all he could do to clear his throat. "Coffee?"

She took his cup, reappearing a minute later. As she carefully set it down, she asked, "Is anyone else here?"

"No, I think we're alone except for the women."

"Are you really going to have to fight him?"

"Yes."

"He wants to kill you. Did you see the way he looked at you?" She shivered.

"I saw." He reached out and squeezed her hand quickly before releasing it. "He can't take me down."

"You won't underestimate him?"

"No." Hearing the front door open followed by voices, he said, "You'd better get back to work."

Without another word, she fled. Thinking about his last glimpse of her face, Spencer had a bad feeling he'd failed to reassure her. And the truth was, he'd spent most of his time in the military belly down, with an eye to a scope and his finger resting gently on the trigger of a rifle. He'd wrestled and boxed, sure, but had never tried out any martial arts.

He didn't picture Joe Osenbrock embracing martial arts, either, though. They required discipline he lacked. He was a brute force kind of guy. Joe lost it when he got angry enough or things weren't going his way.

Spencer had to count on cold determination defeating blind fury.

Leah kept sneaking peeks down the table during dinner. Spencer acted as if nothing at all was wrong. He ignored Joe, but not so obviously that he was doing it as an insult. More as if… Joe just didn't impinge on his awareness at all.

Joe ate, but she doubted he knew what he was putting in his mouth. He barely took his burning stare from Spencer. Everyone else noticed, which made for awkward conversation and uncomfortable silences.

Shelley Galt had reappeared for the first time in days to help with dinner and join them at the table. Leah could see immediately that she hadn't been sick at all. She'd been beaten. She still moved stiffly, her left wrist was wrapped in an ACE bandage, and while the long-sleeve tee probably hid bruises, the foundation she'd plastered on her face wasn't thick enough to disguise the purple, yellow and black that enveloped her cheek, temple and part of her forehead, wrapping around an eye that wasn't yet quite all the way open.

Leah knew exactly how that felt. Just looking at the other woman made her shake with fury. Once she saw Spencer's gaze rest on Shelley's face. His expression never changed, but she knew what he thought behind the mask.

After dinner the group broke up more slowly than some times. As usual the women took turns refilling coffee cups or bringing second servings of one of the desserts. Helen was the first to be able to leave. Dirk took her hand and led her out the back door. That he didn't mind people seeing him touch Helen, or his tenderness toward her, said a lot about him. Too bad he was part of a group planning some kind of major attack meant to shake the foundations of Americans' faith in their government.

Shelley left alone. TJ had told her to go, she said. No kindness there. Twenty minutes later most of the rest departed en masse, leaving Leah by herself in the kitchen. She peeked out to see Spencer and Colonel Higgs sitting across from each other at the table, engaged in a conversation that even an outsider could see was intense. What were they talking about? The morning fight? Or the attack that was to be the climax of all this planning and training?

She sat on a stool in the kitchen and tried to think about something, anything, except Joe and Spencer slamming their fists into each other, twisting and tangling in combat. Would the other men surround them and cheer on their favorite, like middle-school boys excited by a fight? She shuddered, imagining the rise of bloodlust, and wondered if Joe's death—or Spencer's—would satisfy the audience.

She knew, *knew*, that Spencer would never concede, not with her life at stake. As terrified as she was of being left to Joe Osenbrock's mercy, that wouldn't be the worst part. How could she ever accept Spencer's death?

She couldn't. Wouldn't.

As a woman who cried when an animal hit by a car didn't make it onto the vet's operating table, she wasn't used to wanting to hurt anyone. But there was no doubt in her mind.

If Joe somehow won, she'd make him pay. No matter what it took.

They were barely inside the door of the cabin when Spencer groaned and snatched Leah into his arms. Leaning back against the closed door, he held her tightly, his cheek pressed to the top of her head. This had been one of the most hellish days he could remember.

He should have taken her and fled already, to hell with his job. Yeah, he'd had two breakthroughs today, but the price was too high. He'd been so cocky, too sure he could protect Leah. He still believed he'd come out the winner tomorrow...but what if he didn't? Or what if he won but was injured badly enough that he was unable to keep protecting her? Joe wasn't the only threat.

She burrowed against him. His resistance to making love with her had hit a low. He needed that closeness, that relief, and thought she did, too.

"Leah," he muttered.

She lifted her head from his shoulder, letting him see the tears in her eyes. "I don't want you to do this."

Desperately, he said, "Let's forget it all, just for a while. Can we do that?"

Even with her eyes shimmering wet, he'd swear she saw deep inside him. He made himself wait until she whispered, "Yes. Oh, yes, please."

He tried to start off gently. They'd never kissed before. His good intentions lasted maybe thirty seconds before one of his hands was on her ass, the other gripping her nape. His tongue was in her mouth, her arms locked around his neck, and she seemed to be trying to climb him. He ached to have her cradle his erection. Her taste, her softness, her acceptance and eagerness, her vulnerability and strength, combined to blast his good intentions to smithereens. He wanted to strip her, lift her up against the door and take her without any finesse. He actually started to turn her and gripped the hem of her T-shirt to strip her when he remembered that damn uncovered window.

He couldn't do it like this. A monumental shudder racked his body. The effort of persuading his fingers to release her shirt tore another groan from his chest. Wrenching his mouth from hers, he said rawly, "Bedroom."

Her green eyes were so dazed, he doubted she understood.

Too frantic for her to wait, he bent to slide an arm beneath her knees and swing her off the floor. Since he started kissing her again, he blundered more than walked across the small living room.

As he turned to fit her through the opening into the bedroom, some part of her body thudded into the door frame and she cried, "Ouch." The next second she pressed her lips back to his and the kiss became deep and hungry again.

Once he laid her on the bed and came down on top of her, they slid into the dip at the middle of the mattress. Spencer didn't care. All he could think about was getting her clothes off. As he tugged her shirt over her head and groped for the fastening for her bra, he wished he'd thought to turn on the light so he could see her. Much as he wanted that, he couldn't make himself leave her.

He had to rise to his knees to untie her athletic shoes and peel her jeans and panties down her legs. While he was there, he took care of his own clothes. He barely had the sanity to remove a condom from his wallet. She was trying to touch him but wouldn't have been able to see well enough to put the damn thing on. He felt clumsy, and realized the dark wasn't responsible. His hands were shaking.

Too much tumult, fierce need and the knowledge that they could fall any minute off the knife-edge that constituted their only safety, all combined to rob him of any patience. The incoherent, needy sounds she was making—moans, whimpers, he didn't know—told him she was as ready as he was.

Sliding inside her was one of the best feelings of his life. Tight, slick, she welcomed him by planting her feet on the mattress and pushing her hips up to meet every thrust. He set an urgent, hard pace that couldn't last. Her spasms, the way she cried out his name, pulled him with her. His throbbing release seemed to last forever. He collapsed, unable to find the immediate strength to roll off her slender body.

For all the joy and satisfaction he felt, Spencer hated

that she hadn't cried out his real name. That she didn't even know it. She'd just made love to a man playing a role, not him.

Whoever I am, came the bleak thought.

Chapter 11

Leah woke up to find herself alone in bed. She didn't hear a sound. Not the shower or a whistling teakettle or the creak of a floorboard. Where was Spencer?

They'd made love a second time, slower and more tenderly, his voice deep and almost velvety in the darkness, the Southern accent strong as he told her how beautiful she was, how soft. He called her strong, defiant, smart. He hadn't said how he felt about her, but that would have been expecting too much. Really, how could either of them know so quickly?

Just for a minute she pushed back at the sense of dread that would swallow her if she let it, and instead remembered the feel of Spencer's callused fingers, the raw hunger in his kisses, the way he filled her until she felt complete. She wished…she wished so much, but her chest suddenly felt as if a band squeezed, tightening until she couldn't draw a breath.

He wouldn't have left her behind when he went to meet with Joe, would he?

Horrified, she threw back the covers, struggled out of bed and only grabbed a dirty T-shirt of Spencer's to throw on before she rushed out of the bedroom.

Spencer sat on the futon, feet on the coffee table, appearing his usual composed self. He held a coffee cup in one hand and gazed at her in mild surprise.

She lurched to a stop, her heart hammering. "I thought…"

"I might be gone?" His voice was low and tender despite his impenetrable expression. "I wouldn't do that to you."

"What…what time is it?"

He glanced at the steel watch he wore. "We have twenty minutes."

"I didn't know you'd set a time."

"Higgs did. He wants us to get the fight out of the way before breakfast."

"Oh, God." Her sense of impending disaster wasn't alleviated. "I need to take a shower."

She should have done laundry yesterday at the lodge, she thought in that part of her mind still capable of mundane thoughts. Rooting through her suitcase, she found a pair of jeans that she'd only worn one day and a clean T-shirt. Her last pair of clean panties.

Right now she couldn't care less if she was filthy. Even the shower was only a way to put off facing what was coming.

Clutching the small pile of clothes, she went to the bathroom without looking again at Spencer.

What if…? But she couldn't let herself think that.

She stayed under the thin stream of water only long

enough to get clean before drying herself with the pitiful towel and hurrying to dress. She combed her wet hair, then looked down at herself. Her battle armor didn't seem adequate.

Taking a deep breath, she went back out, set on not letting Spencer see how scared she was. What he needed from her was trust and confidence. She should have felt both wholeheartedly, but the dread remained.

As soon as she appeared, his gaze landed on her. "I've been in fights before," he said calmly.

Some of her fears had to be leaking out, like too-bright light between the slats of blinds. "Don't hold back," she begged him. "He'll do anything to win."

He still looked unfazed. "Cheat, you mean?"

"Yes!"

"Let's go out on the porch."

He rose effortlessly to his feet. Bemused, she followed him. He closed the door behind them and leaned against the porch railing. Leah desperately wanted the chance to soak in the comfort of his strong arms around her, but they could be seen.

Not heard, though, she realized, at least not from a bug inside the cabin.

Confirming her guess, he spoke very quietly. "There's something you need to know. You're imagining that I always take the high road. I don't. I've long since lost count of the number of men I've killed. I told you I was military, but not that I was a sniper. I saw those dying men's faces." Gravel roughened his voice even as he kept it low. "Some of them will haunt me for the rest of my life, but I kept doing what I thought I had to do. If I have to kill Joe Osenbrock today, I won't hesitate. Do you understand?"

"Yes," she whispered. "Maybe I shouldn't be glad, but I am. It's not just for my sake that you need to win, you know."

The bones in his face seemed more prominent than she remembered. "I do know."

She nodded.

"We need to get going."

He touched the back of her hand lightly as they descended the steps. She studied him, bothered by that seemingly unbreakable calm. Today he wore black cargo pants and a gray T-shirt that showed his powerful pecs and biceps, as well as flexible black boots that would allow him to move fast. He wouldn't be able to kick or stomp the way Joe would, but speed was surely more important. At Spencer's belt, he wore his usual black leather holster holding a steel-gray and black handgun. The men here seemed to go armed all the time as a matter of course. Maybe as a law-enforcement officer, Spencer always did. Leah hoped not, that he could sometimes set that part of his nature aside.

The minute they started down the porch steps, she saw the crowd gathered in front of the lodge. Were they excited about the entertainment? Or were some worried about the outcome?

"If you get out of here and I don't," he said in that same low voice, "the attack's set for November 11, Veterans Day. The president is set to speak, although the location hasn't yet been identified. And they have the components to make a dirty bomb. Remember that."

She opened her mouth in an instinctive protest but closed it. Nodded. "Will you tell me your real name?"

He cut a glance at her sidelong. His hesitation was infinitesimal but real, replaced by a flicker of amusement. "Alex Barr. Alex, most of the time. But stick to Spencer."

"Thank you."

That was the last thing she had a chance to say. They'd reached the crowd, now re-forming into a circle. She followed in his wake until she was close enough to the front to be able to see.

Joe Osenbrock already waited in the center. Not patiently; he was pacing, rolling his shoulders, acting like Leah vaguely thought heavyweights did in the ring before the bell.

Spencer stopped to unclip his holster and hand it and the gun to Garrett Zeigler. Then he walked into the clear space within the ring of bodies and stopped, still seemingly relaxed. Despite appearances, he had to be poised to explode into action.

The mood was more subdued than she'd expected. Even low-voiced conversation stopped when the lodge door opened and Colonel Higgs appeared. He walked forward, took in the scene with one sweeping glance, then asked, "Are they both disarmed?"

"Yes." Del Schmidt held up one weapon. Zeigler raised Spencer's.

"Good. Let's not waste too much time with this." Higgs studied the two men in the ring, his thoughts hidden. Then he said, "Go."

It all happened so fast, Leah wasn't sure which man moved first, only that within seconds they were toe-to-toe, fists swinging. Grunts of exertion and pain rang out. Blood splattered.

Spencer swiped blood from his face with his forearm, then stepped back to let Joe charge past him. When their bodies collided again, they fell hard to the ground.

Spencer got a headlock on Joe, but only briefly. They rolled, pummeling each other, grappling for any advantage, punishing each other brutally with fists and holds that contorted their bodies in ways that had her whimpering.

They fought their way back to their feet.

A few men called out. Occasionally a warning, sometimes a "Good one!" But mostly they were silent, so intent on the battle in front of them, she could have plucked a gun from one of their holsters and started spraying bullets.

Except…she couldn't tear her eyes from the savage fight, either.

Twice she had to step back along with the entire side of the circle when the two men flung themselves in that direction. Mostly, she knew she was begging, or even praying.

Please, please, please.

After a strike against his neck, Joe roared with rage and seemed to redouble his attacks. Spencer countered them, once tripping Joe, who crashed to the ground, somersaulted and came back up.

Spencer spat out some blood and jeered at his opponent. "Getting tired?"

With another roar, Joe charged forward like a three-hundred-and-fifty pound linebacker ready to drop the quarterback. But Spencer was not only fast, he was as big a man if not quite so muscle-bound. A quick side step and an elbow to the gut sent Joe to the ground again. He seemed slower to get up, pausing with one knee still down, even his head slightly bent. Was he done?

Spencer came at him with a kick that sent Joe sprawling again, but he latched on to Spencer's leg and brought him down, too. And suddenly, something metal flashed.

"Gun!" somebody yelled, but it wasn't. It was a knife, and he slashed at Spencer. Blood didn't just spatter, it spurted.

Ready to leap forward herself, she saw Spencer grab Joe's wrist and wrench his arm back. Spencer's teeth showed in a snarl; Joe fought that powerful grip in silent agony.

A couple of the men did surge forward, but before they reached the two combatants, Spencer flipped Joe, slammed his hand on the ground to force him to release the knife, and slugged him in the face so hard Joe's head bounced.

The next second he'd gone limp.

Spencer rolled off him and lay on his back, his chest heaving, his clothes blood-soaked.

Above the tumult of other voices, she heard Higgs's. He'd descended into the crowd and now raised his voice. "Wyatt's the winner. Tim, Brian, haul that cheating scum up to one of the bedrooms." He jerked his head to indicate the lodge behind him. "Shawn, Rick, you're responsible for getting Spencer back to his cabin." Higgs looked around, spotting her. "You've had practice sewing up wounds. Make yourself useful."

Oh, God, oh, God. Her teeth wanted to chatter. Somehow, she managed to say, "Do you have a first-aid kit?"

"Townsend, you know where it is."

It took three men to lift Joe and carry him up the porch steps and into the lodge. Leah only peripherally saw them go, Joe's arms flopping. On her knees beside Spencer, she snapped, "I need something to stop the bleeding."

Spencer watched her, one eyelid at half-mast. The socket holding his other eye was grotesquely swollen, purple. His teeth were clenched, and she'd swear what skin she could see was gray beneath the tan. Or maybe it only looked gray as an accent to the shockingly vivid color of the blood.

She bent her head close to his. "You'll be all right. You won."

One side of his mouth lifted as if he was trying to smile but couldn't quite make it work.

Two bare-chested men thrust cotton T-shirts at her. Neither looked very clean, but they were the best she had. She wadded one and pressed it hard against Spencer's thigh, looked around until she saw Del Schmidt and said, "Can you hold this?"

He dropped to his knees and complied. She pulled up Spencer's shirt, used the second T-shirt in her hand to wipe at the blood until she saw a narrow slit over his rib cage, and pressed it down. Panic scratched at her. If there were more wounds, they'd have to wait, but what if one she hadn't found was fatal? The slit frightened her the most. That one was a stab instead of a slice. She hadn't seen it happen. What organs lay beneath?

Out of the corner of her eye she saw someone pick up the huge knife lying in the dirt. Blood dripped from the double-edged blade.

A man ran up carrying a metal box big enough to look as if it held fishing tackle. "Do you want it here?"

"Take it to the cabin," she decided. Three men prepared to lift him, Leah ordering Del to keep the pressure on his thigh while she did the same on his muscular torso.

They moved slowly, awkwardly, with five of them bumping into each other, but finally made it up the two steps onto the porch.

"Not locked," Spencer growled.

The man with an arm under his shoulders—Rick Metz, built like a boulder—fumbled for the knob with one hand and got the door open. Once inside, she said, "Can we pull out the futon?"

Del did it while she used her free hand to maintain pressure on Spencer's thigh, too. The mattress looked grungy enough she wished desperately for a clean sheet to lay over it, but hadn't seen one. Pain tightened Spencer's face until it was all bones and skin stretched taut between them. He groaned when they laid him down.

To her distant surprise, the men continued to follow her orders. One put on water to boil on the single working burner here, while another ran for the lodge to boil more. A third went for any clean bedding and towels he could find.

Spencer never looked away from her.

He couldn't die.

Through the pain, that was all Spencer could think. Leah needed him. *Don't give in. Don't lose consciousness.*

A couple of times she whispered, "Stay with me," and once he even managed a nod. He didn't know if she meant stay in the sense that he had to remain conscious, or that he couldn't abandon her by dying. Either way, he hung on. At least he was done with Joe, who was as good as a dead man.

The guys around him seemed to be doing their best for him. He wasn't even sure who *was* here. He'd have had to look away from Leah to be sure, and he couldn't do that.

He managed to tell her he had pills in his duffel. At least, he thought he'd told her.

Don't give in. God, that hurts. He wanted to curl up to protect his belly, sensing that wound was the most dangerous. If the knife had sliced into his guts, all the resolve in the world wouldn't save him. Half-digested food would be spilling into the abdominal cavity, introducing bacteria where it didn't belong.

But Leah looked focused and determined in a way he didn't remember seeing her before. She was fighting for him, and he could do his part.

Don't give in. Trust her.

He floated in a sea of pain as she worked. There had to be broken bones.

Paper ripped. Somehow, she'd come to have a wicked-looking pair of scissors in her hand and was cutting most of his clothes off him. Wet washcloths, hot enough to have him jerking involuntarily, ran over his legs.

"I'll need to stitch that one up," he heard her say to someone else.

All he felt was pressure on his thigh again.

Once, they rolled him. His back hurt like hell, but in a generalized way.

"Man, he's going to be one solid bruise," a familiar voice said. Del.

It went on like that. He hazily understood that they were searching his body for knife wounds.

"Think the blade hit a rib," Leah said. "If it went very deep…"

He lost the thread of what she was saying.

Eventually, something cold was sprayed on his thigh. Her face appeared above his. "This should numb you enough to help," she said.

Still gritting his teeth, he nodded.

He felt the needle pricking in and out of his flesh. Pricking, hell; stabbing. The spray hadn't numbed anything, but he fought to hold still.

Then on his torso, almost on his side. He couldn't stop a raw sound from escaping.

They produced ice and what he vaguely saw were bags of frozen vegetables to lay on his face and half a dozen other places on his body. The worst bruising? He didn't know, only that the cold burned.

Time passed. He wasn't always sure he *was* conscious. Leah was his anchor, distressing him when she moved out of his line of sight a few times. Dripping ice packs and frozen veggies were removed and replaced at least once.

Rick—yes, that was Rick Metz—was the first to leave and not reappear. Given his lack of emotional content, Rick was a strange one to tend him with care.

When Spencer was able to roll his head slightly, he saw Shawn Wycoff and Del Schmidt. They were more logical as nursemaids. He also became aware that when Leah asked for something, they jumped. Funny that Higgs had appointed her medical director early on. The first day? He didn't remember. Spencer hadn't guessed *he* would be the one to need whatever trauma-care expertise she possessed.

He had to get her to safety so that she could go to vet-

erinary school, the way she deserved. Since the slightest
move brought stabbing pains—yeah, that was a pun—
he couldn't figure out how he'd protect her, but he'd do
it. Somehow.

He surfaced to hear her thanking the two men,
sounding almost tearful. Del shrugged. "Let us know
what you need."

Say, *I need to go home. Help me get away.*

Of course she didn't. "I will."

The door closed quietly behind them. The mattress
shifted enough that he knew Leah had sat down beside
him. Her fingertips stroking his forehead was the first
good thing he'd felt.

No, he could wriggle his toes with no pain. In fact,
thanks to his boots, his feet seemed unscathed. That
was good news. If they had to walk out of here, that
was what they'd do, he decided.

"You with me?" she asked softly, her eyes so vividly
green he would have been happy never to look away.

"Yah," he mumbled.

Her smile lit the room like the sun coming out from
behind a cloud. She sobered faster than he liked.

"Thank heavens you didn't lose consciousness! Even
so, I'd give a lot to be able to send you for X-rays, or
even a CT scan. I think your left wrist might be broken, although I can't be sure. It's wrapped tight enough
to immobilize it."

He arrowed in on his wrist. Yeah, that felt like a
break. Ribs, too, he guessed, although those might be
only cracks or even just bruising.

He could hope.

"It's really lucky you had that oxycodone. Aspirin

wouldn't have helped much." She gave an exaggerated shudder.

He shared that gratitude. So he had told her. He hadn't quite realized what those pills he'd swallowed were.

"What will they do with Joe?" she asked, worry carving lines in her forehead. "Should I go volunteer to look at him?"

"No." That sounded almost normal. "Don't shink—" he tried harder "—*think* he'll survive."

"Why? Did you—" Comprehension changed her face. "You mean…"

He managed a tiny nod. Best not to say it out loud.

"Oh, dear God," Leah whispered.

He somehow lifted a hand enough to lay it on her arm. She looked down, then up to meet his eyes, and understood. *Careful.*

"Later I'll have Del and Shawn or somebody else move you to the bedroom. I know the futon must be horribly uncomfortable. But if we were going to ruin one or the other with blood, I decided it should be the futon."

He absolutely agreed. After last night, he'd developed fond feelings for that bed.

"*Could* somebody take you to an ER?"

She meant, would it be allowed. "No," he said. Steeled himself and added, "Okay."

That earned him a wrinkled nose. "You're a long way from *okay*. But I suppose you must have been injured during your years in the military."

Another slight inclination of his head, although even that set off fireworks. He had to close his eyes momentarily.

Yes, he'd been hospitalized several times. Strange

to think that he might have come closer to dying today than he had from bullet wounds or shrapnel from an IED. If that knife blade had plunged deeper, or struck higher or lower, it could easily have been curtains for him, given that the best medical care available was from a veterinary technician with access only to a basic first-aid kit. He'd been damned lucky, and he wouldn't waste that luck.

He really was done with undercover gigs. No hostage rescue for him, either. He'd transfer as soon as he could—once he'd taken down Colonel Higgs and his hatefully misguided army.

And Leah. If she wanted him, he'd do what he had to do to have her in his life, too. He could transfer to the Seattle office, or the office closest to wherever she would be attending grad school.

All good plans. Unfortunately, right this minute a soon-to-be-needed trip to the bathroom reared ahead like Kilimanjaro. Only positive was, he knew he was thinking more clearly.

These injuries would buy him a day or two off from a role that he hadn't been able to set down in months. That said, would Leah still be expected to cook and clean rather than care for him? That would leave her vulnerable…although he thought Higgs had been pissed off enough about Joe's behavior to lay down the law where she was concerned.

Maybe.

Spencer grunted. What he needed was to get back on his feet as quickly as possible. For starters, he wouldn't have a chance to pocket the key to start the Jeep unless he rejoined activities, even if only as a spectator.

A good place to start was with that short journey to

the bathroom. The hell he was going to piss in a jar and make Leah dump it out.

Despite the explosion of pain, he started to shift his body toward the edge of the futon amid her cries of, "What are you *doing*? Stop!"

Chapter 12

The stubborn man insisted she lay a sheet over the dirty, blood-stained futon mattress and bring him some pillows so he could spend the day out there. Leah would have argued more vehemently, except he was right that he could get up and down more easily from the futon than the sagging mattress in the bedroom that fought every attempt to escape it. She'd had to stick her head outside and ask the first person she saw—someone named Jack, she thought—to bring bedding and towels from the lodge. Actually, she said meekly, "Spencer wants some bedding for the futon, and, um, our towels are all bloody. I'm afraid to leave him yet. Do you think...?"

The guy complied.

Spencer refused to let her fetch help for him to go to the bathroom. Pain aged his face a decade or more as he pushed himself to his feet, leaning heavily on her. Two hours ago she'd never have considered that he could shuffle even this short distance on his own.

Needless to say, despite the fact that he was swaying in front of the toilet, he evicted her until he was done and flushed.

Around midday she did leave him alone long enough to walk to the lodge for food. She slipped in the back door, where all the women surrounded her and, whispering, demanded to know what had happened. Leah gave them the CliffsNotes version, then filled a bag with a few dishes, a saucepan and some silverware as well as sandwich makings, cans of soup and desserts. She didn't see a single one of the men as she hurried back to the cabin.

During her absence Spencer had gotten to a sitting position again on the edge of the futon. Stress on his face eased the minute he saw her.

"What took you so long?" he asked. With his lips grotesquely swollen, words were hard to make out, but Leah found she got the gist.

"I wasn't gone very long." She set down the two bags on the short stretch of counter next to the tiny sink. "Jennifer and everyone wanted to know about the fight. They were all ordered to stay in the kitchen and missed the whole thing."

"You get an update on Joe?" A note in his voice she didn't recognize had her turning to look at him.

"No. They served breakfast like usual, and when Lisa asked if she should take a plate up to Joe, Higgs snapped at her. Said he isn't in any shape to eat."

"He wouldn't be," Spencer agreed slowly.

Was he wondering if he *had* killed Joe? Or disturbed

by the possibility of his death, however it came about? Yes, she decided, that was it. She wondered if, instead of becoming numb and inured to tragedy after all the death he'd seen, Spencer still had the capacity to grieve. There'd been nothing about Joe Osenbrock she could sympathize with, and yet... Who knew what his childhood had been like? What had made him so violently inclined and insecure enough to need so desperately to win?

And if Spencer's suspicion turned out to be true, she really hated the idea that one of those men she'd gotten to know was willing to steal upstairs in the lodge—perhaps to the very room where she'd been held captive—to break Joe's neck or slit his throat or... Leah didn't even want to think.

It bothered her even more to picture one of the men who'd protected her or helped Spencer today as the one willing to commit cold-blooded murder. Del? Shawn or Garrett? Chilled, Leah thought, *surely not Dirk Ritchie.* And yet...all of them intended to commit mass murder in the near future. Why balk at killing a single man?

"Will you eat something? I thought you might be able to drink soup from a cup."

"Not hungry."

She turned in alarm. What if the knife had reached his intestines or...maybe his liver or kidney? The pain relievers could have masked the effect that was only now catching up with him.

She evaluated him, deciding that his color was much better than it had been when they first carried him to the cabin. His eyes—well, eye—looked clear. If she made him open his mouth so she could look at his gums the way she would an injured dog's, would they be a healthy color or worrisomely pale?

"Will you try?"

He grunted and very carefully rested against the extra pillows Jack had included in the pile he brought from the lodge earlier. Spencer lifted each leg individually, using his good hand to guide it into place so he could stretch out. Only then did he say, "Yah."

She warmed cream of tomato, thinking it would go down easily and that milk would be good for him. When she took him a mugful and sat beside him to help prop him up, he did slowly drink it all.

Relieved, she had a bowlful herself.

She checked his watch, sitting on the old coffee table that had been pushed aside. "It's almost time for another painkiller. You won't try to be a tough guy and do without, will you?"

On a face that had suffered that much damage, it was hard to be sure, but she *thought* his expression was sardonic.

"No. Not tough."

When she gave him the pill half an hour later, he swallowed it, and after a period of staring broodingly up at the wood-paneled ceiling, dozed off. Leah tried to read but couldn't concentrate. Fictional adventures—or the very real ones during World War II—couldn't keep her attention when her current situation was so perilous.

Spencer was fighting his infirmities with a willpower that awed her. If the damage had been limited to the punches and bruising, however massive, she thought he'd be up and around in only another day or two. As it was, he'd lost a lot of blood, and she couldn't help fearing what harm that knife blade thrust between ribs might have done.

Had Spencer been ready for them to attempt an escape? He'd obviously learned a lot of what he'd been sent to find out. Now...how could they get away?

Was it possible for someone to get to any of the car keys?

Helen was the only one of the women Leah could imagine being willing to try to help her, but she wouldn't betray Dirk by helping Leah steal his truck, even if that was possible.

She and Spencer couldn't possibly set out on foot. Certainly not for days.

Her worries went round and round, but even when he was awake, she didn't vocalize them. Didn't need to. He was surely running the same scenarios and coming up with the same dead ends.

We should be okay for a few days, she told herself, but didn't quite believe her own assurance.

Spencer had a hell of a time sleeping. No position was comfortable. Once Leah dropped off, she couldn't prevent herself from rolling into his aching body, or her arm would flop across his torso, and it was all he could do to stifle a bellow. Her head on his shoulder awakened sharp pain.

He didn't think he'd ever been battered from head to...not toe, calves before.

Come morning Spencer woke feeling as if he'd just regained consciousness after being run over by a semi-truck with lots of huge tires. He tried not to move a muscle. Even breathing hurt. When he assessed his body, he found several places that felt like burning coals against the more generalized pain. Wrist, left cheekbone, the site of the stab wound, a searing strip down his thigh and his rib cage on the left.

All those could be managed, he convinced himself, and he knew from other times he'd taken a beating that the day after was the worst. Then the body would start healing itself.

Okay. One more day before he seriously considered an escape plan.

Leah stirred beside him and he had to grit his teeth. "Are you awake?" she whispered.

"Yah." His mouth was still swollen, making it difficult to shape words. But he got out the two that were most important. "Pain pills."

"What?"

He had to repeat himself before she said, "Oh, no! I should have woken you up earlier to take those. I'll get them right now."

She had to separate herself from him, the mattress rocking as she clambered out of bed. Teeth clenched, he held back the groans.

She hurried back. Sitting up enough to swallow the pills was agonizing. He needed the bathroom, but his bladder had to wait.

He caught glimpses as she got dressed, but as much as he normally enjoyed being tantalized by the fleeting sight of her curves, he didn't dare lift or even roll his head.

Wait.

It was a full half hour before the rigidity in his body eased enough, he was able to get up, shuffle to the bathroom and then lie down on the futon. As uncomfortable as the thing was, he needed to be out here where he could keep an eye on Leah and any possible entrances. He was able to half sit against the pile of pillows, so if something happened he could easily reach for his handgun.

Leah poached eggs for him and poured him a glass of orange juice. He was swallowing it when there was a polite knock on the door.

He called, "Who is it?" before Leah could reach the door.

"Del."

Spencer nodded at her and she let Del and Dirk in.

Del's gaze flicked to the gun then back to Spencer. "I'd say you look better, except..."

Spencer might have grimaced if that wouldn't have hurt. "Colorful?" he got out.

"Pretty as a rainbow," the other man confirmed. "You on your feet yet?"

"Sure." Spencer gave what was probably a death's head grin. "Hurt like hell today, though."

"Yeah, ain't that the way."

Dirk looked at Leah. "Anything you need?"

She succeeded in looking shy and even submissive. "I think we're okay. I went over to the lodge yesterday for some food and dishes. You know."

"Helen said you'd been by."

Spencer couldn't help asking. "Joe?"

Del answered, voice expressionless. "Died during the night."

Leah pressed her fingers to her lips to stifle a gasp. Both men glanced at her before returning their gazes to him. Dirk wasn't hiding his perturbation as well as Del was. He didn't like knowing Higgs had ordered—or even committed—the murder.

"Whatever I said about killing him, I didn't mean him to die," Spencer managed to get out.

Del obviously made out what he'd said because he nodded. "Figured. Ah…the colonel says he'll stop by later."

"Good. It'll be tomorrow before I can walk as far as the lodge." And, damn, he wished that wasn't true.

Leah saw the two men out, closed the door and waited through the thud of them descending the few steps before she turned around, distress on her face. "You were right."

"About Joe?" He was careful to sound…indifferent. "He wasn't in good shape when they hauled him away yesterday."

"Neither were you," she said tartly.

He let himself smile, although it couldn't look good. "I had the services of the only medic on site."

She opened her mouth, no doubt to remind him that she'd volunteered to look at Joe, too, but was again smart enough to let that remain unsaid.

"You were restless last night. Why don't you try to get some sleep?" she suggested.

He might do that. She'd wake him up soon enough when Higgs came calling. "You'll be here?"

"Won't go anywhere." She sketched a cross over her heart.

That made his misshapen mouth twitch.

He drifted in and out of sleep for much of the afternoon, helped along by the pain meds. Leah made sure he ate a little for lunch, and did wake him up midafternoon when Higgs came knocking.

He didn't have a lot to say, probably thanks to Leah's

presence. "Shame about Joe," he remarked, his tone holding not a smidgen of regret.

Spencer met his eyes. "Sure is."

"We picked out a place to bury him. Can't let authorities get involved."

No shit. Couldn't let the body stay in the lodge long enough to start decomposing, either, Spencer reflected.

He stiffened when Higgs looked at Leah. "We're missing you in the kitchen. I suppose Spencer needs you today, but he should be on the mend by tomorrow. I'm hoping you'll make that cake again."

Her eyes glittered with dislike. Her acting had some limitations, it appeared. But she said, "I'll be glad to make it again."

Spencer spoke up. "I liked it, too."

To Higgs, she said, "Did Jennifer talk to you about picking huckleberries? We could make some great cobblers and pies with them, and stretch supplies, too."

He looked surprised. "No. I noticed some ripe berries. Wasn't sure whether they were edible."

"They're delicious. The mainstay for birds and bears and probably some other animals."

"I'll set it up," he said, glanced at Spencer and added, "Hope there's a big improvement by tomorrow."

Was that an order? Irritated, Spencer didn't show how he felt. "You and me both. I'm not built to sit on the sidelines."

A monster cloaked in an average body and mild manner, Colonel Higgs left. Spencer ground his teeth a few times to keep from verbally venting his anger.

Leah didn't like it, but he started doing some stretches and getting up to walk for a few minutes every half hour or so. They could not afford for him to stay down.

* * *

The next morning they took the short walk to the lodge slowly. Leah stayed close to him, but Spencer didn't reach for her. His face was so blank, she knew he was intent on hiding how much pain he was still in. Somehow, he walked evenly, betraying no need to favor one side or the other. He had allowed her to rewrap his wrist, and of course his face was at its worst: still swollen and vividly colored. The black eye was barely slitted, his mouth distorted.

Something like halfway, he said out of the blue, "Know how to hot-wire a car?"

"Hot-wire...?" She sounded startled. "Unfortunately, no. To tell you the truth, I'm completely ignorant where cars are concerned. Beyond how to start and drive them, of course."

He grunted.

"What are you thinking?"

"The Jeep." He'd mentioned it. "Want to get my hands on the key, but if I can't..." He frowned. "I can hot-wire it myself. Old vehicles like that are easy. Plus, the Jeep is back behind the lodge. We'd have a chance of getting a real head-start. I was thinking just in case."

Just in case he was dead or captive and she had to run by herself. Sick to her stomach, she said, "The Jeep is out if I'm on my own."

He nodded, almost matter-of-factly. "We'll make sure it doesn't come to that."

Oh, good. She was completely reassured. She didn't have a chance to comment, though, because Arne Larson emerged from his cabin and fell into step with them.

"Good fight," he said admiringly.

So much for what had appeared to be a friendship

with Joe. This was a guy who wouldn't have felt at all squeamish watching one gladiator troop mop up the other in the Colosseum. Spencer put on a front of being unemotional about what he'd had to do in the army and now, with the FBI, but she didn't believe in it. He still had a human reaction to events and people. He must; she couldn't be falling for him if he didn't. He wouldn't be so ready to sacrifice himself for her.

As for Arne...she'd swear she saw a trace of envy and dislike in his eyes.

Spencer didn't comment, probably saving his energy for mounting the lodge steps.

He felt on edge all day, starting with finding out that Leah had been sent with two of the other women—Shelley and Lisa—to pick huckleberries.

"Galt will make sure no bears get 'em," Higgs told him, smirking.

"What's he going to do if a bear charges them?" Spencer asked.

"Shoot it, what else? What are you worrying about? Black bears are supposed to be afraid of people."

"Not all. And they're big enough to be dangerous, you know. Bullets from a handgun wouldn't even slow one down. And then there are the grizzlies. No matter what, you wouldn't want to get between any bear and her cub."

"Grizzlies? What are you talking about?"

Spencer looked at this idiot. "Grizzlies were reintroduced to the north Cascade Mountains years ago. They're around. I've seen plenty of pictures of them browsing through thickets of berries."

Not sure his slurred speech had gotten through, he

was satisfied to see Higgs alarmed and studying the tree line covertly. Spencer instead looked around at the empty range. "I thought the others would be here."

"I had them stop to pick up the new rifles and ammunition."

He'd have to find a way to involve himself in returning the weaponry to the armory at lunchtime.

"You're pulling my leg, aren't you?" Higgs said suddenly.

"Pulling your leg?" Ah. "Nope. We'd have seen any bears around if we'd been careless enough to leave out food."

Colonel Higgs scowled at him. "Why didn't you say something?"

Spencer pulled off surprised. He hoped, given the state of his face. "You'd already chosen this site. I assumed you'd done your research." He shrugged. "I've heard guys talking about bears. Anyone from the northwest would know."

"You're not from around here."

"No, but I've climbed mountains here and in Alaska." He let the silence draw out a little before adding, "You're right that bears are mostly shy. If you stumble on 'em, they can be a problem, but we make enough racket to warn them off."

But the women picking berries wouldn't be, unless they maintained a conversation, something that was unlikely with TJ Galt standing over them with his sneer and his Beretta M9A3 semiautomatic, a shade of brown that went with his favorite desert camo T-shirts and cargo pants. Spencer found his sartorial taste especially ironic since TJ was one of the few men here who had never served in the military.

"You up to trying out the new rifle?" Higgs asked. "I'd like your take on it."

"Tomorrow," Spencer said. "I'm one solid bruise right now. Getting up and down is a chore, and any recoil wouldn't help me heal."

Higgs accepted his answer, which made Spencer grateful that some of his injuries were so visible.

He did take one of the rifles that were supposedly being tried out by army rangers. The balance was okay. The optics were as good as anything he'd used before, but not an improvement. He only said, "Interesting," staying noncommittal as he handed it back to Ken Vogel. Then he glanced around.

"Where's Fuller?" He frowned, realizing a couple of other men were missing, too.

"More supplies. Fuller took his wife along with Jones."

Damn it. What did they need so soon after the last shopping expedition? Only food? This group did eat like hungry locusts. Still... Spencer tried to remember what day he, Lisa and Del had gone down to Bellingham. They'd seriously stocked up. Wednesday, he decided after counting back. Only five days ago.

Mine is not to reason why, he thought flippantly, before remembering the rest of the quote. *Mine is but to do and die.*

That seemed to sum up his current situation all too neatly.

Chapter 13

After giving the other women instructions on how to tell which berries were ripe, Leah kept a sharp eye out for bears while they picked. For what good advanced warning would do. Either a black or grizzly bear could outrun any human over a short distance, should it feel inclined.

She ignored TJ, even when he wandered by her.

Otherwise, as she plucked berries and dropped them into a plastic bowl, she pondered the others, starting with him and Shelley.

If he wasn't such an unpleasant man, TJ would have been attractive: tall, broad-shouldered, fit. He walked like an athlete, had medium brown hair and hazel eyes. His nose had clearly been broken at some point, which didn't detract from a handsome face…except she couldn't help thinking he'd probably deserved to be slugged. She was ashamed to find she actually hoped that was what had happened, rather than a collision on a soccer field or a baseball pitch delivered too high.

She had only enough abstract knowledge about the dynamics in abusive relationships to understand why Shelley stayed with him. Real understanding eluded her. The dullness in that poor woman's eyes, her body language, the way she cringed whenever TJ came close... Leah would be willing to bet Shelley had grown up abused as a child, too, or at least watching her mother being hit by her father, or even by a succession of men. If somehow she escaped TJ, the odds were good she'd find another abusive man.

Jennifer was deferential around Tim, but not scared in the same way. Helen lit up when she saw Dirk. Lisa Dempsey... Leah was less sure about her. She wouldn't think of challenging Del or any man, but Leah had heard Lisa talking comfortably to him a few times, and his low voice as he actually talked to her, too.

It felt weird to imagine them all under arrest, diminished by convict uniforms and handcuffs, the women seeing their men only through glass if they stuck by them at all.

Shelley would, Leah knew, and Helen, too. The others...she was less sure.

How on earth had all these men gotten sucked into an objective so horrifying? She wanted to be able to hate them all, but discovered it wasn't that simple. Colonel Ed Higgs, she could hate. *He'd* dreamed up this evil, a betrayal of the nation that he had supposedly served. *He'd* recruited all these guys, who were fearful of a changing America but not necessarily fanatical until then. *He* could coolly and with a secret smile say, *Shame about Joe*, when he had ordered him to be executed.

Rick Metz…lacked personality. Did he need to be told what to believe? Maybe he'd been at loose ends until Colonel Higgs gave him a clear objective and whatever nonsense justifications he used.

She sifted through the names of the men she knew best, finding it harder than it should be to label them evil, or even bad. Del Schmidt pretty much ignored her, and Lisa sometimes shrank from him. Beyond that, he mostly seemed decent. He'd been courageous defending her. Same for Garrett Zeigler and Shawn Wycoff.

Except…she wondered if any of the three had been thinking about *her*. Maybe all they'd been doing was currying favor with Spencer while Shawn at least could enjoy poking a stick at Joe.

Dirk Ritchie seemed downright nice.

Arne Larson wasn't nice; Leah remembered him slamming her against the wall and groping her while leering. And she hadn't forgotten how brutally TJ Galt had tackled her when she tried to escape, slugging her before hauling her back to face Higgs, their unlikely alpha wolf, without a semblance of gentleness.

Gee, could that be why she hoped someone had, once upon a time, slugged *him* hard enough to permanently dent his nose?

There were others she definitely didn't like, and a whole bunch who treated the women as if they were barely useful. Did they really feel that way? Or were they just blending in, the way school children were sometimes cruel because they didn't have the courage to stand up and say no?

Spencer must know them all a whole lot better than

she did. Did he regret what would happen to some of these men? Or had he become inured from previous undercover investigations? Nobody was all bad or all good; she did believe that. Even though Spencer must use people he was investigating to achieve his objectives, he'd have to stay focused on the crime they'd been willing to commit—or *were* willing to commit, in this case.

"Leah!" A heavy hand gripped her shoulder and spun her around.

Wide-eyed, righting her bowl before the berries spilled, she realized it was TJ.

"What were you doing, spacing out?"

She knew what she had to do. Bow her head, hope her hair fell forward to partly veil her expression and grovel. "I'm sorry," she mumbled. "I... I was worrying about bears."

The other women stole surreptitious glances at their surroundings.

"Their bowls are full. Yours is, too," he said impatiently. "Time to get back. This is a waste of my time."

Except she knew perfectly well that all he'd do once they got back was lean against the wall in the kitchen and watch them with both contempt and suspicion.

She bobbed her head and hurried toward the lodge, Lisa and Shelley keeping pace with her, TJ silently following. So much for using a berry-picking expedition to make a run for it. That scheme had been downright delusional.

From partway down the table during dinner, a low voice carried to Spencer.

"...get down where I can have internet access..."

He didn't turn his head, making himself depend on peripheral vision. For once Higgs hadn't taken a seat near him. Instead, he'd grabbed a place beside Tim Fuller, and they'd had their heads together ever since. Damn. Had Fuller and the others gone to Bellingham at all?

"Don't like losing you for two days…" Higgs's voice got drowned out. Surfaced again. "…think it's important enough."

Fuller's fervor made the hair rise on the back of Spencer's neck. Probably whatever nugget of information he so eagerly sought had nothing to do with Spencer or Leah—but there was a lesser chance that it did.

Higgs seemed unconcerned, though. Even talking quietly, his enthusiasm could be heard. "…more like the SAKO TRG 42…big jump forward from the…"

Spencer couldn't hear the rest, but didn't need to. The SAKO TRG 42 was a Finnish rifle, much admired among the sniper community. He knew guys who'd sworn by it. Except for the unusual stock design, which did indeed remind him of the SAKO, he couldn't say anything special had jumped out at him about this latest weapon sent to army spec ops for experimentation. Arms makers did that often. Most of those rifles didn't prove themselves any better than what snipers were currently using or regular infantry carried.

When Higgs called down the table, "You handled that baby, Spencer. Tell Fuller what you thought."

Spencer dredged up a few admiring comments that got all the men excited, even though most of them lacked the skills to take advantage of a cutting-edge weapon.

What worried him more was the disappearance this

afternoon of two of the men along with Higgs. Spencer had seen them coming out of the makeshift armory, expressions satisfied. He knew from background checks that Ken Vogel had spent a decade on a police bomb squad, while Steve Baldwin had been expelled from Stanford's physics program for reasons no one had wanted to talk about. Another Ph.D candidate had hinted that he'd been caught walking out with materials too dangerous to let out of the secure labs.

Spencer knew how most of these men had hooked up with Higgs: the internet. As fast as one fringe site that urged violence and revolution was shut down, another popped up. Like recognized like. He'd also done enough research to know that quite a few members of the group had been at a crossroads in their lives when they saw an opportunity that gave them a sense of purpose.

Baldwin was one example. No other grad program would take him. He must already have been working out what he could do with his knowledge, education and possibly some stashed-away dangerous material. Vogel had just gone through a divorce during which his wife claimed he abused her and the children. His visitation with those kids was to be supervised. He'd have seen that as an unforgivable insult; not only an attempt to humiliate him but also to steal *his* children.

Higgs, of course, had been forced out of the military for his views. Likewise, Arne Larson, given a dishonorable discharge that would limit his job opportunities.

And so it went. TJ Galt had had an unapologetic, vile presence on alt-right websites for several years.

Spencer had to make guesses about a few of them. Leaving the military to find themselves qualified only for poorly paid, low-end jobs, maybe. Don Durand's wife had left him, too. Dirk Ritchie's father had disowned his "embarrassment" of a son.

Yeah, most of these guys had been desperate to latch on to something that would salvage their self-esteem, make them feel important. Not hard to understand.

They wouldn't like prison, he thought grimly.

Even if he was knocked out of the equation, the investigation had been going on long enough, and these men, the pawns, would go down. It would be a shame to see them taking the fall for the scum financing Higgs's great dream, or stealing munitions from the United States.

Dinner was ending, people drifting away as the women cleared the table. Spencer took his time finishing a sizeable piece of Leah's cake and his third cup of coffee. When Higgs, bringing his own coffee cup, slid down the bench to join him, Spencer said, "Did you see Durand today at the target range? He's showing a real knack." Which was, unfortunately, true. "I may try him out at two hundred yards tomorrow. Get him working on positional shooting. It's never safe to assume you can settle in prone and not have to move. Plus bullet trajectory, zeroing in and understanding his range finder." He paused. "Is there any reason to focus on night observation devices?"

"Shouldn't think so." Higgs mulled that over. "If we have time, it probably wouldn't hurt."

Apparently, the plans were still in flux. Or else Higgs knew his small army might find themselves pinned down into the night.

Spencer nodded.

Looking frustrated, Higgs asked, "Is Durand the only one with sniper potential?"

Spencer waggled a hand. "Jason Shedd is getting there. He wasn't a hunter and didn't have comparable experience to the others with a rifle coming in, but he does have patience, an understanding of things like bullet trajectory, and a soft touch. He just had further to go."

"Given his experience as a mechanic, some of that makes sense."

"You don't mind me cutting the two of them out of the herd for more intensive training?"

"No, I'm lucky to have you. Originally, I thought I had two other former snipers on board, but one of them…" He shook his head. "Art Scholler. He was too glib. I got a bad feeling."

"You think he wanted in undercover?"

"Yeah."

Art Scholler *was* FBI, although of course that wasn't his real name. Spencer had been brought in when Art got cut off cold.

"The other guy?"

"Didn't think he'd take orders. The guy had serious issues."

Spencer grunted. "After enough deployments, a lot of men bring home a cargo plane full of issues."

The colonel grimaced. "True enough. The anger is useful. The rest of it gets in the way."

From a man who'd been a member of the "Chair Force," Higgs's know-it-all attitude rubbed Spencer the wrong way. He knew plenty of airmen who'd been in war zones, but Higgs didn't impress him as one who'd gotten his hands, let alone his boots, dirty. As usual, he stayed agreeable and emphasized how invested he was as they discussed problems concerning a couple of other men on the team, including TJ Galt.

"He makes me think of a pit bull trained for fighting. Keeping him on a leash takes some effort," Higgs observed.

The guy did have a gift for reading people, which wasn't uncommon in predators. Talk about useful skills. In this case… Galt made no effort to hide his anger. If he had PTSD, it likely dated to his childhood. Spencer hadn't uncovered any adult trauma that would explain it.

They parted amicably, which didn't entirely settle the uneasiness Spencer felt, awakened by the half heard conversation. All he could do was pack it away with all his other worries. The weight of them, he thought, was like the kind of hundred-pound pack he'd once thought nothing of hefting. The cargo plane…well, he had other issues, too.

The next day passed in what Leah thought of as deceptive peace. Tim Fuller took off on some errand of his own, which surprised her. This was the first time since she'd been here that any of the men had left alone. Had he been sent to make phone calls for Higgs? Or might he have something personal he had to take care of? She had the uncharitable thought that he could have a meeting with his parole officer.

Along with the other women, she baked, cooked, cleaned and waited on the men. Her real life had come to be out of focus enough to seem hazy. She told herself she was better off that way. She was surprised when she counted back to realize she'd been here nine days. It seemed longer. Well, she couldn't afford to dwell on resentment or have an outbreak of rebellion.

Spencer couldn't afford for her to blow it, either. She suspected he was hurting a lot more than he let on, especially once he joined the other men. His eyes met hers briefly before a large group left for the shooting range. She read reassurance in that instant, but who knew?

In a few minutes the quiet would be shattered by the nonstop barrage. Were these guys really getting a lot more accurate, or were they just wasting ammunition and scaring wildlife for a mile or so around? It spoke to the isolation of the resort that nobody at all had heard the gunfire and reported it to the county sheriff's department or a ranger.

At lunchtime the men inhaled cheeseburgers, baked beans and apple pie *à la mode*. During the afternoon they seemed to break up into smaller groups for—who knew?—hand-to-hand combat training, lessons on stealth?

Or were some of them building a bomb?

That made her shiver.

Dinner was Jennifer's lasagna, loaves and loaves of garlic bread, and a grated carrot and raisin salad Leah made. It was sweet and substantial enough to appeal to men who wouldn't touch a green salad or plain broccoli, but still mostly qualified as a vegetable.

As if she cared about their nutritional intake. But everything she could do to blend in, to make herself valued, was good.

She was first setting out serving bowls when Tim Fuller walked in. Higgs didn't notice at first; Tim ended up sitting at the far end close to the women. The colonel glanced that way but didn't comment.

In her intense dislike, Leah thought, too bad the mythical parole officer hadn't found cause to lock up

Tim and throw away the key. She must have smiled, because she discovered he was looking at her with an ugly expression. He and TJ Galt were two of a kind. With Joe Osenbrock, they'd made a vicious triumvirate.

With dinner over, Spencer stayed at the table with his usual refill of coffee, tonight talking to two men she hadn't had much to do with. Jason something and… She couldn't remember the other man's name at all.

The swelling in Spencer's face was going down, she noted, but the bruises had turned a multitude of colors. As she poured coffee from the carafe into Jason's cup, Spencer was saying something about wind, his speech much clearer than it had been even that morning.

The three of them weren't alone; a bunch of the men lingered, happy to hang out with friends, she gathered. During her last trip around the table to refill coffee cups, she shivered at the way several of the men watched her. She wasn't *afraid* of them, exactly—certainly not with Spencer present—but she could tell what they were thinking, and it gave her the creeps.

If there was another demand for more coffee, one of the other women could handle it. Clearly, Spencer wouldn't be ready to go for a while yet, so once she put leftovers away in the commercial refrigerator, she borrowed a sweatshirt hanging on a hook and slipped outside. She'd stay close to the door so she could hear Spencer calling for her. She knew eventually someone would notice she was out here. Sometimes, the other women took breaks like this, only to be chased inside when one of the men came to check on them.

The crisp evening air felt good, and when she tipped her head back, she saw the first stars appearing against a deep purple sky.

It had to be a lot later than usual, to be already getting dark. Fine by her; her new domestic tasks didn't exhaust her, but she'd barely sat down today except for perching on the bench to gobble each meal. Besides…she'd seen a glint in Spencer's eyes when his gaze strayed her way while she was wiping down the table. If he was feeling better enough…

Uncle Edward had built a couple of crude benches back here, wide boards laid over cut-off tree stumps. She chose one and sat, knowing she was almost hidden in the shadow of a cedar that would soon have to be cut down if the lodge was to survive. The roots probably already burrowed beneath the foundation.

Male voices drifted to her, abruptly becoming louder. Leah stiffened, ready to hustle back in the kitchen door if they came any closer.

One of them was Ed Higgs's, she realized.

"You're *sure*?" It was a demand; he didn't want to believe whatever he'd been told.

"Positive. It took some serious searching, but I found a picture. He was coming out of a courthouse, wearing the typical FBI getup."

She quit breathing. *Oh no, oh no.*

Tim Fuller was ebullient, really glad to be able to bring down a man he'd deeply resented. "You know," he continued, "black suit, white shirt, shiny black wingtips, blue tie. He was identified as Special Agent Alex Barr. Chicago office then. Now, I don't know."

"God damn." Anger threaded Higgs's weariness. "I can't believe it."

"Believe it," Tim said. "I printed the picture. Left it in my cabin."

Leah rose to her feet and began feeling her way toward the two steps up to the kitchen door. She stopped just short. No—the minute she opened it, light would spill out. Slip all the way around the lodge, she decided. Spencer might have only minutes.

The last few words she heard before going around the corner of the old log building were "no choice."

Chapter 14

Spencer had stood to go looking for Leah when the front door opened. He turned automatically to see who'd come in. It was her, and the flat-out terror he saw on her face had even the hair on his arms rising. An instant later she'd mostly blanked that out, and he hoped the two men with him hadn't seen her naked emotion.

"I'm ready to head back to the cabin," he said easily. "See you two in the morning. We'll do some more work on setting up shots from different vantage points."

Both appeared eager. Neither had let ego get in the way of learning all they could from him. Amidst the "good-nights," he walked toward Leah.

"Ready to go?"

"Yes." The tremor in her voice would have had him on full alert even if he hadn't already shot straight to maximum readiness. He took her arm as they went out the door and descended the stairs. Then, seeing no one, he bent his head and asked softly, "What's wrong?"

"They know." It tumbled out of her. "Even your real name. Tim told Higgs he'd found a photo of you coming out of a courthouse somewhere."

"Where were they?"

"Out back."

The wheels in his head spun. "We don't dare go back to the cabin." He started hustling her in the opposite direction, to the nearest tree line. Thinking aloud, he said, "The Jeep."

"But...it's dark. And don't you need some tools to hot-wire it?"

"Got the key today," he said, more grateful than he could remember being for anything, except maybe seeing an unconscious Joe Osenbrock being carried away. He still didn't like their only option. The minute anyone heard the sound of the engine being fired up in back, the hunt would be on.

Their best hope, he concluded, was that neither Higgs nor Fuller had had a chance to spread the word. The other guys would wonder, maybe think someone was using the Jeep to drive out to the range to collect something that had been forgotten earlier.

The longer the hesitation, the more chance he and Leah would have to make a clean getaway.

The bigger, more powerful vehicles wouldn't have much, if any, advantage over the Jeep during the first mile or two. The rutted, winding gravel road on the edge of that steep plunge to the river had to be taken with care no matter how hot the driver was to catch someone ahead of him. Unfortunately, he'd have to drive cautiously, too.

Once past that stretch, they'd be overtaken quickly unless they got a big enough head start.

A plan forming in his head, he said, "We have to go for the Jeep. Pray nobody noticed the missing key."

Leah didn't say anything, just jogged at his side. He was glad to see that she'd put on a sweatshirt over her T-shirt; borrowed, he thought. He didn't have any equivalent, which meant he'd be damn cold at night, but the temperature hadn't dropped below freezing anytime this past week, so they should be all right.

He didn't want to even think about how long it would take for them to walk out to the closest neighbor or tiny town where someone might have a working telephone. Shit, why hadn't he kept his own with him, even if it was useless up here? He might have had coverage before they got as far as Glacier or Maple Falls.

Or…what would happen if they headed north for the border? He tried to envision a map, but had a bad feeling that was even rougher country. And it wasn't as if they'd know when they reached the border, or that the entire thing was patrolled 24/7. No towns or highways within remotely easy reach of where they'd emerge, either.

At least heading for the Mount Baker highway, they'd be going downhill. Given his condition, that was a real positive if they had to eventually go on foot.

He stopped Leah as close to the armory as they could get without stepping out in the open. As they stood in silence, he searched the ground between them and the lodge. The only movement was the dart of bats. A faint "whoo" came to his ears from somewhere behind them.

"Okay," he murmured, "I want you to turn around and go back to the head of the road leading out of here."

The moon had risen enough to let her see where he was pointing. "When I get there, I'll stop for you to jump in."

"Why don't I just get in the Jeep with you now?" she asked.

He shook his head and talked fast. "There's a chance they'll be waiting for me. If so, you need to take off on your own. You can't follow the road—they'll find you. Traveling in the dark is hard, but try to get a ways before you hide. Got that? I know you can do it. You know this area, wildlife. Better than they do."

"Do you really think we can outrun them?" she whispered.

"No, but I have a plan for that, too."

She pressed her lips together, but nodded instead of arguing as he felt sure she wanted to. Her resistance to the idea of abandoning him to save herself was a part of why he'd fallen for her so fast.

Right now all he did was give her a quick, hard kiss and a push. "Go."

She went, slipping away and disappearing more quickly in the thick darkness beneath the big trees than he'd expected.

He had no choice but to cross the thirty yards or so of open ground to reach the back of the armory. Hating to be so exposed, he did it at a trot. Reaching the back wall, he flattened himself against it, pulled his Sig Sauer and took a moment to slow his breathing.

Then he slid like a shadow around the side, instinct throwing him back to when he'd been a soldier, letting him place his feet soundlessly.

There were no voices. The only light came from lodge windows and, more diffused, the first cabins.

The Jeep sat where it had been since Higgs moved it out of the building.

Spencer stepped from the cover of the building, just as another man appeared from where he'd hidden behind the low branches of one of the old cedars. Spencer froze, weapon trained on the man.

"Is what Fuller says true?" asked Dirk Ritchie.

Finger tightening on the trigger, Spencer sweated over what to do. If he fired, men would pour out of the lodge. And, damn, he didn't want to kill Dirk.

"How did you know I'd be out here?"

"I saw you take the key," Dirk said simply. His hands remained at his sides, even though he was carrying, too.

"Did you?" Spencer said tensely. "You and Helen need to take off, too. Use the confusion after I'm gone."

Dirk stayed quiet.

Spencer pitched his voice low, yet filled it with intensity. "Do you really want to be party to slaughtering what might be hundreds of people who are just thinking about going to their kids' parent-teacher meetings, or the guy they just met, or a sick parent? Remember the Oklahoma City bombing that killed *fifteen* preschooler children?"

Somebody else would come out any minute. He had to *go*.

He took the last steps to the Jeep. "Stop me, or don't."

Only a few strides separated the two men now. Shooting Dirk would feel like murder, but if he didn't—

Dirk stepped back. "Get out of here."

"Thank you."

The other man turned and walked toward the lodge, not hurrying. Switching his attention to the Jeep, Spencer had a sickening thought. What if Dirk had told Higgs he'd seen Spencer pocket the key? What if the Jeep had already been disabled?

He couldn't hesitate. Didn't have time to think of a Plan B. What were the chances he'd make it to the tree line? Gripping the overhead bar above the seats, Spencer swung himself in behind the wheel, grimacing as the quick movement tugged at his stitches and ignited pain in his ribs. No need to open or close a door. He pulled the key from his pocket, inserted it, held his breath and turned it.

The engine roared to life.

The porchlight above the back door into the kitchen came on. A voice called out.

He put the Jeep in gear and slammed his foot down on the gas pedal.

Leah hadn't quite reached the meeting place when she heard the engine start. Spencer had gotten that far. Thank God. Thank God.

Running, she crossed the weedy gravel to reach the other side and turned to see the Jeep racing toward her. The headlights switched on just before he came even with her. He braked, she grabbed for the door handle and yanked. Metal squealed, but the door refused to give way.

"Jump in."

What she did was fall in, but it worked. The Jeep was rocketing forward long before she untangled herself enough to sit up. If there was a seat belt, her groping fingers didn't find it. Instead, she gripped the edge of the seat with one hand and flattened the other on the dashboard.

The feeble, yellow beams cast by the headlights didn't illuminate the road ahead more than ten or fifteen feet.

"I hope you know this road," she heard herself gasp.

"I do."

He'd been aware from the beginning that there was the possibility he'd have to run for it, she supposed, which meant being ultra-observant about little details like the only outlet from the resort. Spencer sounded awfully tense, though.

"Do you hear—?"

He didn't have to finish. Yes, deep-throated engines had been started. Aside from her own car, every vehicle she'd seen up here dwarfed this old Jeep. The giant SUVs and pickups could almost run right over the top of it.

She craned her neck to see behind her. Bright lights appeared.

Spencer mumbled a few obscenities.

"You have a plan." How did she sound even semi-calm? The cold wind whipped her hair and made her eyes water. Gravel crunched beneath the tires. She dreaded the moment when they reached the stretch above the river.

She ought to be thankful it was dark, and she wouldn't be able to see the valley floor.

"I'm going to take a few curves," he said tersely, "brake long enough for you to leap out and run for the woods, then try to set up a skid so that the Jeep goes over the edge and down into the river. They'll think we screwed up."

"What if you can't jump out?" she said numbly.

"I don't have time to try to find a heavy enough rock to brace the accelerator."

"There's something behind the seat." She'd caught a glimpse when she was facedown after her tumble into the Jeep. She didn't know what she'd seen, but now she got on her knees and felt down in the cavity. "I think it's a car battery. They're heavy, aren't they?"

"'Yes. Damn. That should work. Can you pick it up?"

"I think so." Her position was completely unsafe, crouched instead of sitting while trying to heft a heavy object between the seat backs. If he started that skid too soon… Laughter almost bubbled up. Unsafe. *Right*.

She tugged and rocked it until she got her fingers beneath the rusty metal, and then twisted, plunked onto her butt and lowered the battery to her lap.

She sensed Spencer's quick glance.

"We're coming up on a good place to let you out. Just beyond, there's a gap where the guardrail has rusted and broken. That's what I'll aim for."

Leah's head bobbed as if she was just fine with any of this. "You'll find me?"

"Yes." He braked, skidded enough to have him swearing again and stopped. She scrambled over the door, leaving the battery on the seat. He accelerated again before she started running.

This would all be for nothing if the Jeep hung up on a stubbornly intact stretch of guardrail, but he had no time to waste to scout ahead to be sure he knew where the break was. All Spencer could do was judge distances from his memory.

Here.

He braked, cranked the wheel hard, then lifted the battery over the gearshift. Got out.

The sound of approaching engines was too loud. No time.

He slipped the gearshift into Neutral and shoved the battery down on the accelerator at almost the same moment. The Jeep leaped forward, the open door whacked him and he tumbled free.

Without looking to see if he'd succeeded, he ran full out for the bank on the uphill side of the road and scrambled up it. There, he paused only momentarily, turning. The Jeep had disappeared, the sound of its engine drowned out by approaching vehicles. Had the steering somehow corrected itself?

Then he heard metal tearing, screaming in agony… followed by an unholy explosion.

Just as the first set of headlights illuminated that stretch of road he faded back into the forest.

Deep in the trees, Spencer couldn't see any better than he would have in a cavern a mile below the ground. He should have set up some kind of plan for him and Leah to find each other when separated. If she didn't stick pretty close to the road, it would take sheer luck for them to stumble onto each other.

Swearing silently as the receding shouts faded behind him, he made his way uphill, trying to stay twenty feet or so from the road. If the sound of pursuit reached him, he wouldn't be able to keep doing that. At least he could be assured he *would* hear anyone chasing him on foot; it was impossible to pass through the tangle of vegetation without making some noise.

Something swiped him in the face. He shook his head and spun. A swag of lichen, pale even in the limited light, still swayed.

He had a memory of telling Leah *not* to follow the road if she had to take off on her own. Surely to God she'd use common sense and realize they didn't have a prayer of finding each other if she didn't.

He kept moving, pausing every ten feet or so to listen. Uphill, he heard a muffled cry. Animal? Bird?

Some thrashing followed.

Moving as quietly as he could, he headed that direction. What if she'd hurt herself? he thought suddenly but pushed the fear aside.

Quiet closed around him. Maintaining any orientation took determination, and Spencer wouldn't swear he wasn't veering off a straight line toward a sound that could have been a porcupine waddling through the forest, or a bear crashing on its way.

Guessing himself to be close, he finally said, "Leah?" All he could do was hope he wasn't too close to the road—and that Higgs hadn't been smart enough to have men walking it, listening and watching for any indication that someone was in there and not dead on the rocky bank of the low-running river.

"Spencer?"

"Hold still."

She didn't answer. He stepped forward carefully. He felt renewed irritation at himself; if he'd had his phone, he'd have also had a flashlight—although he wouldn't have dared use it now.

He put out a foot and found only space, teetering before he drew back.

A woeful whisper came from the darkness. "I fell in."

Spencer crouched. His eyes had adjusted well enough for him to see fern fronds waving wildly. Presumably, they disguised a hollow. Maybe a giant tree stump had rotted into nothingness; who knew?

"I'm here," he murmured. "Are you hurt?"

"I don't think so."

"Okay." Relief flooded him. He held out a hand. "Can you see me?"

"Yes." More stirring among what he thought was mostly lush clumps of sword ferns. A slim hand seized his, and he exerted steady pressure until she scrambled out of the hollow and fell against him.

Her arms wrapped his torso even as he held her tight, ignoring the pain in his wrist.

Against his chest, she mumbled, "I was so scared! And afraid I couldn't find you, and—"

Exhilarated because they *had* found each other, he chuckled. Her hair stirred against his cheek.

"I was getting a little worried myself," he admitted.

Her head came up. "What *happened*?"

"The Jeep sailed over the cliff and exploded when it hit the rocks at the bottom. Last I knew, the SUVs coming up behind us stopped there. I heard voices. Whether they bought it entirely… I don't know. I'm betting they don't find a way to get to the Jeep until daylight, though. Whether they're taking into account the possibility we weren't in the Jeep, I don't know."

After a moment she nodded. "Now what?" she asked, sounding as if she was running through options in her head.

That was an excellent question. From where they stood, downhill would take them southeast. They'd almost have to hit the highway. Even so, he'd give a lot for a topographical map. And, hey, food, warmer clothes, possibly a sleeping bag, the flashlight and phone, the absence of which he'd already regretted, and probably a lot of other things that hadn't yet occurred to him but would as soon as he or Leah needed them.

He winced. Like the bottle of pain meds. Except, he'd stuck two of them in his pocket, meaning to take them with dinner but decided not to show his vulnerability so publicly. He'd hold out as long as he could before taking them one at a time.

Preferably after they came on at least a trickle of water.

Right now...

"Two choices. Keep going, away from the road. Or hunker down for the night. If we're going to do that, you found us a great place to hide."

He kind of thought she made a face before saying, "I agree. What's your preference? You okay?" She glanced at his still-bandaged wrist.

Reluctantly, he said, "I'm fine. I think we move on. We're too close to the road here. By morning, if not sooner, they'll be looking for us. I haven't had the impression that any of them are real outdoorsmen. A few say they've hunted, so maybe I'm wrong. Still, most outdoor experience doesn't prepare you for a temperate rain forest."

"Have *you* ever spent any time in the north Cascades?"

"Yeah, did some climbing here years ago." Over the course of several leaves, a buddy, Aaron, and he had ascended seven mountains altogether, from the Rockies to the Teton Mountains and here in the Cascades. Spencer hadn't gone climbing since Aaron had been killed in a firefight.

"What about bears? I know what they can do, remember."

He decided not to remind her about porcupines, also nocturnal. "They're rarely aggressive with humans, as you know."

After a minute Leah straightened away from him. "I'm ready."

Conscious of his many aches and the sharp pain in his side and thigh and wrist, he'd have liked to sleep for a few hours. But he wouldn't feel any better tomorrow morning, the next day, or the next. Even a little distance covered tonight would give them a head start tomorrow.

He nodded and led the way, hoping like hell he was going approximately in the right direction—and that they wouldn't stumble out on the winding road where someone might be waiting for them.

The parable about the blind leading the blind crossed his mind. Aesop? Just as well he couldn't remember how that story ended.

Chapter 15

Because of his recent wounds and undoubted pain, Leah insisted they take regular breaks to rest. He didn't argue, but gave away his tension by regularly pushing a button on his watch to check the time. She didn't bother asking how long they'd been on their way, and he didn't offer the information. The day's stresses had caught up with her ages ago—and if she found out that was really only half an hour ago, she might scream—but really she was grateful to be so tired; she couldn't do any concentrated worrying. She just followed in Spencer's wake, knowing at least that she wouldn't tumble into another hole unless he did first.

The ground was soft and uneven, though. Squishy in places, more from the depth of the moss and decomposing organic matter. They clambered over and walked around fallen trees, some that might have come down last winter, others already rotting and serving as nurse logs for saplings. In some of those places faint rays of moonlight found them, and she glimpsed tiny distant stars. Much of the time enormous trees reared above them, blocking out the sky. She had a vague memory of Uncle Edward talking about some true old-growth forest close by and wondered if that was what this was.

It might be, because at some point the walking became easier since they weren't having to fight the ferns and salmonberries and who-knew-what that scratched and tripped them. The darkness was almost absolute, the boles of standing trees enormous. Not that the ground didn't remain uneven, the extreme dark hiding obstacles that would cause Spencer to growl under his breath before he helped her around or over them.

She walked right into him when he stopped.

"I'm beat," he said. "I suggest we get on the other side of this log and try to sleep a little."

Since she was very close to sleepwalking, Leah thought she could do that. And she knew Spencer must be dead on his feet to actually admit to needing a rest.

They had to go around this time. Taking her hand, he guided her. The trunk must have been six or eight feet in diameter. Even decomposing, it reared above her head. On the back side, he advanced slowly before stopping, seeming to feel his way. "This looks as good as anyplace."

Looks? *She* couldn't see a thing, but she wasn't about to quibble, either.

Once she'd squatted and then plunked down, she tried very hard not to think about what insects inhabited a rotting log. Would there be snakes around? Not poisonous ones, she was pretty sure. Her hand bumped something that sort of…crumbled. Recoiling, she made out a lighter shape against the dark backdrop of loam and moss. Mushrooms. Now, *those* could be poisonous, but she didn't plan to eat one.

She heard a groan as Spencer carefully lowered himself beside her. Oh, heavens—she should have helped him. Given the possibly broken wrist, he wouldn't lean any weight on that arm, and the gash in his thigh had to hinder him.

Too late.

"God, this feels good," he said after a minute.

"Uh-huh." Except she felt herself listing sideways until she came up against his big, solid body. "Can we lie down?" She was slurring.

"We can."

They shifted, she squirmed, he wrapped her in his arms and they ended up prone. He spooned her body from behind. His arm made a perfect pillow. Her eyelids sank closed, she mumbled something that was supposed to be "good night" and fell asleep.

Cradling this woman he suspected he loved, Spencer wasn't as quick to drop off to sleep.

When things went to shit, it happened fast.

If not for the damn fight, he'd be in a lot better physical shape and thus more confident that he and Leah would make it safely out of this densely wooded, uninhabited forest. If he'd had even ten or fifteen minutes' warning, he could have filled a pack with food, first-aid supplies, flashlight and more. As it was, they were screwed if either of them so much as developed blisters on their feet. His boots protected his ankles, while Leah's athletic shoes were fine for walking, but wouldn't keep her from turning an ankle.

They just about had to move during the daytime rather than at night even though they might be spotted. Especially given their physical condition, they had to be able to see where they were stepping. In fact, they were lucky no disaster had already occurred with them blundering around in the dark.

He cast his mind back to that brief encounter with Dirk. Spencer had had no idea he'd been seen pocketing the key. If it had been anybody but Dirk…if Dirk had told Higgs, or when he saw Spencer at the Jeep had opened his mouth and yelled… No point in going there now.

He hoped Dirk *had* kept his mouth shut and did find a way to take off.

His thoughts jumped again.

How the hell had that idiot Fuller stumbled on the photo?

He actively tried not to be photographed. With the press sticking their noses in everywhere, he'd been unable to completely evade them given that he had to testify in court. Most outlets were good about not publishing those pictures, but he knew of a couple that had made it into newspapers or TV news stories. There were undoubtedly more online. In fact, the one Tim Fuller had described in Leah's hearing had to be one of those.

His ascendancy in Higgs's estimation had rubbed Tim, in particular, wrong for months. But had he made mistakes that gave away his law-enforcement background? Spencer shook his head slightly. He had no idea, and at this point that was irrelevant. Permanently irrelevant, if he declined to go undercover again.

Tim had to have sensed/heard/seen something to make him do that kind of online prowling. Or, hell, had he contacted a friend who was more of a computer wizard? Maybe, Spencer concluded.

For all that things had gone to shit, he and Leah had made their getaway and, right now, were fine. They wouldn't starve to death in the next two or three days.

The tricky moment would be when they had to approach a road.

He nuzzled Leah's silky hair and let sleep claim him.

His body's demand awakened him before Leah had so much as moved. In fact, it didn't appear either of them had made any of the restless shifts in position normal to sleepers. Her head still rested on his biceps; he still spooned her.

He'd have enjoyed the moment if he didn't need to empty his bladder, and if his body wasn't reporting multiple other complaints. His shoulder ached, his arm was stiff, his wrist felt broken, his thigh throbbed and his whole left side was on fire. In a general way, he felt like crap. What if he was coming down with a cold or the flu?

Stuffing a groan back down where it came from, he gently shook Leah. "Time to rise and shine."

She whimpered, stirred and whimpered again. "I'm stiff. Although I don't know why I'm whining. You're the one who is injured."

He didn't say so, but he dreaded getting up.

Leah did get to her hands and knees, then to her feet. She suddenly said, "I need—" and bolted for a nearby tree.

Since he'd rather she not see him dealing with his

infirmities, he got up, too, in slow increments. Water or no water, he was taking one of those damn pills. Just as she reappeared around the tree, he shuffled toward a different one.

There, he used the facilities, then did some stretches before returning to Leah.

"Turns out GrubHub can't find us to deliver that Denny's breakfast," he said. "Guess we'll have to do without."

Her smile rewarded him. "There are berries ripe, if we can find a clearing."

"Stumble on one, you mean."

"At least we can *see*."

That was an improvement, he'd concede.

He started out. He got the pill down, but was left with a foul taste in his mouth. Walking loosened muscles, and the pill did some good, too, but he felt as if someone was stabbing his thigh with a red-hot poker. All he could do was block out what he couldn't change and go on.

By the time sunlight made it to the forest floor, it was diffuse, soft, even tinted green-gold. He still had to watch carefully for the best places to set down his feet, which made for slow going. Common sense did battle with a sense of urgency; what if finding out they were being dogged by the FBI inspired Higgs to launch an early attack?

Helplessness didn't sit well with Spencer, but practically, there wasn't a damn thing he could do to prevent any immediate action Higgs took. He doubted a bomb had actually been built, but the debacle during the Boston Marathon had demonstrated how much damage could be done by really primitive bombs. He was afraid Ken Vogel, with his bomb squad experience, could put together any number of lethal explosive devices even without input from a budding physicist with an interest in nuclear fission.

Until he got his hands on a phone, he had no way to alert his office that the operation had blown up on him.

Then focus on the moment. Except for my aching body. Best not to think about that.

Deciding it was time for a short break, he spotted a moss-covered rock more or less the right height to let them sit.

Once they did so, Leah looked at him with worry in her eyes. "What do you think they're doing?"

"Right now?" He checked his watch. "Struggling upriver to the wreck. That'll take them at least a couple of hours from the best place to leave vehicles."

"And then?"

Trust her to echo his concerns.

"I think there are two logical options for Higgs. One is to pack up and leave, probably have the others disperse until he can line up an alternate place for them to train. The other is to go for an immediate attack."

"Immediate?"

"Once he realizes we're on foot, he may decide to have the men hunt us for a day or two. Catching us would solve their problem with timing." He didn't have to say, *executing us.* "Otherwise, he could pull together a plan for an attack that might not be quite as spectacular as he intended, but those rocket launchers alone give him the firepower to threaten a gathering of politicians or even the president himself."

"You know him. Which is more likely?"

He didn't hesitate. "Dispersing. He likes the pieces to fit together. He'll want the big bang, so to speak. To accomplish that, the attack was to take place on a lot of levels. Bomb or bombs, rocket launchers, snipers picking off counterattackers or survivors trying to get away. Maybe even sending in a squad of men who don't have the range to be snipers to mow people down."

Leah looked more horrified by the minute. "That's why he wanted you."

"He needed a sniper to train others. That's what I was doing."

The urgency tapped on his shoulder, and he rose to his feet. "I'll stiffen up if we stop for long. Let's get going."

They continued in silence, Spencer straining to hear any sounds unnatural for the forest. Every now and again, a bird would flit by, most unidentifiable, a few common enough he recognized them, like the crow and later a jay, although that had unfamiliar coloration. They weren't plagued by a lot in the way of insects. Mosquitoes and even flies would prefer moist areas, butterflies open meadows with flowers. The rotting logs were no doubt rife with crawly things, centipedes, sow bugs and the like. Nothing that stung, as far as he knew.

And, on a glass half-full note, it wasn't raining. He knew from experience that rain wasn't uncommon here even in July and August. Some water to drink would be welcome; in fact, thirst was increasingly making itself known. But getting wet and having to keep going, pants chafing their legs, even socks soaked, that could be miserable.

"I hear something," she whispered.

He stopped and cocked his head. Speak of the devil. That had to be running water.

He turned, held a finger to his lips and progressed

with even greater care. The small stream they found took enough of a tumble over rocks to have caused the delicate rippling sound. A deer that had been drinking saw them and bounded away.

"Oh, my."

"This water will likely make us sick," he told her, dredging through his memory. "Giardia is the problem, as I recall. If we could boil it…"

She wrinkled her nose. "No stove handy."

"Nope. I don't think symptoms will catch up with us for at least a week or two." He hoped that recollection was accurate. "We'll need to ask for treatment once we have a chance to see a doctor."

If she doubted that time would come, she didn't comment.

Spencer splashed his face to cool it, and wished for a water bottle, too.

If wishes were horses…

His head had begun to throb. He debated taking the last pill now versus waiting, deciding on the latter. He might need it more come morning.

Leah's stomach growled. She pressed a hand to it, hoping Spencer hadn't heard. He had enough to worry about, and given the toll his injuries took, he needed fuel for his body even more than she did.

He'd gotten quieter as the day went on, too. Pain tightened his face whenever he didn't remember to hide it. The flush she saw on his lean cheeks above dark stubble made her more uneasy. Even with all the willpower in the world, pushing himself to get back on his feet as soon as he did couldn't have been good for his recovery. She'd known all along that his risk of infection was high. She'd been able to don sterile latex gloves, and the gauze, scissors, needle and suturing material were sterile, too. Unfortunately, the blade of that black-handled knife Joe had used on him wasn't. Then there were the dirty shirts used to stem the bleeding. This was an awful time for the infection to appear. Dumb thing to think—was there a time that would have been *good*? If only there'd been antibiotics in that first-aid kit, or Spencer had stocked them along with the pain meds.

He was capable of going on with a fever, at least for now, Leah convinced herself. But what if they hadn't found their way out of the wilderness two days from now? Three?

He did go on, and on, hours upon hours, until her thighs burned and she'd quit thinking about anything but the next step. She'd thought of taking the lead but decided against it. With Spencer in front, he was more likely to stop when he needed it, while she might misjudge his stamina.

Just then Spencer stopped, Leah stumbling to a halt just before she walked into him. Blinking, she realized the light had changed without her noticing, deepening into purple.

"We risk getting injured if we continue in the dark," Spencer said, his voice rough. "I'm sorry we didn't come across any berries."

She took the hand he held out. "Going without for a day or two isn't that big a deal. Isn't fasting supposed to be good for you?"

"I've read that. I'm not convinced."

"Me, either." Studying him anxiously, she said, "I should look at your wounds while there's still some light."

"Why?" He let her go and lowered himself to another mossy piece of ground with a few pained grunts he apparently couldn't hold back.

"Why? Because—" She didn't finish.

"I'm not sure we even dare wash the wounds out in a stream," he said wearily. "What if that introduces different microorganisms into my body? And, in turn, I'd be introducing bacteria into the stream that might be deadly to fish or mammals downstream that drink out of it. What's more—" he continued inexorably "—we have no supplies to rewrap my wounds and especially my ribs."

The ribs might be hurting him more than anything, she realized. The binding did offer some support. Yes, she could tear her T-shirt into strips, say, but the knit fabric would be too stretchy to provide the same kind of support.

"I'm sorry." She sank down beside him. "I wish I could do something."

"I'll be okay. I just wish—" He shook his head as if regretting having said that much.

"Wish?" Leah prodded.

"I was sure I'm not leading us astray."

"Short of your watch converting into a compass, I don't see how you can know. You're not Superman, Spencer." Then she stopped again and frowned. "Why am I still calling you that?"

"You don't have to." With a sigh, he rolled his head. "But I might not answer to Alex."

"Really?"

He managed a smile. "No, I'm kidding, but I've even been thinking of myself as Spencer. It's like… Do you speak a foreign language?"

"I'm pretty fluent in Spanish."

"You think in it when you're speaking it, right?"

"Yes."

"When I go undercover, I immerse myself to that extent. I'm not Special Agent Alex Barr. I *am* Spencer Wyatt. I can't slip."

"I can see that," she said slowly, even as she wondered how he could possibly do that. He'd said something once about not being sure who he was anymore, and how he'd done things, bad things, he didn't name. Not raped women, she felt certain. If he'd beaten men to death, or shot them, she believed he'd had adequate provocation.

Apparently losing interest in the subject, he said, "I think I'd like to lie down."

He let her help him, which said a lot about his condition. He encouraged her to join him, and soon they were curled up together. As the temperature dropped with nightfall, he had to be cold on top of everything else—unless he was burning up, of course. Leah rubbed his bare arms and lifted his hands to her skin beneath her sweatshirt. That he didn't protest told her how lousy he felt.

She kept thinking about a man who'd spent—she didn't know—much of the past several years, at least, undercover with violent fanatics who wanted to remake the country into their twisted ideals. She hadn't heard any slurs from him, as she had from some of the other men, but he must know all the right things to say to allow him to blend in.

How jarring it must be to return to his real life, whatever that was. An apartment? How homey was that, when it stayed empty for months on end? He presumably had no pets, he'd said he wasn't close to family and she didn't believe he had a girlfriend or fiancée waiting patiently for him. Spencer Wyatt—no, Alex Barr —wasn't the kind of man to make promises to one woman and have sex with another.

Feeling him relax into sleep, she thought, *I do know him. Of course I do.*

He'd been willing to give his life for her. That said enough about him to erase even fleeting doubts.

Hunger pushed off sleep for another while, but she was exhausted enough to drop off eventually.

Waking suddenly, the darkness unabated, she lay very still. What had disturbed her...? The answer came immediately. A wave of convulsive shivering seized Spencer. His back arched and his teeth chattered before he could clamp them shut.

Terrified, she realized there wasn't a single thing she could do except hold him, and keep holding him.

Chapter 16

A murky haze that made Leah think of smog had settled over the usually crystal-clear silver-gray of Spencer's eyes. Or maybe it was more like a film. All she knew was that he couldn't possibly be seeing as well as usual. He couldn't hide that he was still shivering, too.

She watched as he staggered out of her sight to pee, returning a minute later. His usual grace had deserted him. How could they keep going? If they'd been on a smooth path or the road, maybe, but as it was…

How can we not *keep going?* Leah asked herself bleakly. It wasn't as if he had a twenty-four-hour flu bug. He wouldn't get better until he was on powerful antibiotics. If they didn't reach a hospital, he might die.

Even if they'd both been healthy, each day would be more grueling than the last, considering that they were able to drink only occasionally, and had nothing whatsoever to eat. It surely couldn't be that far before they reached the highway.

"You ready?" he asked gruffly.

Leah nodded. "Let me go first today."

He stared at her for long enough, she wasn't sure whether he was really slow in processing what she'd said, or resisting the idea. But finally, he nodded. Good.

She had to look around before deciding which way they'd come from, and therefore which way she needed to go. Some feature of ancient geology had formed a shallow dip here, and the forest was dense enough, she couldn't see very far ahead. As they started walking, her thighs let her know when the land tilted downward again.

Once, she said, "Oh, did you see that?" and turned, for a minute not seeing Spencer at all. Her heart took a huge, painful leap.

He plodded around the trunk of one of the forest giants. He hadn't heard her, and the small mammal she'd seen had long since dashed out of sight. His teeth were clenched, his eyes glazed, but he was able to keep moving.

No choice.

From then on she made sure to look over her shoulder regularly to be sure he was still with her.

The pace seemed awfully slow, but she felt sure that raw determination was all that kept Spencer moving.

A distant sound caught her attention. She grabbed Spencer's arm to stop him and listened, momentarily confused. That could be a river, but if it was the Nooksack, that meant they'd also reached the highway that followed it. Of course there were tributaries, like the one that flowed from the side of Mount Baker, running past the resort to meet the larger Nooksack, but the water didn't rush like—

It was a car engine. It had to be.

Traffic on the highway? Or had they unintentionally come close to the resort road?

Leah wished she could be sure where the sound came *from*, but her best guess at direction wasn't even close to precise. It wouldn't be so bad if they spotted the resort road, would it? At least they'd know where they were.

She glanced at Spencer, and fear gripped her. He looked bad. Really bad.

Maybe she should take the gun from him, start carrying it herself. If one of the men suddenly appeared in front of them, was Spencer capable of reacting quickly enough?

Could I? she asked herself, and was afraid she knew the answer. There was a reason cops and soldiers were supposed to spend so much time at gun ranges. She'd never fired a weapon in her life. To aim it at a person, one she knew, and pull the trigger—and that was assuming the gun didn't have a safety, which she had no idea how to identify.

Keep going. She had a very bad feeling that, if they took a break and sat down, she might have a hard time getting Spencer up again. She wouldn't be doing it with sheer muscle, since he had to outweigh her by eighty pounds, at least. There had to be a way…but he was still walking.

The light began to seem brighter ahead. They emerged from the trees between one step and the next. Stumps and the kind of mess left by logging told her this land had been clear-cut, probably a couple of years ago. Some scruffy small trees grew, alder and maple, she thought. And a wealth of huckleberry bushes, many growing out of rotting stumps.

"Berries!" she cried.

Spencer bumped into her. For the first time in several

hours, comprehension showed on his face. She steered him to a bush covered with purple-blue, ripe berries. Once she saw that he was able to pick them himself and stuff them into his mouth, she started doing the same.

They shouldn't eat very many; the last thing they needed was to end up sick, but oh, they tasted good, the flavor bursting on her tongue. And she was so hungry!

Within minutes her fingers were stained purple, as were Spencer's. But who cared?

Bushes a short distance away shook. Hand outstretched for more berries, Leah stared. It kept shaking, and that was an odd sound. Sort of…snuffling. Or grunting.

"Spencer," she whispered.

His head turned, his eyes sharp. He had to have heard the alarm in her voice.

He stared at the trembling leaves, and in a move so fast it blurred, had his gun in his hand.

"We need to back away," she murmured.

He nodded agreement.

"Probably won't pay any attention to us," she said, just as quietly.

A stick cracked under her foot. She'd have frozen in place if his hand hadn't gripped her upper arm and kept her moving.

Craning her neck, she saw brown fur. An enormous head pushed between bushes. Supposedly, bears didn't have very good vision, but it was staring right at them. And, oh, dear God, it kept pushing through the growth, canes snapping.

"Not too fast."

The bear wasn't charging, but Leah would have sworn it grew to fill her field of vision. Seeing the hump between the shoulders had her already racing pulse leaping.

"Spencer!" she whispered loudly.

"I see."

Another step, another. The head swung back and forth. Leah would swear the small eyes looked angry.

Suddenly, Spencer cursed, and she, too, heard a deep-throated engine cut off. Car doors slam.

"I see them!" yelled a voice she recognized and detested.

TJ Galt.

The racket off to the right made the bear even more agitated. It took a few steps toward them. Ignoring the two voices Leah now heard, Spencer held her to a slow, steady retreat.

Until the scrubby growth toward what had to be the resort road began to shake and snap as the men trampled through it. One of them yodeled, "Got you now, traitor!"

The grizzly lowered its head and charged.

"Run!" Spencer ordered. She didn't hesitate, racing as fast as she could back the way they'd come. It was a minute before she realized he'd split away, probably intending to draw the bear's attention.

But a gun barked. Again and again. TJ and Arne intended to shoot them down.

She heard a crashing behind her and dared a look back. The bear had stopped and swung toward the two men who were yelling gleefully. One took a shot at her that stung her arm. Spencer… She saw him trip, recover his footing and keep running.

The grizzly charged the men. One of them bellowed, "Bear!"

As if she'd stepped into a noose, Leah pitched forward. She didn't land gently, but didn't even acknowledge pain. Pushing herself to her hands and knees, she twisted to see what was happening.

Gunshots exploded but didn't slow the bear. Screaming, one of the men went down. The other stumbled backward. Even from this distance, she saw his horror.

"Keep going!" Spencer roared.

She used her position like a sprinter on a starting block to run, gasping, hurting, horrified by the snarls and terrible screams she heard behind her.

Leah hadn't gotten far into the woods when she slammed against a hard body. Even as she fought, she couldn't stop herself from looking back.

"Leah! It's me. It's just me."

She was whimpering as she took in his face. If she'd thought he looked bad before, it was nothing to now. He was as sickened as she was by what was happening behind them.

"Come on." He all but dragged her forward. She jogged to keep up with his long strides. Then she realized which hand he gripped her with.

"Your wrist."

"To hell with my wrist." He still held his gun in his right hand. "Let's circle around. If they both went down, we might have transportation."

The words were barely out of his mouth when the engine roared to life. Tires skidded on gravel as the driver floored it.

There was one more strangled scream.

Spencer's lungs heaved like old-fashioned bellows, and his heart was trying to pound its way out of his chest.

He and Leah had slid down an unexpected drop-off and collapsed at the bottom, their backs to a big tree.

She breathed as fast as he did, her eyes dilated, each exhalation sounding like a sob although she wasn't crying. "TJ," she gasped. "That was TJ."

"Yeah," he managed. "And Arne."

"He took off and left him." She sounded disbelieving.

He and she had taken off and left TJ to a terrible death, too, Spencer couldn't help thinking. They'd had more motivation to run even than Arne had, but Spencer also thought sticking around to try to rescue the grizzly's victim would have been useless and possibly a death sentence.

Shaking from reaction or the damn fever or both, he got out, "You okay?"

"I...don't know."

He wasn't a hundred percent sure he hadn't been shot. In fact, he bent his head to search for blood. He saw some, but on Leah, not him.

With an exclamation, he laid down his Sig Sauer and reached for her arm. "Does this hurt?"

She tipped her head to peer dubiously at the bloodstain on her upper arm. "Something stung me."

Yeah, there was a rip, all right. He parted it enough to see that the bullet had barely skimmed her flesh. Its passage might leave a scar, but the blood flow wasn't worrisome. Her face was decorated with some new scratches strung with beads of scarlet like polished rubies crossing her cheek and forehead.

He lifted a hand to smooth her hair, tangled with leaves and twigs. "Damn," he whispered. "I thought that was it."

"Me, too." She blinked against some moisture in her eyes. "TJ sneered at me when I said I was watching for bears. You know, when we were picking berries…"

"We'd better not stick around," Spencer said after a minute. As shitty as he felt, he wanted to kiss her, and maybe more. Nothing like a shot of adrenaline to fire up a man's blood and clear his head. Unfortunately, adrenaline didn't hang around long, and he'd crash when it dissipated. "That bear has to have taken a bullet or two. It'll be mad."

"It won't die?"

"I don't know. Not immediately, I'm guessing. Probably it just thinks it got stung by some yellow jackets."

Gutsy as always, Leah nodded sturdily. She got to her feet faster than he did and picked up his gun for him. Holstering it, he said, "I guess we found the road."

"Yes, and I'm pretty sure we're close to the turnoff."

"We still have to be careful, you know."

Her head bobbed. He had the feeling she was checking to see how *he* was, even as he did the same for her.

She looked like she'd been in a cat fight. Scratches, new and old, on her face and hands. Hair a mess. Her clothes, ripped and dirty, hung on her as if she'd already lost weight. Horror darkened her beautiful eyes.

He hadn't taken very good care of her.

They were alive, he reminded himself. Unlike TJ Galt.

An hour later they had circled around the clear-cut land and saw the resort road. It was paved here, which encouraged him. Not that far to go.

They hiked on, trying to move parallel to it, just near enough they could see it occasionally. Twice they saw a black SUV driving slowly along the road, once heading out, then coming back up.

"They still think they can cut us off," he said.

"What if the driver let off a couple guys who are on foot out here with us?"

The possibility was real, but there was nothing he could do that he wasn't already. He fought to stay in the moment while fighting a blinding headache, chills and a tendency to find himself in other times and places.

A kid, hiding in the woods near his house after his father had used his belt on him. Rage and fear and shame filled him. Sunlight in his eyes, and he was baking in the heat of a street between mud-colored buildings in a village in Afghanistan, feeling eyes on him from every direction. Skin crawling.

Turning his head to see Leah anchored him, so he kept doing it. She needed him. He couldn't let her down.

"I think I see someone," she whispered.

He stared hard in the direction she was looking. Yeah, that desert camo didn't quite work in the green northwest forest.

He nudged Leah, and they very, very quietly retreated, then turned east to parallel the highway, heading toward Mount Baker. Should have known they couldn't pop out right here. Had Higgs sent out his minions to drive up and down the highway, too? Should they hunker down and wait out the day, not try to flag anyone down until morning?

Might be safer...but Spencer bet that by morning, Higgs and the others would have decamped. He would very much like to round them up here and now. Brooding, he thought, yeah, but what were the odds of getting a team here in time?

Even if the sheriff's department had a SWAT unit, could they stand up to the kind of weaponry Higgs's group had? An image formed in his head of the flare of rocket fire followed by a helicopter exploding.

He grimaced.

And, damn, as disreputable as he and Leah looked, how long would it take for police to be able to verify that he was who he said he was, and take action?

What if his head was in Afghanistan or Iraq when they reached a police station? Hard to take a crazy man seriously.

They trudged on, Leah in the lead again.

Her head turned. "I hear a car."

Pulled from the worries that had circled around and around, he listened, too. That was definitely a car, not an SUV or pickup. Which would have been good news if they'd been close enough to the highway to stick out a thumb. Also, if they could convince some backpacker on his way back down to civilization to hide them on backseat and floorboards so they weren't seen as they passed the resort road.

He realized he'd said that out loud when Leah said, "What if we *cross* the highway and follow it until we're past the resort road?"

It was lucky one of them had a working brain.

Her idea had sounded practical, but preparing to run across the empty highway, she was almost as scared as she'd been with a grizzly charging after her and bullets flying, too.

She and Spencer would be completely exposed for the length of time it took to slide into a ditch, climb up onto pavement, race across the highway and get across another ditch and into the woods on the far side. SUVs and pickup trucks with powerful engines could approach fast. Yes, but they could be heard from a distance, she reminded herself, even out of sight around a curve.

She stole an anxious look at Spencer. "Ready?"

"Yeah," he said hoarsely. "You say go."

"Okay." She took a few steadying breaths, tensed and said, "Go!"

Side by side, they slid on loamy soil into the ditch, used their hands to scrabble their way up to the road and ran.

Not until they plunged on the other side through dangling ropes of lichen and the stiff lower branches of evergreen trees did she take another breath. They stumbled to a stop, momentarily out of sight from the highway, and Spencer grinned at her.

Her heart gave a squeeze. That smile was delighted and sexy at the same time, and it didn't matter how awful he looked otherwise. When he held out his arms, she tumbled into them, wrapping her own around his lean torso.

She might have stayed longer if he didn't radiate worrisome heat.

"We're not safe yet," she mumbled into his shoulder.

"No, but we're one step closer."

Stupidly teary-eyed, she was smiling, too. Swiping her cheeks on his grungy T-shirt, she made herself lower her arms and back away.

"I don't know about you, but I'm starved. I vote we get going."

The jubilant grin had become an astonishingly tender smile. "I'll second that."

Chapter 17

Two hours later they passed the turn-off to the resort without seeing a single vehicle or any camouflage-clad, armed men hiding in wait. They'd heard a fair amount of passing traffic, but chose not to attempt to stop anyone yet.

Their pace grew slower and slower. The trees weren't as large here, resulting in dense undergrowth. Leah's body had become more and more reluctant. Her legs didn't want to take the next step. She quit diverting to avoid getting slapped by branches. Stumbling, she'd barely catch herself before she did another face-plant. She had never in her life been so tired—and she didn't have a raging fever. She kept checking on him, sometimes slyly so he wouldn't notice. Despite a sheen of sweat on his face and glazed eyes, he plodded on.

Neither of them spoke. What was there to say?

Spencer glanced at his watch. She went on without bothering to ask what time it was. Occasional glimpses of the sun showed it still high enough to give them a few hours before nightfall. If she was wrong...they'd stop. Curl up together and sleep.

"Hey."

Hearing his rough voice, Leah didn't make her foot move forward for that next step.

"Let's get in sight of the road. It's time to flag someone down."

"Oh." How long had it been since she'd seen him check the time? She had no idea. "Okay." She turned right. Just the idea that they might catch a ride and not have to walk anymore inspired a small burst of energy.

It only took a few minutes—five?—to find themselves a spot to crouch barely off the highway, but probably not visible to passing motorists.

The first one they saw coming was traveling east toward Mount Baker. A red Dodge Caravan, it had a rack piled with luggage and kids in the backseat.

They let several more go.

"I'd be happiest with a sheriff's deputy or forest service," Spencer said.

Of course, they had to identify those quick enough to give them time to burst out onto the road, waving their arms and probably jumping up and down.

Vehicles passed. She began to wonder if Spencer was too sick to make a quick decision. Maybe she should make one.

But suddenly he said, "That's it," and launched himself forward.

She stumbled behind, finally seeing what he had. It was a white 4X4 with a rack of lights on the roof. Spencer waved and so she did, too. A turn signal came on, and a siren gave a brief squawk. The vehicle rolled to a stop only a few feet from them. From here Leah could see green trim and the sheriff's department logo.

Spencer didn't wait for the deputy to get out. He jogged along the shoulder to the passenger side. So a passing motorist might miss seeing them, she realized.

The deputy climbed out and circled the front bumper. Probably in his thirties, he looked alarmingly like the men they were fleeing: fit, clothed in a khaki uniform and armed. In fact, his hand rested lightly on the butt of his gun.

That changed in an instant when he saw the gun holstered at Spencer's waist. In barely an instant, the deputy pulled his gun and took up a stiff-armed stance, the barrel pointing at Spencer, who immediately lifted his hands above his head. "Set that gun on the pavement," the deputy snapped. "Do it *now*."

Moving very slowly, Spencer complied. With his foot, he nudged the handgun over the pavement toward the cop. The deputy never took his eyes from Spencer when he moved forward and used his foot to push the gun behind the tire of his SUV.

"You're not a hunter."

"No," Spencer said. "I'm not carrying identification, so I can't prove this, but I'm FBI Special Agent Alex Barr. I was undercover with a violent militia group training at an old lodge near here. Ms. Leah Keaton—" he nodded at her "—recently inherited the lodge from her great-uncle. She decided to check on the condition of the buildings, and surprised the men who'd taken it over. They took her captive."

The guy watched them suspiciously. "You took her and ran?"

"Eventually. One of them found a photo of me online leaving a Chicago courthouse. We were lucky because Leah overheard two men talking about it. We didn't dare even take the time to grab supplies or my phone, just ran. I urgently need to call my team leader. These guys have some serious weapons, including a couple of rocket launchers."

"What?"

Leah spoke up. "I saw one of them. That's when they decided they couldn't let me leave."

"Some of their weapons are US military, stolen by a like-minded active-duty army officer. The leader of this group is a retired air force lieutenant-colonel. We need the FBI to handle this, not local police."

The deputy studied him for a long time. "No way I can verify this story."

"I don't see how."

Leah said, "The resort was called Mount Baker Cabins and Lodge. My uncle's name was Edward Preston. If you're local, you might know about him. He died last fall. I'm his great-niece. I'm…a veterinary technician."

The deputy eyed her. "We drove up to check on Mr. Preston now and again. Annoyed him, but we kept doing it."

"That sounds like him," she admitted. "Mom tried to get him to move to somewhere less isolated, but he refused."

Looking marginally less aggressive, the deputy said, "Special Agent Barr, will you agree to be handcuffed before I give you and Ms. Keaton a lift?"

"Yes."

"He's wounded," she interjected desperately. "He has a knife wound in his thigh, and another between his ribs. I think the ribs are broken, and his wrist, too. He's fighting an infection."

The deputy's eyebrows rose and his gaze snagged on Spencer's wrapped wrist before moving to the blood soaking the upper arm of Leah's sweatshirt. "You appear to be hurt, too."

"Yes, I was shot, but it's just a graze. Spencer's wounds—I mean, Alex's wounds—are infected. He's running a high temperature. It's a miracle he made it this far. Please don't—"

"I'll be okay," Spencer said gently. "We need to get off this road."

He had to explain why she'd called him by two different names, and why it would be a bad thing if they were spotted by any of the men fleeing the lodge.

The deputy cast uneasy glances up and down the highway, patted them both down and made them sit in the back—in the cage, she thought was the right terminology—but didn't insist on the handcuffs. He took Spencer's gun with him when he got behind the wheel, and did an immediate U-turn to head west toward Bellingham and, presumably sheriff's department headquarters. Then he got on his radio.

Less than two hours later Alex had set the ball to rolling. In his own imagery, he'd tapped a domino, which would knock down the next and the next, until the last fell.

He was rarely in on the grand finale, although his reasons this time were different. In the past, when he'd completed an undercover investigation, it was just as well not to show up days later as his alter ego, Special Agent Barr.

This wasn't the first time he'd had to jump ship, so to speak, but he'd never before had to help someone else make the swim to shore. It *was* the first time he'd been injured badly enough, he had to be hospitalized.

That partly explained his frustration. He did not like being stuck flat on his back in a hospital bed where he was allowed no voice in how the cleanup was run. He was pretty irked at Ron Abram, who'd delegated much of the response to someone at the Seattle office. Since Alex didn't have his phone, the only update offered to him came via the clunky phone on the bedside stand, and that was from Abram, not the agents who'd joined with the local police to raid the compound—yeah, that was what they'd called it—only to find it deserted. According to Abram, they were packing his and Leah's stuff and bringing it down, as well as having someone bring her car once they figured out how to get it moving.

Alex couldn't help thinking that Jason Shedd could have fixed the car in less time than it had probably taken him to disable it.

The Tahoe Alex had borrowed for this operation from the Seattle office had started, once they reconnected the battery. No surprise it had been disabled. He doubted they intended to return it to him. He guessed he'd have to find his own way to the airport.

Truthfully, he still felt like crap, although the pain meds had helped. He wouldn't be released until morning, at the very soonest. He was on some kind of super-powerful antibiotic being given by IV, along with the fluids the doctor thought he needed. They wanted to see how he responded to the antibiotics before they cut him loose.

What had him antsy was Leah's absence. He wanted to rip the needle out and go looking for her. They'd been taken to different cubicles in the ER and he hadn't seen her since. There wasn't any chance she'd been admitted, too, was there? He couldn't believe she'd leave without finding him. Anyway, she'd need to wait for her purse and phone, even if she was willing to abandon her car for now.

He'd tuned the TV to CNN, but had trouble caring about the latest congressman embroiled in a sexual scandal or tension in some godforsaken part of the world. With a little luck Higgs and company would be rounded up, weaponry confiscated and their entire scheme would become little more than a note on a list of terrorist operations thwarted. No breathless reports on CNN or any other news outlet.

Recognizing the quick, light footsteps in the hall, he turned his head. Since hospital security had been asked to vet any visitors to his room, he wasn't surprised to hear a man's voice and then a woman's. A second later Leah pushed aside the curtain. Her hair was shiny clean and dry, shimmering under the fluorescent lights, and she wore scrubs.

"Spencer?" She sounded tentative, as if unsure he'd welcome her. Then she wrinkled her nose. "Alex."

"I'd really like to shed having multiple personalities," he told her.

She chuckled and visibly relaxed, coming to his side. When he held out his hand, she laid hers in it.

"Will you sit down?" he asked, tugging gently. The

minute she'd perched on the edge of the bed, he said, "You saw a doctor. What did he say?"

She reported that, like him, she was being treated for potential *Giardia lamblia*, the microorganism commonly found in otherwise crystal-clear waters in the Cascade Mountains. A dressing covered the bullet graze on her arm, and she was also on an antibiotic for that. Otherwise, she'd been able to shower, a nurse had produced the scrubs for her and she'd been given a chit to pay for a meal in the cafeteria.

"I couldn't eat nearly as much as I wanted," she concluded ruefully.

With a smile lighting her face, she was different. Her eyes sparkled, her mouth was soft, her head high and carriage erect but also relaxed. Seeing her now was a reminder that he didn't know what she'd be like when she wasn't abused and shocked. She could have a silly sense of humor; she might be a party girl; she could habitually flit from one interest to another. Maybe she'd already dropped her determination to go to vet school and come up with another way she could spend any money earned from her great-uncle's legacy to her.

No, not that, he thought. That was unfair. He'd seen her unflagging determination. Her courage. Her strength and intellect.

Her smile had died, and she was searching his eyes gravely. "What about you? What did the doctor say?"

Was that the caring expression of a woman at least halfway in love with a man? Or caring only because the two of them had gone through a lot together?

"Nothing unexpected," he told her. "It was the gash on my thigh that was infected. Strangely enough, this one—" he started to move his free hand to touch his side before remembering that it was now casted "—appeared clean. One rib is broken, one cracked. My ulna is fractured close to the wrist." Rueful, he lifted the casted arm. "They expect a complete healing, but I may need physical therapy once this is off."

"I don't know how you kept going. You saved my life, over and over."

He shook his head. "You saved mine. Over and over."

She didn't seem convinced, and said, "Oh, you mean when I heard Higgs and Fuller talking."

"And when you treated my injures," he reminded her.

"Which you got because you were protecting *me*."

"You also knew enough to find berries to eat, to keep that bear from seeing us as dinner, and you led us to safety when I was too feverish to know which way we were going."

"I don't think any of those measure up to a knife to the—"

He smiled crookedly. "We'll call it even."

Leah laughed. "Not even close."

"Did anyone corner you with more questions?" he asked.

"Oh, yeah. A pair of FBI agents. Apparently, the doctor wouldn't let them go at you, so I got grilled instead."

He was the one to laugh this time. "Grilled?"

Her severe expression melted into a smile. "Okay, asked questions. Only…they wouldn't tell me anything. Do you know what's happening?"

The reminder renewed his irritation. "Not as much as I'd like. As we speculated, Higgs and his crew absconded with all the weapons, down to the last bullet." He told her the rest of what he'd learned, and she appeared relieved to know she'd get her possessions back soon.

"I was worrying about my car," she admitted. "I hated to have to call my insurance agent and say, 'Well, see, these domestic terrorists got mad at me, so they blew it up with a rocket launcher.'"

Laughing, Alex realized he hadn't felt this good since the last time he'd made love with Leah, and then the astonishing pleasure was transitory. They'd both been all too aware of the frightening reality awaiting them.

Before he could say anything else, he heard voices in the hall, followed by one that said, "Knock knock," even as a hand drew back the curtain.

The visitor was Matt Sanford, the deputy who had picked them up off the side of the highway. He had a black duffel bag slung over one shoulder and was pulling a small suitcase with the other hand. "I thought you might like to have your stuff," he said cheerfully.

Leah beamed at him. "Yes, please. Is my purse there somewhere? You do have my phone?"

He let her seize the suitcase handle from him. "I'm told your purse is in the suitcase. The phone, I don't know. If anything is missing, I'll follow up on it." He looked at Alex. "And I take it this is yours."

"Well, the bag is."

"Do you want your phone?" Leah asked, starting to reach for the zipper.

"Eventually. Unfortunately, I don't dare use it until we know it's clean. Somebody was supposed to bring me—"

The deputy pulled a phone from a pocket. "I'm the somebody."

"Turned you into the pack mule, huh?"

"Beats my average day. You introduced some excitement into our lives."

Alex's eyes met Leah's. "More than I ever want to experience again."

"Amen," she murmured.

"Thank you," Alex added. "You don't know how glad to see you we were."

"That's what they all say," Deputy Sanford joked, but he also smiled. "I'm happy I came on you when I did. Oh, I forgot to say I have an update."

Both focused on him.

"I hear the FBI has caught up with four men. A guy with a Scandinavian name…"

"Arne Larson?"

"That's it. He was with a Robert Kirk."

Leah's hand tightened on Alex's. "I don't remember a Robert."

Alex wasn't surprised. Unremarkable in appearance, Rob had never seemed interested in pushing himself forward.

"The other two were Don Durand—his truck was loaded with rifles, they said—and Garrett Zeigler."

"Those two were together?"

"Not from what I heard."

"I'm glad someone is willing to tell us what's happening."

"Yeah, I figured." Sanford sounded sympathetic. "I put my number in that phone. Call if I can do anything."

They expressed more thanks. He left, leaving silence in his wake.

This silence felt awkward to Leah. She wouldn't try to leave until morning at the soonest, Saturday if it looked like she'd have her car by then, but…should she hang around and keep Alex company now? Or make this breezy but plan to stop by in the morning to say goodbye?

Would she hear from him someday?

"I almost hope Del and Dirk get away," she blurted.

He grimaced. "Me, too, but that won't happen with Del. He got himself in too deep. Dirk… I'll try to keep him from being charged if he followed my advice."

He'd told her about the confrontation with Dirk and what he'd suggested. "If he didn't, there's not much I can do for him."

"How will you know?"

He ran a hand over his rough jaw. "As long as he doesn't have any stolen weapons on him when he's stopped, I'll assume he's running from Higgs, not still taking his orders. Dirk saved us by keeping his mouth shut."

Leah nodded. "They didn't let you shave?"

"Wasn't high on their list of priorities, but, damn it, I itch."

His disgruntlement made her smile. It also, for some obscure reason, made her sad. *Just ask*, she told herself.

"You'll be going back to Chicago, won't you?"

An emotion she couldn't read passed through his light gray eyes. "For the short term," he agreed. "I'm in no shape to be useful here."

"No. Um, I'm expected back at work Monday. So…"

"Have you talked to your parents?" he asked.

She scrunched up her nose. "Yes. Mom was next thing to hysterical. I could hear Dad in the background reminding her that I'm okay."

Annoyingly, amusement curved Alex's very sexy mouth. "Did you mention getting shot?"

Feeling sort of teenaged, she said, "I figured that could wait."

He laughed, but there was something intense in the way he watched her. "Leah..."

"Yes?"

"I don't want to say goodbye."

"I don't want to, either," she whispered, praying he didn't mean that in a "We had quite an adventure, and I'll miss you" way.

"Are you still serious about applying to vet school?"

"Yes, except...there's still the money issue. I suppose I should talk to some real estate agents tomorrow. It might be a while before they can actually take a look at the resort, though, huh?"

"I'm guessing a week or so," he agreed. His gaze never left hers. "I want to keep seeing you."

Her heart did a somersault. "But... Chicago."

"I'm done with undercover work. I can apply for a transfer to be near you."

He meant it. Suddenly, tears rolled down her cheeks. "I was so afraid..."

"I've been afraid, too," he said huskily, tugging her toward him.

Leah surrendered, lifting her feet from the floor so she could snuggle on the bed beside him, her head resting on his shoulder, her hand somewhere in the vicinity of his heart. The familiar position felt *right*. She hated the idea of going to bed without him.

"I had the terrifying thought that you might like nightclubs," he murmured.

She actually giggled at that. "Not a chance. Please tell me you don't bag a deer every year."

This laugh rumbled in his chest. "Nope. Guess that wouldn't go over very well with an animal doc, would it?"

"No." Her cheeks might still be wet, but Leah was also smiling.

"Now that we have that covered, I guess we know everything we need to about each other," he said with an undertone of humor.

"I guess we do." No, he wouldn't be able to go home with her to meet her parents immediately; she could only imagine the kind of debriefing he'd face. "Is there a Portland office?"

"FBI? Yeah, a field office. That's what I'll aim for in the short term. If you want me to."

"I do." She was in love with this man who was willing to make big changes in his life to be with her. The sexiest man she'd ever met. A man who just never quit.

"Good," he said. A minute later his breathing changed as he relaxed into sleep. Apparently, she'd removed his last worry.

Not planning to go anywhere, she closed her eyes, too.

Epilogue

Ten days later Alex strode off the plane at Portland International Airport. Leah had promised to be waiting for him at baggage claim. In part because of the cast he still wore, he carried only his laptop case. He'd taken a two-week vacation, the best he could manage until a transfer came through. This was a "meet the family" trip. Even as alienated as he often felt from his own parents, he supposed he'd be taking Leah to meet them one of these days, too. They loved him, if not in a way he'd want to replicate with his own kids. For the first time he was seriously thinking he'd like to start a family.

Only two days ago he'd gotten word that Higgs had been captured trying to charter a boat in Florida. When the local FBI located the beach cabin where he'd been staying, they'd surprised two other men: Steve Baldwin and Ken Vogel. They'd also found two rocket launch-

ers and a small amount of uranium as well as evidence
that the men had been constructing a bomb.

Higgs wasn't talking, but under pressure, Baldwin
admitted they'd intended to sail to a Caribbean island
where they wouldn't be found until they were ready to
make their strike.

Alex felt sick, imagining what might have happened
if the charter operator hadn't had an uneasy feeling he'd
seen Higgs's face, and not in a context he liked.

Yeah, the FBI had ended up putting Lieutenant Colonel Edward Higgs on a watch list, and released his
photo. This time it had paid off big.

They had also quietly arrested army Colonel Thomas
Nash, the man Alex recognized when he and Higgs met
the suppliers. Turned out Nash and Higgs had been
friends for years.

Of course, the single arrest was the equivalent of
peeling open the proverbial can of worms. Nash couldn't
have stolen that quantity of weapons on his own. Even
with help, procedures were designed to prevent things
like this from happening. It was fair to say that army
base would be crawling with investigators for months
to come, making a lot of people's lives miserable.

Dirk had been picked up and released, at Alex's rec-
ommendation. They'd spoken last week, Dirk shaken at
his weakness in letting his father push him into something so hateful. He and Helen were getting married
and moving to Montana, where he'd found a job with a
well-drilling company based in Billings. Alex intended
to stay in touch. He and Leah might not have survived
if Dirk hadn't listened to his conscience.

Suddenly, he didn't want to think about any of that.
The baggage claim carousels were just ahead…and his

gaze locked on a woman hurrying toward him, her face alight. Relief and something more powerful flooded him. He let the laptop case drop to the floor and held out his arms.

Leah flew into them, saying only his name. His real name.

* * * * *